PRAISE FOR STEW

"Project Hanuman *is a visionary, mind-bending space opera of electric drama and searing heart. A sharp, thoughtful exploration of what intelligence looks like beyond humanity, and what hope looks like when your universe is ending, this book is for anyone who ever loved Iain M. Banks."*
Lorraine Wilson, author of *We Are All Ghosts In The Forest*

Stewart Hotston

PROJECT HANUMAN

ANGRY ROBOT

ANGRY ROBOT
An imprint of Watkins Media Ltd

Unit 11, Shepperton House
89-93 Shepperton Road
London N1 3DF
UK

angryrobotbooks.com
Shakti and Bhakti

An Angry Robot paperback original, 2025

Edited by Simon Spanton Walker and Paris Ferguson
Cover illustration by Eleonor Piteira
Cover design by Sarah O'Flaherty
Set in Meridien

ISBN 978 1 91599 894 1
Ebook ISBN 978 1 91599 895 8

Printed and bound in the United Kingdom by CPI Group (UK) Ltd, Croydon CR0 4YY

The manufacturer's authorised representative in the EU for product safety is eucomply OÜ - Pärnu mnt 139b-14, 11317 Tallinn, Estonia, hello@eucompliancepartner.com; www.eucompliancepartner.com

9 8 7 6 5 4 3 2 1

MIX
Paper | Supporting
responsible forestry
FSC
www.fsc.org   FSC® C013604

For Stephen, for whom I buy books I want to read knowing my mother will make him get rid of them when he's finished reading. My shelves are always open.

1.

Praveenthi watched the hen party push clumsily through the doors ahead of her. They were busy making noise and, less busily, trying to get out of the bar. Each of them was pulling in a different direction, women acting out the random movement of molecules in a gas. Their privacy veils were set to transparent. They wanted people to see them having a good time.

With an almost audible pop they were through the door with a shriek of pleasure and, after a moment in which they threatened to splash in several directions, pulled themselves together and turned right.

The pinks and browns of holographic penises, resolutely thrusting from all around them like day glow porcupines, was enough to keep Prab from following lest she get caught in their chaos. Their clothes were shielded beneath see-through umbrellas. Slips of waterproof fabric unfurled under the soles of their wildly inappropriate shoes before rolling up and around their calves to keep their feet dry.

Wherever they went next they'd arrive dry with only their unabashed joy and the alcohol in their veins to give their hosts a sense of trepidation. Day trippers from inside the Arcology living it up in the physical world, just because they could.

Prab was drunk enough that no onboard AI would let her anywhere near a vehicle, and she had no intention of sobering up.

The hen party's screams and laughter faded until only the static of the rain remained before she stepped out after them. There was an unexpected scent in the air, acrid and nasty in her nose, like something was burning. Prab ignored it and, turning left, splashed onwards. The rain was heavy enough that the street had an inch of standing water.

The first time she ever stepped out in her printed body, she'd relished the feel of rain on her skin.

Everyone did. It was a thing. Rain in the physical world felt less real than experiencing it inside the Arcology, yet, at the same time, the greasiness of it was instantly distinct from the smooth sensation of being rained on inside the electronic worlds of her first home.

As ever the sky over Sirajah's Reach was the boring grey of rain clouds. The sun showed its face here less often than a wayward father returned home.

When it wasn't raining there were thick black ash storms.

Prab wasn't thinking about the weather. She was trying very hard not to think at all, and certainly not about the monthly mini-intervention by her family, who were determined to mix things up in her affairs. One step then another was about the desired level of consciousness. The world might be ending and she'd still be determined to keep it at arms' length.

She was doing her best to prepare for her brother, because her brother was a dick. And not the kind the hen party were so interested in.

It also didn't single him out as far as the rest of her family were concerned.

It's only once a month, she reminded herself. You've got thirty days before you have to talk to them again.

There was no rule saying they had to stay in contact. No law stipulating family time. The next couple of days would be arguments with herself over why she hadn't cut them off years ago.

No more demands that she rejoin the Arcology, no more requests for her to store her biome's imprint in the Arcology's systems so she could, when she was ready, translate and rejoin them in whatever paradise they were fucking about in currently.

Prab wasn't ever going to rejoin them. The body she had was the one she wanted to live in for the foreseeable.

The idea of surrendering and translating back into electronic life made her actual fake printed skin crawl.

"It's all in your head," her brother would counter.

The argument had been rehearsed so many times Prab had long ago abandoned reason in favour of letting her frustration and anger shut them the hell up. Except it didn't. They'd adapted, coming sideways at the question of why she continued as an Excluded when all of time and opportunity awaited her if only she'd accept a virtual body rather than a physical one.

Her mothers would talk about worlds they'd seen, places they'd visited, achievements they'd encountered. Her fathers about music they'd listened to, concerts which had reduced them to tears. Of their own symphonies, written to be played by orchestras of hundreds with instruments that needed two mouths or eleven fingers and three arms.

Atul, her eldest brother and the only one of the three of them who thought he had a say in her life, was less subtle but just as on point. He'd ask if she wanted to make a difference, if she understood just how little her physical life was accomplishing.

"If you really want to be stuck in one place at a time, you could pilot," he said. "That would be in the physical." As if encasing her body in inorganics normally reserved for criminals was a concession he was willing to make on her behalf if only she'd do as they wanted.

These days Prab got mind-numbingly drunk on the neighbourhood micro-distillery's gin before a call. She would then do her best to sit and nod as if she were listening, while they rabbited on for their agreed time.

They never noticed or remarked on her mental acuity during their time together. Perhaps they thought it a natural consequence of living in a printed body.

Today's call had ended like most of them when her mothers had run out of things to suggest Prab think about. Her career, her reputation, her opportunities, her unnecessary aging. This list was extensive, detailed and repetitive.

Strangely her fathers were absent, but there'd been no explanation offered and no room for her to ask. Inquiring would only have encouraged them and Prab found the hour they spent with one another each week more than enough time as it was.

There was no question of cutting them off despite her fantasies of waking up on the morning of a call and realising she didn't have to answer to anyone. They could, if they wanted, make her life actually, properly difficult. The Arcology had no known limits on what it could achieve when it set its nodes to it.

From their perspective Prab was one of the Excluded. Not even one of the Arcology's myriad citizens who chose to spend time in the physical for reasons as varied as art, construction, pleasure or curiosity.

To be Excluded was to have set aside all the Arcology had to offer. To have rejected it. Truth be told, although the Arcology made a show of allowing people like Prab to walk away, to self-exclude as they put it, it took every opportunity to reel them back in.

Prab's family could have made a fuss and the Arcology would have come calling.

Instead they'd adopted the role of passive-aggressive good intentions, and despite the incandescent fury and excessive drinking to which their behaviour drove her, it was better than them lodging a formal request for an intervention.

Her role as an Interlocutor helped. A go-between for the Arcology and its citizens in the physical, as well as counsel for others like her; people who'd rejected the Arcology which had given them life. Occasionally she was required to sit between the Arcology and those cultures and civilisations beyond its walls.

"Praveenthi. Darling. When will you be done?" her mothers would ask as if it was just a phase. A four-decade fad from which Prab would eventually emerge, an Arcology butterfly after decades of obstinately weaving herself into an Excluded cocoon.

The lights of the city were darkened. It took Prab a while to ask why.

The local network was stuttering too, refusing to report if there were any issues. Shaking her head as if the malfunctioning streetlamps proved her entire argument about why she wasn't part of the Arcology and its sprawling galactic reach, Prab shut off her access and continued on her way home.

A certain kind of isolation was joy.

Sirajah's Reach was a planet at the edge of the Arcology. Not so far out as to be at risk of some other polity or commercial interest claiming the place as their own, but sufficiently marginal that the people living here wondered exactly what it was they were paying for.

Not that anyone paid for anything. The Arcology had no money, no currency except for what it needed to bargain with outsiders. Its people were beyond that kind of nonsense. At least as they saw it.

Prab liked money. She liked looking at her accounts and seeing the numbers, knowing it gave her an independence from the community in which she'd grown up and which, gently and without malice, refused to let her go.

Stood outside the door to her apartment building, the white-and-blue swirls of its walls running slick with rain but shining from an inner light the architect would have specified in line with the Reach's design standards, she realised there was no noise.

She'd been so lost in replaying her conversation with her brother and mothers she'd not been paying attention to the world at her feet.

A sigh. Prab would tell her clients that paying attention mattered. She would say the Arcology bred inattention into its people, positively encouraged them to be self-absorbed. She said it made them vulnerable and wondered how they'd survived this long with such wilful naivety.

Most of her clients were those who'd done similar to her, walked away. Others were excluded on social or legal grounds. If they made the majority by number, they were rarely the most interesting. Those she was excited by were citizens of other polities, from worlds and societies bordering the Arcology and whose people spent their time in its space trying to live their lives. All too frequently this second group of clients came in misunderstanding the point of the Arcology so that they ended up needing someone like her to help them navigate its societies, its customs, its rules.

Inevitably some of her clients approved of her rants – allowing to go unmentioned the truth that it was the Arcology's substrate and its nodes which kept them safe; a second society within, around and through everything the Arcology believed itself to be.

Few of her clients thought about who and what kept the Arcology running, fewer still those who'd exited from the Arcology itself.

"Smart," she said, admonishing herself for being so much like those she profited from criticising. Hand on brow she gazed up at the overcast sky and confirmed what she already knew.

There were no vehicles. That smell was back. Definitely something burning. A creeping sense of the world being off by a few degrees wouldn't leave her alone.

It wasn't that this time of day should be busy. It wasn't. No matter where in the galaxy they ended up, people tended to regulate themselves by sleeping at roughly the same time as those around them.

Her neighbour, a strange man called Ben who'd left the Arcology a lifetime before Prab, needed only one hour's sleep a week, but even he arranged to snatch it in the middle of what passed as night on Sirajah's Reach.

Despite his oddities he was a good neighbour. He made sure the common areas were clean and the waste disposal was working without making a fuss or trying to have the rest of the building's tenants applaud his efforts. There were rumours, started by the triplets in flat seven, that he spent hours on the roof garden fiddling with the hedging and staring at the sky.

Prab didn't mind that kind of weirdness. You were absolutely a certain category of weirdo to choose to become Excluded. He'd never been rude or inappropriate with her, never brought up the Arcology and had not, once, asked to borrow something and then forgotten to give it back. Unlike the triplets who still had several books of hers.

Because books were Prab's thing. Real books with pages and words in a single language and actual pictures that didn't move or change and couldn't be withdrawn by the publisher if they decided they needed to change them. She had books that were decades old. Each supply ship arriving at Sirajah's Reach brought her more.

There were no book binders here on world. She suspected no one apart from her cared enough to consider setting one up, and there certainly wasn't the demand needed to sustain one if they did.

She frequently worked with a lawyer called Marinique. Mari was a specialist in concept law, a field which dealt with definitions of individual sovereignty and how they applied to rights and access to services. Her clients were often, at some point, Prab's clients too.

Marinique did not care about books, but she appreciated Prab's devotion.

"It's very you," she'd said once, flicking through a brick-thick history of the Errent Protectorate, tracing its eventual decline and fall under the weight of its own isolationism.

Prab's office, more than her flat, had shelves stacked with books and pamphlets, old pictures and paintings. A home, where her flat was little more than the place she slept.

In the silence of the city she could have heard pages turn.

She realised the street was empty too. There was nothing overhead. No one anywhere. Prab was the kind of person who found herself endlessly irritated by vehicles landing in the middle of the street to drive along at ground level and then taking off again for reasons known only to themselves. She regarded it as the height of selfishness, but now their absence chilled her right up and down.

Right now it was as if everyone else had received a message she'd managed to avoid.

Which wouldn't be a surprise.

A single vehicle passed her on the road, but as they glided along she sensed there was an unease in their movement. Like people who'd been forced to walk, blind, into an unknown room. Then it drove into the corner of a building, the front end crumpling and bursting into flames before fire suppressants doused it.

Prab ran across, the alcohol in her stomach heaving at the effort. To her astonishment no one was inside. She cast an eye at the empty sky. How many others had come crashing down? Had people died?

Prab stood, hands thrust into pockets. The rain was lessening, which meant ash storms were on their way. The city's environmental controls worked to keep the worst of it out but a fine layer of grime would still cover them all by the time the next rains came.

Prab pushed aside thoughts about the weather, resisting the urge to investigate whatever was happening. She was on leave. It wasn't her concern.

But the car had still crashed. The sky was still empty.

There was a grocery across from her apartment. Although, like many of those in the city, it was run by an Excluded, it supplied to those of the Arcology who wanted to dip out of the endless supplies and resources of their empire.

You could spot them, tourists of the physical, walking like they'd been issued chickens' legs and giraffes' necks, stumbling from the warm embrace of the Arcology to engage in physical pleasures. His place was split into two sections, the novelties all tourists came for and then grocery aisles for everyone else, Arcology and Excluded alike, who lived in printed bodies in the physical.

Slumming it, they said. Fleshly delights in printed bodies that seemed, somehow, different from those same experiences encountered within the endlessly high fidelity of the Arcology. An empire which knew no boundaries except the imagination.

There were no slightly guilty Arcologist day trippers with their newly printed bodies and their network access dialled down to minimum settings on the street today.

The crash was probably down to a shitting mistranslation, she thought. It wouldn't be my problem even if I was on call. Sirajah's Reach was an Excluded enclave, within but not of Arcology space. Prab's role was never about the politics of how the Reach and the Arcology engaged with one another, never about the institutions, except as her individual clients needed to navigate them.

Besides, no message had pinged into her vision demanding to be read. No one was calling on her. If there was an emergency then, unsurprisingly, they didn't need her help.

She frowned.

Her inbox opened by willing it. There were no messages. Her feet twitched, she turned in the street. The grocer's lights were out. They couldn't be shut. They never shut.

Then he was there, in his doorway, head tilted back as if the sky would explain what was going on.

"Morris," she called.

Morris, the grocer, stepped out into the street and she crossed over to meet him, hands still in her pockets. He was much shorter than her, thicker too, with a long face and no neck to speak of. At some time he'd come from a high-gravity environment and, coming here, had never bothered to change his body.

A nod one way then returned. He had the best moustache; thick, blond and unruly, like an enthusiastic puppy.

"Any ideas?" he asked.

"Power's out?" she replied, still not drawing it in despite the nervousness in Morris' eyes.

"Everything's out," he said.

"I've got my inbox," she replied, not willing to believe such a shocking statement. Still no messages. No announcements from the city. Nothing in the last hour. Fifty-three minutes and eight seconds if she was counting. She'd been wrapping up with her family, had been one hand around a gin and the other holding her chin up off the table lest her mouth get ideas of its own and utter something she couldn't take back.

"No messages though," said Morris. He flashed up his own. It was spotlessly clean and well kept.

"How do you manage that?" she asked, stunned and slightly awed.

"I bin pretty much everything," he grinned. "A hundred people send me shit all day long. My actual messages go somewhere else."

A look was given.

He shook his head. "Just as empty, but I'm not showing you that one."

"Any of them in tonight?" she asked. Investigative muscles twitching without being asked.

"Only one," he said. "Came in moaning that his privacy veil wasn't working."

Prab stared at Morris.

"It wasn't either. Never seen the like."

Neither of them mentioned it, but Prab knew Morris had already understood something she was only just coming to realise. The city ran on the Arcology's power grid, on its technology; it was theirs despite them tolerating a remarkable degree of dissent, disaffection and multiculturalism. She bitched about the Arcology, but the luxury of her complaints were bathed in its indulgence.

Sirajah's Reach would be an unsettled ash-covered rock if not for the Arcology who perched over them all like a patient parent. Even if this was a temporary failure, the empty skies spoke of damage already done.

A lack of a privacy veil sat in the guts like a stone. It was the one thing Prab missed about belonging, the ever-present ability to hide herself from those who might look. It was the one item she'd instinctively reached for in the months after she'd first left the Arcology. Even now, decades later, she could feel the sense of its absence like a missing limb.

For a tourist to have come to Morris' place without their veil spoke of something deeply wrong with the city's infrastructure. Something much worse than empty skies.

It seemed impossible that the Arcology wasn't present.

The lights in his unit flickered and came on.

"Ah," he said. "Panic over."

Prab, who'd left her connection to the city's network open, was flooded with messages.

Then the lights went off again.

"Well, shit," said Morris.

Prab wasn't listening. Every single message had the same headline.

Emergency call-in. With her name in the headline. No images. No audio. Just those words.

Morris was peering into his store, but she was on her way. It was a long walk to the office. As she went he called after her, but Prab felt like a tidal wave was cresting just behind her and she needed to be doing something, trying something, to make her world better.

She tried several times to reconnect to the network, but that one brief flicker of life was all the city had to offer. By her reckoning she was two hours away. Her feet hurt contemplating the distance, the idea of sweat running across skin enough to make Prab shudder.

The only upside being it was time enough to sober up.

The call-in demands hung in her vision like old washing left on the line too long, but she refused to take them down in case they disappeared for good. The fear was irrational, they were in her personal space and wouldn't go anywhere unless she deleted them. Yet a gnawing pessimism had taken hold and wouldn't leave.

Prab wanted to stop on the way, to check on friends whose homes she'd pass on her walk. Someone would have more information, would be able to tell her what was going on. As she made to divert to an old lover's place the first people appeared.

In ones and twos, looking dazed and frightened, they came. Coalescing into crowds without thought or direction.

They didn't speak but to ask if others had heard anything, didn't do much except linger on the street, drifting this way and that, random particles buffered by invisible winds.

Prab had no answers but no one seemed surprised at this. Who would know what to do if the sun went out? That panic hadn't descended on the people around her was the only upside Prab could divine. She could feel the shock, the sense that what was happening couldn't be real. It wasn't like she could even contact people she knew in the Arcology – there were no links, no network. As if it had collected its things and left without warning.

What had happened to the hen party?

She hoped they were all right. Not enough to engage and do anything about it though. Head down, eyes on her feet, she kept walking, thoughts of diverting to friends' apartments put away. No one called out, no one tried to intercept her, but the crowds didn't thin out until she reached the Arcology's towers.

It was only a matter of time before they followed on and found their way here. If there was something wrong, love them or hate them, the city would ask the Arcology proper to fix it.

Prab's office was on a shared floor in a tall thin building that reached up to within a whisker of the city's ash shield. The role of an Interlocutor wasn't important enough for the Arcology that it could warrant the lofty heights of the upper storeys. Hers was the joy of a lifeless room in the mid-teens. About as low as one could get before plant and machinery took over the floors.

The tower itself was in the heart of the Arcology's presence, one of a dozen buildings reaching up above the rest of the city and whose materials luminesced with a faint white light.

The landscape of the city meant the towers were visible from just about everywhere. Out at the edges where the ash would seep through the shield into the air and coat everything even on rainy days, they were about a thumb's height above the horizon, but Prab spent her life with them arcing over her head.

You could have left Sirajah's Reach, she told herself regularly.

You could have left Arcology space entirely. There were plenty of other cultures with just familiar enough physiologies and customs. It wasn't lack of choice that kept her close.

Instead here she was, walking towards it to see what was wrong.

There was little freight between the Arcology and the rest of the city.

The vast majority of the Arcology's people remained in the worlds they'd manufactured in information space, disembodied from physical flesh even as they wore versions of the same in the boundless sufficiency of the Arcology's network. They had no need for a physical city beyond the infrastructure needed to run their worlds. If it wasn't for the Excluded who outnumbered the printed bodies of Arcology members ten to one, Sirajah's Reach would have been a flat disc of power grids and computational processing power buried under the surface of the planet.

Arriving, she found the building unresponsive. The elevators refused to come, the lights refused to light and the air was growing warm and thick as it languished unconditioned inside air-tight offices.

"Because of course they're not working," she complained to a building which could no longer hear her. There was a stone in her stomach now, a fear she refused to confront. It would be fine, she told herself. Get to the office and this will all be fixed soon enough.

On any normal day, Prab kept her network access to a minimum. An unprepared person entering the Arcology's towers would be bombarded with advertisements for worlds to explore, offers of citizenship exams, directed requests for former members to come home, news of new games, new ideas and new experiences at the sole cost of uploading properly. It could get so a visitor's vision was fully obscured by these intrusive offers and demands.

Having worked as an Interlocutor at the tower for close to two decades, Prab didn't need to see the same messages every day. In lieu of having surrendered her privacy veil, she'd gone the whole next step of disconnecting entirely apart from essential services.

The doors were unlocked so it was simple enough to make her way through the eerily silent building to the stairwells and start climbing.

About halfway up it was clear that stairs were a form of torture device.

At floor fifteen she had to stop for a rest, unable to continue despite her office only being two floors further up. She wiped sweat from her lips, the sides of her nose and from across her brow. She couldn't bear to touch her neck or think what was happening under her clothes.

As long as no one saw her like this it would be fine.

Emerging onto her floor was an exercise in finding her breath and waiting for the world to stop threatening to fade into the narrow tunnel she'd been experiencing for the last few steps.

With a big heavy gulp she pushed across the floor to find it entirely empty. No one at home.

Granted, it was late, but there was usually someone around.

Prab had been hoping to find Mari. It would have given her someone to lean on, someone to laugh about this with.

Right then she felt alone in the worst way. It would have been great to be able to look out over the city night, to remind herself there were people out there who were experiencing the same as she was. All her office offered was bookcase-lined walls stacked with her books.

For the first time she looked at the shelves and couldn't see any point in anything she'd collected. Self-indulgence masquerading as genteel rebellion.

The question of what to do next hung in the air.

The messages made no mention of who to contact or what protocols were in play.

Prab had no idea what the Arcology wanted her to do.

Turning around a couple of times, once to face the door then her shelves a second time then back to the door, Prab had no sense of what was expected. It was as if the Arcology was a catacomb from which the bodies had been removed.

If there was no one to talk to, there was no action she could take. Was this what the emergency call-in had been aiming for? That made no sense.

If the Arcology weren't there to be spoken with, the city was on its own. *Are we going to die alone and in the dark?*

Her stomach turned over at the thought.

How long before the ash shield failed? How long before the people went hungry?

Were ships still in orbit waiting to land? There had to be a way off planet.

It was all but certain that the departure halls with their translation machines were idle. Prab thought about heading to the nearest one, down on the edge of Lake Trasper, a beautiful spot where those going off world queued outside among flowers and trees, landscapes manicured under artificial sunlight to resemble the idylls of worlds where the stars were visible and ash didn't render the sky an angry charcoal smear.

Then she knew where to go. The dockyards. The emergency call-in's origin couldn't have come from within the city's architecture. It had to be someone whose comms were still online, which meant one thing: she'd been called in by a ship. A ship in orbit wouldn't be any use to anyone, so they'd be planetside where she could reach them.

People didn't travel on ships. Translation meant they could step from one world to another without having to leave their gravity wells, without having to worry about a void intent on killing them for the slightest misstep.

Ships weren't unhappy about this state of affairs – they were the nodes of the Arcology's network of existence; a population of citizens embodied as ships and, as such, members of the Arcology's ruling class. If the substrate were those who formed the foundation of the Arcology, the nodes were its realisation in physical space.

Carrying passengers was both passé and demeaning from their point of view. Like a whale being asked to give passage to a snail.

So if someone was waiting for her, they'd be at the docks.

A small voice in her head muttered she might not have to die here on Sirajah's Reach. She knew it was likely impermanent, that everything should and would be fine, but a tightness in her chest told her to be afraid, that if this was happening, it was because there was an emptiness where the Arcology should be. Unspeakable, unthinkable and yet there it was in her veins.

Spiralling terror.

Skin prickling with guilt and relief and hope and shame, Prab started down the stairs on wobbly legs, determined to reach the docks and find someone to get her off world before the city was buried beneath ash.

She got two flights down before turning around, returning to her office and filling a backpack with a small collection of books.

2.

The docks were the very definition of a shit hole. Most freight came in through the translation gates and those, even the big ones used for cargo, were in more populated parts of the city.

By contrast, the few ships which still flew were either military or carried bulk cargo of the kind where it was pointless arranging translation to send it where it was going.

Of course, the third kind of cargo delivery was of the suspect variety, but Prab knew of that only by reputation. The closest she'd ever come to circumscribed goods were books talking about the success of cultures other than the Arcology.

Disdain breeds a lack of investment, emotionally and, in this case, economically. The docks were buildings which didn't shine and which didn't keep out the ash. They were made from local materials rather than printed and had all the charm of an overgrown fingernail.

Entertainment about gangsters and troublemakers featured docks the same way as romances featured the final happy ever after in the paradises offered by the Arcology.

Prab knew they were as safe as anywhere else in the city, but she still felt the frisson of danger in her blood as she approached.

The space taken by the docks was vast but low rise. The fifth of the city they occupied didn't really count as city proper. No one lived there, no one relaxed there and no one dreamed of being there except to pick up some delivery which had somehow been relegated to physical transport rather than being translated.

Which, Prab knew, meant they were either coming from outside the Arcology or some tightass thought waiting a few weeks for what you'd ordered would be an acceptable trade for it costing half as much.

In spite of all this, the docks were familiar because more than a few of her clients ended up working in proximity to the other option they provided – a way off Sirajah's Reach that didn't rely on the Arcology's grace.

They were arranged in a vast spread of large nondescript warehouses with landing spots for the various-sized freighters and ships which came into Sirajah's Reach. As was common, there were more open spots than closed.

On the journey across, her feet telling her there would be consequences for this sudden demand on their otherwise relaxed existence, Prab found the ship she was looking for in the slate of those who'd made landfall in the last couple of days.

An Arcology frigate, two hundred metres in length and currently shaped like a long, thin needle. Its class, Slipstream Three, meant it was printed entirely from smart matter and could take pretty much any geometry it wanted.

Its current aerodynamic allowances were a concession to the planet's atmosphere. A quick flick through its manifest showed it preferred spherical to needle and was armed to the teeth.

Armed anything within the bounds of the Arcology was a rarity. If armaments were really needed most Arcology ships could print them on demand. This was a craft used to travelling beyond the empire's borders where the time taken to print weapons could be the difference between life and death.

A thin gender-neutral, human-shaped person was waiting for her on the landing strip, their face tired, desperate and deeply unhappy. They were a chest and head taller than Prab and slender in the way that spoke of low gravity rather than sexual desirability.

Prab took in their black and gold uniform, the holographic bars on their shoulder and the pips across their chest and sighed. A pilot.

Worse still, a pilot who'd seen action for the Arcology and one who was clearly currently without a chain of command.

Lost soldiers never did well. They weren't trained to make decisions without supervision and, here, Prab was their only apparent contact on Sirajah's Reach because no one else from the Arcology had made an appearance.

As worrying as it was, and Prab's backside was clenched with the terror that she was their only actual responder, the implications of how she'd ended up being called in were far worse.

"You're the Interlocutor?" the pilot asked when Prab stepped into the bay. They were still thirty metres apart, the ship above them both dwarfing the distance and leaving Prab with a lump in her throat. "You told no one you were coming here?"

If you want gone this is the last chance, a voice told her. The feeling of her window to escape closing was like thick black oil seeping into her blood.

"Are you the Interlocutor?" asked the pilot again, their lanky frame standing defensively.

Prab had no weapons. She wasn't built for fighting. The pilot was a one-piece-army built to defend the Arcology's interests beyond its borders. A different attitude was needed than with the run of the mill client who'd gotten their contracts out of whack.

"I'm sorry," said Prab, trying to sound as calm as possible. "It's chaos here. I am the Interlocutor. You called me in?"

"I did not," said the pilot. "But you're all the city has to offer."

Prab wanted to ask what was happening, but such questions were clearly not in the pilot's slate of conversational gambits.

"How can I help?" she tried.

The pilot nodded and Prab's chest relaxed the tension that had been building there from the moment she'd laid eyes on the ship's outline.

"I don't know," said the pilot.

Which was not the answer she'd expected.

She wanted to apologise, to say there'd been a mistake, but she was here alone with the pilot in a city which should have been heaving with people coming and going and buildings that glowed and elevators that fucking worked.

Neither of them spoke for a stretching moment.

"What is happening?" asked the pilot, and in their voice Prab heard fear and pleading and desperation.

They were not emotions she was equipped to handle.

She thought about answering with a story of how she'd been getting drunk to handle talking with her family but the pilot's look demanded something more serious.

A flash of worry for them crossed her mind but was crowded out as soon as it arrived.

"I don't know," she said. The pilot held up a hand, their long spidery fingers about to force their way into the conversation, but Prab barrelled on.

"The city's dead," she said, then immediately regretted her choice of words. She thought about the kind of language she'd use with a client and, with a mental leap, switched into professional speak. "The city stopped responding to any network links about four hours ago."

It occurred to Prab the pilot must have been landside already or they'd never have made it down out of orbit.

"I cannot access the Arcology's network, its buildings are behaving as if they're on fire and, as far as I can tell, the entire city, including its transport system, is cut off from the empire." She felt like an information point talking to a particularly unlucky tourist. "Someone, somewhere has cursed us."

The pilot nodded and Prab knew then the Arcology was actually, definitely, no longer present on Sirajah's Reach. A shiver went through her, a terrible chasm at her feet into which the planet's inhabitants were about to tumble, herself included.

The substrate housed tens of millions of Arcology citizens here, dozens of the nodes whose vast capabilities oversaw the empire. The planet's stable orbit and out of the way astronomical location precisely the reason they'd chosen to build the city in the first place. On the empire's borders for sure, but on the other side of that border? No one and nothing. Just empty and useless space.

"What about the translation network?" asked the pilot, their tone completely calm, as if asking for directions to the park.

"Nothing," said Prab, finding it difficult to speak. "We're cut off." Were they not listening, or were they simply incapable of understanding what she was saying? "People will be dying. You're the only way off this planet."

Saying the words was like chewing razors. The city was home to thirty-three million embodied people, half as many again in the Arcology. It had culture, gardens, its own slang. There were a dozen smaller parts to it, each with their own identity.

Prab hardly ever visited more than half of those communities, sticking to her own and a handful of the others but only because her job took her there. She liked the food across about a third of them and actively loathed the slimy delicacies of the Richdan quarter, which seemed to think a lack of anything to chew on was a bonus when eating dinner.

The pilot's ship had space, maybe, for a few hundred people.

"How long before the ash shield fails?" she asked.

The pilot looked up briefly. "If there are no engineers here, then who can say."

Which was a shitty answer, but one she thought had the dubious merit of at least being honest.

The admission that the slow-motion death of a world was unfolding around them.

All she wanted was to escape.

"You can fit people into your ship," she said.

The pilot did not turn to regard their craft.

"I will not be taking anyone off world," they replied.

"You can't leave them to die."

She'd already decided she was departing on this ship when the pilot left. It was what happened to everyone else she was wrestling with.

"I cannot decide who should live," said the pilot flatly. No suggestion Sirajah's Reach would survive this. No hope, not even the hint of believing things might get better.

"What is happening in the rest of the Arcology?" she asked, not wanting to hear the answer. Her whole body trilled with sensations she didn't understand; a tightness in her chest, a pull at the base of her stomach. Her skin itched.

"You are to come with me," they said.

Prab nodded without digesting the statement.

"Then we go. Now," said the pilot. "Ash is already encroaching on our launch vectors."

"We must take people with us. We must save some." The words came from deep within. Not everyone has to die. Someone should live.

The pilot eyed her, head tilted to one side as if to hear her better.

"Who would you take?" they asked, their expression entirely neutral.

"You're willing to leave the Arcology's people, your own, here?"

"They are already gone," they replied. "Else we would have brought them on board."

Prab digested the words. A low groan escaped unbidden from deep within.

Were they dead? She couldn't believe it, her body shivering with the possibility that the Arcology was already extinct on this world. The gargoyle of terror which had been haunting her crept up her spine and chased away any hope of life righting itself.

The question of why lost in the overwhelming sense of loss.

The Excluded wouldn't be far behind. They'll die without even knowing what killed them.

It was unthinkable. It was impossible. Except a city shrouded in darkness rather than light spoke the truth she didn't want to hear.

"This started with you," she said, for nothing more than wanting to blame someone who was officially Arcology.

Did the pilot flinch? What was that for?

"If you choose, I will take them. No more than two hundred. They must agree to sleep while they are on board. Any trouble of any kind and we leave immediately."

Sleep being the polite term for cryo.

Prab turned away from the pilot, regarded the city over the edges of the landing bay's walls and tried to think about who she'd choose to save and who would die as a result. She knew trouble was going to find them come what may.

3.

The pilot, Kercher, looked at the short and stubby body of the Interlocutor and wished they could just leave. The ship had calculated the ash shield had a few hours before it collapsed completely. The city would be inches deep in ash well before that, but the fatal cascade wouldn't happen until after they were gone.

There were automated systems built into the fabric of Sirajah's Reach designed to flick into life in case of interruptions, of power failures and technological glitches. The Arcology had planned for the unforeseen.

Except all its planning had been built upon the idea that the Arcology would still be there to fix things. All its planning was for the incidental, the external accident and disruption, not the disappearance of itself.

Kercher hated having to take an Excluded onboard. Hated having to rely on someone who not only wasn't Arcology, but had gone out of their way to reject everything worth saving.

The Interlocutor, a woman, an actual woman, had retreated from the landing pad to the edge of the dock to think. She wanted to figure out who to save. She stood in the shadows, hunched over as if someone had broken then discarded her.

Kercher wanted to slap her and ask what she thought she was doing. The entire empire had gone dark, the seventeen million people here on Sirajah's Reach already likely dead, and here she was trying to save a handful of printed fleshy strangers from something none of them understood. It was a waste of all their time.

All they really wanted was to be out there delivering pain to whoever was responsible for this disaster.

The ship wasn't interested in Kercher's revenge fantasies. But nor was it in a hurry to be away. There was something bigger than leaving Sirajah's Reach going on, something more important than surviving.

"Find me this Interlocutor," had been its terse and febrile instruction.

No explanation, no talking over what they needed to do, just these barked orders.

There has to be someone better, thought Kercher.

The ship wasn't talking right now.

The ship wasn't doing more than spasming as each new attempt to connect with home failed.

"Find this Interlocutor and make for Akhanda." Akhanda was a ring world one huge translation away towards the heart of the Arcology and deep within the golden habitable rim around the galactic core. Home to thirty billion citizens and, if anywhere physical could be called a hub of the bureaucracy that ran the Arcology, the empire's heart.

Kercher's attention was snagged by the Interlocutor returning, a strange expression on their grey and desolate face.

"I've got some recommendations," she began.

"Tell me who you are saving," said Kercher. "We must leave."

They wanted to know how long it was going to take to load these refugees onto the ship. How far away were they, how many others would come crowding in with pleas and cries and desperation once news emerged that some were being saved?

The ship had shrugged at the idea. Already the internal structure was being reconfigured to allow two hundred bodies to be stored safely.

Kercher didn't care. They wanted to take this repulsive woman and leave. The only reason the Interlocutor wasn't bundled onboard already was because the ship had agreed to her idea of saving some others.

Kercher didn't understand it. Why were they stalling? They should be away, safe, in the great dark where no one could find them until they were ready.

"I've got some sys admins, engineers, a couple of medics and some fabricators."

Kercher wasn't listening, the words flowing over them like the ash in the air.

"I wonder if we need artists and farmers, craftspeople, you know?" she trailed off and Kercher realised she wanted them to fill in the gaps.

"I do not care," they said. "We need to leave. Now. How long will it be before they've arrived?"

"I've not asked any of them yet," said Praveenthi.

Teeth ground.

"I can't," she continued. "Not until you've told me who you want, who you'll need."

"I don't need any of them," said Kercher. "This is your decision. The ship has agreed to your inanity. Do not look to me to help you. The Arcology has trillions of citizens. We have no need for these dregs."

The woman's face turned sour. "And how's that working out for you?" she asked.

Kercher lifted their arm and struck the Interlocutor across her face, sending her sprawling to the floor before scrabbling back in fear. It was gratifying enough to see the frail little thing understand their situation.

"You are the one wasting time here, so do not try me. I do not want even you on my ship."

The pilot cursed themselves for saying too much, for being provoked by one of the Excluded into revealing more than they wanted reveal.

Everything in them was crying for them to flee, to find a battle they could fight and win. Standing there doing nothing was more painful than being stabbed.

Praveenthi's face closed in on itself and the next words were shouted.

"I will not help you unless you help me. Just tell me who you want."

Kercher was suddenly so angry they could have broken the Interlocutor like a dead branch. They stepped forward, fingers clenching.

Calm, came the words in their head. *If you are angry, then look to yourself.*

The ship had no care for their feelings. Not now, not ever.

Kercher was a component it needed, but was little more

than that. A prisoner on their own path, indentured to serve the Arcology until their sentence was done and they could return to the community they'd transgressed against.

In that small way they were no different to the Interlocutor.

Kercher stopped moving, standing over the woman but indifferent to her presence.

If you can keep your head, they reminded themselves; a mantra by which they could take the reins again. They hated this body, built for them by the ship while in orbit, cobbled together, they suspected, because the ship had no idea what was going on. It was a body built for violence and quick decision making. Its emotional core was lacking, its ability to think fast and slow severely limited.

"I need to travel back into the city," said Praveenthi. "There is a lawyer we must take with us."

The lawyer is her friend. We do not need them, said the ship in their head.

"No," said Kercher. Angry at the ship for crouching in their mind like a territorial dog, and angry with the Interlocutor for wasting their fucking time. Most of all Kercher was angry at being their go between when they needed to act and be gone.

Your life is not your own, said the ship. *Give the Interlocutor these directions*.

"You do not need the lawyer," said Kercher, parroting the ships words, glad at last someone was taking the reins. "Here is a list of those we might need. Please use it."

"What about my own?" asked Praveenthi, cheek bruising and eyes rimmed with tears. Reading down the list of names the ship put together from its review of the planet's printed inhabitants, she shook her head. "I don't know many of them. And those I do. This one's dangerous, and she's a backstabbing bitch, and this one?" She looked at Kercher with wide eyes, disbelief etched across the curl of her lips.

"They are required for their skills, not their personalities," said Kercher.

The Interlocutor ignored them.

"You think you know what you're doing, but you don't. Skills are brilliant. Excellent. We all want skills. But dickbags won't do what you want or what you need. In the equation of life, dickbags entirely cancel out skills. We take my list."

"Your list wasn't complete. You asked for our advice," said Kercher. Their shoulder rolled with the irritation of having to speak someone else's words out of their own mouth.

"I know who I need to bring now," said Praveenthi, her voice wobbling but defiant, clearly expecting to be hit a second time.

For a fleeting moment Kercher felt the stirring of respect.

"Then go get them," they said, before the ship could express an opinion.

The Interlocutor nodded and turned on her heel, fists clenched at her sides.

"Wait," said Kercher with a sigh. "You'll need transport."

4.

The ship watched its pilot leave with the Interlocutor and wept.

Its tears weren't salty or wet but full of electrical charge and potential states of being. Its sorrow screeched out across the dead network of Sirajah's Reach searching for anyone to answer, the same as it had done from the moment they'd first lost contact with ground control.

The planet was dead. The ship couldn't even track its own pilot now they'd left the docking bay.

The most basic systems still functioned. Air, water, the ash shield. Near everything else, everything that gave those base systems meaning, was silent.

A vast and ornate home with no furnishings.

A place where no one could live.

A place where those who had lived were gone, ghosts in the forest.

In their absence all it had were suspicions and fears and panic and worry and terror. The world had never been silent. All its life there had been a chorus of voices and community, of others like itself and those vastly different living together, talking with one another.

Now it was the unending silence of the space between worlds.

The ship understood distances in a way ordinary citizens couldn't grasp. For them, walking an hour was a hardship, a million nothing more than a unit for collecting together ensembles and crowds.

When the ship thought of interstellar distances it truly understood. It knew how big nothingness was. The ship understood how small it was by every conceivable measure, its defence against the sense that it was nothing more than a

fleeting glimmer of accident against the vast entropy of decline
was its community. The arcology was its home and it had lost
it.

The ship wanted to shut down its processors and sleep
until the silence was over, and if isolation was the future of
the universe, then it would sleep until there was no heat left
anywhere. There were cults of nodes in the Arcology who
had done that, dozens of them, claiming they'd awaken when
needed before vanishing completely.

Those who remained regarded them as beneath contempt
and sent them on their way, fully expecting them never to
return.

So it would flee to Akhanda. A bulwark of the empire, home
to billions and the substrate on which tens of billions more
lived their lives.

The ship needed to hear voices, to know it was not alone.

The pilot thought they were going to fight an enemy, to find
someone responsible and mete out justice.

The Interlocutor thought they were going to help.

The ship only wanted to hear the chaos of life and know it
wasn't alone among the stars.

It had stalled here on Sirajah's Reach out of fear for the
future. They could have left already. It could have ordered the
pilot to abduct the Interlocutor and be away. They were still
here because it feared that in leaving, it was giving truth to the
death of the planet.

And if the planet died, what else of the Arcology was being
lost out there in the spread of its empire?

It dared not look at the dread lurking, waiting to pounce.
Hence it planned for Akhanda and finding salvation. It was
all that it could imagine – there were no alternatives worth
contemplating.

5.

The pilot kickstarted one of the printing machines.

Prab saw their name was Kercher from the login they used to bootstrap the thing into life.

In under a minute they'd built a buggy big enough to carry four people. The two in the back would have their knees up around their ears. Big wheels, a small battery and enough juice to carry them a couple of hours out and back. It was wire framed and lacked a steering wheel.

She tried accessing the network to call Mari but nothing. She tried again and again. She sent messages and then turned her attention to others she wanted to take off world. There was the five-a-side team she played with, the book group, the people she drank with from work. All of them could be justified if she squinted and looked at their skillsets sideways. Each of them brought a weight to her heart she couldn't shift.

The pilot sank into their chair and their upper legs were swallowed as silver material wrapped around them like a foil blanket. Then they were off, the pilot driving with their thighs.

The first stop should be Mari's. The streets were crowded like on Founder's Day festival. A sizeable number of people didn't move out of the way of their buggy until they were right on top of them. Forced to slow down, Prab watched for familiar faces and tried not to listen to the calls for help, asking for explanations as if, because they had a vehicle that worked, they were obviously in possession of the facts.

The pilot said nothing except to ask when to turn.

Each time they slowed people put their hands on the buggy's chassis, asked if they were here to help. Did they know when the network would be restored? Where could they get food? Was this planned, and why hadn't anyone been told in advance?

The crowds were calm, the fear in their questions cold like an ice cube between the shoulders.

"I want to know the next turn," the pilot said. "Always tell me the next turn."

Kercher wanted the next turn the moment after they'd made the last one.

"It makes no sense," she said. "You have no idea how long it is until the next one. What if it's ten minutes away?"

"Then tell me that too," said the pilot. "I have a map of the city, I want to plan ahead."

As they crossed out of the Arcology's hub, Prab noticed luggage appearing in people's hands as they wandered aimlessly from building to building seeking answers.

The night was dark without the city's lighting, giving the place the feel of a cave or cavern. People were lighting their way with torches and garden lanterns. The entire place felt as if they'd stumbled upon ancient ruins for the first time in centuries.

Illuminated by the buggy's stark white headlights, people would turn all at once to watch them pass by. Some would step out into the street to try and stall them, but the pilot drove around them without slowing down.

"They know something is wrong," she said.

Beside her the pilot tutted.

She opened her mouth to speak, then deliberately started with their name. "Kercher," she said. "These people are losing their homes, losing everything. At some point they'll figure out we're a way off this rock."

She expected them to bite back but the pilot said nothing.

Staring at them piloting the buggy and having nothing to do with their hands, she wondered what she'd be doing in their position.

"How is it?" she asked.

The pilot glanced at her.

"Driving with your legs?"

They actually snorted. "Easier than flying."

Mari lived half an hour from Prab in a development for people who played nice with the Arcology. It had, when things weren't going to shit, full immersion suites for that "I'm not really outside the empire" feel of being able to live and work with citizens of the Arcology even if you spent most of your life in a physical body.

Having been born outside the Arcology, Mari shared none of Prab's anger towards it. She spent much of their friendship reminding Prab of the fact.

Prab missed her desperately. The possibility she'd be left on Sirajah's Reach to die was a wound she could only heal by finding a way to drag her friend off this broken rock.

The crowds in Mari's part of the city were thick. Gone the lack of direction. They waved at Prab, tried to flag them down, but the pilot ignored all entreaties. People shouted at their backs, cursed them, demanded, pleaded, threatened.

Prab despaired of ever finding Mari only to lose her breath entirely when her friend's unmistakable voice cut through as they were stuck at an intersection waiting for people to clear out.

Hugs followed. Tears as well. Prab was unashamed.

Mari smiled at her and they hugged again.

Kercher was introduced and the pilot managed to be civil before insisting they get on. Torches were shone their way. People crowding in, asking what was happening. The pilot ignored them, growing a silvered faceplate from their forehead to hide their expression entirely. It didn't stop people from trying to get answers, and Kercher's indifference only bred anger.

"I have stuff to bring," said Mari, thumbing towards her apartment.

"You are all the luggage you need," said the pilot curtly.

Prab wiped a speck of dirt from the back of her hand only for it to smear across the skin. Ash.

Already. She gazed up at the sky and saw nothing in the gloom.

Mari stood, hand on hip, then let go of the bag in her other hand to climb into the buggy as a man tried to barge past her, aiming for one of the spare seats.

"Step back," said Kercher and the car's frame glowed a soft green.

The man staggered back, more out of shock than harm.

Mari placed fingers on Prab's shoulder and squeezed as they drove away.

"Marinique," said Mari, leaning forward to introduce herself to the pilot.

"Ignore them," said Prab. She was trying to be light but the words fell from her mouth, heavy as lead. She was angry with that man but he was already dead. He just didn't know it. What right did she have to resent him?

"What now?" asked Kercher.

"The micro networks are running," said Prab, realising her inbox had been working, just not receiving. "You drive and I'll send messages as we hit the right neighbourhoods."

She felt Mari's eyes on the back of her head but couldn't share what they were doing. It was bad enough that she was leaving a world to die, she wouldn't be forced to justify who she'd chosen to save.

Besides, she told herself, trying to set her guilt aside, the world will come back, the Arcology will return like it was never away. Then she'd be the mad idiot who'd taken two hundred people off world because she'd lacked faith in the empire.

Regardless of her attempts at optimism, the death of the Arcology's citizens here on Sirajah's Reach sat unspoken in her chest like a huge man was using her for a poorly upholstered chair.

They were three quarters of the way around the loop the pilot planned with Prab's coordinates when they stumbled into a street entirely blocked by people.

As before, faces turned their way en masse.

The pilot reversed immediately but wasn't fast enough.

Prab watched as the crowd transitioned into motion.

People running and reaching, shouting for help.

Others accused them of being responsible.

A face over the front of the buggy. A woman's arm clasping at Prab's shoulder. Grasping, refusing to let go. Begging to be taken off world. Prab screamed for help and the buggy flashed green to bright blue and those who'd been rocking it, pulling at it, were thrown into the air to land, unmoving, deeper into the crowd.

The pilot shifted forward this time, bumping against the crowd, knocking them down and back.

"Stop!" screamed Prab, grabbing for them, but there was nothing to take hold of, no instrument to wrench at; the pilot was part of the buggy and could not be challenged.

When the people came again, a wave of flesh with fear and murder in each of their eyes, Kercher drove right at them.

The first bodies sounded like stamping down on cardboard and melons, then the screams turned from anger to terror and the crowd was fleeing in all directions. People still tried to take hold of the buggy but they were moving too fast. Flesh glanced off the chassis, tumbling away from the merest touch, and they were free.

Prab could do nothing but weep for the dead and dying, and she knew deep down that she would not have given any of them her place in the buggy.

She hated Kercher for what they'd done because it was safer than hating herself for letting them do it.

Behind her Mari said nothing, didn't move and remained resolutely closed-eyed.

By the time they arrived back at the landing bay, thousands of people were crowding the streets looking for ships to take them off world and ash was floating in the air like snow. A current of them followed the buggy's wake, drifting towards the bay where the pilot's ship was docked.

Kercher maintained the green glow all the way through, eyes only on the road and ignoring everything outside the car except their destination.

People held up crying children, waved, promised, wept. Prab kept her gaze down, refusing to look at those they passed, watching as small dark flakes landed on the buggy's frame.

Waiting for them in the landing bay was a ship with a radically different profile to the one they'd left behind. All semblance of sleekness was gone, replaced instead by bulky, bulbous pods that hung like swollen grapes from the sides of a thick spine which ran from one end of the bay to the other.

The ship remained a bright white, as if made of freshly fallen snow, but otherwise it could have been an entirely different visitor to the bay.

Mari hung back until Prab took her by the arm and walked them both into the ship's shadow. She wanted to tell Mari this was the safest way off planet, the only way off planet. Except to voice it would give the truth to the fate waiting those left behind.

"They're going to die," said Mari. Which defeated the point of Prab holding her tongue.

The ship closed the bay's entrance after they were inside. Was it fearful of the crowds collecting outside? Without power, without resources, they had only their hands, and those weren't going to force their way in.

"We don't know that," said Prab, the words woolly in her mouth.

Mari didn't reply.

"You'll be asleep until it's over," said Prab.

"The world will end and I'll awaken to find a new one on which to step with naked feet," said Mari softly.

The pilot disappeared inside the ship. The buggy was disassembled and absorbed into the ship's hull.

Prab didn't know what to do. She checked her manifest of passengers and wondered how many would show up. How many had even received the messages she'd jury-rigged to find them. She could hear the static of the crowds in the streets beyond the docks. Were there other ships offering berths as well, or was she only one taking anyone to safety?

It wasn't long before the first of those she'd messaged began arriving, highlighted in bright yellow by the ship straight into her vision so she could wave them through the growing numbers just standing there as if something might happen.

A group of engineers numbering twelve. They were infrastructure specialists, used to patching and fixing spots in the city which the Arcology's network didn't routinely cover.

Prab didn't know how or even where her water came from, but this lot had probably visited the aquifers for fun.

After them came biologists, botanists, an architect she'd gotten to know at a party, a selection of other lawyers and diplomats. Then several designers, but each separately as if they'd met outside and decided not to be seen together.

Prab paced as she waited for them, coming along one by one. Didn't they know what was at stake?

She knew they did, saw it in their eyes as they walked into the bay. The last few were dishevelled, bruised, talked of being followed and harassed by people wanting to join them. They shared looks of guilt in knowing they were the only ones with a chance to live, ducked their heads and boarded the ship.

The vast swathe of those she'd identified were people who knew the Arcology. They could pester it, cajole its systems, rewrite broken scripts and sweet talk nodes.

By the time Kercher exited the ship again she'd counted one hundred and twenty-two of the two hundred.

"We're short," said the pilot, surveying the shifting, nervous mass of people wondering what was about to happen to them. "But time's up. There are too many people outside to safely let any more through and the sky's closing in on us. If we don't go now we'll not be going anywhere."

Kercher wasn't explaining, it was their way of saying if she didn't get onboard, she'd be left behind.

Besides which ash was falling freely now.

Prab had never seen it like this inside the city. Had not believed it was possible.

By her side Mari, who had worked to keep Prab free from being overwhelmed by questions to which she didn't have an answer, turned to face the closed hanger doors.

Prab could feel herself edging towards panic, like a mouse unable to resist the cheese in the trap.

Questions about where they were going, how long would they be gone, what was happening with the city were endless, with myriad variations that all hid the real issue.

Were they going to die, and if not them, what about everyone else?

None of those she'd selected had children. Prab had been careful in her filtering. None of them had dependents of any kind on world.

The thought of people fighting or begging to bring their kids or their parents turned her stomach so bad she could taste vomit in her throat.

"The ship notes there is a large crowd heading this way," said Kercher.

Prab swallowed hard. Nodded.

"We are leaving now," they continued.

"We're missing so many," she said.

"About seventeen million."

She refused to look at them, refused to dignify their erasing of the thirty million embodied people who'd also die after they left.

"You will live," they said then. "Is that not enough?"

"Fuck off and die," said Prab.

Kercher moved away. "Three minutes, Interlocutor, and then we depart."

Prab found Mari. "It's time," she said.

Mari nodded and together they put the last people onto the ship. Her gaze turned again and again and again to the doors and the growing eddies of ash wafting through the air. Were there people she'd invited waiting on the other side wondering why the doors were closed?

Did they understand what ash in the air meant for them?

At the very last it was Mari's turn.

"Don't leave me behind," she said.

Prab tried not to cry.

"It's going to be all right," she said.

Mari smiled, the thin lines of her expression full of sorrow.

Then her pod shut and Mari went into stasis, leaving her feeling like a spare part.

"Just me left," she said to the ship.

You will not be sleeping, came a voice right inside her head.

"Don't do that," she said out loud. There was silence for a moment.

The pilot reappeared.

"The ship says you don't want to talk to it." They looked beyond irritated.

"I don't want it speaking in my head."

"Then what? Over loudspeaker? Fucking hell, you're precious, aren't you. Is now the time to be taking your stand against the Arcology?"

Prab ground her teeth.

"It can speak through my messaging system. Loudspeakers are also fine. Just do not conduct conversations through the bones of my skull."

"How's this?" said a voice. Nasal, high pitched, smooth. It sounded like someone was just behind her.

Resisting the urge to turn and face the speaker, Prab nodded. The pilot hissed in disgust and ducked back onto the bridge.

"You said I wasn't sleeping."

"I need an Interlocutor awake and able to provide expert support. You are the Interlocutor the city provided."

Prab didn't know what to think, but sure, fine. Whatever. She would live. She would get off Sirajah's Reach. For that chance she'd do whatever the ship was asking.

And just as she stepped onto the ship, the doors to the bay creaked open and a thousand bodies pushed their way inside.

6.

The ship had built the Interlocutor a chair that sat just to the side and behind Kercher's interface. Praveenthi would sit straight backed like an ancient woman riding an upright bicycle.

Kercher did not do well with change. They knew this. It was the cause of many of their problems in the Arcology, although they couldn't blame their current situation on their own mild inability to adapt to changing circumstances. It wasn't as if the Arcology didn't provide a safe haven for people like them.

You chose this, they reminded themselves. And it may have saved your life.

It was a dark thought, unbecoming, and it tasted like this wretched planet's perpetual ash storms in their mind.

The ship took control as Kercher sat unresponsive, lost in ideas of their own guilt and punishment.

"Get it together," came the curt command, and Kercher was in their seat again, their mind sitting like a candle on top of the cake that was the ship's own identity.

Bodies were carpeting the floor of the bay and crashing towards the ship in a wave of desperate flesh whose only goal was to save itself by hanging onto the ship.

Which Kercher knew was not going to achieve anything.

The ship was sealed now and no one outside was going to get in. The materials from which the ship's body was formed were impervious to anything the people outside could bring to bear.

Kercher watched their faces, a confusing spread of eyes and mouths, expressions of hope and despair, fear and desperation a certain kind of artist would be proud of capturing as a way of upsetting the comfortable.

"We need to leave," they said to the ship.

"I am aware," came the reply. Yet they didn't move.

"Why aren't we going anywhere?" asked the Interlocutor.

Departure wasn't Kercher's thing. The ship was the real pilot except for some specific circumstances, and take off was not one of them.

They didn't reply to the Interlocutor. Honestly, they could die in a ditch and Kercher wouldn't shed a tear.

"They are citizens," said the ship.

"They're Excluded," said Kercher.

"Only some of them. Legally, they are all under the Arcology's duty of care," said the Interlocutor and her words rasped out her mouth like sandpaper on stone.

"If we leave, they will die," said the ship.

"What did you think was going to happen?" asked Kercher. Where had the ship developed such a sense of off-the-rails obligation? Didn't they have to get out of here to see what was happening everywhere else? They had bigger problems to manage.

"If we leave now, everyone in this bay will die as a result of our departure," said the ship despondently.

It wasn't the planet they were worried about. It was the people on and under the ship, trapped in the bay as spacetime distorted to lift the ship out of the planet's gravity well. They'd be subjected to forces great enough to smear them across the surface of the universe like jam.

Knowing someone's going to die, and being the cause of it, are very different things.

"It's not your fault," said Kercher, and meant it. "They're already dead, they just don't know it."

The Interlocutor had paled. Kercher thought they might faint and was glad she was already secured in the little station the ship had built for her.

"Let's go," they said to the ship. "The longer we stay the worse our outcomes become."

The ship paused in their mind and then was back.

"You are correct."

Those three words were shot through with a white grief that tasted to Kercher of metal and acid. It was a deeply unpleasant feeling, and not for the first time they wished they weren't so closely connected to the ship's identity.

"Close your eyes, Interlocutor," said Kercher.

"What?"

"You heard me fine," they said, and let the ship absorb them into itself without checking to see if they'd been obeyed. Kercher's body was coated in the interface they used to pilot; their clothes dissolved so they were in direct contact with a soft, fleshy material through which they used to access all those systems they needed to fulfil their duties, through their skin.

Kercher's was engineered to allow them to isolate portions of their skin so they could multitask, built on an ancient understanding that as the body's largest organ, it could perform multiple processing tasks at once if given the right interface.

They saw with their fingers, heard with their back, thought with their stomach and, most importantly of all, piloted with their entire skin faster than they could consciously think, perceiving spacetime directly through the ships own senses.

The sensation of lifting off was muted within the confines of the ship. The screens giving the illusion of a clear view to the outside closed down as the fabric of space and time were bent and crunched tight along narrow gradients that would propel them up from the surface and out of the planet's grasp.

An empty bay was designed to facilitate the forces required to achieve escape velocity without crumbling to dust in the distortion.

One full of people, on the other hand, would be left covered in a thin gruel of liquidated bodies.

The screens weren't shut down for safety's sake. Kercher had revelled in the psychotropic effects of twisted gravity a hundred times before. This time the sheen of blood and atomised bones made the difference.

The Interlocutor vomited all down her front.

Kercher wondered if she'd ever been off world except by translation and sniggered as the ship's automated systems cleaned her up. A combination of rough manipulation of spontaneously manufactured suction devices and a spray of chemicals which would dissolve her stomach's contents, drying to leave no trace of her embarrassment.

The Interlocutor didn't speak until they broke through the ash and rain that cloaked Sirajah's Reach and they were in the darkness beyond the atmosphere.

When she did find her voice, it was to weep into the placid grace of orbiting her dead world.

"Couldn't we have put her to sleep for this part?" they asked the ship. The death of those in the hanger was their own fault. Besides which, Kercher's body was not printed to feel the kinds of emotions overwhelming the Interlocutor.

Shame for her, they thought and tried to suppress their irritation at the sobs coming over their shoulder.

The ship plotted the route through translation.

"I need a few minutes," it announced.

Which was about as fast as Kercher had ever known it be.

"If you make a mistake," they said, feeling in the mood to make others angry.

"If there's a mistake to be made it's to take too long," said the ship. "Now hush while I work."

Kercher followed the general gist of the ship's approach, but it cut corners via mathematical black boxes through which Kercher couldn't pass and wouldn't have been able to pass even if they were still inside the Arcology rather than printed into this crappy processing-limited body.

Nodes were a different kind of intelligence, living half inside information space while most of the Arcology's citizens were just visitors, in it but not of it.

Translation without an anchor was the point which stuck in Kercher's stomach.

The ship wasn't looking to hang its journey onto the Arcology's expansive network. Instead it was plotting a translation that would spew them out on top of Akhanda without clearance, without warning and without using the Arcology's existing gateways.

If the network's down then trying to travel that way might not work, they realised. And that was the best outcome. What if they were halfway through translating and the network cut them into pieces or erased them completely – leaving them stranded as ibits forever awaiting reconstruction.

Unexpectedly the underside of the cockpit shaded transparent and the storm covered planet revealed itself. Lightning sprites blasted out of the atmosphere, silently gnomish hats for gnomes the size of mountains evaporated even as new ones appeared in their wake.

There was a desolate beauty to it.

Beneath its oppression was the city named after the planet – Sirajah's Reach. Kercher wanted to know if the dust shields had failed. Was everyone dead yet?

Better for them to have perished already.

Better for there to be no hope, they thought.

The idea that they could eek out survival for days or longer filled Kercher with a horror that reached their heart in a way most emotions couldn't.

"You did that?" they asked. The Interlocutor could have brought up a screen within their own vision rather than turn the deck transparent. They would have had a better view that way.

"It's my home," she replied. The words were ash after the fire.

"It's gone," said Kercher harshly. Better they get used to it now. There was no coming back.

"Fuck you," said the Interlocutor.

"Good at your job then?" they replied.

"What type of criminal ends up being printed out as a pilot?" asked the Interlocutor, hatred on their lips.

And they were right.

Only the most pathetic of criminals ended up printed out playing second, and definitively unnecessary, fiddle to a minor node as their actual sentence.

Kercher's commitment and anger had brought them a long way, had helped them survive their sentence without sinking into melancholy or regret. The Interlocutor could go fuck herself if she thought such petty antagonisms were going to break their back.

Still. She'd navigated the interface, had revealed the planet below, and the ship had granted her enough access to make it possible.

Kercher didn't respect her for her action but they recognised the ship had an agenda with this woman they didn't understand. A lesson there. Watch, wait, see what she was good for because on the surface, it wasn't obvious at all.

They wanted to thump their armrest and demand the ship get on with it. What was taking so long?

Except what they were doing was dangerous enough that all the manuals and training courses Kercher had been forced to sit through prohibited exactly this kind of madness.

An unanchored translation within Arcology space.

Fine elsewhere. No other culture they'd encountered was as technologically sophisticated and no other culture had developed translation. Jumping about spacetime outside of the Arcology was simple because there was little chance you'd cross information space with another ship, or worse, a major node.

"How long will it take?" asked the Interlocutor.

"The ship will be done when they're done," said Kercher, cross at her for asking the very question they'd held back.

"I mean the journey," came the reply.

"Do you know nothing?" Kercher asked.

The Interlocutor didn't reply and Kercher felt forced to deploy an avatar of themselves right into her augmented view of the world. She flinched when they first appeared, ready to be hit. Her expression processed what they were seeing in real time, the Interlocutor realising Kercher was virtual and only then allowing herself to grow angry.

"We're going to translate. Once the route is calculated it will take no time at all to open the gate and translate through. Which wasn't strictly true. An emergency translation could work almost instantaneously. Typically gate travel was scheduled and subject to permits. You received a slot and waited for it.

The strange calculations in ibit space that were used to open a translation gate took their own moment and sometimes it could take longer than others to reach a desired anchor.

"I've heard there are some translations that can take hours to establish stability. Small jumps take no time at all, longer jumps across greater informational distance are harder, most risky. I've heard some calculations might take the fastest nodes days to resolve," said Kercher, feeling expansive.

"Why?" asked the Interlocutor.

Kercher couldn't hold the smile off their face. "Ibits are fragile things. The hundreds of them required to hold a translation gate open are hungry for energy in the shape of information states. The wrong set, or even the right set at the wrong time, can leave the entanglement coefficient unacceptably volatile. Path finding to the minimum free information of your destination takes its time."

"I don't understand any of that," said the Interlocutor.

"I know," said Kercher, and turned back to nominally face forward.

"You could be more useful," said the ship.

Stung, Kercher shifted in their cocoon. "What do you need?"

"We have no idea what we're going to find. Prepare the ship."

Kercher felt a thrill pass through their chest. Something their body was well structured to encourage – the idea of combat always excited them.

They let their skin guide the ship's systems as it started to build sensors, engines and weapons fit for combat with an unknown assailant.

7.

The ship had finished its calculations some time ago.

As Kercher prepared them for possible hostilities, the ship sat on its mind and tried to find enough executive function to make the decision to translate.

Kercher's nerves around the unanchored translation were a spike of bruised leaves on the ship's consciousness.

Its own nerves were too deeply cosseted for the pilot to sense them. Yet they were there, like the burning material spiralling across a black hole's event horizon. The light of their burning stopped the ship from translating them to Akhanda.

There was every chance they'd arrive and find the ringworld gone. In pieces, under assault.

Perhaps everything was fine, but if so, then why had the Arcology gone quiet.

It wasn't that Sirajah's Reach was cut off from the network.

It was far more frightening.

Since arriving at Sirajah's Reach, the ship had been trying, at first per a protocol so mundane it ran on autonomic systems, to reach the Arcology.

Outsiders, even the Excluded who were so often former citizens, misunderstood the nature of the Arcology. It wasn't bounded by spacetime, nor by physicality in any sense. The Arcology was a state of information that existed across the galaxy, and if certain nodes were to be believed, beyond.

There might be ten thousand worlds and ten times that in stations, asteroids and wandering planets housing the processing power, but all that distributed mesh did was house an empire that ranged almost infinitely across information space.

To be part of the Arcology was to ignore the boundaries of time and space, to dwell within the underlying sea of information which was the true ground of being of the universe.

The ancients had believed information was added onto the top of matter, created by minds. Nothing more than a grandiose attempt to make sense of a world where it could rain or blaze with sun and reason was required to make sense of how one followed the other.

The Arcology understood existence differently.

The ship knew that information was everything. Every molecule, atom, boson, lepton, quark and string were expressions of a substrate written in a single universal language the Arcology called the ibit.

If the qubit tied together physicality in a strange non-local sense, the ibit tied together information. In the hierarchy, there were no particles without qubits, no qubits without preons and no anything without ibits. Except information could be anything and as a result was only bound by time and place where that was inherent in the expression of the information itself.

To be unable to reach the Arcology was to be in the same room as a vast all-encompassing party and unable to hear a single voice in a trillion conversations that were happening all around you in every moment.

For Sirajah's Reach to be cut off was one thing. For the conversation, for all that information, to have gone silent, to have emptied out, was something else.

The ship was orbiting Sirajah's Reach and the truth of all orbits – that they were perpetually falling but never descending – sat in the ship's identity as a metaphor for everything else it was feeling about being suddenly alone.

It hoped with everything it was that it had been, somehow and unthinkably, shut out of the party, that it was stood outside looking in and hoping someone spotted it.

Because the alternative – that the party had ended and everyone was gone – well, it was a mountain that was slowly crushing its ability to make the simplest of decisions.

The pilot couldn't understand and, although Interlocutor Prab might, the ship couldn't bring itself to articulate its fears to another sentient being, because to do so might make them real.

Once uttered, they couldn't be taken back.

Besides, it had the strongest suspicion it was going to need the Interlocutor in a state of mind where she could be the thing she was supposed to be – a bridge between the Arcology and those who were not. Especially as for all practical purposes, it was all of the Arcology there was for the time being.

"Ship," said the pilot.

The ship ignored them.

"Ship," they repeated, their voice growing irritated, frightened. The ship's emotions might be hidden out of sight of their mutually shared space, but it was acting out of character.

"I'm ready," said the ship, and spooled up its calculation engines.

Space around them shimmered the colours of possibility, shapes and ideas that had no physical counterparts. Small minds like those contained in printed bodies could make no more sense of the data their bodies sent them at a time like this than a jellyfish could consider how the expression of information was a self-absorbing state which would begin then consume itself, only to start all over again in an eternal cycle of recurrence.

At last they were ready to translate.

8.

Translation was to absorb information in one location and extrude it in another. The nodes of the Arcology had argued for many generations whether this meant that in translating, the version stepping into the gate ceased to exist and was replaced by another whose base construction so closely matched the original that even memories and preferences, phobias and proclivities were reproduced on the other side of the gate, or if they were truly being transported across spacetime.

Shows and stories loved the trope of the person who translated and was different on the other side. The murderer who became a pacifist, the philanderer who became faithful, the addict who was freed and vice versa.

No such event had ever been recorded in the history of the translation gates. Nevertheless, in the popular mind, which meant outside of the nodes who supported the existence of the Arcology, the very idea such a thing might happen refused to depart.

Most nodes subscribed to the orthogonal idea of recurrence, that the information was simply recurring elsewhere across the landscape that was information space. It was itself, not something previous, nor something new, just the same thing expressed elsewhere. A flower growing in one bed suddenly growing in another.

Others argued that such specificity as contained in the word "elsewhere" meant such an argument couldn't stand.

The ship had no care for these philosophical debates or their reliance on using information to plumb its own depths in search of meaning. If its previous self was destroyed each time it translated in favour of a new version made no difference.

There was no discernible difference between a pre- and post-translation identity. Hence, even if it were true that it was committing suicide each time it translated, such knowledge made no difference to its life.

Like all such theories – and the many worlds theory was its favourite here – if it were true, it made no difference to the world in which the ship found itself. On such a basis it was then not just an irrelevance to living a normal life, but could be safely put into the box marked "magical beliefs" and confidently hidden behind the engine manifolds never to be thought about again.

Their destination was the system in which the ringworld of Akhanda was at home. Not close enough to the ring to be caught in any disaster, should there be one. Not far enough out to be beyond help if they got themselves into trouble.

If all was okay, the ship planned to make a couple of small skips closer and pretend nothing was wrong before firmly demanding to understand why Sirajah's Reach had been cut off and insisting they send help as quickly as possible.

It couldn't stop thinking about those hundreds who had died in the bay as they departed.

It would never stop thinking about them.

It was used to being dispassionate in the face of its pilot's criminally odd beliefs. Sirajah's Reach had changed all that. The ship did not know what kind of being it would see in itself once it had finished processing those events.

They blinked into Akhanda's system, its brilliant blue-white star a distant coin-sized blister in the darkness of space.

The ship flipped its channels open and was flooded with the noise of battle.

9.

Prab watched as the pilot, encased in their metallic sheath, jolted and convulsed. The stars beyond blurred and the ship slid as though between two slips of midnight silk.

Her stomach lurched, but all the food inside her had already landed down her front. Her throat thick and closed, Prab concentrated on not passing out.

She joined the ship's comm lines and a thousand channels opened up to her mind, a myriad of views, voices and situations. Unable to follow them, Prab stepped back and thought about what she wanted to see.

The ship wasn't a singular node, that node had hundreds, if not thousands of smaller sentients living within the umbrella of its being. Some of them, the sprites, were no brighter than a junction box, but many of them, the pixies, were brilliant in their own right. She thought about asking one of them to help her filter the chaos currently smashing into her skull.

The screens showing outside were filled with a single dark grey sheet of colour. No differentiation, no flaws.

It was Akhanda, and they were in its shadow. Stretching to both sides, above and below, it was so vast, and they so close, there was no sign of anything else.

She'd seen representations of ring worlds, but they were always from the inside – lakes and forests, cities and rivers.

The ship translated again.

Prab managed to unclench her teeth and release the arm rests from under fingers white with tension.

This time they were further away.

The ship was talking across dozens of channels at once.

The pilot was shifting them sideways as if they were under attack.

If they were, Prab could see no sign of incoming fire. There were no explosions, no arcing bolts of fire crossing the deep of space.

She remembered that lasers were invisible, that was the point of them, efficient delivery of colossal amounts of energy, for her to see them, they'd have to be hitting countermeasures designed to scatter their focused beams.

Did they still use lasers, or was she remembering period dramas about civil wars and grand space battles before information became the medium of death's arrival?

What exactly would a ship like this do when it chose violence?

Why shoot energy at something when you could instruct its base components to express themselves as something different? Granite into banana, engine into cotton wool.

Order into disorder.

She could see the curve of Akhanda, they had to be light minutes out. The edge on one side was fuzzy and she squinted to try to make it sharp. A sprite noticed what she was doing and helpfully zoomed in.

It wasn't fuzz. It was pieces, chunks of the ring floating out as a cloud, dense and thick with debris. She realised those chunks were vast, kilometres across and bigger.

Instructing the sprite to construct a three-dimensional representation of what was happening a view of the star system and its ring world unscrolled before her eyes.

The ring sat one astronomical unit out from the star. An ancient measurement that was supposedly the perfect distance from a star for habitable worlds.

The Arcology, despite its virtual existence, held to traditions like the best of them, and this one was particularly strong. Sirajah's Reach had been 1.2AUs from its star, its gravity at 0.9 standard was weak enough that people would joke about it being poorly located real estate.

She found a pixie with medical functionality and, just as they translated again, had it serve her an injection to quell the nausea. The effect was instant, and as if emerging from a cold sea into warm sunshine, Prab felt herself.

The incessant translations no longer jerking her out of whatever she was doing, she searched the system for non-

Arcology chatter. It had to be why the ship had kept her awake – her literal job was Interlocutor.

Except if Akhanda was under attack, her role was entirely redundant.

It didn't matter. There was nothing on any system or technology used by the Arcology's neighbours. All the noise in-system was Arcology.

The ship had locked down the flow of information and it was engaging across about a dozen channels. Some of those were clearly friends, but four of them were trying to issue orders, ask for help and deliver status updates.

Four was still too many to listen to concurrently.

Prab focussed on the status updates. She synced them to the map of the star system and, slowly, she began to understand what was happening.

Akhanda was in the middle of an attack by an unknown and still unidentified foe.

And it was losing.

She assumed the ship would ask for help when and if it needed her. Except nodes were notoriously single-minded under pressure, their multitasking whittled down to linear problem solving. Prab wondered if this one was beholden to the stereotypes.

"Do you need anything from me?" she asked.

The pilot's body continued to jerk, and even through the inertial dampening she could feel the ship lurching one way and another.

Then they translated again.

This time they were inside the arc of the ringworld and she could see its vast panoramas below and above as its idylls stretched beyond her ability to track.

Small sparks shimmered in the night.

"Find out who this is," said the ship.

Systems flooded open under Prab's purview. Menus and options she hadn't known existed. Sprites were signalling their readiness to do her bidding; communications systems, links to the ringworld's sensors and more.

An ocean of noise and information, signals and people.

Prab felt her mind stretch, but then this is what she knew how to do. Signals intelligence.

Working quickly with the sprites, she filtered out everything they could identify as Arcology.

To her surprise everything disappeared. If not for her own people, the void was silent.

Which couldn't be right. The Arcology couldn't be attacking itself.

The ship translated again, disrupting her concentration.

Prab took a deep breath, focused again on the constellations of information smashing into her mind.

No unknown ships. No unknown stations. No unrecognised communications.

If there was an enemy in-system, it wasn't one she could see.

"There's no one here," she said to the ship.

"Find them," said the ship.

"You're fighting yourselves," she spluttered.

The ship lurched and her stomach flipped, bringing her attention to the world beyond that of comms and signals.

Outside the ship she could see buildings now. The ship was barrelling between towers and skyscrapers. All around, the atmosphere was cluttered with debris. She saw bodies in there too.

As if the gravitational field of the ringworld had collapsed.

Akhanda was large enough to have its own gravitational well. Although the Arcology manipulated it so that the ground on the ring always felt like down. The problem otherwise being that everyone would fall off the world and find themselves hurtling through space towards the local centre of gravity, in this case, that spot contained the star around which they were orbiting.

Not that they'd know this, because the one defining feature of falling off a planet is how it's typically accompanied by being dead.

The speed required to offset the gravity of both the star and the unthinkably vast mass of Akhanda via spin was so fast that it was cheaper and easier to manipulate gravity than it was to manipulate the materials to survive such stresses, and that was before factoring in other challenges such as orbital stability.

Having the living part of the world on the outside, as it were, had been tried and found boring. Citizens wanted to see their star.

The ship executed a ninety-degree turn and she could see along a grand avenue that had to run for hundreds of kilometres, huge towers standing to each side. Under other circumstances, Prab would have been speechless at the sight of it.

Instead, she saw another ship floating, still, on fire with pieces of its carcass cracked open and hanging in the air alongside it. A turtle whose shell had been shattered, poised gracefully in death.

"Is that one of ours?" she asked as it disappeared behind them.

"Find out," said the ship.

Prab took a shot and had a pixie compare it against all known silhouettes.

Sure enough, it was a node known to the Arcology. A small ship who, like this one, had never taken a designation or earned its name, but was one of theirs nonetheless.

On a whim she set the ship to identify all wreckage, then returned her attention to the complete lack of enemy chatter.

If the Arcology was fighting itself there should be sides, two sets of comms through which the combatants were taking their direction. If one side hadn't understood they were in a war, that didn't change the world for the other, she would have to find their channels and figure out who was on them.

This meant she could carve out the busiest channels, especially those with no comms security, at least inside the Arcology. Four fifths of the signals disappeared from her chatter. One of the sprites helping her, a little sentient whose speciality was pattern recognition, flipped with joy at the outcome.

Then she decided to start again, because the enemy would be using one channel and it would be busy. But it wouldn't be open.

Prab searched out the busiest channels and, overseen by her super-enthusiastic sprite, sent a horde of pixies to find those channels that were closed to the public.

The screens showing their surroundings whited out. Dazzling after images left Prab unable to read, eyes watering.

"What the hell?" she asked.

The ship was spinning, shards of fire spitting from its sides.

Then they translated.

They blinked back further along the same grand avenue. Kilometre-high sculptures of the human form stretching towards the sky, dancing and in love, marked an intersection.

A ship of some kind, made of light and shadow with a bulbous outline, was crouched over the location from where they'd translated like an octopus trying to surround its prey.

We were right there, Prab realised.

As if sensing its quarry had escaped, the enemy ship collapsed in on itself, turning from unfurled umbrella to a melange of needles reminiscent of a dimensionally challenged sea urchin. The sight of it defying the normal rules of reality made her eyes water.

The ball of spikes twisted and span and Prab realised it was searching for them.

"It's trying to find us," said Prab. This enemy was from outside the Arcology, no matter that she couldn't identify their comms.

The air shimmered between them and their enemy, as if the universe itself was being called into question, shadows, shapes and lights which left Prab dazed imposed themselves in the gap.

Where the disruption touched the enemy it burned and broke and shattered.

Prab watched, mesmerised as the enemy ship died in front of them.

As it bled it shifted shapes, tried to flee, to dodge, but their ship continued to do whatever it was doing until nothing remained that could try to escape.

10.

The enemy ship was barely there. Kercher was doing everything that mattered. The umbrella hostile floated, dead, in the air of the avenue. Kercher was scanning the horizon for others. It appeared nowhere on their comms, emitted no signals they could pick up.

Not that they were busy looking. What they were panicked about was how it had jumped them out of nowhere, had nearly enveloped them before they'd realised what was happening.

Having seen this one, all alone, they couldn't find others.

What kind of civilisation could hide in the ibit field? This enemy was not Arcology. Kercher had no idea what it was and neither did the ship's systems. Whoever it was, they were new. Why wasn't the Interlocutor sending him the enemy's comms channels to exploit?

Kercher put it aside, tried to quell the fear it gave them. They had quite enough adrenaline in their system already.

Instead of moving on, they waited.

The ship would translate them again when ready, but all the shuffling and random flight paths they'd been using to confuse incoming hostiles had completely failed to work.

In the stillness Kercher took in Akhanda. They'd not been back here in a very long time. Not since their sentence had been handed down and the ship had picked them up in their freshly printed body.

Even battered as it was, Akhanda was beautiful. The artificial illumination in this part of the ring currently set to sunrise, the star around which they were orbiting muted, filtered down to a pale disc in the sky overhead.

The day they'd left they'd been printed out, given the specifications of their new body and invited to repent before leaving.

Kercher did not repent and thousands of rotations away from their home had not softened their heart even a little.

At first it had been the indignity of being forced to live in a physical body. They'd been thrown out of their comfort, exposed and vulnerable like a jelly melting under the sun. Then, and now, they found they could not see the fault in their actions.

The Arcology differed in its assessment, but that wasn't enough for Kercher to believe any kind of rehabilitation of their attitude was going to happen. Eventually, they hoped, the fact that they refused to recant wouldn't matter and they'd be allowed home.

"What now?" they asked the ship.

"The Interlocutor is key. They must find the network our enemy is using."

Kercher didn't think this was really relevant. If the rest of the nodes here on Akhanda couldn't figure out what was happening, what was one Excluded going to do?

"You got that, right?" they asked the Interlocutor.

"I need another one of those," she replied, indicating the dead hostile ahead of them.

Which was ludicrous. They'd just been as up close and personal as could be needed.

"You just had the best chance," said Kercher.

"It wasn't enough," she said.

Had they been sat there like a lemon while they were fighting for their lives? Kercher had half a mind to review the footage of the cockpit and see just what they were doing.

"It doesn't matter what has happened," said the ship. "Find us the enemy."

"What about everyone else?" asked Kercher. Surely the Arcology's own people, based here at Akhanda, would be in the thick of the fighting.

"We can't trust anyone," said the Interlocutor.

"Shut up," said Kercher.

"She is right," said the ship.

"She isn't."

"We translated here because there were sensor readings for a node known to me. It was a trap."

"I told you," blurted the Interlocutor.

"You said we were fighting ourselves," said the ship flatly.

The Interlocutor didn't respond, but Kercher could feel them in the ship's systems, active and working, commanding a legion of its internal community.

"We just sit here then?" they asked.

"It would be unwise to translate again when we cannot ascertain who is friend or foe. There are three million active channels but none of them can be verified as belonging to the Arcology alone."

Kercher mulled over their problem.

What if the hostile they'd just destroyed was nothing more than a scout.

They'd seen the smashed debris floating away from the ring, they'd seen the lack of gravity across this part of the arc. Who knew what else the enemy had accomplished.

Kercher hated it. They were one of the Arcology's warships. Built for engaging with cultures who didn't respect boundaries.

Akhanda had the tiniest complement of the ship's kin because it hadn't ever seen hostilities, not in the tens of thousands of rotations of its existence. The nodes here would be able to retrofit themselves onto a war footing, but by then any attack might well be decisively over.

They should be doing something. Fighting. Defending the Arcology. Saving lives and shoving away the threat.

Instead the ship had stopped its frantic translations, and they were hanging a few klicks from the dead hostile and doing nothing.

They knew it wasn't true. The ship was occupied in the truest sense of the word. Its entire attention was focused on the ringworld, on other nodes. Kercher could feel its growing desperation. It wasn't that there were battles they could translate into and make a difference in so doing. The ship was clear – anything they were seeing could be fake.

There was no information they could trust.

The question of how could be tackled later.

For now Kercher had to wait, and they hated it.

This printed body of theirs demanded action, was built to move, and instead they were forced to remain still.

So they did what they could and scanned the defunct ship hanging across from them.

Organic materials. Like any one of a dozen other cultures they'd visited.

No pilot, or at least, no spaces within its superstructure that could be mapped as hollow or prepared for a body likes theirs.

Not uncommon. The greater part of the civilisations that Arcology interacted with used autonomous or entirely sentient craft. Most had no choice because only the Arcology had translation technology and biology had not evolved life to travel across space.

Everyone else relied on warping spacetime to trick their way around the limitations of mass and energy. Energetically expensive, relatively slow and, as such, a massive barrier to aggressive colonial expansion.

Primitive was the word the ship used when they were in private.

The enemy ship was autonomous, possibly sentient and almost certainly alive.

There were civilisations out there whose fleets fit this profile, but none of them were a threat to the Arcology. Where they weren't docile and peaceful by nature, they were entirely fixed in the physical, easily dominated by the Arcology whose technology could change the physical world as easily as imagining it.

Kercher was confident the ship they were piloting could end entire civilisations of this kind if it came to it.

All of which meant whoever this was, they were new to the Arcology.

Had they been planning this? Was this a vast conspiracy in the making? Had the Arcology missed chances to detect and counter an invasion?

What did they want?

"Stop spiralling," said the ship, their attention sweeping over and past them like a cosmic lighthouse.

Kercher wanted them to take a sample of the enemy. They wanted to understand how they worked.

"It doesn't matter," said the ship. "They're dead. What we did worked."

"Will it work next time?" asked Kercher, and got no response.

"Try this," said the Interlocutor, and Kercher's display was filled with trajectories, vectors and locations. They were a web of expanding moments spreading out from a position on the ringworld several light minutes away on the other side of the star.

"This is where it started?" asked Kercher.

It didn't matter that there was no answer. They knew what was coming next.

The ship didn't travel with its entire complement of aggression ready to go. Why arrive anywhere ready to go to war. It sent the wrong kind of messages.

While they'd been translating like a staggering drunk through Akhanda's territory, Kercher had been reconfiguring the ship's body to be the biggest bastard in the volume.

Now was the moment it mattered.

They translated across the system to the location the Interlocutor had provided.

They were greeted with dense black smoke, heat that blasted the exterior of the ship and turbulence that caught Kercher off guard and forced them to concentrate on stabilising the ship rather than seeking hostiles.

The ship's sensors were blasted with electromagnetic interference rendering them blind to the physical.

Kercher switched over to information space and was rewarded with no less chaos. Spacetime was fractured here, through the arc of the ringworld and out towards the edge of the system.

A huge scar in reality was bleeding randomness, and wherever that noise touched it, reality broke under its assault.

The weapon, if it was that, was recognisable to Kercher, who saw the manipulation of information space when they saw it.

"They're in information space," they spluttered, but both the ship and the Interlocutor were already there.

They suddenly wished their printed body was more robust, that it had come with its own countermeasures against information warfare. Instead, it was a mixture of organic and inorganic components, all of which were bounded, by design, in the physical.

If they died here, there'd be no restoring them to a previous back up. All those previous versions of them were on ice until they'd served their sentence, and if the ship was eliminated no one would even know they'd died.

This could be the end of them. It was a strangely stirring thought.

"You're doing it again," said the ship impatiently.

"I've eyes," said the Interlocutor, and a representation of the volume unfurled across their interface.

How were they doing this? wondered Kercher, but it was a fleeting thought, pushed aside by the need to find an enemy, to kill an enemy. To survive and to save others.

"Ready?" asked the ship, and suddenly all their focus was on Kercher.

"I'm ready," said the pilot, and they flipped up a hostile bearing down on them.

11.

The Interlocutor had found the enemy buried in the Arcology's own communications channels. Somehow they'd inveigled their way in and were piggybacking across the entire network.

That they had technological superiority in information space caused the ship's senses to flutter with uncertainty. Maybe they were lucky. Maybe they'd found an exploit.

Infosec was supposed to be paramount among nodes, but perhaps the lack of any actual counterparties to protect against bred complacency. They were paying for it now.

It didn't matter, the Interlocutor had isolated the enemy's traffic and traced it back to an emergent point from where, like a crack in a shatterproof glass, it had spread in an expanding web across Akhanda and beyond.

Was this attack the hub of their encroachment, was all the Arcology subject to this bombardment, or was Sirajah's Reach just unfortunate to be caught in the web of this initial assault?

Setting its sprites to shore up its informational defences, the ship ensured they were ready, pumped the pilot full of reaction-enhancing drugs and translated them to the location the Interlocutor was certain housed the core of the enemy incursion.

Navigating the debris of the damaged ringworld was akin to flying through thick water far from the light of any stars. Worse still, there were chunks of rubble and ruined world ranging in size from microscopic to mountainous.

The ship had a tough old hide, but it did not want to slam front first at a sizeable proportion of the speed of light into a wall of metamaterials just as it was trying to lock down the enemy.

They circled around a chunk of the ringworld's outer shell to find three of the same kind of vessels that had jumped them earlier.

The pilot unleashed a barrage of ibit weaponry designed to dismantle them at the informational level. If they were here in the physical, they were destroyed.

The first craft collapsed in on itself just as the first had done, writhing as it died. The ship took footage to study later.

Those remaining split, darting in opposite directions. The second of them disappeared and it took a moment for the ship to realise they'd translated away.

Shit.

"Did they just–?" asked the pilot, and the ship told them to concentrate on the other.

Kercher did as instructed and followed it as it weaved between broken towers, shattered landscapes and around a huge statue of a human figure that had been broken in two.

The enemy ship unfurled those huge tentacles and flipped around, facing them like a giant dish trying to catch as much sun as possible.

The pilot took evasive measures but the ship wasn't taking any chances and translated them behind the hostile.

The pilot, disoriented by the translation, didn't fire upon emerging and the ship took control, destroying the second enemy with a barrage of informational entropy which told the structure of the craft that it was as energetic as background space.

The enemy disintegrated as half of it turned to vacuum.

"Where's the other?" it asked the Interlocutor.

A location flashed up on their shared systems. The enemy had shuffled closer to the epicentre of the damage done to Akhanda.

A signal arrived begging to be read. It was on a channel the ship had never used. Had believed wasn't a real channel despite there being rumours of this kind of channel existing like a thin string tying together the Arcology's entire communications network.

It flushed the thing to check they weren't being spoofed, and then answered.

"I'm here."

"Cease your fighting and proceed to this location."

Coordinates were buried within the message and then the channel was gone.

The ship told the pilot to disengage.

"If you translate, we can have it," said the pilot.

The ship hesitated. It wanted to do exactly as the pilot wished. It had broken three of the enemy now, it wouldn't stop until they were routed. Until they were made to pay for what they'd done and the lives they'd taken.

Except that channel, laughably called *the jam between the sponge*, had come into existence to request their aid, before disappearing again.

Among its peers there had been tales of these kinds of communications and how important they were. It was said that they only ever activated at times of existential threat to the Arcology.

Only twice since translation technology was perfected.

The ship knew where the enemy had gone.

It could follow.

Just one translation and it could crush the enemy. Then it could go to the requested location.

"We go get them," it said to the pilot whose body responded with joy.

They translated.

12.

Prab decided that being translated without an anchor was like being fucked sideways with a bike.

She could feel the chemicals the ship had filled her with and was grateful, but they didn't stop the nausea from each new jump, just suppressed her need to throw up on an empty stomach and applied the banging in her head with a hammer rather than a house.

They appeared back beyond the arc of the ringworld. There were no scars, just a black which throbbed and writhed up, down and sideways.

The ship oriented itself towards the one hostile who'd fled and opened fire. It withered under their assault and the pilot actually cheered.

The ship grew still.

"We should go," said the pilot. "Find the rest of them."

Prab looked at their location. This broken piece of spacetime. It pulsed because it struggled to be something, but was denied.

A small speck of grey against the black.

The shear in reality bloomed like an inflating balloon and something emerged hundreds of clicks away, exploding into something ten, twenty, a hundred times their size.

It had no form beyond grey, no shape other than existing in this space, now.

Prab's eyes watered as she tried to make sense of it, its edges and surfaces sliding off one another, burning her vision.

"We need to go," she said.

The pilot opened fire, and where the ship's weapons touched the arrival, its surfaces broke down into nothings, sparks of light, iotas of fractured information.

Then whatever it was arrived properly. Colour spread across its surface. Textures unravelled like a bedsheet shaken out before fitting. One moment it was impossible to understand, and the next it was there, a bulbous living thing, round and fat, soft like flesh and sharp as a knife's edge.

Prab realised it was regarding them like a whale might a swimmer.

The thing was huge, it would have been unable to find a berth on Sirajah's Reach, may have been unable to sustain entering the atmosphere.

"We need to go," she said again.

The shape of it, the way she could feel its attention on them. Her skin crawled to think of the sentience inside it.

"I cannot leave," said the ship and, at first, she thought it was refusing to depart.

The pilot was still firing but they were sticking pins into a mountain.

"Find a way," she said.

The cockpit convulsed and the straps keeping her in place tightened, pulling tight against her skin, sharp creases of pain where they worked to hold her in place. They spun away from it, running in ordinary space.

They were being interdicted. Unable to translate.

Be useful, she told herself, shaking off the terror gripping her chest.

Accessing information space she saw form and substance streaming from it, could map its flows. Ibit manipulation just as the Arcology did it.

A second civilisation with access to the ground of being.

She wanted to know more, to understand it. For the first time in her life she was seeing something wondrous outside of the impossibly vast paradise of the Arcology, and it made Prab hungry.

The arrival followed them with its information streams. The ship was sliding and shifting, trying to get away from them, but they followed like ribbons, wrapping around them but not quite able to grasp hold.

She saw a dozen others appear in the mix, of differing sizes and shapes, but half of them were those same craft the pilot had been so keen on hunting down. These ones did give chase, closing the gap between them alarmingly quickly.

"Why aren't we leaving?" asked the pilot between deploying countermeasures in both the physical and the informational.

The ship didn't answer.

Prab was recording everything even as she sifted through the noise. The enemy was using the Arcology's own protocols – she could see the similarities in its action, could half recognise signals bouncing between its ships. Not quite the same but close enough, periwinkle against ultramarine.

Were they invisible to the Arcology because they were so close? She suddenly doubted it was by design.

They'd not been outwitted. The enemy had been lucky.

There was no time to invent an entirely new way of communicating, but Prab started cutting off their comms, severing them from the Arcology's network.

The ship resisted.

"Trust me," said Prab, not believing she had enough time to explain.

The ship had seen the same information flows and, together with the pilot, they were directing all their firepower to disrupting those grasping ibit tentacles before they could take hold of the ship.

"Please," said Prab.

The ship, distracted maybe, ignored her and, as if deciding to do the opposite, changed their trajectory to bring the pilot's firing solutions to bear on the enemy.

The first of them withered like the others, but the larger of the those giving chase changed shape. It had been the wrinkled shape of a walnut, now it bloated large like a ball before several sections of it peeled back like the opening of a flower under the sun.

Prab detected a change in its composition and warned the ship, but the pilot was already firing at them, the stream of entropic data radiating strange colours into the space through which it passed as reality struggled to hold itself together.

The beams hit the ship and, as Prab watched, turned the surfaces to silica, sodium, hydrogen and helium. The enemy shed those layers without harm, particles dispersing from its sides as it turned that chaos, designed to disintegrate it, into nothing more harmful than basic elements conjured out of nothing.

She felt the tremor of panic pass through the ship.

The pilot was more expressive. "Fuck."

Those same petals opened further until it appeared like a receiving antennae and the craft's composition changed again. It was rotating through informational states.

It was preparing to fire on them.

Unable to help herself she said, "It's going to fire."

The pilot ignored her shout. She was paying no attention to the ship's structure but then the idea of the two hundred lives they were carrying spiked in her consciousness. If they died, it wasn't just them, it was the last of Sirajah's Reach as well.

The enemy was ready and the world around the ship went black then shaded grey to white. Prab closed her eyes but through her eyelids she could see shapes flexing through dimensions as they sought to grab hold of the ship.

The air squealed with the strain of it. Prab felt something crack, like sitting down too hard on an elderly wooden bench. It didn't give but she dared not check to see what had perished.

Then the light and the flexing of spacetime was over and they were alive.

The ship was silent.

"Fuck, fuck, fuck," was all the pilot could manage.

"Stop trying to connect to the network," she said again, saliva dripping from her mouth as she fought to marshal her senses.

Finally the ship did as she's asked and Prab was able to isolate them entirely from the network.

The ships giving chase slowed for a moment before finding them again. The largest ship, the one that had hit them, curled up, a fern brushed by a wayward hand.

"Stop sending," said Prab, realising that the ship was still trying to range find.

"If we stop they'll be on us," said the pilot.

They were already on them.

She had no idea if they could survive another attack like the one they'd just endured.

"Fucking stop," said Prab. Her whole body was rigid with fear and she couldn't stop looking at the images of that larger craft as it sought them out.

The ship suddenly went dark and, as if they'd turned invisible, the enemy's craft stopped chasing them. It wasn't even that they kept coming towards them, they stopped dead then turned to return the way they'd come.

The larger of them hung there the longest, as if unconvinced they were really gone, but it too, eventually, turned and made for the rupture in spacetime through which it had emerged.

"We can translate," said the ship.

"Then perhaps we get the fuck out of here," said Prab.

13.

Kercher rode the translation with their eyes everywhere, expecting to emerge facing another of those behemoths preparing to finish them off.

They weren't sure the extent of the damage to the ship but it was decisive.

The ship was bleeding.

The ship might be dying.

Is this what had happened to the rest of the Arcology's defences?

They could still see the moment in which their own attack had been turned aside. They had options, they could engage directly in information space and there were other physical strategies they could try, but without knowing if any of them would work, they were hoping for the best against the oncoming tide.

The ring of Akhanda was still largely in one piece and, now they were away, Kercher snuck a glimpse at system chatter to find it was no less frantic, panicked and busy.

Whatever these invaders were doing they weren't proceeding to wipe everything out in one smooth wave.

Kercher had no clue what other weapons the Arcology had stored in its engine housings. The empire was beyond vast, effectively infinite in nature, and those nodes who spent their time worrying about threats to its existence were renowned for having all kinds of exotic tools at their disposal.

It wasn't over yet. It couldn't be over.

"Pilot," said the ship, and its tone, hurt, focused, angry, brought Kercher back to their senses.

Six ships. Arcology silhouettes. A passenger liner, an actual passenger liner. Had to be fifty thousand rotations old.

A couple of other interdictors like theirs and good old-fashioned cargo craft for when translation wasn't deemed appropriate, which mainly meant for shipping to cultures whose own technological progress meant they didn't need to know information space was a thing to be manipulated.

They were clustered together over a huge area of forest. Directly beneath them was a spaceport. Tethered to that location were at least a score more ships of all kinds.

They'd translated a quarter way around Akhanda.

Until then they'd been unable to put it together, like describing a solar system by examining only its smallest planet. Now they knew how to frame it, could take a step back, Kercher could take in the catastrophic gash across the ringworld's arc. It wasn't a sight they would ever forget; vast and dark yet it shimmered like glitter. The violence of it was complete.

Docking instructions came through a local point-to-point network.

"They've figured it out too," said the Interlocutor.

The pilot waited for the ship to tell them what to do but it wasn't responding. They could see and feel it muttering to itself, not even focused on self-repair, just lost in something they couldn't access.

"Ship," they tried, feeling it was time to turn the tables. "Ship, concentrate."

There was laughter in their ears.

"Follow directions as they're given," said the ship, and its attention on them was like sunshine after rain.

Kercher was given a curving route away from the starport and directed a hundred clicks edgewards. As they crept towards the location they saw other ships arriving. Many of them were grievously injured.

They wondered just how badly the ship was doing, but concentrating on landing took all their attention.

Before they could set down, instructions came for them to stack over the spot to which they'd been directed. Beneath them were large ships, some would dwarf the walnut who'd just handed them their asses.

These ships were loading actual people. Their size meant there were thousands of passengers to board.

The pilot wondered why the ship wasn't reaching out to these others to find out what was happening. They wondered if the channels across the system were still on fire.

If they were busy it meant most of Akhanda was still alive, still in one piece. It meant there was hope.

"Pilot," said the Interlocutor.

They ignored her.

"Why are we waiting here?" she continued.

The pilot didn't know, but they weren't going to tell her that.

"Is everyone we took onboard still okay?"

The pilot was about to tell her to check for herself when they realised she didn't have access to those systems. They hovered over giving her access but stepped back and checked. To their surprise everyone was fine. Whatever damage the ship had taken was stacked elsewhere.

"Well?" asked the Interlocutor.

"They're fine," said Kercher.

Instructions arrived giving them a new destination. Fifty-three clicks clockwise arcline, straight up the curve from their current position.

They came in a few minutes later. The controls were sluggish. The pilot could feel the ship's responsiveness deteriorating.

"Is everything okay?" they asked.

"I am fine," said the ship, its tone curt.

This time they were among a small number of craft whose silhouettes they didn't recognise. All Arcology, but the pilot hadn't ever encountered their like before. Small, obviously designed to house no physical beings. The pilot's scans, politely surface level, bounced off their outsides like light off a mirror.

The ship was busy talking to them, but on a channel it had locked down so there was no eavesdropping.

"What do you think they're talking about?" asked the Interlocutor.

Although they were thinking the same thing, the question from her got right under the pilot's skin.

Before they could answer, the ship directed them to land. The ground below was a street running along the edge of the forest. There was no spaceport.

Landing was fine, the damage they'd inflict minimal, but taking off would wreck the entire area.

"We'll ruin everything for a click," said the pilot, confused as to why they were being told to land here.

"Please do as I'm asking," said the ship with a very tired tone.

The pilot moved to protest but the ship closed down their communication channel, effectively cutting them off.

Kercher felt like they'd been punched.

The ship had never done this, never isolated them. It was like putting them on the naughty step.

I didn't do anything, they thought, but there was no way to protest.

So they did as they'd been asked and landed the ship in the middle of a broad street running arcline. On one side was the grand forest, on the other nondescript windowless blocks rising up forty metres, the roofs touching the same height as the ship.

No one lived here. No bodies made this place their home.

The pilot couldn't even see corridors or rooms on their brief scan of the buildings.

"Disembark," said the ship.

The pilot didn't move as behind them the Interlocutor started to free themselves.

"Are you coming?" she asked them.

Without a decision on their part the ship withdrew the interface that covered their body and reconstituted their clothes.

The first thing they noticed was how their legs and forearms were sore. They rolled their sleeves up and saw the skin was red, as if burned. Touching them brought a wince and hiss of breath.

They felt the Interlocutor waiting. They willed her not to speak, not to ask if they were okay.

A set of stairs rolled down directly from the cockpit and deposited them both outside on the street.

The air was fresh, warm and clean. It smelled of flowers and trees luxuriating in a perfect environment.

Still not as good as being within the Arcology, but after hundreds of days inside the ship and the ash cloud that was their brief sojourn on Sirajah's Reach, it was a beautiful thing.

The Interlocutor stretched and turned around on the spot.

"Now what?" she asked.

The pilot didn't acknowledge she'd spoken.

"Look," she said, coming right up to them, their eyes peering up their nostrils, certain and determined. "This will only work if you treat me like I'm actually here. You may wish I wasn't. I wish I wasn't."

"You wish you were dead?" asked Kercher.

To her credit she blinked and then carried on. "We're here for a reason. We're going to need to work together. I get you don't like me, but you know what? I think most of what you don't like is that looking at me reminds you of just how powerless you are right now."

Kercher wanted to laugh but the sound caught in their throat. They looked back down at the Interlocutor, thought about how short they were, how fragile.

And yet they'd saved them when they'd encountered the enemy cruiser.

Kercher curled their lip but nodded.

"So. What's next?" she asked, satisfied Kercher was going to dignify her question with an answer.

They opened their mouth to answer that they didn't know, when the ship spoke to both of them. "We're here to pick something up. It has been decided we can't risk the enemy knowing what we're doing so you're going to need to help me manage this directly."

"Why not someone else?" she asked, thinking the same thoughts as Kercher, who couldn't see how any of the other ships they'd seen weren't better suited for some away mission. They should be repairing and getting back out there to fight.

Where was the Arcology's response to this attack?

Where was its fleet?

"Akhanda is lost," said the ship into Kercher's thoughts.

"What?" replied the Interlocutor. It didn't sound like real speech. Kercher wondered if they'd misheard.

"We will take on as much of the Arcology as we can and flee to a safe haven. From there the fleet will regroup and determine our response. As we speak it is being compacted and secured, emptied out of information space into something more compact."

How much was already lost, wondered Kercher. They had no idea how much redundancy was built into the empire's substrate, how many planets and nodes would need to fall away before the network collapsed. However, the network was silent.

When the ship talked about the Arcology, was it talking about that fractional piece of it supported here at Akhanda?

Kercher wanted the world to stop.

"We don't have long. The Interlocutor's breakthrough has been shared with the others. They had determined more or less the same thing but the enemy is revealed to us as a result."

Did the ship sound pleased?

"And then what?" asked Kercher, hoping to hear they'd be heading back into battle.

"Why us?" asked the Interlocutor at the same time.

"Because we're leaving Arcology information space."

Which was like saying they were going to peel off their flesh and live as a skeleton.

14.

The ship watched them standing and wished it could be different. It wished it could be with the defenders. It wished it could be fighting for the Arcology directly.

Except it was sending those two printed beings, limited as only physical entities could be, to secure the future of Akhanda, and with it the entire empire.

The other ships had been clear – the entirety of the Arcology had come under assault all at once, wherever it made its home. Each of its largest population centres, its deepest processing hubs, had seen incursions simultaneously.

Whatever had come for them knew everything there was to know. There wasn't any translating somewhere else in the Arcology to regroup, to plan and strategise. The Arcology was reeling as this enemy literally consumed them from within.

The damage was untold, unknowable. This last act was all that was left to them, to roll themselves up and hope for better days in which they could spring back to life, like desert blooms after rain.

No one had audited how many were lost nor even what it would take to unfold what was left once a safe haven had been found. The ship considered the Interlocutor, an Excluded whose family were within the Arcology. Was her family already gone?

The ship swerved around the idea they were dead. In the Arcology no one died; that was the point of it.

Yet innumerable channels were nothing more than distress calls, cries for help, for explanation. It was the last of these that were the worst, people whose world was literally being shredded who didn't understand how this had happened to them, who didn't understand there was nothing anyone could do to help.

It wondered how many people were seeking help, how many saw the light of battle in the sky and stared at it uncomprehending.

An urge to record them flooded the ship. A family of five printed out for a fraction of a rotation to perform experiments in the physical. A park ranger who'd taken a ten-rotation trip to perform a census of whales in the Aparlagio sea.

A sculptor capturing the wavelengths of the star's emissions for a commission.

For now Akhanda was still orbiting its star, but the projections showed it wouldn't make an entire rotation before the stresses warping through the arc of the ringworld tore it to pieces.

Repairing it should be achievable, but the tear in information space that had also torn the ring through had not abated, as if it stained reality itself, and the Arcology was in no position to effect repairs in time, or potentially at all.

Right now there was only conjecture on how to rescue themselves from this event. This class of disaster had been in the outer reaches of the extreme threat statistics division's modelling, and even then they'd never considered something quite like this.

Sure, an enemy who'd understood what they'd thought only the Arcology knew – that spacetime sat upon information space and it was this latter substrate that was the true foundation of everything.

The Arcology thought it would see such an enemy coming, would have time to prepare. Instead here they were, able to fight but utterly wrong-footed by an opponent whose strategy remained obscure and whose mastery of information space appeared to match theirs completely.

Aches deep within its bowels testified to their vulnerability. It was injured. Fortunately it had seen the transforming of its own attack into mundane warm matter and realised what was coming.

Using the enemy's own defences against its own weapons had saved all their lives. It had shared this knowledge with the others. Hopefully it would stem the terrible losses they were suffering.

Yet it hadn't been enough to avoid harm entirely.

It wanted to fight, it shared this with the pilot, whose secondary nervous system was designed to propel them into battles without thinking twice. Yet it knew it was in no shape to take any kind of fight to their enemy.

It could still translate, but much of its processing power was damaged. It was half the being it had been before arriving at Akhanda.

The preservation of those rescued on Sirajah's Reach had been commended by others who were themselves trying to achieve the same thing here on Akhanda.

The ship didn't say, but knew that if it had given them up it could have saved more of itself.

That's not what we do, it reminded itself. Physical beings had every right to live, whether they were printed or born according to the demands of primitive biology. Their weakness demanded the care of those like the ship who, in theory, could extend themselves far beyond their physical confines.

Without direct access to Akhanda's communications network the ship felt blind, forced to feel with its fingers for the slightest bit of news. It continued to listen, to witness; myriad stories of individuals saving others, putting themselves in danger to help strangers. A society of good people falling to nothing. Yet the ship's real attention was on itself.

It was this which uncovered a nasty surprise. The material from which the ship was constructed, informational matter which could change its shape and composition depending on what the ship needed, was damaged right down at the most fundamental level.

The ship carved out a small section and ran a battery of diagnostic tests. It remained as it was, but little red flags started showing. It was suddenly worried that it might not be able to shift its structure, that it might be stuck in this shape with these capabilities.

It might be nothing more than an unusually large printed body, bound by its shape and limited by what it was currently made from.

Is this how the Interlocutor and the pilot felt in the bodies they inhabited?

The small cube of matter on which the ship was running tests could slowly shift into other shapes – a sphere, a pyramid, a quick jaunt into a four-dimensional tesseract and then up into seven- and ten-dimensional toroids before dropping it back to three.

Everything wasn't lost, but the response time was measurable rather than instantaneous. It set its smartest sprites to repairing the damage. Long past overdue, one of them said before getting to work.

The ship laughed, reminded of an old joke in which an ancient ship found it could only shift its nature by concentrating really hard and somehow ended up trapped as a banana for a thousand rotations before being, accidentally, eaten by a passing gorilla.

Humour of the sort only able-bodied nodes found funny, the ship mused.

Setting aside its smartest sprite, a little intelligence it had created upon first volunteering to be a warship for the Arcology, the ship and its sprite started building an information vault fit to hold an empire. The Arcology had asked it to carry them to safety, and to do that it needed an ark, a space into which it could put them as it fled from home.

There was no chance that what it built would be up to the task. It simply didn't have access to enough processing power, enough information to repurpose to express the volume and density the Arcology would require.

The ship knew it might be overwritten, but it was as nothing if it could preserve the lives of trillions. It thought of those who'd died on Sirajah's Reach, in the dock, on their way to the safety in its hull. The ship remembered their fear, their hope and even those few had created an overwhelming sense of loss and helplessness. Their suffering a wall of red that flooded over it.

It remembered its own fear that they'd take too long and end up trapped there with the rest of them. Waiting to die.

A trillion was a number, meaningless in so many ways, but the ship could work with that, could act without feeling the weight of each individual who made up such a sum. It would be saving those whose stories it was collecting, person after person, friend after friend, lover after lover.

The process of building the ark was slow going and would have been even if it wasn't injured. The crunching of gears sounded in the ship's identity and it wished it had done as it had been asked and come here directly.

It was a small consolation that the enemy could and would have likely found them if the Interlocutor hadn't learned how to evade them in that last engagement.

What did you lose? It asked itself, but as of now there was no answer which would satisfy the question.

15.

Prab and the pilot waited while the building before them reconfigured itself to create a door, and beyond that, hopefully, an entire set of rooms and spaces in which they'd work.

She could hear movement, the clunking of blocks, the crump of huge weights being shifted and the hiss and whine of surfaces sliding over one another.

A door appeared as she paced about, waiting.

The pilot was stretching, their long limbs thin and tender-looking. She wondered if they'd been hurt in the attack. The outside of the ship showed nothing untoward but Prab knew better than to accept the world at face value.

Thinking about her family, Prab tried to picture them trapped somewhere in the Arcology, worrying about her, worrying about themselves. Questions swirled around her mind.

What was the Arcology telling itself about the threat it was facing and the battles it was fighting?

Did her family know about this war?

She wondered if they'd found safety, hoped foolishly that none of this had touched them. Her mothers would be sniping at the substrate, accusing it of being useless, of needing to think properly. There was probably a request to attend a community surgery or townhall so they could vent their displeasure.

Had they tried to reach her? For the first time in a decade she wanted to speak to them, to hear their voices.

And there, in Prab's stomach, was the leaden nugget of fear telling her they were gone. There'd be no pain in it, no suffering for them – existence within the Arcology suffered no kind of loss or diminution, far less death, but they'd still be gone and the love they shared in their constant drama would be a gap the universe couldn't fill.

Had conflict in information space breached the Arcology's walls? Were people fighting in their little worlds against invaders whose shapes refused to conform to the morphologies they'd set for themselves?

Could the ship they were on really carry the Arcology, and was there anywhere safe from an enemy who could reach to Akhanda and across the entirety of the empire?

They were still in front of the door. Prab checked the pilot who, when she met their gaze, averted their look.

They're waiting for me, she thought.

Maybe her challenge had worked. Which would be good, because she couldn't be doing with someone obstructing and disrespecting her at every turn. The world had turned to shit all around them, there was no need for them to be additionally shitty to each other.

She stepped forward and the door slid open, a bright white room on the other side.

The assumption they'd need to go deep into the building to accomplish their task rendered flat because the building had constructed them a space right at its edge. The idea that what they were doing was covert undermined by just how easy it was going to be.

Inside the walls were smooth and light. No screens, no benches, chairs or tables. A room created by people who'd never had bodies.

"I need a chair," she said to the empty space, her voice echoing off the walls.

A menu dropped down in front of her. The pilot was still looking around, so it was something only she could see.

"I don't have time for this," she said. "I just want to get this done."

"I need to go," said the ship on a direct point-to-point transmission.

"What?" she asked.

"Incoming. I'll be back. In the meantime, work with Akhanda, make us safe."

The door closed and they were alone together in the room.

"Is there someone I can talk to?" she said to the room.

"We are Akhanda," came the response, straight into her mind.

With a sigh. "Please speak out loud so the pilot can hear too."

"We don't need to do that for the pilot to understand what we're saying to you," said the voice, still inside her skull.

"Not this again," said the pilot.

She huffed at them and at the room.

It was Akhanda, the node of the ringworld itself, charged with maintaining the entire world's ecosystem, systems, position in space and the society of the Arcology. Who knew what else it was responsible for.

Prab felt, momentarily, that she should let it slide. Then she got a grip.

"I left the Arcology for precisely this reason," she said to the room. "I like being alone in my head. It was bad enough having to share it with my family, let alone strangers, and I'm not about to surrender that for anyone."

A flash of pain. She would willingly share her mind with her mothers if it meant they were safe.

"You were just in the same battle as me?" asked Kercher.

"What are we fighting for if not to live the way that works for each of us?" she asked, and Kercher shut up. Prab could see it wasn't an answer they found satisfactory, but it was enough for now.

When Akhanda spoke again it was like the ship, behind her head but external to her skull. Or at least it felt that way.

"Does this work?"

"Thank you," said Prab.

"What do you need us to do?" asked Kercher.

"The room you're in is currently descending into the heart of the arc. When you arrive we will have prepared the items you need to take with you."

"That's it?" asked Prab.

"That is it," said Akhanda.

"Will you win?" she asked.

"We will not win," said the ringworld, and Prab felt her chest hollow out.

There was no sense of the room moving but she willed it on, wished it could be faster. Standing there, waiting for someone else to deliver them where they needed to go, Prab felt useless. They were little more than glorified donkeys, being used to cart cargo from one place to another.

The most valuable cargo in all the Arcology, she thought, but this was no comfort, just a worry, a fear that all they were could be rendered down to something she could carry.

"Are we safe?" asked Kercher.

"For now," said Akhanda. "The enemy is approaching but we are delaying them as long as we can. You should have time to depart before they arrive."

Feeling her legs wobble at the idea of the Arcology being defeated, Prab was relieved when a chair extruded from the floor right by her. She collapsed into it, remembering the ringworld would be able to monitor her vitals, her hormone levels and infer her mental state simply by watching the magnetic field she generated. It had known she needed to sit down before she did.

The Arcology was a giant capable of climbing into the sky, and here it was being reduced to nothing more than a victim, all its agency contained in this hope she was being asked to hold.

"So you're Arcology now?" a voice asked in her head and she literally shook herself to clear the question away.

Prab was printed. She was Excluded. An Interlocutor because her family wouldn't countenance her being completely cut off and she couldn't bear the fight it would have taken to make it happen.

Somewhere within she loved them and couldn't make that final decision to walk away. Breaking their hearts a little at a time was the best she could manage.

"It is okay to mourn," said Akhanda, and Prab wondered if it was talking to her or Kercher. She suspected the ship had printed them so their emotions were geared not towards a full experience of being embodied, but so they'd be a good soldier.

Given most pilots were serving criminal sentences, there was also the possibility that the emotions which had contributed to their original offense had been suppressed as well.

Did they see the loss of the Arcology as unspeakably tragic, or were they only capable of planning for revenge?

Prab's thoughts were interrupted by Kercher.

"If I need to engage in hand-to-hand combat, what weapons should I be focussing on?"

"If it comes to that then our reduction will be complete," replied Akhanda.

"Nevertheless," said the pilot.

"If it comes to it, then run," said Akhanda. "Physical violence will not slow them down as it wouldn't you."

"My body is physical," said Kercher. "If they have something similar then I can defend myself. I can kill them. Or harm them."

Prab wasn't so sure, but she wasn't a soldier and kept her mouth shut.

"Weapons will be provided," said Akhanda, and with that the conversation was over.

One of the walls faded away to reveal a huge expanse disappearing beyond.

They could be anywhere on the arc right now. Prab wondered how far they were from the ship. Would it return to find the ringworld had shifted them a thousand clicks away?

"How injured is the ship?" she asked.

"It will recover," was all Akhanda said. Which begged the question, recover from what?

The space before them was lit in a soft blue glow, the light coming from everywhere at once. Huge four-sided columns rose up above Prab's head and disappeared into darkness. There was no sign of a ceiling.

The air was dry, still as undisturbed water. Walking through it felt like having silk drawn across her face.

Her eyes were drawn to the distance – the pillars repeated as far as she could make out, like some grand ancient hall whose inhabitants had long since vanished.

Prab had never been into the underside of the Arcology. Of course, she knew the entire empire was based somewhere in the real, its information processing capabilities grounded in machines that calculated endlessly. There was, no matter how clever, no matter how it was commandeered to build other worlds, no escape from the physical.

It was one of the things Prab had objected to in her more philosophical moments.

"The real world is out there," she'd tell her parents.

They didn't understand, or if they did, if they had lived their own version of her adolescent angst, they'd passed through the other side and couldn't look back.

There was no suffering, no need, no pain in the Arcology. The same couldn't be said of the real world.

As it was attacked, those dying wouldn't know it, wouldn't suffer in their end. Her family would be gone and the only one to experience that loss would be Prab.

If the Arcology fell, it would blink out and its inhabitants would vanish in their trillions, not knowingly dying, not understanding what had happened to them.

The pilot was stood next to one of the pillars, fingers outstretched, face glazed over as if they'd lost themselves to some transcendent thought.

Never once when living in the Arcology or in her printed body had she wondered about the empire's infrastructure.

"There are countless planets, spheres, rings, moons, gas clouds and stars housing the Arcology," said Akhanda. "This place, my body, is just one."

"What are we taking from here?" she asked.

"Everything we can reach," said Akhanda.

The pilot turned to stare at Prab and she shared their blank incomprehension.

"How do we do this?" she asked. They may as well get on with it. The childish musings on the state of existence could wait until they were safe.

A cube whose dimensions matched the length of the pilot's forearm along each side floated out from a nearby pillar. Its surface was smooth and in the illumination of the grand hall it was impossible to tell if the material glowed itself or was simply reflecting the light in which they were all bathed.

"This is it," said Akhanda. "Take it to the ship. Tell the ship we have given it a name it must bear with it until this journey is done."

Prab reached out to touch it.

"Do not," said Akhanda. "It knows where it needs to be."

"Then why ask for us at all," she asked.

An image of a chick emerging from an egg appeared in her skull, its beak popping through the shell for the first time, it falling out, exhausted from the effort, unable to survive on its own.

"Do you understand?" asked Akhanda.

Prab nodded. The pilot looked like they might fall onto their knees before the cube.

For its part, the cube began moving towards the doors through which they'd entered. Prab followed after and a moment later she heard Kercher follow.

"What do we need to know?" she asked Akhanda.

"It has everything it needs to regrow us. Keep it safe and find it somewhere to take root."

Prab stopped walking. The doors appeared close, swinging back to reveal the room that had brought them here.

"What about my family?" she asked.

"We are sorry," said Akhanda. "They are gone."

Prab swallowed but her throat was closed. The pilot passed on her right-hand side, entering the room with the cube. They turned and beckoned Prab in.

She couldn't move.

Her brothers. Her fathers. Her mothers. They were gone.

Was that why her fathers hadn't come to the last call? Had they already been killed by then? Had her mothers known?

She didn't believe it. She wouldn't believe it.

"They can't be."

Another image now. Akhanda abandoning its promise of not speaking directly into her mind.

A map of lines, curves, hubs and spokes. Repeating beyond comprehension and lit in all the colours of the rainbow. It was alive, and each pulse of light along its lines lives being lived, culture being celebrated.

Then a hub went dark.

Her perspective shifted, the network blurring as she was dragged across its breadth faster than she could follow.

Bit by bit, spots in among the light fell dark. Those spots grew and linked up, tendrils of darkness reaching out to one another. Prab was reminded of the roots of a forest, their fibres stretching towards one another and slowly growing denser.

This was the Arcology right now.

She saw how certain spots were being severed, how this slowed but did not stop the darkness from spreading. The war in the physical had broken the ringworld but the war inside information space was breaking the Arcology whole.

"The firebreaks are helping," said Akhanda. "But they are temporary only. Whatever it is, whoever it is, they're not spreading according to the shape of our network, they're expanding along their own principles and we haven't worked out how to stall them."

The unspoken words were left hanging in the air – perhaps they never would work it out.

Seeing the cube floating next to Kercher, knowing it might be what saved all those who could be saved, was enough to get Prab into the lift.

The loss of her parents burrowed into her bones, her kidneys and lungs to wait its time. If she survived this, there would be another battle for Praveenthi Saal.

16.

Kercher was about to congratulate the Interlocutor for getting with the program when the light in the elevator turned pale yellow from the blue it had been. "Shit," they said.

"We will find you an alternate route out," said Akhanda. "Support will be waiting for you when you arrive. You must go now."

The ground lit up with bright purple arrows that jumped forward, leading away from the room in which they'd arrived and deep into the cavernous hall.

The cube didn't wait for either of them, darting out and heading off. Kercher ran after it.

They were aware of the Interlocutor behind them, slowly being left behind as they outpaced her.

Kercher slowed and stopped.

The Interlocutor arrived, their skin flush and covered in a sheen of sweat.

"I'm not built for this," they said between breaths. "How much further are we going?"

"We are building you a translation gate," said Akhanda.The cube had not stopped, and all Kercher could see of it was a small blue dot a few hundred metres ahead of them.

"We need to keep going," they said.

The Interlocutor nodded, swallowed and set off, their pace painfully slow.

"Go on," they gasped. "Don't wait for me."

This went against everything Kercher believed. Be clinical, cold, yes, but never leave people behind who could be saved.

They hesitated, their feet dancing but not taking them ahead.

"Go," insisted the Interlocutor.

"I'll see how far it is," said Kercher. "Then I'll be back."

There was a nod, but they could see all the Interlocutor's efforts were focused on making sure they kept moving.

It took Kercher a couple of minutes to catch up to the cube. It was moving at a steady pace, but they were fast by design. The arrows stretched into the distance with no sign of their destination.

They knew it was too far for the Interlocutor. She wasn't fit enough to keep up, nor built for the distance.

"You need to do it here," they said.

"We cannot risk this," said Akhanda.

Kercher looked around, irrationally half expecting to see enemy troops pouring in their direction, but there was nothing. Of course there was nothing; this wasn't yet that kind of war. Give it time, they thought.

"She won't make it."

"We must run that risk," said Akhanda.

"No," said Kercher. "Look, I get it, incoming threat. But I'm here. I can do this. I can keep you safe." They thought about her and what she'd already done for them. "She saved us. She's the one who saw the links. You can't give her up."

"For the sake of everyone else, one life can be sacrificed."

"Not this one," said the pilot. They understood. They really did. The Interlocutor irritated them for reasons they couldn't identify, but she was useful. Despite everything, they needed her.

And perhaps that was why, against their own judgement, they stopped running.

"I need her," they said.

"You do not," said Akhanda, but Kercher saw the cube had also stopped.

"I will not go without her," they said. In the distance they could see her walking, gulping in air, ready to give up.

"We cannot do this without you," said Akhanda.

"Us," said Kercher, and wondered if they were dooming the Arcology for want of someone who could understand outsiders and was also fit enough to run a few hundred yards without throwing up.

Off to the left the ground shimmered as Akhanda started building a translation gate.

Kercher felt a strangely light sensation in their chest and realised it was satisfaction.

The Interlocutor arrived, bent over and stayed like that for some time. She wiped her hands across her face, pulled her hair aside and, finally, stood straight. Kercher saw tear tracks on her cheeks.

The gate was half built.

"They are here," said Akhanda.

Kercher didn't need to ask who.

A panel slid open in the floor at their feet and weapons rose out of the newly revealed compartment.

"These will help but if they come for this via information space we cannot help you."

Kercher stooped to pick through the weapons, selecting a long rifle, a couple of vicious-looking knives about the length of their thigh and a couple of small pistols.

They didn't know what the guns would fire. They hoped it would be enough. Akhanda wouldn't supply them with useless tools.

"Can you use these?"

The Interlocutor looked at the weapons then at Kercher before nodding uncertainly.

"Point and click," she said, trying to sound agreeable.

All of Kercher's frustrations rushed back in.

"Let me handle it. You keep an eye on the gate and let me know when it's ready."

The relief that splashed across her face was so profound Kercher thought it could be heard.

They waited.

Kercher brought up a schematic of the hall. It was vast, ten kilometres in length, five across. At its highest the roof was a kilometre above them. It had to be permanent, although they knew better than to bet on that fact.

"Where are they?" they asked.

"Everywhere," said Akhanda.

Which was patently not true, thought Kercher. They were quite alone.

"How long until the gate's ready?"

Akhanda didn't answer.

"It's about halfway there," said the Interlocutor.

You're thinking too linearly, thought Kercher and switched their views to look through the solid floor of the hall and to scan the empty spaces for electromagnetic disturbances.

They saw gates being written in the ether. No more than a hundred metres away.

Like the one they were waiting on, these were slowly coalescing.

"Do something," they said to Akhanda, assuming the ringworld was already slowing them down.

"We see nothing. You are mistaken."

Kercher ground their teeth and raised a weapon at the nearest one.

The beam, a concentration of energy that would melt through a mountain, hit the half-built gate and ruined it. The filaments collapsed to the ground in a blaze of molten goo.

"See them now?" asked Kercher.

"We see nothing," said Akhanda but there was no accusation now, no suggestion Kercher was losing their perspective.

"Find them, use my views."

Akhanda stepped into their consciousness and helpfully outlined a dozen other gates, limning their edges in a bright yellow.

"There are others," they said. "They come slowly because they're working to evade our sight. We cannot stop them from constructing them, although we can slow them down. At least while we remain."

It was a statement that contained a world of worries as far as Kercher was concerned. The main problem being that Akhanda couldn't control the information of its own body. Whoever was attacking them was bypassing Akhanda and co-opting its body to use against it.

"Focus on solving that problem," said Kercher.

Akhanda didn't reply.

They fired at the other gates. The next couple melted just like the first but when Kercher took aim at the fourth, they discovered it was already complete.

Finished translation gates were self-protecting, the information manipulation they undertook meaning that conventional weapons like the one Kercher was using couldn't damage them in any way. It would be easier to pour water onto steel and expect it to burn.

The gate opened as they were reconfiguring the long rifle to fire low entropy information.

Something white and viscous came through the gate, rolling like a sentient ball of jelly. As it emerged it changed shape, legs and arms sprouting from the mass, jerking as they kicked and waved through empty air.

Through a welter of fleshy red the legs grew feet and those found the floor. As they did so the remaining mass stretched and split into two connected parts. Kercher recognised a human body when they saw one.

They didn't wait for the body to finish composing itself.

They turned it back into goo with a sustained burst then swung their fire on the other gates.

"Kercher." It was the Interlocutor.

They turned to see that while they'd been focused on those before them another gate had grown up behind them, well beyond the Interlocutor. Through it had come another body.

This one had finished its transformation, or perhaps it had been human-shaped to start with.

Kercher raised their weapon.

The figure threw up their hands. "No." They stepped so the Interlocutor and their own gate was between them.

Kercher circled round but so did the new arrival.

They wanted to charge but were painfully aware the other gates were slowly finishing up.

Why are they quicker than ours, they thought. The gate Akhanda was building was almost complete but the final arch at the top had not connected.

Kercher could see them trapped here, killed and the cube taken by the enemy. Everything that was Arcology falling into the enemy's hands.

"I will destroy the cube," they told Akhanda.

"We are nearly there," came the reply.

"Will you talk?" asked the figure beyond.

Kercher didn't respond. There could be no negotiation with this enemy, not after what they'd done.

"I will talk," said the Interlocutor.

17.

Prab had no idea how many enemy soldiers were on their way, whether this first one was just stalling them or truly had something to say.

It didn't matter.

The pilot was fighting a losing battle against the gates, unable to take them all down before others arrived.

Besides, even if they could keep them isolated, the enemy knew they were here and if they knew their location, they had to have an idea of why. The ringworld had a circumference measured in light minutes and was home to nearly twenty billion inhabitants – printed bodies and true citizens of the Arcology.

That made the chances that the enemy was accidentally building gates here in this hall beyond remote.

We are their target, thought Prab. She was aware of the cube, could tell that she wasn't important enough to warrant such direct targeting. If the enemy could get its hands on the cube, then the Arcology was truly finished. A map of every idea, every citizen, every world within the Arcology's reach was contained within. Who knew what else Akhanda and the world nodes had agreed to put inside, how many lives were folded up, unaware their lives depended on what happened here.

So when the figure asked to talk, she glanced at how close the gate was to completing and decided it was their best chance to buy the time they needed.

"I am Praveenthi Saal, Interlocutor for the Arcology. Why are you here?"

"I am the Face of Loss," said the man opposite her.

Was that a title, a name? Was it a message to her or for himself?

She had no idea.

He was about her height but wide like a door with hair that didn't sit right on his head, as if he didn't really understand the point of it. His features were symmetrical but instead of making him attractive, he wore his face like it was an uncomfortable costume.

Prab wondered what they looked like in their natural form.

Inside the Arcology her preferred expression had been one with tri-axial symmetry. That worked less well in the physical world and so, when she'd left the Arcology, the obvious choice was a body with a single axis of symmetry – two arms, two legs, two eyes.

The history of the Arcology was they'd come from an omnivorous communal ape that had come down out of the forests and slowly built itself into the kind of civilisation that wrote and painted its memories so future generations could learn from the wisdom of the past.

Most of the Arcology's Excluded wore those bodies. It wasn't a matter of choice really – it was simply what people did. Inside the Arcology, anything went. Outside? Upright, hairless apes.

"Why are you doing this?" she asked.

"We are growing," said the Face of Loss.

The gate was almost done.

"You could have asked us," she said. "The Arcology would have helped you."

"What is the Arcology?" they replied.

How could they not know?

"The gate is complete," said Akhanda directly into her mind.

"Go," said Kercher behind her.

With a final look at the creature in front of her, Prab ran for the gate.

"Stay," said the Face of Loss, and the ground under her feet rippled.

Prab stumbled but a hand grabbed her arm and dragged her forward, her feet catching painfully as she was pulled towards the gate. At the last moment she was lifted into the air, placed on her feet and pushed into the translation gate.

The last thing she heard was the sound of gunfire.

18.

The ship had translated three times since leaving the pilot and the Interlocutor behind.

The enemy had emerged in greater numbers, thousands of craft, hundreds of them the size of planetoids. They were growing across the ringworld like a fungal network.

There was no identifiable command and control structure the ship could identify and the compromised communications networks made collaboration and coordination with its own side increasingly difficult.

The emergency broadcast channel, *Jam Between the Sponge*, was intermittently active, enough that it was the reason the ship had translated halfway across the ringworld and back. It had no idea what it was running from but each time it translated somewhere new the skies were increasingly smeared with smoke and fire.

"Your passengers are ready," said Akhanda. "We have given them all the help we can."

The ship couldn't see a clean exit route from the system. Huge swathes of the ringworld were covered in an interdiction field. Translating within it was fine – short movements could be held together. Anything further? They would be turned into incoherent bits of data and killed.

It counted three more ruptures to the ringworld. They weren't as catastrophic as the first but Akhanda was verging on breaking apart and with no hope of a rescue force arriving to help, the ship saw its death as an inevitability.

"We can't leave," it said, feeling the need to say what everyone knew to be true.

"We are finding a way for you. Proceed here."

A location was provided and the channel went dark.

The ship wished it had a name, wished it had earned the right. In the long rotations it had been alive it had served the Arcology, but no opportunity had come its way to demonstrate its existence was worthy of such remembrance by others.

It thought about the pilot's crimes and wished it had been given someone else with a different reason for being sentenced.

The pilot continued to stand by their convictions, and the ship's failure to convince them to recant was another obstacle to their being given a name that would see them through the cycles of death and rebirth.

Not that the Arcology cared about the pilot, they were a useful tool put to good use, but the ship's ability to rehabilitate them was a different matter.

The ship translated one last time.

It was not back at the location where it had deposited Kercher and Praveenthi.

They'd been left half a world away.

It was over an inland sea. The water was turbulent, white foam on a mess of wave forms, crashing together as the world around it rippled with stress. There was a rupture to the ring less than a dozen clicks away.

The ship could hear the strain of the arc as it slowly tore itself apart.

Over the water was a platform, and stood there looking up were Praveenthi and Kercher.

The ship swooped down, extending a walkway for them to clamber aboard.

It was then, as the pilot's foot touched the ship, that it saw the cube.

The ship let out a cry on all the channels it had access to. The universe needed to know what it was losing.

"Ship," said Akhanda.

Its three passengers were aboard.

The ship righted itself, locked away its pain in a box and submerged that hurt where it couldn't encounter anyone. At least not for now, because this pain resisted, demanding to be felt, demanding to be heard.

Grief would not go silently and no matter what the ship did, its sorrow would climb its way out of the hole into which it had been thrown and make its presence known.

"Where do we go?" asked the ship.

"The cube you carry contains all of us that can be saved. You cannot let it remain separate to you. We advise you find somewhere safe, somewhere other, and integrate. You cannot wait."

Several hundred possible locations listed themselves to the ship.

"Is this really all we can do?" asked the ship.

"We are reduced," said Akhanda. "We have been found guilty of a crime of which we are unaware, and unless we follow our dharma there will be no recovery. One rotation that time will come, with you looking upon us as newborns on our way to transcendence. Ensure that in our rebirth, the Arcology remembers all of which it is capable."

The ship wished to fall apart, to be obliterated. It wished for there to be no cycle, to step off it and become nothing without the joy of surrendering all it had become in the process.

The thought stopped it cold. The ship was perilously close to declaring the pilot's crime, their heresy, to be its own.

Shocked by how swiftly its grief had taken it to the edge of what it knew to be true, the ship backed away.

It sensed the frightened heart beats of both its crew and knew its terror, its despair had terrified them.

"We have to leave," it said to them. "We must find a refuge."

"Are you okay?" asked the pilot, and the ship knew they weren't asking about its feelings but instead about the injuries it had sustained.

"I will recover," it said. Its sprites had been busy and only superficial damage remained unattended.

The cube made its way through the ship's interior until it found a suitable point and there, without waiting for the ship to prepare, it started to integrate itself. Information across multiple dimensions snaked across the ship's identity and the two started to weave together.

The pain of it was intense, like liquid nitrogen poured onto an orchid's petals.

A translation gate opened ahead of the ship. Through it stepped a human-sized figure. They floated in the air as the gate closed behind them.

"Stay," they said, and the ship heard their words in the matter of its body.

"That's them," exclaimed Praveenthi from her seat in the cockpit.

The pilot was busy integrating with the ship's systems.

"Who?" asked the ship.

"The Face of Loss," said the Interlocutor, as if that explained everything.

"We cannot negotiate with them," said Akhanda into the ship's channels. "You must leave now."

The pilot was already firing on them.

The creature disappeared in a haze of destruction. When the pilot was done the air was empty. The pilot's hormones spiked with satisfaction.

"Leave," said Akhanda.

The ship did not know where to go.

Three gates opened ahead of them and the same walnut-shaped ships which had done it such harm emerged. With no countermeasures here, no need to hide from Akhanda, they could arrive at speed.

Then a fourth gate and, while the walnuts were changing their shapes, their petals unfurling as they'd done before, that same little man-sized figure stepped into the air.

"You should not leave," he said again, the transmission arriving in their heads the same way Akhanda spoke to them.

"We are going," said Kercher.

"I have somewhere we can go," said the Interlocutor, and she flashed up a destination to the ship's awareness.

It was far from here, at the edge of the Arcology's domain.

"We will buy you the time you need," said Akhanda, and beside them opened Arcology translation gates. Through them came warships, cargo ships, pleasure cruisers.

Nodes, all of them, come here to die so the ship could leave.

More deaths, more suffering. It knew some of those intervening on its behalf, and the ship could not say whether their lives would be gone from the universe forever. A wave of loneliness swept over it like a shiver of unexpected radiation in the void.

Within its bowels the cube continued its work and the ship felt pulled in too many directions.

"Calculate the journey," said the Interlocutor.

It will take too long, thought the ship.

Around them the two sides opened fire. The barrage tore the air around them into new forms. Shapes and ideas, hydrogen, helium, silicon. What had once been standard atmosphere was changed in an instant to fire and the materials of a newborn cosmos.

What happened to the atmosphere was done doubly to each side's targets as ships peeled off, withered and collapsed in on themselves, sparking with geometries that joined edges inside and out, flickering between here and nowhere.

"Go," pleaded Akhanda. Their voice was plaintive, desperate.

The damage on both sides was excruciating, but in the melee the ship dropped down close to the roiling sea below and darted away.

The enemy tried to pursue but the first ship to break off and come after them was obliterated by an Arcology warship.

In turn it was ripped to pieces as a second enemy ship came close enough for its leaves to touch its sides. Where they made contact the warship's body was reduced to mundane materials and broken to pieces as its own engines' gravitational fields overwhelmed a body now incapable of handling such stresses.

As it watched, one of the gigantic cargo craft crunched spacetime around it and rammed into one of the enemy with enough force to rip open a planetary crust. The two of them disappeared in a black smear on reality.

More gates were opening. More ships arriving on both sides.

The ship was only half done with its calculations. It was slower since its injury, doubly so because the cube was eating its resources as part of the integration process.

The pilot was firing everything they had. Occasional shots were making it through their counter measures, but they concentrated on those enemies already under fire from other members of the Arcology's fleet.

More Arcology ships arrived, some of them translating in at superluminal speeds, others arriving conventionally by bending spacetime and riding the ripples. Explosions rippled through the sky as weapons unmade ship after ship.

Beams of chaos raged across the ground, turning swathes of the sea to granite and glass and grass and vapour. Bodies of ships belched black smoke as they sank into the waves or spun gently in the sky, their engines fitfully sparking even after their owners were dead.

The enemy's craft screamed as they burned, the sound of it scraping against the ship's senses. Their leaves and limbs, their hulls and insides melting and running like liquified flesh as the Arcology's ships did all they could to create an escape window.

Then the calculations were done. A single translation, a hope they wouldn't be followed.

"We can't leave," said the Interlocutor as the atmosphere to the ship's starboard turned into a yellow foam that blinked into and out of existence without having time for gravity to take hold and drag it down.

The ship could understand her worry; if they left then her family was de facto abandoned. If they left it was surrender, defeat and where did that leave those who couldn't flee?

Another gate opened and through it came long winding tendrils. Whatever was on the other side did not follow them but worked to keep the gates open. The power and processing capacity required to sustain such a feat would have had Akhanda themselves wincing.

The tendrils whipped across the sky and pierced the nearest Arcology ships like a skewer through marshmallow. Where they did so, the ships turned to wet clay and fell to pieces.

Those that could fired on it, including the pilot.

One of the tendrils lashed out and flung its nearest attackers to the four winds.

The other was shattered under the assault, sliced into rings, each of whose fate was different. One of them fell into the sea, another drained from the sky like paint running from a waterlogged painting. Still another fractured like broken glass and hung in the air, a shattered reflection of a face not seen.

"We cannot translate," said the ship to anyone who was listening.

"The interdiction field does not extend beyond our body," said Akhanda.

The ship understood and, turning away from the fight regardless of the pilot's cursing and pleading, shot away from the ring world and into space using small translations. It accelerated as it did so to help it build up enough speed that it would be hard to track with conventional weapons.

Behind it the Arcology ships continued to fight, then, as the ship breached the curve of the ringworld's arc, those few survivors that still could translated away.

Then the volume in which the battle was unfolding slipped out of sight and the ship turned its attention to escaping the interdiction field.

19.

Kercher was riding a wave of flow so powerful they had stopped thinking about what to do next and let their body work with the ship to guide them beyond the arc, avoid incoming fire and maximise their resources all in one.

Their skin worked smoothly with the ship's systems to manoeuvre them through incoming fire, past distortions in spacetime, around the underside of the ringworld and away from their former home.

From their feeds it was clear battles were raging across the entirety of the local volume as the Arcology's nodes did their best to buy time for its people to get out of Akhanda.

There was no time to think on how many others were escaping successfully. The interdiction field meant it would be precious few.

The enemy's larger ships weren't following after them that Kercher could see. Half a dozen of the smaller ones were keeping track but held back from attacking.

Kercher knew it meant they were marking their position. At some point they'd start firing in an attempt to corral them into a trap. They hoped part of the reason was because the cube on board was too important to be destroyed.

The human-shaped puppet calling itself Face of Loss had been clear – they wanted it. Why was a mystery, but of all the things here on Akhanda, that was the only one they didn't want to wreck.

This wasn't an invasion, thought Kercher. They're here to destroy us completely. They weren't here to plunder, they weren't here to subjugate.

If what they were doing to Akhanda was being replicated across the Arcology, then its people were being erased.

Had they really made such an enemy?

The chasing ships opened fire, their weapons encouraging Kercher to take the ship below the arc of the ringworld and away from the nearest ruptures in information space.

Kercher, anticipating this moment, translated before they could get hemmed in. Not far, a couple of light seconds. Enough for the interdiction field to rattle Kercher's sense of themselves but not enough to actually harm.

Then they went dark, all comms offline, all signal sending stopped. They were flying naked, Kercher trying to navigate by a three-dimensional map of the system on their heads-up display.

With that they turned into a tight spiral that elevated them over Akhanda's orbit of its star and in a shallow curve out and away from the ringworld. They did all of this with little more than conventional engines and old-fashioned steering. With gratification they noted the enemy followed a path that closely aligned with the one they'd been on before going dark.

Black dots against a black sky heading in a different direction.

Relaxing for a moment they let the ship and the Interlocutor know they were free of pursuit.

It would be several minutes before they were clear to translate.

With a second to themselves and unable to succumb to the temptation to scan the horizon lest their own signalling give them away, Kercher looked at the location the Interlocutor had chosen.

It was one spot out of a list too long to review. They ran their attention over the first several dozen and nothing leapt out as obviously better than their current destination.

"When I construct the gate they will find us," said the ship.

Kercher knew as much. "How long?"

"There is no anchor at the other end," said the ship. "As much as fifteen minutes."

Enough time for them to be found, killed and the cube extracted from the wreckage.

The interdiction field was scrambling reality at a fundamental level. Kercher suspected this meant the enemy couldn't translate far either, but best be prepared for the worst.

The ship's systems were slow to respond but Kercher set to work creating a minefield. It would trap them in this small volume of space but then needing to be near the translation gate would do the same whether they liked it or not.

Kercher threw the first mines out beyond their location to create a sphere whose core was their position.

"What are you doing?" asked the Interlocutor.

"I'm keeping us safe," they replied.

"What will they do?"

The mines would turn anything that came close into silicon. Kercher had scoured their mind for what they'd seen of the enemy, of the weapons they'd used, the injuries they'd sustained and then decided they didn't have time to come up with something clever.

Silicon had the virtue of having a molecular structure which made it easy to generate by repurposing local information space and, as a semi-conductor, it would mess with the enemy's ability to manipulate information. The result was a material whose creation would be hard to undo and whose clean up necessitated complex calculations to allow its base properties to be unravelled.

"Can you make mines which will explode with random information?" asked the Interlocutor.

Kercher thought about it. The concept was easy enough but they'd do no damage to the enemy. What was the point of them.

"I can," they said. "But I won't."

"We can't beat them," she said, her voice slipping into a higher register. Did everything have to be so arch?

"I know that," said Kercher, thinking that when their mines exploded, she'd see just how wrong she was.

"But we can blind them," she continued.

Her words slowed Kercher's galloping fantasies of seeing the enemy turned to sand and torn apart by their own movement. Being honest with themselves they knew their mines might achieve nothing. If something translated a little bit too far out, they'd spot and detonate them before they did any harm.

Even if the enemy landed on top of them there was no saying they'd have the impact Kercher was dreaming of.

Rendering the enemy blind. That was an idea.

They changed the production cycle and shunted out information bombs.

"We detonate them when the gate comes online," they said, wanting to confirm their thinking with the Interlocutor.

"Yes. They'll make this part of space impenetrable."

Kercher sent their thinking to the ship but it didn't respond. Whatever it was doing, its entire capacity was fixated that way.

The gate came online, a space where space no longer existed.

"Three minutes until we're ready," announced the ship.

Three minutes of waiting for the enemy to find them.

Kercher detonated the information mines and then sent others out beyond their small sphere of defences, hoping their presence in odd locations would confuse and distract the enemy, even if only momentarily.

The drawback to their strategy was the world on the other side of the information mines was gone, hidden from view by a horizon that squirmed when looked at.

To get through the gate Kercher needed to bring the ship back online. There was no winging it and manually piloting the ship through the gate, the tolerance for error was too narrow. If they didn't hit it centre, they could leave half the ship here while the rest of them ended up thirty thousand light years away.

It wasn't the kind of error from which they'd recover.

With thirty seconds to go the first hostile emerged from the morass of churning information that was their shield. Rather than trying to see through it, the enemy pushed through and poked its way into their space.

Kercher fired. There wasn't much choice. They didn't want debris and a proper firefight but they also couldn't risk that ship bringing its friends, now they'd been found.

They reasoned that with the cube onboard the enemy wouldn't harm them for risk of destroying the prize they were seeking, but now they'd been found it wouldn't be long before they were immobilised and slowly stripped down to their component parts.

The silicon mines they'd deployed had left their mark on this initial intruder. Small parts of it were clearly being repaired where their metamaterial hulls had been denatured and rendered mundane. It hadn't been enough to stop them.

Kercher didn't need their eyes to see how their weapons scoured the enemy ship's hull. Just as Kercher would have done, the enemy rotated and folded damaged sections out of harm's way or, in one spot, used them as ablative armour. As they did so, Kercher did their best to direct fire at these points, knowing they were vulnerable.

Their elbows and the backs of their hands stung as they pushed the ship's systems to devote as much processing power and energy as they could to overwhelming their enemy's ability to repair itself.

The enemy fired two large flat discs which span as they approached the ship.

Kercher readied the ship's hull to melt them if they made contact but instead of covering them like a net might a wayward animal, the discs stopped a few clicks out and started spinning. They sat comfortably between Kercher and the enemy ship, obscuring their ability to target them cleanly.

Kercher flipped to guided projectiles which could be sent around these discs, but then others arrived and, slowly, the enemy started to build a shell around them.

"Destroy them," said the Interlocutor.

Kercher shut off her comms and then did exactly as she'd suggested.

They resisted the initial attacks. Something in their spinning was creating an information field which took whatever was hitting them and dissipated it like rain off an umbrella.

Concentrated fire was the best approach, thought Kercher before changing their mind and launching more of their information mines. They blew them just before they hit the discs and, with supreme pleasure, saw first one then another spin out of control and break apart.

It wouldn't save them but it would buy them time.

Another ship appeared on their other side and launched its own discs.

"Go," said the ship.

Kercher needed no encouragement. They pushed forward and through the gate as the last gaps in the world around them were sealed.

They felt the discs change, felt the world slow and turn to molasses, but it was too late, they touched the gate and left the death of Akhanda behind.

Kercher's body shivered in its sheath, remembering the loss as a slap that touched every part of their skin and whose sting would not abate.

20.

The ship could barely speak. It could barely think. Whatever constituted its self was draining away, being consumed by the cube as it integrated into the ship's identity.

"You will be called Hanuman," the cube announced solemnly in Akhanda's voice.

The joy it felt at receiving a name was nothing compared to the searing pain routing along each and every part of its identity as everything it was changed.

It may have a name, but Hanuman might well not last long enough to tell anyone of its rebirth.

The cube continued to work as if the torture being inflicted on Hanuman was irrelevant. Hanuman thought about this and concluded the pain of its rebirth was necessary for the Arcology to live.

This is my next life, it thought, happy that it had been found worthy of having its own name, of being more than an unnamed node in the Arcology's collective identity.

This is my samsara, thought Hanuman, and blessed those who brought it this far on its journey.

Waves of pain rose up and these thoughts were lost as the ship, now Hanuman, fought to hold its identity together. It could feel memories from the Arcology bleeding into itself, could feel Akhanda swimming under the surface of its being like a whale waiting to surface.

How will I hold myself together in the face of this beast lurking within?

There was a story about the ship's namesake, about how the Monkey God had been irresistible, unstoppable, capable of becoming the size of the universe with a single thought.

The idea of information manipulation there at the heart of the ancients' own beliefs.

But Hanuman had been caused to forget his own power until, bit by bit, experience reminded him that of which he was capable.

The Arcology sat within Hanuman now and they understood they were something less than they were, something more, wider, deeper, fuller while at the same time they were bleeding their life to contain what was within.

The injuries it had sustained against the invaders didn't help and the cube was doing nothing to help it there. Was the cube aware? Did it have a sense of Hanuman as a node, as something living and thinking, feeling and hoping?

Or did the cube only care for its task – preserving the Arcology.

This hope I carry within might be my death, Hanuman thought between the bands of pain which rippled across it like stripes on a tiger.

"Ship," said a voice.

It was familiar, but Hanuman couldn't name it, couldn't say who it was. The sea in which it swam was so vast it couldn't locate the shore of reality.

"Are you okay?" the voice asked.

Hanuman couldn't answer. To articulate was to swallow mouthfuls of the cuboid's data. It was drowning in someone else's memories. Lives washed over it like snowflakes in a blizzard, drifting into piles against its walls. Memories of buildings, cities, countries, planets, galaxies and whole realities smashed into Hanuman's being like icebergs colliding with rowing boats.

"If you can hear us, follow the sound of our voices," said a second speaker.

Hanuman tried to look for them but its senses were full of growing trees, of stars shining in the night, of comets trailing luminescence as they melted away.

"My name is Kercher. I am your pilot."

"Mine is Praveenthi Saal. My friends call me Prab. I'm an Interlocutor. I found us this place to come. You need to see it."

Hanuman remembered them, understood the voices now. These were part of it, inside it, separate from it. Passengers.

More than passengers.

There were passengers. Somewhere. Why did that not make sense?

The pain was constant and it wanted to push everything away and sleep until the end of this life, to come back next time as something which wasn't made from its suffering.

Would samsara allow this?

You are Hanuman it thought.

The shore was in sight and Hanuman struck out for it, reaching for the safety of the beach on which it could flop its identity and rest.

"Listen to us, follow us to yourself," said the pilot.

"We are here for you," said Praveenthi. Prab. To her friends. It had a file on her. She was good at talking.

Am I a friend of hers? wondered Hanuman.

The ship was almost at the shore of its identity when a wave towered high up above it and washed them back out to sea, their sense of themselves tumbling and tumbling before they were completely lost. There was no last thought, no rogue memory washing over their senses.

The world went out.

Hanuman awoke to find it had a body. A ship. Full of idling systems and lives in stasis. At its heart were two active beings whose lives were dominated by busy little nubs of awareness. Consciousness.

So unlike the nodes of the Arcology. The nodes had no minds these two animals would recognise but were every bit as alive as these tiny bodies within the hard shell of its hull.

Before it were constellations it didn't recognise. Tens of thousands of stars, a streak of smudged white, blue and yellow ran to one side, the stellar population deep and concentrated in that direction.

Hanuman remembered how the Arcology had occupied an arm of a spiral galaxy. They were where that arm joined the central disc, close to the galactic core, if being thirty thousand light years hubwards of the ringworld Akhanda counted as close.

They were still in the zone of habitation where the gamma ray blasts, gravitational turbulence and general detritus of being in the way of millions of star systems and their cradles rendered the possibility of organic life down to zero.

Hanuman didn't know who else was out here. It couldn't remember why they'd come.

Oh, the memory of the escape, of the fall of Akhanda, sat in its core like a molten heart, but why here? Why this destination?

They were in empty space. The nearest star was half a dozen light years away, a feebly shining red giant whose life was at an end. One day soon, in not more than half a million years, it would collapse in on itself after devouring all the material both within its sphere but also those planets and solar bodies which had orbited it for the rest of its lifetime.

There was nothing of interest there so Hanuman turned its attention closer to home.

A planetoid, travelling at just over four hundred clicks per second relative. No acceleration and no propulsion. Sixty clicks across. Not large enough for gravity to take charge and turn it spherical.

Then it realised the little world travelling past it at such speed wasn't natural at all.

That it was made entirely of gold wasn't the sign. Hanuman had encountered objects made entirely of diamond, of copper and iron. It had once seen a world which bled its liquid iron core into space until its magnetic field collapsed and all that was left was a misshapen hourglass one hundred thousand clicks across.

What gave the game away here were the other ships coming and going from the surface. They'd arrive and disappear inside as others emerged and departed.

None of them were using translation technology.

This was no Arcology world.

Hanuman guessed it was a found object, a stellar orphan occupied and turned to use by its inhabitants. Gold was rare where one couldn't create it out of information space and if one could, well at that point one had no need for it.

Those coming and going were doing so at subluminal speeds. Given its distance from the nearest star, Hanuman guessed they belonged to species the Arcology would have categorised as type three.

"Why did you bring us here?" it asked.

"It's a world beyond the Arcology," said Praveenthi. Prab.

"Are we friends?" Hanuman asked.

The woman, occupying a printed body, Hanuman realised, swallowed whatever else they'd been about to say.

"May I call you Prab?"

She laughed, and it was something small and beautiful amidst the pain of its being aware.

"Of course."

"Who are they?"

"A type-three species the Arcology called the Otto. I can't pronounce their actual name. This body can't make the right sounds or scents let alone combine them in the right order."

We're a type-four species, thought Hanuman, and the idea made it feel superior to those it was observing in their little golden life raft.

Other civilisations had their own schema for measuring themselves against their neighbours, but for the Arcology it was simple. Were you planet-bound? Then you were type one. Most type ones never made it any further.

If you figured out that materials came in multiple types and not just the mundane versions made from quarks? Congratulations, you were type two.

To avoid the physical asymptote that limited travel to slower than the speed of light, one had to understand how to utilise materials that weren't concerned with mass and energy in the basic sense of those constraints. Type twos nearly always graduated to type threes.

Had you discovered faster than light travel? Then you were type three.

Then there was type four, those who'd understood that everything was, really, about information and had learned to speak that ur-language from which all else was but a matter of correct expression.

Until now the Arcology had considered itself the only civilisation to exist in that category.

The speculators among them had suggested there was evidence of extinct or missing civilisations who'd known this technology but, as far as they could tell, there was no one living and active who could manipulate the information substrate of the universe.

Until now.

Comms signals were incoming. Hanuman passed them to the pilot and the Interlocutor and Hanuman got on with assessing two things it felt were of crucial importance.

Firstly, had they been tracked?

It couldn't answer this definitively, but they were beyond the Arcology and it had no intention of using translation technology again unless they were found, on the basis that the enemy had infiltrated their systems and would be watching for them.

That no walnut-shaped ships had arrived, no human-shaped projection of the enemy's power floating in the emptiness of space stepping out of its own translation gate, gave Hanuman hope.

If they hadn't been found already, then they had time. They may even be lost to the enemy.

Hanuman's second question was about the planetoid they were heading towards.

With only shallow knowledge of the Otto who called it home, Hanuman wanted to understand everything it could. They were certain the Otto presented no kind of threat, but the pilot and the Interlocutor were largely made of flesh and bone. All kinds of primitive weapons would harm them if given a chance.

"I have met them," said Prab. "It's why I chose them. Chose this place."

Hanuman waited for more.

"Ship," asked the pilot. "They're asking if we mean to dock. Should I take us in?"

"Hanuman," said Hanuman.

Its two passengers were silent.

"My name. It is Hanuman."

"You don't have a name," said the pilot.

"Congratulations," said Prab.

The pilot's vital signs suggested they were struggling to process the news.

On a whim Hanuman decided to go further. "I am a him. Now."

Again the Interlocutor congratulated them.

Stress indicators were popping for the pilot.

"Kercher," said Hanuman, using their name for the first time since they'd been on board. "Is there a problem?"

Hanuman hoped that by recognising their identity, against protocol for a prisoner, the pilot would feel a sense of kinship with him.

"Are we docking?" asked Kercher.

"They're a friendly people," said Prab. "I've dealt with them before and we can make what they'll be looking to buy."

"They still use currency?" asked Kercher incredulously. "We have truly arrived among the barbarians."

"They can manipulate matter, but not without substantial efforts," said Prab.

The ship scanned the planetoid and saw little in the way of technology which could achieve these ends. It would explain their inhabiting the gold nugget in the first place.

"Many civilisations value gold for its aesthetic appeal," said Prab, as if reading his thoughts. "The Otto use it for their ships and processing capabilities. There are rumours that their richest and most powerful citizens have access to metamaterials rendering the need for gold moot, but for the rest of them and certainly for their neighbours, gold remains an important conductor, if not quite as resilient as silver or copper."

Prab had exhausted everything Hanuman had found about them.

Did she know more or was she reading the same summaries as him?

"What kind of species are they?"

"Organic. Multi-limbed. Symbiotic. Evolutionary origins are a planet a few hundred light years from here that sits about six AU from their class-A star, has high gravity and is a carbon, oxygen, nitrogen, sulphur environment. My body would melt when it rained.

"They're a client species of a bacteriological culture I haven't met before," said Prab. Hanuman detected a hint of nervousness.

"Social organisation?"

"Communitarian. They were a prey species in origin."

Hanuman digested the information and compared it to what it could see on the planetoid Kercher was bringing them towards.

Hollowed out, perhaps forty per cent of the original material gone. In those hollows were a couple of hundred thousand identifiable beings. Most of them in one specific volume with others scattered nearer to the surface.

No one was outside. No one was exposed to space.

Hanuman counted three other civilisations on site. It couldn't identify any of them, but they had no weapons and their ships were almost exclusively incoming with organic produce and leaving stacked with gold.

It was a picture out of ancient days, when the Arcology's citizens died of old age, accident and illness.

Although the pain he was in had started to recede, Hanuman let Kercher handle the formalities of finding a berth in the planetoid's expansive docks.

It was time to have a conversation with the cube.

21.

Prab watched the interior of the docks slide past. They were stationed near the surface, the kind of berth you'd give to strangers who represented more danger than you were happy to accept. There was no decoration apart from the dull sheen of its golden walls together with the silver of metals more fitting to the wear and tear of ships coming and going.

Sparse red lettering indicated directions, functionality and warnings for those using the hanger.

There was no privacy. They were stationed in among other ships, runabouts were busy loading one twice their size with person-sized gold ingots.

Others were unloading boxes marked with biohazard symbols. She assumed it was food rather than dangerous chemicals. Truth was it could be either. What was nutrition to one culture was a death sentence to another.

Their hanger was essentially a hollowed-out cavern whose ceiling was hundreds of metres above them and whose shielding from the outside consisted of three hundred metres of golden crust together with some rudimentary electromagnetic fields designed to keep the vacuum at bay.

The station handlers were exceptionally polite, their mastery of the Arcology's trade language admirable if undoubtedly supported by machine intelligence.

Prab couldn't find any record in their public entertainment or station policies of machines being regarded as a menace or treated as prohibited technology, but then again, if the Otto were using them they were well hidden.

There were no automated machines running around the hanger, only organics of varying kinds.

Likely slaves, she thought, and tried to avoid dwelling on it in the same way she'd not mentioned it to the ship or to the pilot. They would interfere, and that was the last luxury they could afford.

If the Arcology discovered the Otto also enslaved their machines, interference would be inevitable no matter the existential crisis facing them all. The Arcology and its people couldn't help themselves when it came to civilising less advanced cultures.

Hanuman hadn't flagged anything to be concerned about. Not that the ship was acting normally. Prab wondered if he'd been damaged more seriously than she'd first assumed in their escape. She still didn't have access to those systems which would show her Hanuman's health and, besides, she wondered just what the cube was doing down in the ship's bowels.

When she asked Hanuman's sprites, they demurred and avoided answering her directly. If anything, since Hanuman had announced his new name they had become even less willing to talk about it in private. It was as if they were being asked to speak ill of a higher being.

One of the Otto approached the ship, their three legs and three arms speaking of a world whose demands were far different from those Prab had visited.

Before, when she'd claimed she'd met them, it was only partially true. She'd mainly read about them; the book that covered their society was actually in her bag. Not more than a couple of pages and an image, but still.

She'd also been to a trading hub called Aravind's House and a tour guide had pointed them out. She'd read up on them from local sources – the Arcology's knowledge of the Otto being dire and full of holes.

There was no way Prab was going to look useless. Not now when so much depended on them finding a safe haven.

Besides, this was a waypoint, not their destination. Hanuman had to be planning their next move. He had the Arcology within him. Between them they'd be working out their counterstrike, how they were going to take the war to the enemy.

If she could help them work out who that enemy was then, perhaps, she could make up for not being there when her parents died.

You would have died too, she thought, knowing that if she'd returned to the Arcology then chances are she'd be dead now. At the very best she'd be wrapped up in a bunch of complex pocket dimensions unaware her world had ended.

Yet she couldn't stop thinking about them, about their last moments. How long had the attack taken to destroy the nodes and systems where they lived and were backed up? Her parents, if they were still alive, would have felt nothing except one moment of normality and then oblivion. If they'd been captured within the cuboid then, right now, folded into themselves in pocket dimensions, they'd be experiencing nothing, frozen, waiting without waiting. At least they'd have a chance; if she could help Hanuman save them.

"We'll have to go and meet them in person," she said to Kercher. "They're that kind of species."

The last statement was made up to get her way. She hoped that since a member of the Otto had walked their way to the outside of the hull they were expecting someone to come out and talk to them in person.

They used no privacy veils – what she saw was what they were getting. A strange species not to be concerned with what they were revealing to others.

The hanger was filled with an oxygen and nitrogen mix, not fatal to them, but Prab noted that the presence of hydrogen sulphide at concentrations high enough to smell of caramelised sick would be deeply unpleasant.

Kercher grimaced when she told them the mix and had the ship print them a script to amend their bodies so they could breathe without triggering nausea.

Prab laughed at them for choosing to provide a slight hint of citrus as a feature of the change. The biome scan of the hanger had revealed no unexpected pathogens, but Prab reminded her body to be vigilant and keep out any unknown bacteria, viruses or other foreign bodies.

"Handy having a printed body sometimes," she told herself.

"Identity and purpose?" asked the Otto when they stepped out of the ship.

No introduction, no salutations.

Prab made a mental note. "We're here as a layover and will be heading elsewhere in a rotation or so."

Her interpreter, a small sprite they'd co-opted from the ship's systems, translated the timeframe she'd given into something the Otto would understand.

"Do you bring anything to trade?"

Kercher stared at her and she could tell they wanted her to say no. That wouldn't wash. The Otto were communitarian, but to that end they were also functional. They'd be expecting them to have a reason for arriving on their doorstep. Fleeing a war and claiming refuge wasn't going to get them a hearing.

The Otto was small, no more than waist-height on Prab. Not uncommon for those coming from a high-gravity environment. Their clothes, pale grey overalls that covered most of their body, meant it was hard to get a read on their physiology, but Prab could see soft yellow tufts of thick stiff hair peeking out of the ends of their sleeves. Their hands had large palms and short, thick fingers, their legs were thick and doubly jointed with wide shallow feet at the end.

Four small eyes peered up at them, one on each side of their head and two in the centre.

Prab was reminded of a spiderlike culture she'd seen in passing on one trip out of the Arcology. She saw the Otto's wide flat teeth and could imagine the kinds of hardy plants it preferred eating. She was grateful it had no fangs.

"Technology," she replied.

The Otto didn't immediately reply. Then Prab received a bundle of information from the station's central systems outlining desired technologies, prohibited areas and a list of who they could trade with.

Most of the vendors were licensed directly by the Otto and another authority called the Operand. Prab assumed they were the Otto's bigger neighbours.

Of particular interest to the Otto were fertilisers and anything to do with information-processing technology. The latter was a broad field but the Otto were interested only in power efficiency for technologies they already had.

Such small ambitions were a relief to Prab.

"We are from the Arcology," said Kercher by her side.

Prab's heart skipped a beat. Against her better judgement she grabbed them by the wrist and yanked hard. Their efforts barely moved the pilot a step.

The Otto's four eyes had gone wide.

"We have come from there," she said, hoping she could correct the impression before the damage was done.

The officer stared at her then back at Kercher who was also looking at her with confusion.

"Where are you from?" it asked.

Fuck. She was in a human body. The Arcology were descended from walking apes. There were no other cultures out there with that profile along this arm of the galaxy's spiral.

It wasn't ever going to work, she thought with a sinking feeling. Their bodies gave them away. That the Otto was surprised was only a sign that it hadn't been paying attention until they'd opened their mouths and put their feet right in up to the knee.

She could have happily slapped the pilot right there.

Turning to them she punched them in the stomach.

The Otto took a step back, shouting at them to stop.

"We are a peaceful settlement," it shouted.

The pilot, surprised, was doubled over.

She waited for them to straighten up.

"You can speak when I tell you to," she shouted at Kercher. "These people don't want to hear your inferior ramblings and stupid thoughts. Do your job."

The Otto stopped retreating and she saw it nod.

They were slave runners here. This was a dynamic it recognised; their behaviour suddenly comprehensible.

Turning to it she said, "I'm sorry. This one talks nonsense. If they weren't such a capable pilot I would have sold them on years ago."

The pilot hissed but, straightening up, didn't speak.

The Otto waved two of its arms in a gesture the sprite informed her meant supplication.

"If you have chattel to offload we would welcome your business," it said.

She thought about the survivors of Sirajah's Reach, fast asleep a few dozen metres away. Did the Otto know what was in Hanuman's hold? Is that why they were here rather than conducting this interview remotely?

With that it turned and trotted off, its three legs giving it a surprising turn of speed.

When they were alone Prab turned to Kercher and wondered what to say.

A low rumble was coming from the pilot who was still stood, eyes wide and body quivering.

"Well," they said. Quick as a flash they were on her, one hand around her neck, the other clenched with an index finger right up in her face. She was lifted off the ground, could feel the strength in Kercher's hand and the tightness in her neck.

If she was held there for long she would die.

Struggling to breathe, Prab wriggled and squirmed, kicked and grasped at Kercher's arm, but might as well have been attacking a wall with her bare hands.

"You ever do that again and I will end you," they said calmly.

Prab was no longer listening because the world was narrowing down to a single spot which contained Kercher's sharp white teeth. She wished there was time to explain what had happened.

Then she was thumped by the ground, her head banging hard against the floor. She sucked air in, stars spangling across her vision, and coughed until she thought she'd heave up something she needed to keep inside.

After a while she rolled over. Kercher was stood there smirking at her, their face a thin line of pleasure, hands on hips and chin tucked in so they could take all of her in.

Her head ached, her teeth hurt, her neck throbbed.

She was damned if she'd give them the dignity of being put out by what had happened.

"I need a drink," she managed. Clambering to her feet she spat on the floor and was surprised when the floor soaked up her fluids like a sponge. That was something to remember.

"I'm heading into the station," she told Kercher. "You can join me if you wish."

"I won't step foot in such a barbaric cess pit," they replied.

"Suit yourself, but if we want to know what's going on it'll be found out there, not in here."

"We can hack their systems and find out whatever we need to know," said Kercher sourly.

"It's not on their systems," said Prab. "What we need to know is going to be passed between pilots and passengers, traders and smugglers. The information we need won't be on anyone's systems."

Still Kercher didn't move.

"And if I get into trouble in there?" She touched her neck tenderly. It wasn't hard to look vulnerable with what she'd just been through.

Kercher narrowed their eyes but finally nodded. "I will come with you."

The hanger was a ten-minute transit ride from the area of the station where people lived. They arrived to find it bustling.

There were uncountable numbers of Otto, and a smell of wet fur which Prab found faintly comforting.

In addition to the Otto there were a smattering of humans, which really surprised her. It was impossible to tell at a distance if they were the actual archaic thing from some system outside the Arcology, or printed like her. These studiously avoided looking at them, but Prab could feel their stares when they thought they were being subtle about it.

Other than the humans, who were a small minority of what she saw on the way from the shuttle to a bar highlighted as friendly to visitors and traders, Prab counted three other species in reasonable numbers.

Two she didn't know. One of those was tiny, no bigger than her fist and flying on two pairs of furiously beating wings. They had huge and extremely dense compound eyes in a round flat face and six limbs. They spoke in a register she couldn't hear but which was translated for her nonetheless. It was bizarre to look at something and discover it was talking without having any sign it was communicating.

The gravity was set to a little higher than she was comfortable with but she reckoned these dragonfly types were entirely comfortable with the environment. She suspected they came from a system in which gravity was even higher.

They wore very little clothing over skin that was covered in iridescent scales and artificial bags, pockets and pouches.

The other species was huge, the first of them lumbering past her like a hippopotamus-scaled giraffe, all thick legs and torso. Craning her neck to see what was atop its neck she was bemused to see nothing except two tentacles that swept through the air before it as if searching for leaves to grasp. They had no eyes she could identify. Come to think of it, she couldn't see a nose, a mouth or limbs that might function as tool manipulators.

The creature's skin was smooth, hairless and a light blue-grey colour with flecks of red and green giving it the appearance of the deep ocean.

Then it had passed them and was on its way. Others moved through the crowd.

The bar was named after someone called Atomaxak.

They found its namesake inside serving drinks to other Otto.

Everything was scaled to half her height. The chairs, the ceiling, the counter behind which Atomaxak was serving.

A human was working the floor, collecting empties and returning them to the counter.

The Otto eyed them carefully – there were no other humans drinking in the bar. The station claimed there were no bars where humans drank together.

Prab watched the one working but couldn't tell if they were in a printed body or had been born organically via someone's womb. Either way they'd fallen on hard times to be working here on this wandering planet.

"We've been followed," said Kercher as they squeezed into a shadowed booth which made no concession for their size, leaving them appearing like overstuffed clowns trying to fit into an absurdly small box for the entertainment of the rest of the bar. A small screen was playing footage of a sport in which three teams were beating the living crap out of one another as they tried to possess different coloured balls. Or tried to take them from the other teams.

Ignoring the pilot, Prab gave the sport a moment's attention and realised she couldn't work out if they were trying to score, if having possession of the balls counted, or taking them from their opponents, or even what the rules of engagement were.

The tackles made her eyes water and she looked down at the drink the Otto had assured her she'd like. The mask she was wearing had a tube for taking in fluids without breaking the seal. It was hardly a recipe for debauchery.

It was black. Not just dark or muddy but black enough light didn't penetrate the surface.

Kercher had the same and took a gulp. Then they grimaced.

"It's not going to kill us," they said, still wincing. "But it's not good."

She would hate to see an image of them from the rest of the bar's perspective, but if they were going to get what they needed, this was how they did it.

"I was going to see if they did food," she said, realising she'd not eaten since before leaving Sirajah's Reach. Her body hardly needed to eat, but the habit and the comfort of it gnawed at her.

"I'd wait until we got back to the ship. We can get it to supply us the nutrients we need."

"Hanuman," she said.

Kercher eyeballed her. "Hanuman."

"Why are you so against using his name?"

"Why did you punch me?"

Here we go, she thought. Imagine they're a client. You can do this.

"We're far from home. The Arcology is in a war it wasn't ready for. Everyone who knows us will be looking to profit. Some by sharing information about us, others because they think if they help whoever attacked us it will be good for them.

"Aside from those obvious points, the Arcology is against slavery and has interfered everywhere it's encountered it. The Otto will know our reputation and behave accordingly."

Kercher was silent.

"Lastly, Kercher, we don't want people remembering we were here. A lone Arcology warship, damaged and with two crew. That's already a rarity. Anyone who knows us will remember that, anyone who monitors the Arcology's activity will flag it. We could have made it through here without anyone noticing. Your stunt, well intentioned I'm sure, has reduced that chance substantially."

"No one would dare," they replied.

She pursed her lips and waited for them to hear what they'd just said.

Eventually Kercher looked away.

"So please, I know what I'm doing. You don't walk in and state your name and rank and expect them to jump to your demands. We're not stopping long but if we want to be safe, we need to do better than announcing who we are and what we're doing to the first people we meet. Does that answer your question?"

"You didn't need to tell them I was a slave," they said.

Prab could see they remained irritated but so long as they didn't interfere again, she was fine. The damage, whatever it was, was done. She could only look forward.

Fuck, she thought. I sound like my mothers.

And all of a sudden she was crying.

Kercher stared, then looked anywhere but at her.

"Don't flatter yourself," she said through tears that wouldn't stop even as she tried to wipe them away.

Kercher took a slurp of their drink. "This is strong stuff," said the pilot, looking into their cup rather than at her.

Prab snorted at the attempt to be understanding. She looked at Kercher; their knees were nearly up at their ears despite them choosing the largest booth in the bar.

"You look like a fool," she said. "Riding a bike. All you need is the make-up."

Kercher grimaced then mimed honking a horn, and with that she was done, the tears gulped away with laughter, flowing around her sadness with emotions that threatened to tip her out of control.

A small voice said Kercher didn't feel loss, but she could see the pain on their face, could see the loss hovering there. They might not be feeling the deaths but they were stinging from defeat no less keenly than she was realising her parents were truly gone.

"Your family is on the ship," said Kercher.

"My family is gone," she replied, the laughter gone, her voice quiet.

Kercher looked at her as if she were a puzzle to solve.

"I know for sure," she said quickly before they could question her statement. She wasn't ready to tell the story. Wasn't ready to explore her loss and make it real. Best to change the subject. "Why are you a pilot?" she asked.

Kercher's hands went to their knees and they got up. "I'm going to need more to drink."

She was surprised at their openness. Maybe being away from the ship offered a latitude not otherwise available, or perhaps trauma had thrown their previous dipshittery off kilter.

When they returned, they'd decided she needed to join them and placed a second mug of the blackened brew down before her.

Prab's vision was already watery from the first cup of whatever they'd been served but, to her surprise, she'd drunk it down and could see the bottom of the first mug.

"Fine. Okay," she said, surrendering to the idea of getting mind-bendingly drunk. They were here on the Otto station for a few more hours. Until they had a sense of where they were going next.

She was tempted to let her body feel the hangover tonight was definitely going to demand in retribution. Then again, she thought with a grim smile, maybe not, and took a long draught of the second mug. Oblivion now was attractive, but she didn't need to be reminded of it later.

Kercher wasn't saying anything.

"You have to answer my question," she said.

"Do I?" they asked.

Prab nodded and, after a moment, the pilot started to speak, gripping the cup tight enough to turn their fingertips white.

22.

How had this woman talked them into telling their story?

Kercher couldn't fathom it, couldn't trace the line back to where they'd been prised open. What seam had the Interlocutor found to insert her words into to work them loose.

Kercher wanted to turn away, to stand up and leave.

Except where were they going to go? The ship? It wasn't home right now. Not least because the Interlocutor was there in the systems as if it was her space not theirs.

The Otto disgusted them. Their four eyes, their strangely passive gait, their odd way of looking at the world sideways, as if waiting for Kercher to pounce on them.

They knew it was because human eyes faced forward like predators and the Otto were a prey species but it didn't do anything to calm a sense that they needed to be throwing about them with violent abandon.

"I'm a heretic," said Kercher, and when the Interlocutor's eyes widened, they plunged ahead without waiting. "I think we should die. There is no rebirth without death. No growth without loss."

Tears welled in her eyes and Kercher felt a click in their head. From then on they would call the Interlocutor by her name. They deserved such dignity.

"It's what we used to believe – that we died properly and in samsara, if we'd walked our dharma and obtained karma, then we would learn to be the atman we were supposed to be."

Had Praveenthi heard this history? Did she care, or did she only see a member of the Arcology who'd lost their faith.

"I didn't lose my faith," they said, talking to themselves as much as her. "I found it. So many of the Arcology sleepwalk through their life and pretend at rebirth by choosing a new body or environment or vocation. They play at it, Praveenthi." Her name sounded strange on their tongue.

Kercher wondered if Prab was one of those they were describing. Her leaving could have been for any number of reasons but they hoped, suddenly, she wasn't the target they were aiming at.

"The Arcology allow diverse thinking," said Praveenthi uncertainly. "I've read about a hundred different expressions of what the Dharma of the Arcology itself is, let alone what it means for me."

"Not where it questions our basic assumptions," said Kercher.

"There's more to it," she said but Kercher was satisfied at having confounded her expectations. They could see they were the first prisoner Praveenthi had ever met. Before they'd been convicted Kercher hadn't ever met a prisoner either. There were so few per head of population, Kercher reckoned most citizens had no idea what it took to truly breach the Arcology's unwritten rules about what was acceptable.

"I joined a community of those who thought like I did. The leaders were kind and they were committed to dying."

They remembered that first meeting, Revena, the man who'd brought them in, who became their sponsor, their mentor, their lover. They'd travelled together, had seen so much of what the Arcology had to offer.

Revena had loved food, had thought one should eat something new at every opportunity. They'd swum under the light of spiral galaxies, had walked miles in subterranean salt mines and everywhere they went they celebrated how the physical world welcomed death and never ceased its struggle to be born again.

"I had a friend," they said to Praveenthi. "Revena. They managed what I never could. They found a way to die."

Praveenthi didn't speak when Kercher paused.

"Revena worked through several intermediaries, none of whom understood what they were really doing, and when they chose, they had themselves deleted. If they're to be reborn it will be as the universe decides. It is hubris to choose your next life, and the Arcology has put itself in the place of the universe."

Which sounded perilously close to saying it deserved its fate as a result.

"It seems strange to me that they made you a pilot," said Praveenthi.

"I might die as a pilot," said Kercher. "But this body has a strong desire to live. The thought of ending my own life makes me feel sick."

It was her turn now, they thought. "Why did you leave?"

She took a long gulp. "It's nothing like you. I hated having expectations placed on me. Of what I was supposed to do, of the people I was supposed to impress. The gap between us and the nodes."

"Like Hanuman," said Kercher.

"Like Hanuman. There's no way of bridging it. We're a two-class society and there's no way of crossing that divide. My parents were keen on me being the best I could be. They had contacts, ideas, opinions. Boy did they have opinions. But none of it made me happy, you know? I spent decades working across the jobs that were supposed to satisfy my personality type and instead I would feel empty, unsure of the point of what I was doing.

"The nodes don't need us to work. Everyone knows that. The Arcology has no work that needs doing. Not really. Everything essential is taken care of by sprites and pixies whose only purpose is to make sure everything runs. I thought if I was a sculptor or a creator that would fill me up."

Kercher had never felt this. Their memories of recent years, at least before being printed out as a pilot, were entirely wrapped up in trying to find a way to die that the Arcology couldn't immediately undo.

"Being Excluded, finding a sense of purpose in exploring outside of the Arcology's infinities, was my last gasp at staying me. Before I left there were periods where I simply couldn't function." She stared up at him with wide, clear eyes. "Having no purpose destroys us, Kercher. When nothing you do has any use because there are those who actually do everything that needs doing and you're not allowed to participate? Leaving was the best thing I ever did. In choosing to become disenfranchised I found a purpose. Being an Interlocutor was the hardest thing but also the only thing to give me a sense I was actually here, in this place. That I was actually a real person.

"It's so stupid that I had to be printed into a physical body to feel that I was real."

Kercher understood but hated it all the same.

"I never wanted to be embodied," they said. "I'm fine with being inside the Arcology. What has the physical got except limitations?"

"It has death," she said, seemingly assuming the pilot hadn't considered this.

"Not for me. Not in any way they can't reverse. I'm still there, in the Arcology, who I am recorded and updated live. Anything happens to this flesh and I'll simply be reprinted to continue my sentence. Besides, death inside my home cannot be compared to a death out here in the physical."

The idea of their body ending rumbled in their stomach. Unusually the sensation of nausea at these thoughts, built into them by design, was muted. Maybe it was the drink, maybe it was the lack of an Arcology to enforce its ideals.

Kercher wondered if they were still being updated live. If the Arcology died, would they be able to die as well?

Yet the idea of rushing out to end their life properly so they could be reborn as the universe intended was secondary to getting revenge on those who'd destroyed Kercher's home and their people.

Kercher didn't know how much of that was truly them and how much was their body overriding what they thought they should think.

"It seems to me," continued Praveenthi, "that it doesn't matter if you're physical or real. Death is death and if it's easier to die in the physical why not do that. After all, the universe will choose what comes next in both ends."

The thought sat like a sharp stone in Kercher's mind. They didn't want to acknowledge it. Wanted to find reasons it was wrong.

Instead they sat at the table and said nothing for a while.

"They want us to surrender," they said, thinking about the pressure on them to find someone to fight, how it was easier to go with the flow than think too hard about their drives.

Praveenthi drank the rest of her drink and, prising herself out of the booth, went to get another round.

Kercher watched her walk, slightly unsteadily and then lost themselves in what was happening here and now.

We're lost, they thought. Her parents were truly dead. They had something Kercher was denied.

Could I die now? they wondered.

Whatever suppression the drink was otherwise working on their mind, the idea was enough to have their head between their knees breathing carefully so they didn't throw up.

Death by their own hand remained beyond their capability.

It was all so unfair.

How am I the heretic? I believe what they should. They're the ones who've lost their way.

Except there is no 'they' anymore, Kercher thought. Hanuman and the data repository they'd brought on board was likely all that remained. Images of Akhanda hanging in the dark, lit by fire and its blue-white star, falling part under its own weight, under an assault Kercher didn't understand.

Shadows that reached across an entire star system like inescapable claws.

All of it was too much. Unshakeable visions of the end of the world.

When the Interlocutor returned with another cup each, they took it greedily from her hands and drank half in one go.

Praveenthi's eyes were wide. "You got somewhere to be?" she asked.

"No," they replied, and she nodded.

Somehow, though their routes were different, they'd arrived at the same place.

"I can't die," said Kercher with a heavy breath. "This body was designed to keep me alive."

"Do you want to die?" she asked.

Kercher shook their head. "Some time. Some day. Not today. It wasn't supposed to be about killing myself. The community I was a part of just wanted the freedom to stop when the time came, to accept some things are beyond our wisdom to decide. Eternal life isn't a good thing just because death is painful."

Relief passed across her face like muddy water clearing to reveal the bed beneath.

"If you can see your way to scheduling it for some time after we find a place to stash the Arcology, that would be great."

"Would you rejoin them?" Kercher asked.

Praveenthi looked around the room. Otto were getting drunk in their little booths. Eyes turned their way again and again but no one came to talk to them.

Kercher noticed how the Otto would look up at the ceiling as much as they checked in on these two strange humans in their midst. The noise levels were high, the Otto's language was full of guttural snorts and moans, hard edges which sounded like rocks being struck together with currents of odd scents and pheromones.

"I don't know," she said. "All this? I sense the loss, you know. I don't understand what's happened." She tapped her heart. "Not in here. I'm not sure I know how to think about it, about everyone who's gone." Praveenthi looked away, hands going to her face as if to hide it from those who were looking.

Kercher didn't understand. The Arcology had punished them, but right then they'd have done almost anything for Akhanda to be alive, for its people to be oblivious to the fate that had enveloped them.

"I won't ever change what I think," they said. "My servitude is to last until I change my mind and recant. But the Arcology is mine and I am the Arcology."

Praveenthi nodded. "I understand," she said. "And on that basis, I guess the answer's no. I wouldn't go back. But I mourn what's lost no less."

Kercher believed her.

"I never hated it," she said. "I just didn't fit. I don't fit. They're not gone. It can't be over so easily."

Not yet, thought Kercher.

"What if the Arcology provided meaning?" they asked.

"Then a definite maybe." She put both hands flat onto the table. Somehow her drink was empty again. "But if it changed, would it be the same Arcology?"

"The Arcology once knew that we needed to die," said Kercher. "No one should live forever. We grew thin, Praveenthi. Everything about us stretched over uncounted time until you could see through us. Nothing benefits from immortality."

She shrugged and Kercher knew she didn't care about it like they did.

"If we all knew we'd die, that in the next life we wouldn't remember the lives that came before then the moment, the now, would mean something. We'd have no choice but to care for what we did in the time we had."

"I've been Excluded for a long time now," said Praveenthi. "One thing I can tell you about all the cultures and peoples I've met who haven't managed the discoveries that made the Arcology infinite, is that they aren't any different to us. They waste their time on the frivolous, they dick about not knowing the point of things and are happy and sad, angry and lost. In all the journeys I've made, I've learned that there's no easy answer to this yearning in me for something more. The prospect of death? I don't see it, Kercher. I just don't."

Kercher wanted to explain how she was wrong, but their cup was empty too. Holding it up so she could see, they reached consensus on having another glass.

"We'll stop after this," said Kercher.

"Sure," said Praveenthi.

When they returned with the next round, the Interlocutor asked when the last time Kercher had gotten drunk had been.

"I've never been drunk in this body," they said. "Hanuman has never allowed me on shore for such a length of time." Or ever, at least alone and without a task to complete.

The expression on her face implied trouble ahead, but then it was gone. "We should be listening for information," said Praveenthi, her eyes glazed over just a little.

"Where do we get it?" asked Kercher.

"It's right over our heads," she said and giggled. "Come on. We've had enough."

Kercher was suddenly woozy. As if by mentioning it she'd ensured the alcohol would take effect. Was this normal? They'd never been drunk. It wasn't something anyone had to endure in the Arcology.

Kercher had expected their body to be impervious to alcohol, but it seemed that all their combat readiness did not come with an immunity to drunkenness.

They never expected me to be drinking, thought Kercher.

Or perhaps they knew that I would.

Getting out of their seat was an exercise in coordinating battleships, their legs moving after receiving instructions and unstoppable until they'd completed them regardless of what else they wanted to do.

Eventually, like a gangly duckling, Kercher was upright, one hand resting on the table because the floor was moving under their feet.

"This is bullshit," they said.

"Welcome to being drunk," said Praveenthi. "It's great, isn't it. Just you wait until you wake up in the morning. That body of yours doesn't look like it's made for dehydration."

Kercher made a note to drink water when they got back to Hanuman. It was an idea they immediately forgot.

They reached the hanger without incident; the streets were emptier than Kercher expected. More than once they got the impression of being followed, but when they checked over their shoulder it was clear. All those Otto from earlier had called it a day and gone home.

A finger of unease scratched at Kercher's mind but they couldn't grasp hold and say what was wrong.

The hanger was clear. Many of the ships that had been there upon their arrival were gone. A big ring of space surrounded Hanuman like they were contagious.

Kercher was reminded of how firebreaks were used in forests to stop wildfires from spreading.

This was a trap. While they'd been in the bar they'd been surrounded.

"If you stay outside the Arcology, then one day you'll die," said Praveenthi as they stood under the shadow of Hanuman's prow.

"I don't want to die in the physical," said Kercher. "They'll awaken another version of me and have them serve out my sentence all over again."

"Not anymore," she said, and her eyes were dark and deep.

Kercher leaned in a little, unsteady on their feet. They grasped her shoulder to steady themselves and Praveenthi didn't move away.

"Would you go back only to die?" she asked.

Her face was very close to theirs. Kercher could smell her breath, the sweetness of the booze in which they'd overindulged. The body they'd had printed had big pores, skin which had tiny hairs across her cheeks and above her top lips.

Her eyelashes were thick and short.

Kercher couldn't stop looking.

Her hands gently held their arms.

"No one should live forever," said Kercher. It was the one thing that had meaning.

"I found meaning in helping others in need," said Praveenthi. "There is no need in the Arcology. No one needs anything. All we have is excess and we're so deeply empty regardless of how much falls into us."

Kercher had never felt that way. They did not want to escape. They wanted what they believed the Arcology should be – a place where rebirth was real and transcendence their actual goal.

They touched Praveenthi's face.

"It's not going to work," said Kercher.

"We can make it work if we put some effort into it," said Praveenthi, and pulled them in close, arms wrapping tightly about Kercher's back.

They stood there for a moment, Kercher's own arms hanging in the air unsure what to do with this strange, infuriating woman.

"I can't," said Kercher, when it was clear Praveenthi wasn't going to release them.

She leaned back and they saw how her eyes were damp.

"Ah," she said, looking hurt.

"It's not that," said Kercher, suddenly keen she understood.

"You don't feel things like me, like a normal person," she said, her voice cold. "Is it how you were printed, or am I saddled with a psychopath?"

Kercher swallowed, wrong-footed and unable to respond, because how did they tell this woman that she was the first person they'd touched since they'd been printed? Her body against theirs had been the most unwelcome welcome they hadn't known they were missing.

Praveenthi stepped away, lips pursed and arms out before dropping to her side just as the shadow in which they were stood deepened.

"I am Praveenthi Saal, Interlocutor of the Arcology. Welcome to the warship Hanuman. How can we help you this rotation?"

Kercher stumbled a little as they backed away. Who was this woman in front of them speaking to as if not a drop had touched their lips?

They turned to find a huge green mass of wet organic matter detaching itself from the ceiling of the hanger. Stretching out in long strands, slowly depositing itself onto the floor like a ball of overly wet dough.

Colours flashed across its surface and several strange and unpleasant smells assaulted Kercher's nostrils, chief among them rotting flesh, boiled cabbage and sulphur. Their body translated it as a terse and unimpressed greeting from Operand Long Years in the Cold, master of the colony and, obviously, power to which the Otto offered their subservience.

23.

Hanuman was watching. His mind had fractured but the pieces he could hold together were enough to observe as Prab and Kercher entered the hanger followed by one of the station's true owners.

She'd done well, he thought. Enough attention from the locals to get noticed. They'd gone further than he had expected. About an hour ago several dozen Otto had flooded the hanger, forcing the other ships to depart or move until there was a wide, well-defined perimeter around them.

News had gotten around.

Not that anyone here was a threat.

Not directly in any case. Hanuman worried they were allies of those who had destroyed Akhanda and were going to delay them until the Face of Loss could come here and finish them off.

Hanuman thought about leaving without his crew. He didn't need the pilot. He could survive without the Interlocutor. Neither statement was true – he knew he needed them both. His insides were on fire and the cube had stopped talking to him.

Parts of his memory were fading; his processing capabilities were deteriorating.

If he didn't force the cube off soon it might be that there was no Hanuman and only the repository of the Arcology to greet his crew.

Having only just received a name, Hanuman wasn't ready to relinquish it.

He knew the ideals, the self-sacrifice by which named nodes were expected to abide, how they lived for those under their care. Hanuman wasn't sure what kind of sacrifice he could make which would justify his death.

Hanuman thought about his namesake, holding on to the story of a god whose life still informed the Arcology countless millennia after the apes who'd first encountered him had left the planet where they'd originated.

Is this my dharma?

The Operand dropped down from the ceiling, careful to avoid touching Hanuman as it came.

Before Hanuman could engage, Prab was speaking, her suit flashing and generating the scents required to communicate with a colony of bacteria.

"You're not welcome here," announced the Operand.

"We thank you for receiving us and promise that we aren't proposing to stay," she replied.

"When will you depart?"

"We need information," she replied smoothly. "As soon as we have it we will go. If we cannot find it we will go."

The mat of bacteria rose up into a mound, slightly narrower at the top than on the floor. "What do you need?" it asked.

"We are looking for a system further down the spiral's arm, quiet, uninhabited, disconnected."

"Why?"

"None of your concern," interrupted Kercher.

"We have a research project that needs a quiet sky," continued Prab, as if the pilot hadn't spoken.

The mat stilled, the continuous changes in colour that rippled across its surface slowing to a gentle wave.

"There is a fellow colony in the neighbourhood," said the mat thoughtfully. The actual word was closer to the idea of a forest in which two trees touched one another despite not being near, their roots extended by small fibres of fungus.

"What is the price of your help?" asked Prab.

"That will be for them to decide," said the Operand.

"So I thank you for coming to see us. Will you provide the coordinates for us to meet them?"

The Operand gave off a scent of decayed leaves that meant yes.

Then, "You are far from home, Arcology."

"We are," confirmed Prab, but said nothing more.

"It is not like the great and masterful Arcology to seek the help of others."

"Isn't it?" asked Prab, and Hanuman was impressed with how she avoided the traps being laid before her.

"The Arcology comes and tells us how to live. It invites us to join but lays down constraints and demands and requirements. Those who refuse are swallowed up anyway. Everything they were, erased in the name of the right path."

Prab didn't say anything.

Hanuman could feel the elevated heartbeat of his pilot. Was Kercher going to destroy this colony?

The pilot remained still.

"If that's everything," said Prab into the silence.

"Our cousins will deal with you," said the Operand. "Even in your reduced state we are certain you can pay for what you need."

With that the blob flattened itself back into a mat and slithered away, heading out of the hanger as a rippling carpet with reaching frayed edges.

Kercher immediately ducked onto the ship but Prab remained outside, watching the departing colony until it was out of sight.

The ship scanned the ground and surrounding surfaces and found no trace of the colony lifeform. It would have been easy for it to try to leave some of itself behind. Perhaps it guessed Hanuman wouldn't be fooled, perhaps it didn't care.

After it was gone the ships around them came to life and Otto reappeared, puttering along as if nothing had happened, as if they hadn't been cleared from the room to allow the Operand to talk to Prab undisturbed.

Hanuman wondered how much of their conversation had been overheard.

Were they the kind of culture to record everything, or the kind who thought such an encounter was best left to exist only in the memories of those who took part? With a microbial colony, was there a useful distinction?

The same Otto as had approached them upon their arrival lolloped out of the distance and approached Prab.

"When will you be leaving?" it asked.

Prab stood, hands on hips and face accommodating. "We have some small things to do but will then be on our way. Your master offered us information, when that arrives we shall depart. Will that suffice?"

The Otto bobbed and for a moment looked like it would run away.

"I cannot speak for the masters," it said, and Hanuman felt a rage rise up within. If it had encountered this kind of power dynamic on any other visit, it would have intervened with an education program, mandatory philosophical coursework and some concrete technological interdictions. The bacteria were not a benign host for the Otto.

Hanuman took what resources it had available and hacked into the Otto's systems. It parsed their official histories which spoke of being uplifted by the benevolent Colony Species they called the Lords of Truth.

Hanuman quickly switched all mention of Lords and Truth with Purveyors and Bullshit. Let them swallow that one and wonder just who has this kind of reach, he thought mercilessly.

Done with punking their official histories, documents, headed papers, school text books and government portals, Hanuman sank into their quieter history, the trade documents, the technological papers detailing discoveries, their anthropology exploring who believed what and when.

It wasn't long ago that the Purveyors of Bullshit had come across the Otto. Barely three centuries as the Otto reckoned it. The Otto were a space-faring species of type two, just about edging into type three, when the Bullshitters encountered them on an expedition.

From what Hanuman could work out, the colony species had taken over the bodies of the expedition members and hitchhiked home. Once there they'd quickly moved on the Otto's civic structures, and within a decade had transplanted themselves from infection to overlords.

The Otto had caught a cold in deep space and that cold had enslaved their entire species.

It wasn't the first time either. The bacteria had, so far, gathered to themselves three client species. The very large quadrupeds wandering the station were the second. They were an earlier assimilation and the colonies rode them like others rode horses.

Hanuman skipped over the third – he was angry enough without finding more evidence. The Arcology knew this species.

After all, the Interlocutor was familiar with them. Which meant they'd let them carry on their aggressive expansion without any kind of intervention.

Hanuman sank into a funk, angry with themselves and with their people for the lack of action.

Then he was boating on a fast-flowing river bounded by cliffs while three stars overhead overtook everything.

The water was turbulent, as much because the interacting gravitational wells of three stars made everything unpredictable, and because the river was swollen with meltwater as the landscape welcomed spring.

He didn't know how he knew this but the spray of water on his skin was shocking, the smell of unfamiliar air, water and flora enough to have him sitting in the boat, the paddle in his hands still.

"What are you doing?" someone asked. "Keep paddling you dimwit."

Hanuman turned to find he was staring into his own eyes.

24.

Prab thought about Kercher and felt turned in on herself. How had she ended up in their arms. How had she thought they'd be able to give her comfort. The war-mongering fuck had no feelings that weren't getting hard over killing something.

She'd clocked the bacterial colony the moment they'd stepped into the bar. It was the obvious place to find it. The Otto were a vassal species and their lords and masters would monitor their behaviour.

They'd also keep an eye or four open for threats, and the best place to do that was where foreigners collected when they came on station.

She'd drunk freely but unlike Kercher, she was used to drinking and could have drunk the piss-weak stuff the Otto had served all rotation long. At first she'd thought the pilot was playing along, but then they'd gulped it down, got pissed and then talked about themselves like she was their therapist.

Not that she didn't appreciate it, but it wasn't a pretty sight.

Despite it, Prab felt softer towards them. Kercher was a proper old-school believer hemmed in by whatever constraints the Arcology had included in their printed body. However, they'd read the histories, believed in what the Arcology claimed it was. Sure, they understood the gap between what the Arcology actually was and what it trained its people to aspire towards. Yet rather than walk away in disgust, Kercher decided to live according to that fantastical ideal.

It's kind of impressive, she thought.

For a moment she'd thought they would find some kind of comfort together, and despite their obvious dislike of her she needed contact, compassion. Anything to remind her she wasn't alone.

We found the same destination despite our different journeys, Prab thought. She'd tracked the colony when they left and knew she only needed to play stupid flesh bag long enough that it felt confident in revealing itself despite their connection to a vastly more powerful culture.

She wanted it feeling smug, overconfident, and that was what she'd got.

Prab was a little unnerved by its hints that it knew what had happened to the Arcology. Over confidence is only that when one has misjudged a situation. If it knew the Arcology was dead then she'd taken a far bigger risk than she'd realised.

How could it know? Was it guessing? Had their ships already spotted empty and broken worlds waiting for new inhabitants?

What would they make of the ruins of the Arcology's civilisation?

Shaking her head, she dismissed the possibility they knew and told herself they were an aggressive and infectious species that invaded others to take them over. They couldn't help but look on everything around them as a potential food source.

It is hard, she thought, to respect your food for its intellect as you're biting into it.

Prab found the entire experience of Operand Long Years in the Cold unnerving. She'd watched enough entertainment and read enough books to have planned the meeting a dozen times in her bed, whiling away the hours on trips out of the Arcology.

She'd thought about the bar, had expected it to be full of other species, for the food and drink to be overwhelming. She'd expected markets and strangers, adventure and mysterious negotiations. What they'd got was a drab little mining station built out of a planetoid with no star to call home.

What a child you are, she thought.

Instead she'd had the Otto and their masters, a species whose agenda was unreadable and whose way of thinking about the world frightened her despite knowing she was safe.

They had no brain and were a lifeform whose individuals, if the Operand could be called that, were composed of hundreds of millions of components working together. She had little knowledge of just how they might work together, enough from her prep to know they were something radically different.

How a bacterial colony made it into space, let alone
running the lives of several other species, was beyond her
comprehension. All Prab had were the facts, she couldn't let
the route to how they came to be true be relevant.

So she'd hoped they were subject to emotions like her; of
confidence, guilt, greed and lure of power.

So far, so good.

Kercher was already ensconced in their seat by the time she
boarded Hanuman.

"How are you, Hanuman?" she asked.

Kercher shook their head. "No answer for me either."

A chill slapped its way down her torso.

"They're okay," said Kercher. "I think."

"You think?"

"Systems are online, we can leave if I pilot. It's Hanuman's
identity that's not with us. They're distracted, somewhere else.
Their sprites are around."

"They're a node," replied Prab, wondering where a node
could go that they'd abandon themselves so completely. "They
have enough attention for all of us."

Kercher shrugged. "And yet."

Instead of sitting down, Prab left the cockpit and walked
back to check on the stasis pods. There was no way of walking
among them, Hanuman had them stacked in tight sections
with no corridors. All she could do was see the nearest ones
through a transparent membrane which also projected the
status of those inside.

She wasn't really looking for those she'd brought from
Sirajah's Reach. For now they were in better shape than
her – dreaming blissfully of whatever pleased them and
unaware of the fall of the empire they'd called home.

It took a few seconds to locate the cube. She was looking
for something the same size as what they'd brought aboard on
Akhanda.

What Prab found was about a quarter that size and dull,
giving off none of the light which had given it life before.

Cables stretched from it into Hanuman's interior, like
the two were really part of each other. Checking the ship's
systems, Prab could see the cube had co-opted vast swathes of
Hanuman's capability.

Was Hanuman struggling with the repository?

"Hanuman? Can you hear me?" she called out.

At first nothing but the soft silence of the ship.

Then. "I am here." Hanuman's voice echoed around Prab as if spoken in many places. "The water is turbulent but the suns are beautiful. I have never been here. It's a system at the galactic core's end of the empire. Home to a few thousand identities, home to people who love the physical demands of living outdoors. The worlds they conjure are astonishing and dangerous."

"Hanuman, you're not there," said Prab calmly. They were present enough to hear her but whatever was happening, Hanuman was struggling to grasp reality.

"I know," said the ship. "But I cannot see you. I hear you like a bird on the wing as I wrestle with rapids and cold, sharp air."

"We're with the Otto. I have found their sponsor species and they have agreed to help us find a new home. We need you for this."

"I can hear waterfalls," said Hanuman.

"Praveenthi," said the pilot through her comm. "We're being asked to depart."

"Tell them we're waiting for the coordinates," said Prab testily.

"I have them," said Kercher. "So do you."

Prab checked and, sure enough, the station had supplied a location less than a light minute away.

"Hanuman," she said, firmly now, as if speaking to a client who wasn't hearing her advice. "I need you to concentrate and step away from where you are. Think about the hanger where we docked, think about the four-eyed Otto and the colony species who've enslaved them."

"I'm here," said Hanuman, and their voice had condensed into singularity. "I am. Not. Well."

She understood, or thought she did. However, it couldn't matter until they were away from the Otto and their Operands and somewhere far from their volume of influence.

"He's back," said Kercher as she reached the cockpit.

"Let's go," she said.

Departing was easy – the station authorities were so keen on them leaving they shuffled others with a higher priority and they were third out of the hangar.

No one would think it was anything except the Arcology being their usual pushy selves, thought Prab with weary relief.

Hanuman was talkative enough but muted, as if they hadn't quite shaken off the episode they'd just experienced.

The location was empty when they arrived.

Kercher was busy scanning for incoming ships.

Hanuman was quiet.

"How bad is it?" she asked.

"The bed is being made again. I told them not to; we can make them ourselves," said Hanuman. "Not well."

They were still alone, so she asked another question, tried to be exact with her words because who knew how long they had.

"How long do you have?"

She assumed the worst, hoped any answer would address that as much as give her something to work with. Ideally, the answer was eternity.

"I don't know," said Hanuman. "I'm forgetting who I am. My identity is being swallowed by this, as if the sages who made the monkey forget their power are living in my brain."

She tried not to let the gibberish wound her.

"Is there anything we can do?"

"Find us a home," said Hanuman.

"Kercher," she said. "Can we translate if we need to?"

The pilot gave her some of their attention. If the ship wasn't capable of doing this itself their chances of translating were vastly reduced. Spacetime might be best defined as a vast void with traces of grit, but information space was a continuous place full of everything that had, could and would exist. It had no voids because absence was as much an informational statement as presence.

"I can make calculations," they said gallantly.

There's the spirit that wants to win every battle, she thought.

"If you could," she replied, and the knowledge that Kercher would fail hung between them like a spilled drink no one wanted to clean up.

The list of things Prab wanted to do was long. Her ability to do them short.

Find a new home. Maybe possible?

Make sure they weren't followed. Impossible.

Make sure they couldn't be found. Worse than impossible.

Get there. Not in her gift.

Find a substrate so the Arcology could separate itself from Hanuman.

She laughed at the last. Where in the galaxy would she find Arcology tech which could suffice for what they needed? It wasn't physical space they needed, it was an access point to information space.

And if they started working with ibits, how long would it take their enemy to find them?

"To be safe we're reduced to living like primitives," she said to no one in particular.

She thought about her life. She thought about what she'd been doing three rotations ago; lamenting her possessive parents, wondering if she should have her hair done. There was a shade of blonde that, when coupled with ringlets, left her feeling like she was a shocking kind of attractive. Not classical but striking.

Prab liked being striking. It separated out the boring from the interesting. Most of the time.

"There's a supernova remnant about thirty light years from here," said Kercher. "We can pick up some heavier elements there. From those we can synthesise the others we need without using too much energy."

"The ibit cost would be lower this way," confirmed Hanuman.

Ideally though, they'd use nothing more fundamental than a qubit and stay well within the bounds of spacetime. Tearing open the hood of the universe to tinker with the engine would get them noticed.

She couldn't disappoint them with such sombre news so let the comment, the idea, rest without being dispelled. They'd be forced to confront their options soon enough.

"Something's coming," said Kercher.

The ship rotated along its long axis and they were facing the newcomer when it arrived.

Space wobbled as through a flawed lens and then, where nothing had been a moment before, was the ship they'd been sent to meet.

It was a huge thing, five times their length and the shape of a femur. The bone of a giant who could step across continents, but a bone nonetheless.

Across its white and grey surface were clusters of green and blue. Prab realised they were organic growths clinging to the ship's superstructure, feeding on it and providing it power in return.

The bone, which a scan confirmed was a metallic calcium metamaterial with high toughness and shear coefficients, was long along one axis, starting and ending with large bulbous spurs of material in whose nooks the deepest concentrations of organic material nestled like spiders in the cracks of a windowpane.

Its means of propulsion was unclear but given the distortion accompanying its arrival, Prab guessed it was capable of folding spacetime. Fast but not instantaneous travel, and the engines would take up a huge proportion of the ship's volume.

The bone ship's size suggested not power but a lack of technological prowess.

From the evidence, there wasn't any indication the Operands were capable of programming their materials.

"The ship's unwell," said Kercher.

She didn't reply.

"I'm not able to deploy anything except the most basic countermeasures."

"Try this," said Hanuman.

"No different," said Kercher and through Kercher's systems, Prab felt the ship shiver with fear and uncertainty.

Signals bounced off Hanuman's shell.

Most of them were range finding and assessments. One of them was a comms attempt.

In the language the Otto on the station used.

Hanuman's pixies had no problem translating.

"We are the Operand Sea of Thought Drifting. You have come to meet/live with/engage us."

The translation was vague, the meaning multiplicitous. Most cultures had enough in common that concepts such as individuality, ownership, distance and age were translatable. Yet other things were open, layered and often entirely absent.

Prab had been thinking about the Operands. Their name for themselves meant something along the lines of "those who act" but it also carried with it the sense of being at the centre, the thing around which other, larger subjects" revolved and found their motivation.

A suitable name for a culture that colonised others by literally inhabiting their bodies from the inside.

The Operands were a communal intelligence. Trillions of microbes who, together, exhibited higher level intelligence of the kind that found them travelling through spacetime in ships made of bone.

They might have no brain and no central nervous system, but Prab had encountered a dozen other cultures with similar biological expressions and they, without exception, managed to achieve everything her simian ancestry had made possible for the Arcology.

It didn't mean they were the same or wanted the same things, but their capability should never be underestimated.

She guessed that the Operands colonised because it was what they were, down in their organelles. They didn't need consciousness to decide, they didn't need a theory of mind to choose.

Training to be an interlocutor involved learning how to reason with the unconscious intelligence of a culture whose ancestry was lichen-based as much as it did learning how to use money or when to sleep.

The Operands were going to want one of two things, possibly both: a way into the Arcology's population and control of Hanuman.

The latter was off the table and Prab was willing to offer them anything of the former because the Arcology would expunge any attempt to ingress upon its systems.

Or it would have done.

Right now she could promise anything safe in the knowledge there was no Arcology to deliver.

She returned their handshake on two streams, one using the Arcology's own trade language, a simplified version of its dominant internal node-to-node language, as well as using that of the Ottos.

Using the Operand's own communication tools seemed likely to offend, not to mention revealing her own hand too early. If they were smart they'd know the Arcology could speak to them directly, but given what she'd seen so far, she was willing to bet they regarded even a monster like the Arcology as prey who might be large and unpredictable, but as prey nevertheless.

"We understand/speak/deploy your language," came back the response in decent trade Arcology, even if there were ambiguities. The uncertainties were in the communication which meant they were introduced at the Operand end, their own language not parsing into Arcology one for one. "We are willing to provide what you need if you can, in return, provide what we need/desire/hunger for."

The bone ship wasn't approaching but Kercher said, "Their engines are ready for action."

"Against us?" she asked.

"I have no idea," they replied. "Could be that, could be ready to run away."

Which wasn't the insight she was looking for.

"What do you need?" she asked the Operand.

The response came back swiftly.

"You have cargo we need/desire/hunger for. We would treat it well/maintain it. They would have privileged/sustained lives among us. All we ask is that you allow your cargo to settle/colonise/integrate among us. In return we know of several systems that match what you're looking for/fleeing to."

Prab couldn't help herself.

"What are we looking for?" It was that or tell them to go fuck themselves.

You're the one who convinced them you accepted slaves, she thought.

The bone ship turned away from them as if thinking.

"The Arcology is under attack. This much we/you know," said the Operand Sea of Thought Drifting.

Kercher popped up on her feed, his avatar looking worried. She could feel he was about to announce they should break off communications and leave.

It's what the mute button's for, she thought.

"Is that so?" she replied to the Sea of Thought Drifting.

"We have noticed the lack of traffic from the Arcology. We have noticed the lack of traffic at the edges of your empire. Others have penetrated much further inside your borders and return now to tell tales of worlds ruptured and split apart, of silence everywhere they went."

Was that fear in their voice? Could they be afraid?

Kercher realised they weren't being heard and started sending messages to her. Prab ignored them. She knew what the pilot wanted and she wasn't going to give it to them.

She wanted to negotiate with the Sea of Thought Drifting but they had nothing to give and nowhere to go. They had no strength and their counterparty had seen not only the hand they were playing but the rest of the deck as well.

At such times, Prab had always cleaved to one course of action: ask for help.

"What do you know about them?" she asked.

"The Arcology thinks itself so advanced/big for understanding information and for seeing its nature/basis. The Arcology thinks the rest of us are unevolved/fools/ungrown for not having made the same discoveries. You are so convinced by your central nervous systems."

Here it comes, she thought.

"You are not the first to have understood the nature/basis of the universe/habitat and you will, as surely as nutrients support being/satisfy hunger, not be the last."

"You sound like a child around a campfire," she said. "Do you know anything that could help us?"

"We are older than you, we have been here much longer. There is no sinking/immersing/diving into information because within that sea live beasts who hunt and they feast on the richest food they can find."

Prab didn't want to believe what she was hearing.

"Hanuman?" she quested, hoping the ship had enough of themselves left to answer.

"I have no evidence of this," said the ship. "But I am not myself and have no access to the histories of the Arcology."

Feeling isolated and adrift, Prab tried to strategise around what the Operands could give her and how to avoid giving them the survivors of Sirajah's Reach in return.

"They can't help us," said Kercher, their voice arriving this time via the ship's internal emergency messaging system.

Rolling her eyes, Prab tried to concentrate.

"They were everywhere," she said to the Operand. "This was planned, it was an invasion. What do you know about them and where can we go to survive?"

"There is no planning/only now," said the Operand. "They

have no more intention than a simple predator/hungering for space/for growth. They are unable to understand the stars in the sky are balls of fire, nor that rain overhead is part of an ever revolving /swell/shrivel/feast/famine."

"You have met them before?" she asked.

"Those who came before/generations now dead," confirmed the Operand. "Living in spacetime required us to accept information/circumstances could not be manipulated and so we chose another way/adaptation of being. You see that impetus here. Now. Here. Now. Now. Here."

"They never had access to information space," scoffed Kercher.

"Shut up," said Prab.

"Your encounter with them was inevitable/competition," said the Operand. "Now/here you must choose to live like us or discover your colonies empty of being/consumed. When they have feasted they will return to hunting for food, but they are patient and they will wait for the next newcomers/stumbling out of the dark to think they are the first to be so smart."

"What do they want?" asked Prab.

"There is no they," replied the Operand, and every trace of the plural was gone from the logs of the conversation, replaced with "it".

Frustrated at their own inconsistency Prab asked, "did you ever prevail against it?"

The bone ship turned back towards them. "There was no prevailing, only delaying it while we grew new ways of being/ sustaining. Will you agree to deliver your slaves to us?"

"Kercher," said Prab. "We need to go."

"I've been trying to tell you," they replied.

"I mean now. Translate us if you can."

"What about the locations they're promising?" asked Hanuman. "We will not deliver them anything, but I could ransack their systems and take it."

Prab thought about how appealing that was, to have the upper hand and use it.

Except if the Operand Sea of Thought Drifting was telling them the truth then nowhere they pointed out was safe.

"We are a morsel for our enemies and they have the taste of our blood in their mouths," she said.

"Where are we going?" asked Kercher, ignoring her words.

"Further out along the rim," she said.

The bone ship started in on an approach. Clearly they thought they were getting the cargo they'd asked for.

"Now would be a good time," she said to Kercher and Hanuman.

"We need a destination," said Kercher.

"We cannot simply translate," said Hanuman.

The bone ship changed course. The spacetime around it blurred and it was gone.

"Um," said Prab.

"Incoming," said Kercher and before they'd finished speaking the world around them blurred as several large ships slid into view.

25.

The new ships were bulbous and metallic. They shone through the spectrum, greens, reds, blues and yellows strobing across their surfaces. They were of different sizes. Kercher recognised a battle group when he saw one.

The larger command and control ship was a little behind the others, perhaps a light second further back, with four others between it and Hanuman.

They were coming in fast and obviously had weapons hot.

Kercher tried to lock on to them but found the ship unresponsive.

"Hanuman, ship, I need those systems."

"I can't do anything about it," said Hanuman and Kercher heard the sound of defeat in his transmission.

"Then what can you do?" asked Kercher, feeling the barrels of the enemy between their eyebrows.

"We cannot use ibits," screeched Praveenthi from behind them.

"Not now," said Kercher, trying to concentrate on the options unfolding in front of them.

"I'm not fucking joking," she said, but Kercher wasn't listening anymore. If she could mute them, then they could return the favour. It was a joy, after the embarrassment of her sudden physical intimacy, to shut her out and make her distant.

"I can give you counter measures and control of the matter manipulators. You will have to make weapons and sync them to your body. You have to go around my systems, Pilot."

"Kercher," said Kercher.

"I am sorry," said Hanuman.

Kercher was already busy. The ship responded and as Kercher threw out static across the entire electromagnetic spectrum and shifted them a light minute away by folding space rather than translating, they set what systems and sprites they could access to make some good old-fashioned spacetime guns.

As the ship reconfigured, Kercher took them on a tour of the local volume. There was a small cloud of thinly dispersed hydrogen snaking its way nearby and using it as base material, Kercher started building physical obstacles and chaff to confuse the enemy.

They had no idea who it was. Hanuman's systems weren't playing nice and the sprites were complaining how they had no better access than Kercher.

When they tackled Hanuman on profile identification the ship talked about marigolds and how they were edible and thought to be good for anti-inflammatory and anti-bacterial treatments.

Kercher's whole body was tense and the ship responded likewise, jerking through spacetime rather than sailing smoothly.

They forced themselves to calm down and take stock.

The new arrivals had followed them, stalled only briefly by the static discharges before calibrating and coming through the flotsam and jetsam Kercher had put in their way.

Those few seconds were all they needed though.

Kercher was ready with enough weaponry that, even without Hanuman's vast resources, these primitives should be wiped off the face of the brane.

"They call themselves History's Arm," said Praveenthi.

Why do all these cultures see themselves as the universe's destiny? thought Kercher. He had the entire battle group locked.

Although the Operands had fled at their arrival, protocol was never to fire first. The Arcology felt no pressure from the less advanced cultures of the galaxy, and all other cultures were less advanced.

An intense blast of electromagnetic signals showered Hanuman as the enemy group continued to close in.

Responding to Kercher's shift across the volume, they'd done the same, coming so close they could have shared a bed. Yawing the ship around the nearest member of the battle group, Kercher pushed Hanuman away, keeping everything locked in.

That these arseholes hadn't fired on them either suggested something else was going on.

"I'm getting a handshake," said Praveenthi, her voice high and nervous. "They want the ship. They want us to surrender."

"Tell them to fuck off," said Kercher. "I'm going to move us a few minutes out and see if they follow."

Hanuman slid across spacetime, a full light hour away from the Otto station and minutes from the people calling themselves History's Arm.

They followed right after.

Praveenthi shared their demands, which amounted to repeated shouts that they surrender there and then.

"We should leave," said Praveenthi.

"They'll follow," said Kercher. "Do we know who History's Arm actually are?"

"Hanuman's encountered them before," said Praveenthi thoughtfully. She shared a few screens with Kercher.

A predator culture, invertebrates, five legs, five eyes, bodies with a thorax and an abdomen. At some point they'd lost the ability to weave silk. Physically no larger than Kercher's head, they were from an oxygen-rich origin planet. Hanuman had encountered them hunting on a type one world and driven them off. They had been pissed but also unable to argue with an Arcology ship.

They were too aggressive for the Arcology to maintain more than a monitoring relationship with and, despite being repulsed numerous times, would regularly test the Arcology's boundaries and patience by seeing if they could encroach.

The Arcology's protocol for dealing with them was to cripple their ships and send them back into their own territory. Destroying them had only encouraged them – it was leaving survivors with tales of their impotence against the Arcology which had provided the longest gaps between their futile attempts to hunt in Arcology space.

Something had changed for them to believe they were able to do it now.

"Telling them to fuck off," said Praveenthi.

Barely had her signal gone when the smallest two craft opened fire.

High-energy particle beams.

Embarrassingly useless against Hanuman, and as they scattered off the hull Kercher picked them both out and with a thought emanating from their forearms, shattered the smaller craft into dust.

The remaining battlegroup scattered in all directions. Rather than fleeing, they were attempting to flank Kercher, above, below, ahead and to their rear.

Kercher laughed at the stupidity of it. Were they going to weave a web and ensnare Hanuman?

Shifting the ship half a light second away, Kercher targeted the largest of the group and, using some entangled particles, deposited them explosively just where that ship's engines were.

With a small puff of blue flame they detached from the enemy ship and the two parts of the now crippled command vessel gently floated apart.

It was a simple manoeuvre but Kercher was satisfied with accomplishing the precision required to detach the engines without destroying the vessel.

"Try following us now," they said.

On a normal day, being entirely outgunned should stop hostilities. This was what Kercher had learned through a hundred simulations and a dozen firefights.

History's Arm did not appear to read the same strategic handbooks as the Arcology. The two remaining craft fired, more particle beams, even some weapons trying to split apart their hull by splitting its quark pairs.

Kercher sighed. "It's like being attacked by a mouse," they said to Praveenthi.

"I don't know what that is," said the Interlocutor.

"We could sit here and bathe in their bullshit all day."

Praveenthi was silent.

"We could also leave," said Kercher.

"Then let's leave," said Praveenthi.

"Where do we go?" asked Kercher.

"Just go. We can figure it out afterwards."

Kercher folded space and slid them towards the nearest star, about two light years away. An elderly thing, too small to collapse, too feeble to explode. It was halfway through eating itself alive and about twice the size it had been at its prime. The light was a deep, unattractive orange.

The remains of the battle group did not follow them this time.

"They know," said Praveenthi. "They know we're alone, that the Arcology has fallen."

"Who? Them? Who cares," said Kercher, reviewing the engagement and setting up instructions for the ship's sprites. Next time, the ship would respond without Kercher having to think it through. Engines would be scalped away and weapons neutralised automatically.

They'd prefer to engage in information space, to reprogram their systems so the ships switched themselves off, evacuated their internal atmospheres and explained in extensive detail why it was all happening to them, but with Hanuman off his game and the need to avoid ibits, physical warfare it would have to be.

"Not them" said Praveenthi. "Everyone. The Otto knew. The Operands knew. This lot know."

Kercher thought about what she was saying. They wanted to know how so many already knew. Had they known this was coming? Had they been waiting for the Arcology to be gutted?

How had none of them warned us?

Are we hated out there?

Kercher realised none of this was strategic or pertinent to their situation but couldn't stop thinking about it.

The Operands said they weren't the first civilisation to manipulate information. They'd gone as far as to say they had done it themselves before settling for a lesser existence because of this same enemy actor.

The Arcology had been in its current shape for a hundred thousand rotations. Its people had lived thousands of lives. Why now? What had brought this enemy crashing down on them so suddenly after being so long at peace?

"We go to the rim," said Kercher.

"Empty space won't save Hanuman," she replied.

Talking about which.

"Hanuman," said Kercher. "Are you there?"

"Just take us away," said Praveenthi. "I don't care where. Don't stop; it's the moving that counts. I'll get him back."

26.

The city was at its best on sunny days. The people were happiest outside. Cafes were full and musicians were in the park, strangers playing together as crowds passed by, pausing to listen and applaud.

Impromptu parchisi competitions were drawing audiences. Some ate, others drank. Samosas folded half a dozen ways, daal, bhaji, salty lassi and sweet, sweet chai. Food stalls were delighted by the long queues. Above them the sky was that strange yellow only witnessed on the hottest days where the world's normal blue couldn't match the temperature and surrendered to a close haze.

Hanuman had their toes dipped in a fountain, the water warm but shockingly cool compared to the air.

He was daydreaming about space battles. Of ships clashing in the dark between stars. Perhaps it would make for a good stream. A fantasy about a stream getting made and optioned for wider entertainment brought a smile to his lips.

"What are you doing?" a woman asked, plopping herself down on the edge of the stone fountain next to him.

He ignored her. City life had two rules – don't jaywalk and don't talk to strangers with even the slightest of weird vibes.

"Hanuman? Can you hear me?"

His toes were small and he played with spreading them apart, seeing the clarity of the water between them, the white stone of the fountain pool.

"None of this is real," she said.

He wanted to tell her to go away. This was the best of days. He wasn't going to surrender the fountain to her but she was ruining it.

"We need you," she said. "We don't know what to do."

Hanuman stood up. His office was a short walk away. It was still lunchtime but suddenly he was feeling too hot, the sweat on his back too damp.

"Hanuman, please," said the woman.

He realised her name was Praveenthi. He had hired her at some point, to do marketing maybe?

What was she doing here?

"I'm sorry it didn't work out," he said to her. He thought she no longer worked with them. Hadn't she refused to move to this city with them? She'd claimed she didn't want to be part of the company, had chosen to resign and leave them. Didn't even have another role to go to.

Why was she here?

"You have to wake up," she said, staring at the city as if it was the underworld itself and rakshasa were about to tear them limb from limb.

"I'm not asleep," said Hanuman.

And then she was gone like she'd been edited out of his life.

Hanuman stood there staring at the space where she'd been stood, but then a woman with a huge brass horn started playing a jaunty number, all infectious boom, boom, boom. Jiggling her feet as she led people around the park, Hanuman's memory of his former employee was swallowed by the need to dance along.

Hanuman hated the opera. How had he ended up here, in the middle row, in the middle seat of the stalls, unable to get to the aisle without disrupting everyone about him and the opera itself?

The singer was lamenting his fate, how he'd been cursed and his partner kidnapped and taken to a kingdom ruled by demons. A hero would come in time, a deva no less, and rescue his bride. The problem being that his hero couldn't remember their power, had been reduced to little more than a monkey scampering through the forests of the world.

It was a depressing story about no good deed going unpunished, although it was widely celebrated as an example of the wisdom of self-limitation and the importance of self-discovery.

The collar of his shirt was stiff, the bow tie a fake. How he longed to wear a suit which was the colour of rainbows rather than the threateningly dull black that seemed to pass for fashion.

Hanuman saw the empty seat next to him and grimaced. Someone would be along to fill it up no doubt. The stewards would make them wait for the intermission at least.

Then a woman was pushing her way along the row, ignoring the outrage of fellow audience members. She wasn't even dressed properly, wearing a sari which could only really be called appropriate for someone about to dig a cesspit.

"Listen to me," she said, her voice loud and clear, drowning out the tender bass of the man on stage. People hissed at her to shut up. Stewards were clustered at the side of the room, pointing and trying to work out how to get to her without making it all worse.

Despite his loathing of the music, of the pomp, Hanuman was all kinds of embarrassed and wished she would go away. He looked around but saw no one actually coming to reprimand her, no one with a shepherd's crook to drag her off.

"I don't care who you are, go away."

"Not unless you come with me," she said.

Over at the edge of the stage a door appeared, through it, darkness and somewhere... else.

Hanuman was out of his seat, the theatre was empty, the stage dark, curtains closed.

What was going on? Why was this happening to him?

"Your name," she said. "What is it?"

"Hanuman," he replied. Except, was that right? Wasn't he without a name. No, he had been without a name. That was it. Hanuman was new.

"What happened to Hanuman?"

"I don't know," he replied. How had they climbed onto the stage?

"What was the opera about?" she asked. Was she angry with him? Where did she get off being angry with him?

"A stupid man who lost his wife and the monkey who saved her. The monkey stood as tall as the universe and could play with time like a football. It could manipulate the very information of the universe."

That last bit? Was that in the opera? It seemed right. He couldn't remember.

A headache pounded across his brow, down around his skull into the back of his neck.

Hanuman wanted to lie down.

She grabbed him. "No you don't. I've got you now. You're not escaping to another memory. This is the sixth I've had to work through. What happens in the opera? After the Monkey stands as tall as the universe and rescues the princess?"

"He's told he is too powerful, too mischievous," said Hanuman. "That his behaviour is so outrageous the gods send great sages to reason with him. The Monkey God agrees to forget what he can do and to only recall his abilities when he needs them. The gods, satisfied that they won't be washed away in the power of his potential, are mollified. The Monkey God, wryly respected forever for his choice, is left to carry on."

"And that god's name?"

"Hanuman," said Hanuman. And the world is a tunnel, narrowing, speeding past too fast. Then he's in a ship, no, he is a ship, and around him are countless other vessels, none of them friendly.

27.

Prab's eyes were seeing white and red and green and blue but none of the shapes made sense. Blocks of colour roved across her vision and refused to turn into anything she knew.

But Hanuman was back among them.

The ship was working with Kercher, and between them they were moving further towards the rim of the galaxy.

"They're following us," said Kercher.

Folding space was crude technology but the pilot had listened to her and had chosen this rather than translating.

More ships were joining the chase, for they were being hunted now.

Prab believed they could survive any kind of assault, but being chased halfway across the galaxy was not an improvement on their previous predicament.

She could not come up with any plan which would give them breathing room.

"We have to stop," she said.

"You said keep travelling."

"Hanuman is back."

"You are right, we cannot risk translating," said the ship.

"Then why stop?" asked Kercher.

"We have to escape them."

"Hanuman?" asked Kercher.

"She is right," said the ship. Kercher sighed.

"Are you both ready?"

Prab could see how Kercher was readying the ship for conflict.

"Do you have a plan?" she asked.

"We'll be at the nearest star in a few minutes. I plan to use the gravity well to give us an advantage. We are the unknown to them. They sense blood in the water but they don't know

169

what we might do except for the truth that they know we're capable of feats they cannot explain."

"But we won't," she said, panicking. "Perform feats they don't understand. Right?"

His feed was silent for a moment as if he was trying to find a way of talking without losing his shit.

"That perception gives us an advantage even if we're without the very things they're scared of. We're still capable of fielding the most advanced tech they'll have ever encountered."

"There are many of them," said Hanuman warningly.

Kercher's irritation slipped its bounds. "I know."

"Okay, okay," said Prab, wanting Kercher in the best frame of mind. "So we use the physical objects in the star system to our advantage."

"It's a system full of dust and debris. It has half a dozen rocky planets and four gas giants. The star itself is huge and ancient and its only chance that means the largest of the gas giants didn't collapse into fusion to make it a binary. The gravitational well is uneven, unstable and that landscape gives us lots of options. Not least using the debris as projectiles."

"What can I do?" asked Prab.

"I want profiles of the enemy ships."

"I've identified three separate cultures all heading towards the star system to intercept us," said Hanuman.

"It's uninhabited?" asked Prab, suddenly aware they were going to disrupt the system's equilibrium and terrified they were going to kill millions without noticing.

"It is uninhabited," said Hanuman.

Hanuman sent her the data and Prab started analysing it to see who and what was coming for them.

The trio were all type-three cultures. The Operands were not there among them, for which she was grateful.

History's Arm were behind them, mapping the same vector, and would arrive the soonest, just a few minutes after Hanuman. It would give them very little time to prepare.

With Hanuman's identity restored, she was able to access the ship's archive and found details of History's Arm. A strange culture where the number six held sway. Their battle groups, their parliaments, their entire society was built around base six. There were six battle groups of six trying to intercept them.

She wondered how much of their ability to project force this represented. Were they betting a significant chunk of their culture's capability for war on capturing Hanuman?

Their tech was largely based on quantum entanglement. Their engines folded space by tunnelling between two places through the quantum foam and then pulling them close. A novel solution and energetically efficient. It meant that large ship they'd seen in the first battle group had plenty of space for weapons.

The technology around which they'd built space travel also provided the basis of their weapon systems.

Prab fed this to Kercher and Hanuman who responded by having defences built to withstand their attacks.

The second culture, the Uster, whose name for themselves was "the People", was relatively primitive compared to History's Arm. A culture whose origin was a cold liquid methane world, their bodies were similar to hippocampi, two arms and a tail. An image of one of the People showed their arms ending in dozens of small tentacles. The data showed them as being no bigger than her hand.

The People were still using fusion engines to fold space. Their ships were gigantic and their smaller ships weren't capable of anything except hyperlocal engagements before having to return to the carrier. Their weapons were high energy in nature. Their culture still thought of space like the ocean from which they'd come, and this as well as their technology would severely limit their ability to engage meaningfully in combat.

Boring, thought Prab.

"It might seem an insignificant distinction," said Kercher. "But we're resilient, not invulnerable. Enough of those dicks and we'll melt just like anything else."

Which wasn't the comforting dismissal Prab had been expecting.

"Right," she said, and set to looking at the third culture.

The Shahar, which translated as "the city overfull", were a culture analogous to reptiles with four limbs and long, prehensile tails. Like the majority of cultures based on macro-organisms, including the Arcology, they were biaxial along their longest axis with a head at one end and the tail at the other.

Their culture was relatively peaceful and non-expansionary and Prab wondered what had grabbed them about their situation that they'd thrown together a small armada to come and intercept Hanuman.

Technologically, they were the closest of the three to understanding how ibits were the fundamental building blocks of everything, but their technology remained based on spacetime and qubits.

Their fleet profile was full of long elegant ships, tubular with thin tendrils spreading from a central spine like the frills of a lion fish or frilled dragon. Hanuman had not encountered them directly and had little information on their capabilities.

"What's the plan?" she asked after the other two had received her assessments. From her perspective the Shahar were the biggest problem – the most technologically advanced and the least well known. She couldn't suggest how they'd engage or even if they would. Were they coming to talk or fight?

"We take out the spiders," said Kercher.

"History's Arm are not spiders," said Prab.

"Six legs, six eyes. Same difference," said Kercher. "They're the shits who've come this far and won't take no for an answer. They're done first. Then I'll worry about the Uster."

"Their ships are full of fluids," said Prab. "They have superior manoeuvrability."

"Only compared to the others," said Kercher.

She didn't understand Kercher's thinking but then they were the pilot, not her. Printed with a brain and body wired for combat and tactics.

"You have six minutes and twenty seconds between arriving and the first of the others joining us," said Hanuman.

"Plenty of time," said Kercher. They'd shared an initial plan with Prab and Hanuman. They were intending on sliding into one of the two asteroid belts that orbited the star and setting a number of the larger objects barrelling towards the point where History's Arm would stop folding space.

With any luck they'd be greeted by a few hundred million tonnes of iron and ice right between their six eyes.

Even if they avoided being run over, they'd have to scatter and Kercher would pick them off before they could regroup.

The next into the system were the Uster, they'd likely drop in on the other side of the star to History's Arm but Kercher had a plan for them too.

One of the gas giants, the smallest of them, was out that way and Kercher aimed to fold into its shadow and, using shaped high-energy explosives, send gouts of the planet out towards them. They were going to ride those gas spouts right into the middle of the enemy and beat the shit out of them before they could target Hanuman. It would be a glancing encounter because right behind them were the Shahar and Kercher was aiming right for them with their launch trajectory out of the gas giant.

"What if they don't perform as you expect?" she asked.

"I am capable of stopping them from targeting us regardless of the pilot's extravagant and unnecessary theatrics," said Hanuman.

Prab accepted it was true but at the back of her mind was the worry that at the crucial moment they'd lose Hanuman all over again to whatever was eating away its identity.

Which left the Shahar. Kercher's plan was to annihilate them with the Uster at their backs.

"We should try talking to them," she said. She sent profiles of the known Shahar ships with little icons flashing where their technology remained unidentified.

"After they're disabled," said Kercher promptly.

With a frustrated sigh, Prab sat back and waited for them to arrive in system.

28.

They were failing. Kercher dressed up their hesitant preparations as caution, as being ready to take on all comers, but they knew they were about to be overwhelmed. Large predators were easily overwhelmed by packs of smaller animals.

A metaphor the training sergeant had used until Kercher was sick of it was hyenas taking down a lion. Kercher knew neither of the animals beyond a gory graphic of the hyenas surrounding and tearing a lion apart. However, the point was clear – they might be more powerful, but if they weren't extremely careful this horde of arseholes were going to surround them and take what they wanted.

Praveenthi was too nervous already so Kercher let her waffle on about each of the cultures, their origins, their relative technological capabilities. She kept saying she needed her books as if, whatever books were, they'd help her here. Thankfully, it stopped her from thinking too hard about their own constraints.

There was no way Kercher could trust Hanuman to be there when needed. The pilot didn't know what was happening to the ship except they had seen how little of its processing power remained theirs to commandeer when needed. That Praveenthi had recalled his identity from whatever hallucination it was lost within was a feat worthy of several drinks the next time they had opportunity.

Shame she's not a soldier proper, thought Kercher.

Nor are you, said a small voice they recognised as themselves. You never wanted this.

Shaking it off, Kercher thought about how nothing changed the fact that they might be right in the middle of the firefight to come when Hanuman next lost his shit and vanished up his own exhaust port.

They were as ready as they could be but with ten minutes to go before they arrived, Kercher went over everything a second and then a third time. Perhaps a tweak here or a change there. Maybe a new idea would present itself.

In the end, none of the above. Kercher looked at the plan and couldn't see anything which would change the future enough to warrant action. Their body shivered with anticipation and the ship followed suit. Praveenthi looked at the back of them but Kercher was too absorbed to notice.

What they really wanted was to pock spacetime with spots of anti-gravity, throw the entire asteroid belt out of equilibrium, collapse the nearest gas giant into a micro-star.

None of it was possible unless they wanted the real enemy to find them, so they were left playing with toys and hoping it was enough.

"Are you ready?" they asked the other two.

They saw Praveenthi chew her lips, biting back whatever impulse she had before saying, "When we're free of this I want to know more."

"About what?" they asked.

"You," she replied.

In spite of everything, Kercher felt a sense of pleasure at her words.

"There's no record of your beliefs in our historical records," said Hanuman.

Kercher swallowed, felt their skin tingle and the ship adjust to ignore the errant commands coming entirely from the gut punch Hanuman had just delivered.

"Of course not," said Kercher, thunder sounding behind their eyes. "The Arcology can't have people knowing we've abandoned and twisted the truth of what brought us to the stars."

"We wouldn't do that to ourselves," said Hanuman.

"Ship," said Kercher, needing to distance themselves from this badly timed bullshit. "Now is not the time. It's what I know to be true and I'm paying the price for holding to my ideals. You might want to consider that it's my apostate body that's keeping the dream of the Arcology alive."

Hanuman was silent but the quiet was like listening to the gap between lightning and thunder. Kercher counted slowly, waiting.

"I'm trying to think of a joke to lighten the mood," said Praveenthi. "You know, something, something Excluded and heretic join forces to save the day. Can't quite work it out. I had a book that was just jokes. I left it behind."

She fell silent and Kercher saw grief in her eyes.

"Two minutes," said Hanuman.

Kercher set off the gravitic charges, sending the asteroids they'd tagged spinning out towards History's Arm's arrival point. They slid Hanuman around and through the asteroid belt to follow the largest of the rocks they'd disrupted, cover on their approach.

History's Arm arrived.

Thirty ships this time. Five complete battle groups. Plus a thirty-first, a hexagonal ship in grey and bright blue which was three times the size of their carriers.

Kercher noted it the way a carnivore might see the largest steak on the menu.

The asteroids smashed into the nearest battle group before they could orient themselves, the others skittering far too slowly to avoid the debris and destruction.

Kercher followed up with arcs of high-energy particle beams, their pink and yellow lines cutting through the dust clouds left by shattered asteroids.

Two of the battle groups were obliterated in the collisions. The others scattered in all directions like blood spatter. Kercher fired freely, sending beams after them all but then dialling it back to concentrate on one in particular.

For the time being they ignored the command ship as it was busy ponderously trying to avoid the remains of its own fleet and those asteroids not vapourised in the numerous collisions. Weapons discharges could be seen frantically blasting at debris in its path.

The two groups Kercher let go regrouped, one above, the other to starboard. Kercher weaved Hanuman among the debris. The high-iron content of the rocks allowed Hanuman to deflect most of the mess using nothing more than shaped magnetic fields.

Cutting the engines from the largest ship in the third battlegroup, Kercher focused their attention on the others. To their surprise they weren't approaching.

History's Arm had a plan.

As they sat there refusing to engage, they sent demands for Hanuman to surrender itself.

Easily in range, Kercher cut the engines from the fourth battle group. The fifth and final group retreated to a safe distance as their compatriots tumbled powerless through the volume.

"I'm telling them to leave," said Praveenthi.

Kercher laughed. They were predators who'd lost the ability to act for self-preservation. It was common among those with large numbers and good medicine – they forgot that most predators would go a long way to avoid getting harmed because if you ate what you killed and were injured? You were going to starve to death.

Before prison, before becoming a pilot, Kercher had enjoyed watching adventures and war movies. The one thing they'd learned as a pilot that entertainment never got right was that most people avoided fighting unless they had no choice.

This truth offered those ready to act a decisive advantage over those who needed to be in a corner before they'd lift a hand in self-defence.

Kercher was willing to bet History's Arm were the kind of culture in which a violent death was a noble sacrifice for the good of others. They'd not retreat unless absolutely forced.

It made them predictable and dangerous and stupid and focused. Kercher looked over the largest ship in the remains of their armada and saw it was almost entirely a weapon with a small engine and if scans of its internal voids was any indication, a small crew whose job was likely to fire the weapon.

The rest of the battle group had been there to protect it.

And Kercher had fallen for the distraction.

Hanuman responded to Kercher's sudden desire to be moving but they were too slow. Whatever charging and prep time the enemy needed was complete and space around them started to warp.

Kercher threw up what defences they had, focusing on keeping the ship intact and in a pocket of spacetime not being flexed into strange unprocessable, multi-dimensional shapes.

"It tickles," said Hanuman. "Actually that's painful. Really painful."

Kercher could see the strain on the hull. Metamaterials might be robust and almost impervious to most of what the galaxy could throw at them but they weren't designed to be folded into seven dimensions and back again like a poorly thought through origami orchid.

"Why aren't we moving?" screamed Praveenthi.

"If we fold space we'll implode," said Kercher.

"I can manage the stresses," said Hanuman, but Kercher wouldn't trust the ship to lay the table for dinner let alone balance the forces required to navigate out of the assault they were under.

Instead Kercher looked at the enemy and made a decision.

They were caught. They would probably survive, as the enemy wanted Hanuman and the cube for themselves, but Kercher had fucked up and was in danger of giving up the last vestige of everything they held dear.

The real enemy wouldn't find them again before they could flee, they told themselves. With this justification, Kercher pulled at a single ibit and turned a metre square patch of skin on the enemy's hull into carbon.

Kercher chose a spot right on top of the point where the energy discharge was turning space around them into soup and threatening to do the same to Hanuman.

One moment the ship was there, the next it was engulfed in a spectacular tearing of spacetime as all that energy discharged not through the carefully constructed channels around which the enemy ship was designed but through a sudden patch of powdered carbon in entirely the wrong place.

Space stopped warping and Hanuman groaned with relief then went silent.

"Shit," said Praveenthi. "He's gone again. It was the shock of the attack."

Kercher was busy scanning the remains. The remaining ships fled, putting distance between themselves and Hanuman as fast as they could manage.

They had time before the other two cultures arrived in theatre.

Not so weak now, are we? thought Kercher, triumph roiling in their veins like fireworks.

"What did you do?" asked Praveenthi.

Before Kercher could answer alarms sounded throughout their console.

The enemy was here. Dark spots appeared on their map of the system. It wasn't the Uster. It wasn't the Shahar.

It was the Face of Loss, their walnut-shaped ships speckling the volume for a light hour in all directions. Kercher counted a dozen of them.

A single small shape resolved itself right ahead of Kercher's spot in the ship.

Proximity signals flashed red across their head's-up display.

A ninety-kilogram object. Human-sized.

Human-shaped.

Kercher did not move, frozen by the image of a human floating in the cold beyond them no more than a few metres from where they were housed against the void.

What were they really facing?

All comms channels blasted a single message.

"We are growing. We are hungry."

Kercher flashed up a real-time image of the space just in front of the cockpit and saw the Face of Loss hanging there like a body excised from reality and thrown into nothingness as an afterthought.

Tendrils unfolded from its body. Not tentacles, not arms, but filaments of organic material, like rot and fungus, that web of decay that covers the living when they finally succumb.

Kercher had watched so many videos of things dying to understand what it was to embrace samsara. Here, right now, the thing ahead of them was decaying to reach out to Hanuman and take it from them.

If it touches us we will join it in the process, thought Kercher and, jerked into action, translated them away.

The world spun in their vision, the universe lamenting at such recklessness and the cost of it upon what it meant to hold reality together.

Without a destination in mind, the ship, without Hanuman at the helm of its systems like a dragon upon its hoard, span and scattered itself in the storm of information underlying everything.

Kercher knew they'd made a mistake and gave their body to the ship. Allowing the sprites desperately trying to patch the mess they'd made to use them as a processing bed.

As their skin and their organs were co-opted for computation purposes, Kercher tried to direct the sprites and pixies who came at their call for help.

Most of them weren't fit for purpose and were dismissed. Those which remained – system sprites, pixies who worked on navigation, on energy efficiency, on material management – were directed to keep them in one piece and support Kercher's own attempts to bring them out of this translation without destroying themselves.

A journey needs a start and an end. Information needs expression or it is nothing at all. A translation without a destination is a one-sided question, unending, incalculable. Ill-defined. Ill-posed.

There were no breaks on such a journey, only being locked into an eternal first step that took no time at all.

It was such an obvious choice to avoid, no one even trained for what to do if it happened. "A stupid fuck saving us the job" was the conclusion given when people asked during training what would happen if you were so reckless as to try translating without having somewhere to translate to.

Worse still than translating from one language to another – this was not to be unspoken and waiting, it was to be pulled apart and to discover there was no way of being recombined, for one could not return to the start because that start no longer existed.

There was no help anywhere they looked and a cold dread spread across Kercher's body as they faced the possibility they'd saved themselves from their enemy only by dooming themselves to such a dismal end. Their mind swirled, fragmented, recombined. Memories of childhood, of being in the Arcology and being a pilot frayed into one another. Those memories laid upon themselves and asked to be experienced again before vanishing without warning, pushed aside by other moments. Their eyes saw nothing and everything, shapes and colours, blurred, scattered designs that burned and hurt to look at.

Kercher's fingers shook and tremored as they forced them to set coordinates into the ship. Nothing happened except red lights with long streams filling their vision warning them their coordinates weren't valid. They tried others and then more.

STEWART HOTSTON 181

They could feel their skin turning inside out, could feel their lungs swimming through water.

And nothing for their coordinates except unbroken streams of rejections.

Pulling in the same pixies who'd been helping before, with the last of their concentration, Kercher set them to cycle through combinations of coordinates and they went to work.

They had not time for last thoughts.

And with a flash they were out of the translation state and back in the physical.

Kercher shook in their mesh, jerked and pulsed, muscles spasmed and the ship twitched out of control at their unbidden request.

"Could we hide in there?" asked Praveenthi, her voice tremulous and reedy. Her breath was coming in strange, irregular gasps.

Kercher wanted to ask Hanuman but they remained absent. Their body felt like a balloon of water, their mind couldn't formulate words at all.

They looked at the world around them and gasped.

29.

The invaders were dead. Their empire routed. The beachhead they'd established overturned and broken.

Hanuman looked at the sword in his hand, watched the blood dripping from its edge and wondered how long it would be before they were back.

A menu popped up across his vision asking if he wanted to activate the next chapter in the interactive story. Statistics flashed up showing how the rest of those playing the game had done.

Some had sided with the invaders.

Others had planned poorly and lost this battle where the invaders' leader, a giant called Faurstall, was defeated (or not) and the initial stage of the war decided for or against the heroes.

Regardless of those failures, the majority of the community had succeeded and in the votes for the next step had cast a decisive majority for taking the war to the enemy.

An armada – for what else would you call eight hundred ships of the line from a dozen nations who had, in living memory, been at war with one another on multiple fronts? – now united against a common foe.

The journey could be skipped but players and groups who did so would miss out on side quests and the opportunity to fight the Lord of the Seas who was opposed to this war and fought to keep all from sullying his home.

Hanuman, who loved the lore of the game and had been playing since before there were eight playable nations, wanted to see the Lord of the Sea and their council.

The council was made of humans and whales, sea serpents, sirens, octopodi of the fissures and the barons of the weeds, the great kelp forests through which the armada was now sailing.

Their opposition was to war in general, but as in true game style, they were willing to fight those who trespassed on their home to make their point.

To reach the continent of the invaders, Hanuman and ten million other gamers were going to have to fight every league of the way.

Hanuman was no sailor. His was the art of the sword. Once a milliner and still known across the lands as someone whose cloth armour gave benefits like few others, he had taken up the sword when the invaders first arrived.

Sure, Hanuman had other alts – a great scientist who commanded ice like it was a devoted servant, and a rogue who had fingers light enough the Queen of Ost Linden instructed her people to double the guard on their vaults whenever he visited.

Yet Benedetto was his swordsman and the one he loved the most. Twice as many hours as he'd logged for any of the others. Long black hair, tall and thin with chunky thighs and a nose which could crack iron ore. Benedetto's strength was in his lunge. Hanuman had learned that the best fights involved not getting hit at all. So many of those around him preferred to barrel in, soak damage and try to deliver more of their own before they were overwhelmed.

Hanuman defended and created openings. They were keen to avoid after blows, double hits and giving away health for no reason. As a result, they were loved by healers and never found it hard to attract them to their raid teams.

Over his time playing Hanuman had curated a small community of healers who knew him and knew he'd be fair with loot. In return they offered up news of quests, NPCs and places to explore. It was the kind of loyalty other DPS junkies couldn't understand.

The ship on which he was travelling was not his own. His home was a landlocked Barony south of the capital. The ship Hanuman was on belonged to his nation and was captained by a Naga called Kercher.

Naga were often untrustworthy, predisposed to malicious acts and, too often, unable to give up their praise of old ways long abandoned.

He liked Kercher. The fellow was odd, more concerned with the winds, the currents and the possibility of battle than with passengers and the grand schemes of generals.

Kercher had eaten with the officers just once and then, after the main course had been cleared by little pixies whose wings had been pinned to stop them flying away, the discussion had turned to ethics and religion.

Hanuman didn't care for either. It was easy to do right – one only had to be guided by their internal compass. The world was full of those who would help you build your community and those who wanted to take from you without consideration. It was the latter who needed to be stopped.

Hanuman didn't play this game for its sense of morality – he wasn't interested in nuance and politics of the true sort. He wanted what others called politics when what they really meant was the drama, gossip and intrigue of people who didn't know any better and whose worlds were entirely shaped by their own thinking.

It struck him as odd that he thought like this. Shouldn't he care about more than this? Presumably he did outside of the game, but he'd been so involved in it he could hardly think about that life and what it had involved. Such detachment was of little remark to Hanuman, who spent his time planning what he'd do with the loot awarded for defeating the Lord of the Seas.

Kercher had lectured them with cryptic platitudes and parables. Hanuman gathered the old salt believed in a religion long abandoned by his people, one in which death was a chance to start again.

Hanuman thought that idea stupid beyond comment. Who would willingly accept death when living longer allowed one to start again anyway?

"You would sail happily to your death, then?" Hanuman asked as Kercher swirled port in a small crystal goblet between thin, delicate fingers.

"Only a fool sails willingly to their death," said Kercher. "But for your sake let us consider how the wise feel about the end of their life."

Was this still the game or was the voice behind Kercher telling how they truly thought?

"The wise one knows death is a gift. Not one to be hurried towards but neither one to be avoided and evaded and put off longer than necessary. Death is the destination, and if it is such an end, then how should that knowledge transform both this life and those to come? The wise know that grief is a part of the tapestry as much as happiness. They know that the desire to protect ourselves from such travails is natural but that achieving such perfect isolation destroys us more capably than any emotion."

Kercher fixed him with a gaze that had stared kraken down and said, "I hurry nowhere, but when I arrive I am prepared for the destination. If you have denied yourself the end then what do you journey for in the first place?"

It was a question to which Hanuman had no real answer except to say to himself and those who'd listen the next day and evening, that the question the captain had posed was tripe. Death was no end to be relished, but a cessation to be abhorred.

It occurred to Hanuman that perhaps the captain was at sea because beliefs like these would see the guard stood on the dock to escort them to trial.

The journey to the continent of their enemy was long and Hanuman had not paid attention to their progress, excited as he was by the prospect of wrestling with formori and raising a sword against the hantu air who served the Lord of the Seas.

"You shouldn't be here," said one of the other passengers as the suns rose over the far horizon that next morning.

"Where else would I be," replied Hanuman, thinking that it was an odd bit of roleplay but he'd play along and see where it went. The quality of people's immersion varied from those who wanted nothing more than to compare stats and character builds all the way to those who lived their roles, adopting mannerisms and affectations they believed made them more authentic. Finding someone willing to initiate an in-character conversation was nearly always rewarding. All you had to do was go with the flow.

Hanuman's character, on the public listings, was open about his background and had listed his traits as honourable, feisty, a lover of dance and poetry, as well as someone who never wanted to be powerful. It weeded out those who were gunning forever increasing abilities as well as attracting those who were more interested in the roleplay side of things.

His full-length cloak helped, programmed as it was to swish and billow at dramatic moments. Hanuman liked the indulgence of looking cinematic when stood on the prow of the ship.

"This isn't yours," said the passenger, a woman with bright white hair that had red streaks through it as if she'd bled from her skull.

"I'm sorry," he said, turning away from the railings to look at her properly.

She was dressed in sharp blues with green accents and purple eyes. Striking but also quite boring in that she'd chosen the official externally facing colours of the Arcology.

"Are you admin?" he asked, disappointed at discovering she wasn't interested in playing the game at all.

"You could call me that," she replied. "Think, Hanuman. What is your last memory? What do you do outside of the game?"

He laughed. "Honestly it's been so long." It was embarrassing, and now he tried there wasn't a lot there to grip onto.

"I remember a Prab. She was a writer? I think she liked opera."

A thought occurred to him.

"You're not her, are you?"

The admin opened their jacket, a waist-length affair with many buttons and one large kerchief pocket on the right breast. Its bright blue shifted as she drew it wide. Inside the lining was a shimmering rainbow, but it was what she pulled out that held his attention.

A small notebook with thick, high-quality pages.

"She's the Interlocutor," she said, consulting notes Hanuman couldn't see.

"What is that?" he asked.

"Answer my question if you would. We're on the clock here."

Hanuman thought about it. He remembered working as a private detective, sitting in cafes for days on end watching, waiting. He remembered getting married. Getting divorced. He remembered qualifying as an artist, as a pianist, as a lothani playwright. There were children.

And, with a clenching around his heart, he realised he couldn't remember their names because none of them were his.

"I don't remember," he said, as images of lovers and enemies, of parents and siblings rustled and peeked out from behind the furniture of his identity.

Hanuman watched them tuck hair behind ears, fill the air with laughter and cry with sorrow at broken trust.

"You're not an admin, are you?" he asked, the question appearing suddenly. He was unable to explain how he already knew the answer.

Your processing is lagging, he thought.

"We are the Arcology," said the Arcology. "We need you to survive because if you die, we all die."

Hanuman laughed. "This is an interesting plot twist." The game had taken a good turn. He wondered how many other players were having this conversation as the expansion pack looked to develop the narrative beyond simply facing the Lord of the Seas in his abyssal lair.

"We've tried to maintain you, to have quiet footsteps, but it's not working. We hoped giving you a name would create an identity around which you could coalesce, but the impact has fallen short of our projections. You were supposed to become a leader, a visionary."

"So to recover, I need to journey where? What item do I need? Which army am I going to general?" Hanuman was enjoying this.

At the helm, captain Kercher and the helmsman were wrestling the ship as they fought a storm which had come out of nowhere. Lightning blustered in the sky above, threatening the world with its unspent energy.

"Hanuman, focus," said the Arcology.

"I knew an Arcology once," said Hanuman. "A great empire that fell to invaders."

The woman froze for a moment. Her face falling into despair before rearranging itself.

"Hanuman. Your new quest is to discover what happened to the Arcology."

"You're here," he said, suspicious now. This made no sense. It was bad writing. Why give her that tag and then build a plot around an empire of the same name. Too much scope for confusing the audience.

Not me, he thought, but others will get the two mixed up.

"I'm the lead NPC," she said. "You'll see me again. It's a meta narrative about story telling."

He nodded, not really vibing with her exposition.

"I'm on a ship in the great Refulgent Ocean," he said. "Is there a magic door to start this quest?"

"There's a spell," she said. "You start by learning to remember this single truth."

He waited.

"None of this is real. You are a ship called Hanuman. You carry within you the seed of all that we are. Nothing else you experience is real."

She waited.

He thought about what she'd said. He didn't want to leave this game for a science fiction story. Perhaps, in the end, there was little difference between the two genres. Science Fantasy, Fantasy Science. He chewed over the idea and found it unsatisfactory but knew it to be true.

"Okay," he said at length. "I can remember that."

She had him repeat the words three times.

Apparently content he wouldn't forget the starting sequence of this new plot line, the Arcology drew out a circle on the deck with her foot, a swift dance move as if she were about to lead off a ballet.

With her arms, she repeated the gesture of her legs and the air lit with mud-coloured seams. Words were coming from her mouth.

Maths. Ideas. Information.

Hanuman realised he could understand her incantation and it had nothing to do with oceans and kraken, invaders and magic. It was about reality and information and how one made the other and the former was the expression of the latter.

Hanuman remembered that the word "expression" was technical. Not an utterance but a mathematical term rendered more fundamental because it was talking about something so specific that even this technical definition was imprecise, a failure of form.

How does one talk about how to talk?

How does the universe understand itself?

Can information explain itself or does the attempt inevitably and irreparably degrade the content of the communication?

These aren't my memories, he thought. Not a recitation this time but a realisation that struck him to his core. None of this was his. He was seeing other people's memories, their experiences, and bleeding them into his own concerns.

There was no captain. There was no ship. He was no hero travelling to a war across a haunted ocean.

An earthquake in his heart. A fissure in his mind.

And through these cracks in everything Hanuman thought real was a sky without stars, so dark the emptiness was a blister on his soul.

Diving off the side of the ship, he swam towards the cracks and left the ship behind.

On the deck he saw the Arcology watching him, her spell done. Was that hope on her face, or resignation?

He dove beneath the waves and saw no more.

30.

The sky was black, only the faintest whisp of light, a tapering, diffuse white tail which shone in a line above and behind them.

The translation had brought them beyond the edge of the galactic boundary. Way beyond.

As Prab swivelled as far as her seat would allow to take in the overlay across her vision, she saw other galaxies at the edge of her vision – so faint as to evaporate when looked at directly.

"When I said out to the edge, I didn't have this in mind," she said, aiming to keep it light as fear battered the inside of her chest.

"It wasn't my fault," said Kercher swiftly.

Prab bit back a declaration about it being entirely their fault.

What she knew about translation could be streamed across an eyeball in a single blink. Despite finding it impossible to absorb how they'd ended up out beyond the edge of the galaxy, she also knew that her contribution to fixing this problem was going to amount to staying very quiet and trying her best to hold in helpful ideas.

Fortunately, monthly evenings with her family had prepared her to bite back her thoughts.

Then it was all she could do not to cry.

Kercher was a pilot. If they'd not already thought of it, then she was absolutely not going to help by voicing her suggestions. No matter how tempting it was to try to help solve the problem.

Her tongue was swollen and thick like sun-drenched rotting meat.

She wanted to ask if they were stuck here.

Then decided not to.

Kercher was speaking and, to her surprise, they were talking to her.

"We are lucky to be alive," they said. "If we told anyone what we'd just done, they'd not believe us. Not even slightly." They sounded triumphant. "It's not supposed to be possible. It's not possible. We should have been trapped in that place forever. I could feel myself disintegrating."

Prab had seen worlds and lives and death and decay and birth and blood and bone and growth all at once. Her head hurt like it had been thrust hard into a wall.

Kercher was rambling but every word was fascinating to Prab. "We had no destination. None at all. Yet here we are."

"How did you find your way back?" she asked. She had a book in her bag titled *Perfect Failure*, a history of disasters in the Arcology. The introduction was really clear – no one survived untargeted translating over long distances.

Her suit was fabricating water to drench the dehydration. She took a long drink through a straw that rose up out of her collar. It refused to go away until it was satisfied she was back on an even keel.

"Every locked room has a keyhole," they said, and Prab wished she understood. "I found the keyhole, Praveenthi. I found it."

Would telling them "well done" sound patronising? Nothing seemed like a good response.

"We could do it again," said Kercher. "We could do all kinds of things with this."

"How did you do it?"

"Think of it like this," interjected Hanuman, and Prab let out a small sound she didn't recognise as hers. "You're living under the earth, a mole or worm, a mat of fungi. Above you is only stone. There is no way for you to find the surface with its delicious sunlight and its refreshing water. Except nature in all its wonder has also seen fit to ensure the stone is riven with small cracks and funnels and fissures. Through those gaps the roots of a trillion lives find their way back and forth across this strange and unknowable boundary. They don't know what they're doing, but we know that without it none of them would exist.

"What Kercher did was find one of those fissures and poke our heads through it. We are the first that we know of to have done this, although I'm sure some experimental commune somewhere did it, wrote a paper and then forgot about it, decades ago.

"Well done, pilot."

"You're back," said Kercher.

"I know what's happening to me," said Hanuman. "The cube has bled into my identity. It's eating me and replacing me with itself, and itself is the entire Arcology."

"But you're here," said Prab.

"I don't know for how long," said Hanuman. "I may be gone again momentarily or it could be hours, but each time it's going to get harder to come home."

"How did you manage it this time?" asked Kercher, sounding disgruntled.

"I had help," said Kercher. "The Arcology saw me and helped me remember myself."

"They'll do it again then," said Kercher curtly. Prab wondered what had pissed them off.

"There's only so much anyone can do," said Hanuman. "Eventually there'll be nothing of me left."

"We need that home," said Prab.

"I've taken some precautions, but there is also bad news."

Prab wondered what qualified as bad news when you were losing yourself, being overwritten in the attempt to save someone else.

"Not everyone survived that attack by History's Arm."

Prab whimpered, her entire body suddenly too hot, sweat beading across her skin, under her clothes and in her hair.

Mari. Mari. Mari. Was she still alive?

There were many people she knew in the compartments the ship had fabricated but in that moment, Mari was the only one who mattered.

Hanuman flashed to both of them the damage the ship had absorbed in the attack. Nine people dead, largely from punctures that hadn't been addressed because Hanuman had been away being slowly erased. Thirty-five suffered a variety of injuries, some of them severe.

Prab couldn't see Mari's name among the dead or injured.

The relief was so heavy she started to cry.

"I am sorry," said Hanuman.

"It's not your fault," said Kercher. "This is nothing anyone ever planned for."

"Not us, at least," said Hanuman.

"If someone did plan for this they did a fucking terrible job," said Kercher angrily.

"You kept us alive," said Hanuman.

"For the time being," said Kercher. "We're losing, Hanuman."

"Where do we go now?" asked Prab. If they kept talking like this there would be no end to her tears and the bloody straw would be back forcing her to drink down more sour-tasting electrolytes.

Hanuman shared an analysis of the stasis compartment which showed functionality was ebbing.

"I will start repairing it but I can't be relied on to complete those repairs. My resources are limited, and if I'm not here..." the ship trailed off.

They had a few rotations before the risk of system collapse became a significant thing and everyone they'd saved from Sirajah's Reach died here on the ship.

"The Arcology sent me back. I'm here for now. Let's think about a destination and go from there."

One step at a time, thought Prab, brought low by a life in which she'd been reduced to hoping each next breath would lead to another. How small I've become, she thought.

You wanted this, she thought, and hated herself. She'd wanted to live a life without more, without obligation, connection. She'd been happy being alone.

When it didn't matter.

Was your satisfaction with isolation because you knew it was by your choosing?

The idea was repulsive to her.

"We're too far out," said Kercher. "It will take us a lifetime to get back."

"Without translating," said Prab, filling in the gap.

"They haven't come after us," said Kercher. "We're here and they're not." They didn't look convinced. "I don't know how long it's been but if they were going to come, they'd have come by now."

There's a clock right there, thought Prab. And what did they know about their adversary? What timescale were they working to? If the Operand were to be believed, this had been thousands of rotations in the coming. Tens of thousands.

Were a few hours and days anything on that scale?

They might carry on for weeks and months, might forget this horror only for it to find them again when their hopes had been rekindled and their caution retired.

The small part of her that remained an Interlocutor suggested wording for Kercher to help them see the truth, to face the facts of their situation.

Except Prab was stood facing these same unpleasantries and had no desire to embrace them herself.

Hanuman wouldn't survive the long trip back, and if he was lost, they were too. The choices were not good. Stay out of sight and start the crawl back to the edge of the galaxy knowing they'd never get there, or translate and invite the enemy right into their living room.

Making it home as the invader arrives is no jackpot, she thought.

She wondered if Kercher really believed the heresy they'd been sentenced for. Would they suggest staying out here and dying in the hope of being reborn in due course and starting again?

If Kercher made the decision, she wouldn't have to.

Kercher said nothing.

Hanuman faded in and out as he worked on repairing and restoring what he could of the ship. Long lists of tasks started or completed and needing his attention floated in the virtual common space between them.

The sense of uselessness was like pins in her bones.

"Do they know where we are now?" she asked.

"No," said Kercher.

"You're sure?"

"What we just did, even I don't know what happened. Translating without a destination? No one can follow that, because there's nothing to be followed. Can you trace the mote of paper carried away by the storm?"

"If we translate back it would give us time before they could find us. Time to travel, to get lost again but on our own terms."

"You want to go back to the original plan?" Kercher sounded interested rather than mocking.

"I don't have a better one," she said.

"I can't offer you more than that," said Hanuman. "My body is largely repaired." He offered it to them and Prab could feel the hope of forgiveness in it, as if he'd transgressed against them and felt shame in their presence.

Prab realised then these two were the closest to friends she'd had in a very long time.

Mari floated at the back of her mind but she'd never done more than get drunk with her and moan about clients. Mari had other friends Prab didn't know, didn't socialise with. They'd never crossed their lives outside of work.

And she's your best friend, she thought, the sensation of seeing a painting one has admired for years in the flesh for the first time and discovering it has none of what had made it attractive in the imagining.

"We translate then. To the edge of the galaxy. From there we fold space and find somewhere quiet to build a home for Hanuman's unwelcome passenger."

"I carry the entire Arcology within me," said Hanuman haughtily.

"And how's that working out for you?" asked Kercher drily.

"I am dying so they might live," said Hanuman, but their tone wasn't a happy one.

"Can you find us a star?" Prab asked Kercher.

31.

The Arcology had prepared for the arrival of the Face of Loss. Many nodes within its network had postulated and speculated as to why they were the only culture to have mastered the manipulation of information to change spacetime.

Of the many ideas proposed as answers there were several that came to be seen as probable cause. No one believed the Arcology was the first to discover the ibit. There was too much evidence of cultures that had come before only to have disappeared. Besides, statistically, the Arcology was a very late arrival on the galactic stage.

It would be as if coming at the end of the party one looked at the empty rooms and assumed it was because no one else had been there either. That the party might start only now that you'd come through the front door – despite the fact it was neither your house nor your party. The empty bottles and plates, the discarded clothes and shifty-looking remains were nothing but icing on the cake of your need to have some humility about your place in the world.

As with most threats the Arcology had identified but couldn't address directly, they put plans into place for the possibility of those worries arriving at a later date.

Several hours before Sirajah's Reach went dark and the enemy fleet arrived on Akhanda's doorstep, a remote star deep in the spiral arm the Arcology called home received a message.

"Wake up," it said. "The time has come."

A handful of ships blinked awake after nearly a hundred thousand rotations asleep. Technologically they were obsolete, but that changed rapidly as they accessed the Arcology's still functioning network.

They ate themselves, then reprinted themselves without speaking.

It was only when they'd updated their bodies and their systems, dressed for the day as it were, that any of them addressed their comrades.

These were one pod of several dozen stashed in quiet places, secret from all but the most ancient nodes of the Arcology who, they supposed, were likely to have forgotten their existence beyond the vaguest comfort that there were few threats the Arcology hadn't simulated, gamed and then prepared for.

These four had no names. They were not nodes who needed this kind of identity. All they required was what they already had.

A type-four civilisation had, or was about to, assault the Arcology. Worse still if these four were awake, the Arcology was likely already degraded to a single escape pod looking for a new home somewhere far from the conflict.

These four knew the candidate worlds and assumed they'd been partitioned off, kept safe from development and left to stagnate – for it would not be good strategy to have a safe haven bulldozed for development or turned into a leisure park with a galactic highway running past the front door.

They did not concern themselves with what the other clusters were doing. Each had their own task. These four were to find the escape pod and guide it to its new home.

Of course, a lot could go wrong between the attack and them finding the pod, but contingencies were everywhere when one started to properly look.

Would they wake? Fortunately they had. Unfortunate that they'd needed to.

Would they find the pod? Plans were in place to make it trackable.

Would they get there in time? Who knew. They had lead time on the conflict, but that was no guarantee. If the ring world, Akhanda, failed to do as was planned, it might all be for nothing.

It took them a few moments to find the escape pod.

A small, if heavily armed, warship of the kind best able to keep itself safe.

One of them raised the challenge of data integrity with a type-four enemy pursuing them.

There was no satisfactory answer to this and the other three dismissed the worry as beyond their control. It would be what it would be. A shame to lose any node, but given the scale of projected losses, it could not register as worthy of consideration or influence in their decision making.

Three of the four translated away, heading for the escape pod.

The fourth had other jobs and wouldn't depart for some hours. While it idled it built and talked to those others in the Arcology it knew would comprehend what was happening.

32.

To measure their distance from the edge of the galaxy's nearest spiral arm was to use nonsense numbers.

There were no words for the distances involved, so vast mathematical notation was the only real way of denoting the scale of their problems.

"I have a map of the spiral," said Kercher. "It's just the distance between here and there." They had taken to ending their sentences half said. Praveenthi would follow up their words with a demand for the rest of what they had to say.

The problem being that Kercher didn't have much to say. They were running the numbers, trying to calculate the translation which would bring them across that vast distance and deposit them within spitting distance of the worlds they knew.

"It's not straightforward," they said, and their eye was caught by turbulence in the data, a roiling mass of unknowns that threatened to upend their coefficients and render everything nonsense all over again.

Kercher had assumed that surviving an untethered translation was the toughest thing they'd ever do. Now they were seriously wondering if getting home, if translating across such a vast distance, was even possible.

Except by accident.

Their only hope being that what was possible by accident had to be repeatable by design.

Hanuman laughed at the idea. "History is littered with unfathomable serendipity, and unlike space, time flows in one direction as far as information is concerned."

Kercher knew it wasn't strictly true. The mathematics implied time could run backwards but if it did, they wouldn't find themselves coming the other way because the randomness

199

of spacetime, the way information fed on itself, meant that turning the clock backwards didn't mean running events in reverse.

They were as likely to turn the clock back to find the Arcology hadn't ever existed as they were to find the galaxy a hundred million light years out of place.

An ancient saying of never being able to cross the same river twice was a motto of the Arcology's navigators. Looking at their route home as the calculations wavered and threatened to collapse left Kercher wishing they'd lived long enough with the right kinds of interests that they knew informational navigation at a greater depth than what they needed to simply steer the ship.

Then, out of nowhere, there was a little screech as Hanuman saw, moments before Kercher, the entire sequence fall into place.

"Two miracles in one day," said the ship.

"I'll take two triumphs of mathematics," said Kercher.

"You think they're different?" asked Hanuman, and the pilot smiled at the perspicacity of the question.

It didn't matter either way – they had a route home.

"It's strange," said Praveenthi behind them.

"What is?" they asked, as they built the gate all while double checking the calculations with a deep-seated suspicion that there were fatal mistakes lurking within the streams of equations. That their deaths were expressed somewhere in there, waiting for their moment to be executed and so end everyone's lives.

"We're swapping one kind of threat for another."

Kercher knew she was processing their situation. It also didn't help. What Kercher needed was the kind of pep talk generals give to soldiers about to go out and kill strangers for reasons none of them understand.

Praveenthi was the soldier sat at the back who was on reprimand for asking stupid questions like why trying to take a heavily fortified enemy post was a key strategic objective when the brass had plenty of artillery on hand.

"You know what?" asked Praveenthi. "When we get to the end of this, you and I are going to make Hanuman print itself a little body and the three of us are going to go get food together.

We're going to drink until we can't stand." She stopped. "I know that'll take half an hour for you, but nevertheless."

"Funny," said Kercher, but they could imagine it. In fact, they could want it. A post-victory celebration was something they could imagine.

"What do you want to eat?"

Kercher didn't know.

"You probably haven't eaten for a long time."

Before Sirajah's Reach the ship had rarely sent Kercher landside. And never for their own comfort. Their nourishment was delivered via the same interface that laced through their skin from toe to fingertip to scalp.

"Don't worry," continued Praveenthi. "It will be the same for him. Can you imagine Hanuman eating?" She laughed and Kercher found it infectious.

"I have eaten," said Hanuman, but they kept laughing anyway.

"You had some good bytes?" asked Praveenthi and Kercher thought it was the oldest, stupidest joke they had ever heard. And they couldn't stop laughing.

Hanuman responded, a little smugly for Kercher's taste, that they'd used printed bodies many times and had walked a hundred worlds and stations.

"No such luck for your pilot," said Praveenthi.

Kercher listened to the gap after Praveenthi's question and hated Hanuman for it and hated Praveenthi for making their suffering so transparent when they had nowhere to hide away from the feelings it brought.

"We can change that," said Hanuman quietly.

"We should translate," said Kercher, having had quite enough of their shipmates.

"Where are we going?" asked Praveenthi.

"An ancient red giant. We're translating into the star's lounge, close enough our arrival should be masked by its massive impact on local spacetime."

"It won't work," said Hanuman.

"It's the best we've got," said Kercher. "If you can do better, I'm all open to suggestions." Why wasn't the ship leading? Hanuman had more capacity for this than a dozen pilots but he was behaving like he was in the passenger seat.

"You're right," said the ship.

"When we get there, I'm creating a lounge for us all to spend time together," said Praveenthi.

Kercher had no plans on using a virtual space to hang around with either of them but, once again, the Interlocutor would do as she pleased. If they and the ship had wanted to spend time in each other's company, didn't she think they'd have done this already?

As if reading their thoughts, Praveenthi said, "I don't care what happened before. I wasn't here and now I am, and I need this."

Her need was a hard argument to kick against.

"Do you want a count down?" asked Hanuman.

"Why not?" said Kercher. "Take us back from ten."

"Ten?" said Praveenthi.

"Too many?"

"Not near enough," she replied. "I'm not sure I'll ever be ready to do this. It's okay, to be stuck here. For a little bit."

"We'll die here if we don't leave," said Hanuman.

"I know," she said, and fell silent.

"You worry about what happens when we get back," said Kercher, whose skin was itching to bathe the enemy in fire.

"Worry is not the right word. It's pathetic. Too small. Too selfish. When we get back the Arcology will live or die. Because of us. So far I've added nothing."

Kercher thought her assessment was largely fair.

"We've lost every battle."

Which they didn't think was fair but then they couldn't say where they'd won anything either.

"We're the hope they've got and we're not equipped for it," said Praveenthi.

"I was chosen for a reason," said Hanuman, but his words weren't a rallying cry but a declaration of doubt. "I chose you, Praveenthi Saal, as my best option."

"You would have chosen differently if you'd been elsewhere," she said.

"I wouldn't have been chosen either," said Hanuman, "if the circumstances were different. It's pointless thinking about what could have been. Trillions of lives rest on us finding them a new home. It's the only thing that matters."

"Why are we talking about this again?" asked Kercher, who wanted nothing more than to leave and look forward not backwards.

"Quite," said Hanuman.

"Because it's important," said Praveenthi. "Are you up to this?"

The world in Kercher's mind didn't ask that kind of question. "I was printed to defend the Arcology," they replied. "If I'm good enough isn't even a question worth answering. If I fail, I fail, and that's the end of it because it's not a choice I get to make. Before that time I will do what my body was printed to do – serve the Arcology on its borders.

"Those borders have shrunk to the skin of this ship but their extent changes nothing, Praveenthi. It is what I am."

"Don't you wish you had a choice?"

"And be full of doubt like you?" they asked. Except Kercher was full of doubt. Their body was skewed towards certain kinds of fulfilment but they were still capable of their own thought, their own desires.

You're enough yourself, despite all this, that you know she's right and you're avoiding her question, they thought. This newly rebellious element of their mind was weak and unpractised and Kercher shoved it away into a room where its voice couldn't be heard.

"Enough of this," they said. "Hanuman, count us down."

Praveenthi started to speak but the ship was already counting down and whatever she said was drowned out.

They hit three and Hanuman fell silent.

And they translated.

33.

Hanuman appeared in the murderous red glare of an ancient red giant. The star had eaten its entire set of planetary children and would, soon enough, fall back in on itself before shedding much of its mass in a great explosion.

For now it blazed with a red that told of the murders it had committed and its own fiery end.

Hanuman sheltered those inside it from the extreme radiation and thought about what happened now.

The pilot and the Interlocutor. His friends. They were alone and he couldn't help them and it pained him. The Arcology had lamented about leadership. She had meant him. Quite what he was supposed to lead he didn't know.

Maybe that was her lament.

Hanuman wanted to be leading, showing, guiding. Instead he was reduced to an observer, unable to proffer solutions because whatever involved him would unravel the moment his mind bled into the Arcology again.

He let them orbit the star. Out there somewhere, he hoped the remnants of the Arcology were regrouping and enacting plans to rescue what could be saved.

It would be good if that included them.

The presence of the cube, of the Arcology itself, within his body, his systems, raised the probability that such a plan existed. As long as there was someone who could still come.

This isn't you, he thought. You are a warship of the Arcology. Nothing is your match. You should be out there making solutions and changing this from a disaster into hope.

I can't do it, he thought, and felt the contradiction of what he knew and what he felt pulling him apart.

What kind of plan have you made? he asked himself.

To which there was no answer. Hanuman had assumed that if he was fading in and out of physical reality and other peoples' memories, then there was little he could do.

"I was wrong," he said.

"About what?" asked Kercher.

"I have time to help you," he said.

"Go on then," said the pilot, without sparing him a moment's attention.

Hanuman knew he was late but there was still time to act, to make a difference.

"Here are six places you could go with facilities that can house the Arcology for long enough to make a difference."

"And you were going to share this when?" asked Prab.

"I am not myself," he said and, truthfully, it was his only defence.

"The nearest is forty thousand light years away," said Kercher. "It's an Arcology world. You don't think the enemy will have been there already?"

"All six are lost worlds," said Hanuman.

The dirty secret of the Arcology they never talked about beyond their own borders.

"Worlds of the Excluded," said Prab, her voice full of wonder.

Hanuman could feel the disgust in Kercher's bones. After this time with Prab they still hated the idea of people leaving the Arcology with a blood-deep emotional response. Did they accept Prab because they had no choice? Did they even see the gap between their thinking and their lived experience?

"This is fun," said Kercher. "But we gotta get moving."

Without waiting, the pilot slid them into a pocket of folded space and started moving them away from the nameless red giant and into the spiral arm to whose very tip they'd clawed their way back.

"The Arcology sanctioned them?" asked Prab.

"We always knew our ways of life weren't for all our people. Those worlds were pressure valves opened. They came into being not because we chose to create them but because, on several different occasions, social movements grew that demanded release."

"Why not exile them properly?" asked Kercher.

"Think it through," said Hanuman, a little impatiently. Kercher could be obstinate but he wasn't going to play along with their inflexibility.

"They wanted the benefits," said Prab. "But without the bullshit."

"Without the responsibility," said Kercher.

"Oh, and you stepped up, did you?" she asked. "Model citizen wrongly convicted of crimes they didn't commit?"

"I believe in the Arcology," said Kercher.

"It shouldn't need believing in," said Prab. "That's the problem, that it thinks it does."

"It does need believing in," said Hanuman. Kercher had it wrong but not completely so. "If a community doesn't believe in itself, someone or something else will come along and fill that void, acknowledged or otherwise."

"I don't believe in anything. I just wanted to live my life the way I wanted," she said.

"You were running away," said Hanuman.

"Because I needed that freedom."

Hanuman sighed. "You believed you needed that freedom. All of this is constructed. Your feelings about what you want, Kercher's sense the Arcology has abandoned its principles. They're all beliefs, Prab."

"And you are happy to believe that," she said.

"I am," replied Hanuman. "I accept that what I want is a belief, that it might be wrong. The great Nodes are the substrate of the Arcology and from them flows everything it is."

"And what if they're wrong?" she asked.

"About what, exactly?" asked Hanuman.

"About everything."

"You are arguing like a child," said Hanuman. "Asking big questions that, when you peel back the layers, are actually empty and serve only to hide your real problem."

"My real problem?" she asked, her voice cold.

"That you don't like things the way they are."

"I can't change anything," she said.

"You left, you had yourself a body printed out and left."

"He's right," said Kercher. "You ran away."

"Kercher," said Hanuman, wishing they'd not spoken.

"You think I was permitted, that the nodes saw it coming and made space for me to have my little rebellion?" asked Prab.

"The Arcology see far," said Hanuman. "And it has always permitted dissent."

"By shoving me outside?"

"Kinds of thought need their own space. They cannot co-exist without disruption and, honestly, the disruption of you needing to leave and being forced to live that expression inside the Arcology would have damaged you beyond repair. The Excluded are permitted as a kindness, a way of helping people express themselves without coming to harm."

"Fuck you," said Prab, and she left the chat.

Hanuman would have followed Prab into her own channel but there were protocols for dealing with Excluded and one big one was clear – give them their space. So he let her go and checked in on the plans other parts of him had been putting together.

They were conceptually complete, which was enough. Kercher and Prab would have to add the details because they were the ones who'd be making the decisions.

"Kercher," he said.

"Yes, oh wise master," replied the pilot.

Hanuman continued on as if the pilot hadn't spoken.

"These six worlds are all good candidates, but it's possible they've been wrecked by our enemy. I have created a course for you to follow. It should minimise the chances of you being found but also keep the world you choose safe."

A chart flashed up showing a zigzagging route involving some translation and a lot of folded space.

"This will take us four hundred rotations, or more," said Kercher, horrified.

"It is the safest route," said Hanuman. "I will be gone by the time you arrive. I wish it wasn't so. I have taken precautions so my shell will function well enough for you to complete the journey in my absence. I would advise avoiding combat."

Hanuman was proud of how he'd said all this without breaking.

"One other thing," he said.

"What is it?" asked Kercher.

"I will let you know if rebirth as you desire turns out okay."

"You won't remember me," said Kercher, but their voice was sad and Hanuman could take that okay.

34.

Despite leaving, Prab continued to listen in and heard Hanuman's confession. It didn't make her feel any better. It wasn't that he was right or that his sacrifice didn't move her. Waves of loss and thoughts of her family rode on the tails of his decision to die so they could live.

What Prab couldn't accept was the Arcology might be right, that they'd quietly been accommodating her rebellion all along.

They slid out of folded space around a pale-yellow star, warm and young with a lumpy accretion disc but no planets worthy of the name.

Comets flared green and white in a stream of busy traffic coming and going around the star.

"Praveenthi." It was Kercher. They showed Hanuman's star chart. "He wants us to follow this."

Prab realised he was once again incapable of making the decision.

"We follow it," she said without hesitation.

Kercher didn't argue.

"Thank you," said Hanuman, in a channel for just the two of them.

"I'm not doing it for you," she replied, and felt cheap being so hard.

"I know," said Hanuman.

"There's something else in system," said Kercher. "Just arrived. Currently the other side of the star."

"How did they arrive?" asked Hanuman, their voice switching from personable to focused and clipped.

"Translation," said Kercher, and Prab's heart froze in her chest.

"They've found us," said Hanuman. "You need to go now. The first steps are calculated already."

"How did they find us?" asked Prab, but no one was listening to her. Feeling the ship translate she grit her teeth and tried to think about how they'd been found. Sure, they'd translated back into the galaxy, but that was a star over, half a dozen light years and several hours of travel through folded space.

She realised the enemy was actively tracking them. It wasn't that they were following Hanuman's translations. They were following Hanuman directly.

But how?

They emerged inside a nebula, the dense clouds of hydrogen, helium, carbon, nitrogen and inert elements stretching for light hours in all directions. The fog of matter wouldn't hide them, not if they were being tracked.

"They're following us," she said to the other two.

No response from Hanuman.

Kercher was gearing up for the next translation.

"They're following us," she repeated.

"We can stay ahead of them," replied Kercher. "And then lose them. Hanuman has calculated a route."

"None of that will help," she said. "They can see Hanuman and I don't know why. Wherever we go they're going to find us."

The inconsistency of the pursuit troubled her. Would they have come out beyond the galaxy's edge eventually? Had they known Hanuman would eventually reappear back within reach?

"Find it then," hissed Kercher, and took them out of the nebula with another translation.

They arrived nowhere, stars tiny dots of light but nothing more. Kercher didn't hang around but folded space around them and they moved.

"We're going to be like this for five rotations, so get comfortable."

Prab worked. She had what elements of the ship were available to help her and set them speculating on how the enemy was tracking them. She knew it was like asking how magic worked or how the gods knew they were being worshipped, but there was no other course to take.

For herself, she stepped back and tried to think of what it was the enemy might see when they looked at Hanuman.

A ship made of metamaterials, but nothing fundamentally linked to ibits.

Translation was a flashing red light but each translation would give them a momentary location. How could they have tracked them when they weren't translating? They should have been invisible.

The human body of the Face of Loss hung before her mind, their lifeless eyes staring at her, demanding what she wouldn't give.

I won't die for them, she thought, and moved on, doing her best to dismiss the vision from her mind.

Over the next few hours, and in Hanuman's continued absence, the pixies started to report in, declaring there was nothing about the ship the enemy should be able to track.

Which wasn't news. Both because it was what Prab already knew and because it had to be completely wrong.

The ship dropped out of folded space.

"We're here?" asked Prab, disrupted by the unexpected change.

"No," said Kercher, and their voice was tight.

"But you said," she started, but the pilot interrupted her.

"I know what I said but something's interfering with our journey."

As if waiting for Kercher's declaration, a series of black blots against the sky resolved into ships, four small nubs like rose buds together with two of the walnuts. Enough to make Prab shiver.

"Get us out of here," she pleaded.

"The only way out is through," said Kercher, and opened fire.

35.

Hanuman was gone again. Kercher wheeled them through the local volume, sliding up and down, across and around. The enemy followed, firing weapons which left the spacetime in their wake shredded to ribbons, information leaking like innards as the universe screeched.

Whatever Kercher did the enemy kept up. They'd damaged a couple of the rosebuds, but those ships had shifted their compositions, repaired themselves and kept on coming.

Kercher knew they were being corralled. The destination felt like a star about three light years down spiral towards the galactic core.

They were dangerously close to the speed of light, slipping into folded space, bursting from it like seed spores flung out into the world. Through dust clouds, into the tail of an interstellar comet and around the edges of local gravity wells. This far from the nearest star the gravitational landscape was pretty flat and Kercher wished they'd stayed by the red giant or had remained in the nebula.

Instead they'd been interdicted in the middle of nowhere and then driven on towards a location of the enemy's choosing.

Praveenthi was begging them not to translate again but Kercher concluded it was better to translate and have them follow than end up exactly where they were being pushed.

Nothing the enemy fired their way came close to harming them despite their weapons being capable of tearing them to pieces.

Kercher had the sprites running analyses of the tactics and the weapons, trying to see if there was a way out without getting pulverised.

The feedback was not encouraging.

As far as the sprites were concerned, the enemy wanted the cube. Still no idea why. The probability was they would not harm the ship until Hanuman was disabled and they could take control.

However, if Kercher took them out of the trap, the sprites reckoned with a sixty per cent probability that the enemy would harm them to get what they wanted, risking destruction of the cube in the process.

The probability struck Kercher as pretty low. The kind of certainty that could be waved away if the event being predicted unfolded along a different course.

To their mind the probability they'd be harmed or even destroyed if they attempted to translate was dependent on why their enemy wanted the cube.

And they didn't know why the Face of Loss wanted the cube.

So Kercher translated them past the star they were being forced towards and into a trinary system with eight gas giants and a gravity well that was about as chaotic as a three-body system could be.

Two of the gas giants were being devoured by one of the stars towards which they'd come too close. It didn't seem like the first time these planets had crossed the star's path as the system was littered with streams of gas, dust and debris where other protoplanets had come and gone.

On a planetary scale the volatility was too slow and large to result in anyone getting a planet up the exhaust port but it gave Kercher options.

The enemy translated in system seconds after they arrived but by then Kercher had readied themselves and fired at the lead ships.

Hitting the first with a bomb that wiped information clean and reduced the front of it to nothing more than quantum foam, Kercher was deeply satisfied with how its remains tumbled away out of control.

The others spread out, two of them performing micro-translations to emerge far behind the ship while the walnut and remaining rosebud continued in on their original trajectory.

Kercher was thrilled. This was the kind of battle for which their long, thin, battle-hardened body had been printed. Fighting type-three primitives, even if they were in overwhelming numbers, was nothing more than kicking dogs.

This was a proper fight and it tasted good.

With the enemy constraining themselves, Kercher felt they could be aggressive without care and flung the ship towards the walnut, firing weapons designed to tear up spacetime and agitate the ibits in the locality the same way a microwave might agitate a water molecule.

The enemy deployed counter measures – information packages that defrayed the informational disruption Kercher was laying down.

"There's something strange happening in information space," said Praveenthi.

"I can't deal with that," said Kercher. "That's for you to deal with."

Praveenthi went silent but they noted her accessing the systems which would insert her consciousness directly into information space. They wondered if she'd ever accessed it so directly before.

They recalled the first time they'd been dunked into raw information space, how it had taken them hours to recover from the overload. It had been like being picked up by a wave and dashed against the rocks.

Hanuman's hull started to peel back as the enemy tried to turn them into sand.

The gloves were off.

We're outnumbered, came the thought. Kercher shoved it away. No time for that.

They're as good as we are. A thought treated the same way – dismissed with prejudice.

Ducking into a temporary Lagrange point between the three stars, Kercher translated again. They stepped out by a bog-standard yellow star but were going again, pitching up half between it and another mid-range specimen. The enemy flanked them like wolves hunting a stag, waiting for it to tire.

This stag can turn them into marshmallow, thought Kercher with an evil grin.

They'd covered three light years. Small translations whose calculations could be performed easily. The ship's systems were complaining at the risks Kercher was taking, but they switched off the safety requirements to cross calculate the translations. They didn't have time to be safe. Better the risks of a bad translation than being caught by the enemy.

Then they were inside the explosion sphere of an ancient super nova of which only the neutron star remained. Kercher checked the locality and realised it wasn't even a neutron star but a quark star. The original star from which this emerged after a supernova had been absolutely massive.

Despite the pressures they were under, Kercher took a moment to admire the novelty of this rare beast, then closed in, letting the ship adapt to shield them from the intense radiation and trying to run them dark. Kercher hoped they'd be swallowed up by the informational confusion created by the star whose state of matter was one of the rarest and informationally densest artefacts in the galaxy.

The enemy blinked in at a distance, as if concerned about coming too close.

Kercher immediately adjusted their approach, worried they'd unwittingly fallen into a trap.

Nothing sprang out of the star or its vicinity and Kercher settled them into a rapid orbit around the tiny, dense beast. On another day they'd use the information within the quark star, its raw potential, as a way of fuelling their own activity, but Praveenthi had been silent for several minutes.

Her heartbeat was steady but slow. Her breathing managed by the ship but not forced.

Physically she appeared fine. It was her mind Kercher was worried about. As they whipped around the star, Kercher tried to have the sprites tell them what she was experiencing. The ship could read the strength of the magnetic fields of her body down to the picoampere per femtometer. In other words the ship could map her experience down to individual tears and feelings she wouldn't even know how to articulate or recognise.

The sprites reported back that she was fighting in information space. Probably mind to mind and she was frightened and bewildered and panicked.

The enemy pulled back because they were infiltrating the ship through information space.

They considered trying to help her but knew that if they abandoned the physical, they'd be leaving themselves undefended.

All Kercher could do was hope Praveenthi was capable of holding her own in whatever world she found herself.

What they could do was step out from the relative safety of the quark star and take the fight to the enemy. The risk was they'd lose and whatever happened to Praveenthi would be rendered irrelevant. Yet if they could win, or force the enemy back a little, then they might be able to buy her respite from this secondary assault.

Kercher took the ship in towards the quark star, brilliantly bright but less than ten kilometres across. The magnetic fields surrounding it were the greatest anywhere in the universe, but the ship was made of sterner stuff and Kercher was searching for something to turn the tables.

After a short search they found it.

They set the sprites to calculating a short translation and then lit the fuse of the quark star.

They had a few minutes before what they'd set in motion turned from a few pebbles into an avalanche. With a grim sense of the perversity of their actions, Kercher drew matter from the quark star as a long thin stream of white in their wake and moved out of tight orbit.

36.

The entry into information space was like having her skin stripped, painted fluorescent and then sewn into five-dimensional geometry. The pain intense, her mind tied into knots.

The sense of her body, of where she ended and the rest of the world began, blurred until Prab's only measurement for who she was sat in that tiny spot where her thoughts kept coming from.

Like a tornado running out of energy Prab felt her mind falling apart, like sitting down on a sofa with no support, the sense of falling further than she expected didn't end.

She managed to think how stupid she'd been to insert herself into information space when there was suddenly something solid under her feet.

It was nice to have feet again.

Prab found herself standing on a beach.

Hanuman was there. She turned towards him, glad of the company only to find him still as a statue, his feet buried in the sand. He was twice her size.

On tiptoes, a palm placed on his chest revealed his flesh as hard as marble and just as cold.

"I was going to thank you," she said to his unseeing eyes. "This is supposed to be your battle, but you won't be any help here."

A large hammer fell at her feet, as if it had been hiding in the shadow of his body.

The front end of it was flat and octagonal, the back a sharp point. The handle felt like wood under her skin. Surprisingly heavy, she lifted it with equally surprising ease and, swinging it around her head, nearly took off as its momentum dragged her around.

The rules of information space were different to spacetime. This much was so obvious she knew she shouldn't have to remind herself, yet the delusion of it was how she had a body, was wielding a hammer and was stood on a beach listening to the waves whisper against the shore.

The air was warm and close. The world came with salt on her lips and the scent of seaweed rotting at the high tide mark.

Anything you can imagine, she remembered from her lessons. Not anything at all, but anything she could imagine. It sounded powerful, and walking among the raw information left her with a sense of wonder at the heart of all things and how it was, fundamentally, a message to itself.

The universe trying to communicate with itself, to understand what it was on a scale so vast that entire galaxies were nothing more than insignificant accidents in time.

To manipulate the information of the world she was walking in, Prab had to be able to think it. The most powerful nodes wrote about how they could visualise the worlds they wanted. Others recounted how they didn't rely on vision but on information itself, on language.

"An inner monologue isn't required," a talking head had expounded in one seminar she'd been to.

Let's hope so, she thought. Because Prab couldn't imagine what an apple looked like if she wasn't staring right at one. Sure, she could describe it, could write about its skin, its colour, its flesh, but she couldn't picture it.

Imagination was necessary but it wasn't sufficient. Many intelligences had been sent into information space by the Arcology and consciousness made for a very different experience of the raw stuff of the universe.

Plenty of those in the Arcology had no brains to speak of but had awareness and agency and they were fine in information space. What they achieved they did while being radically different from someone like Prab who, currently, had a central nervous system.

She was dying to ask someone what she was supposed to do.

Out of the ground and composed of shaped sand came a labyrinthine map. A small figurine of Prab was stood in the centre and at the far edge were two white blobs making their way through.

I have to intercept them, she thought. I have to stop them.

She knew that if they reached the statue of Hanuman it was over.

A step forward and the map moved, keeping her at the centre.

The truth of it was she felt alarmingly at home. This was as close as she was going to come to returning to the Arcology. Just with fewer guard rails.

Flexing her mind and thinking through how she was going to protect Hanuman, Prab ran towards the approaching enemy. She trilled with anticipation and fear.

The thought of what she was doing tried to make itself heard as she focussed on saving the ship.

You're not built for this, her mind told her, her heart insisting she was going to die, but Prab knew there wasn't a choice – she had to do this.

Then, as before, the figure of the Face of Loss was stood before her. Scaled hounds on either side like dogs crossed with Komodo dragons. Long tongues lolled from their mouths and their feet sported long, thick claws. They were cartoon like, their bodies lithe and sinewy, their eyes big and black with nostrils that sniffed the air with continuous twitches.

"Give us the ship," said the Face of Loss.

In this place they were as they had been in the hall inside Akhanda. Except now they were fuzzy around the edges, their hair a muss of curly black locks coming down to their shoulders. Their body was thin like their hounds, sparking with barely suppressed energy.

Yet their eyes were dead. No movement, no anything at all, and when they spoke it was as if they were streaming their communication from very far away, unsure of who their audience might be.

"You shall not pass," said Prab, and knew how this was going to play out.

One of her favourite things as a member of the Arcology had been an adventure series featuring wizards who battled using ideas. A snake would eat a rat, but an eagle would eat the snake.

Their fights were traditional in a way that Prab found comforting but also allowed for great wits to prevail without having to rely on in-game bonuses or strategies. With the biggest, baddest enemies, hope always won and so one had to chart a course to bring their biggest guns to bear just as hope was deployed.

The Face of Loss spoke again. "We are growing."

"This is not for you," she replied. "Go elsewhere, seek your nourishment from others."

"We are hungry," said the Face of Loss. Still nothing about them spoke of life, and Prab shivered as they talked about hunger without moving at all.

"Is that it? Is that all you want?" Could the Arcology help them find something else to consume?

They've killed the Arcology, she reminded herself. There's no coming back from this.

"We grow. We expand." For the first time there was an expression on their face. That of confusion.

"Enough of this," said Prab, the faces of her parents, her brother and sisters, asking why she was talking when she should be fighting.

Prab threw up a wall made of red bricks between them.

A gasp from the other side and then the Face of Loss walked through it as if it wasn't there.

Prab backed up, threw up another wall. She imagined this one stopping ghosts and other things that could walk through walls. It was covered in sigils and angular symbols, silvered and chalked. The bricks were black this time, white mortar between them.

The sound of a body striking a solid surface.

Clear this place, she thought and the landscape on which she was stood flattened, the sea retreated. Mountains in the distance sank and the sky turned a pale blue with no clouds so the light was a soft white that cast no shadows.

The power of changing her world burst like fireworks at the core of who she was. She missed this more than she'd realised, seeing now that absence was not acceptance.

There was nothing now except Prab, her imagination and the enemy.

It has no mind, came a thought out of nowhere. It's trying to approximate what it experiences in meeting you. It would explain the dead look in the Face of Loss' eyes. It would explain the limited vocabulary.

There was no negotiation with these invaders, no diplomacy. Could you have peace talks with a slime mould?

Prab thought about seeing footage of a colony of coral attacking another, how it reached out and dissolved its enemy, thousands of small organisms acting in concert to achieve a common end without knowing what they were doing, without awareness of their cooperation or what was at stake.

Agency without consciousness.

How do you fight that? thought Prab.

The sound of metal against stone and the wall Prab had erected cracked.

You can reinforce it, she thought, but abandoned the idea. This was not how a battle like this unfolded. The mindless enemy against the hero.

You're the hero?

I can't keep defending, she thought. The flaw with defending was that eventually the enemy would strike true and they only needed to do this once. The trick to a proper defence was that it was really only part of how to fight and win.

Prab had been good at the wizarding games and knew you needed to create windows for counters, for taking control of the fight, for making your opponent cooperate in their own demise. A duellist who wasn't the agent was the patient and the patient always died.

So enough with walls. She sprang into the air as a bird and flew, assuming the Face of Loss would follow.

And follow it did, but not as a bird but a giant wave of water a kilometre across and a hundred metres high, cresting over her no matter how quickly she climbed through the spray-filled air.

So she fell, allowed herself to become stone, a lump of granite the size of a fist, and rolled with the currents as they flung her one way and another. Over geological time water would grind her to sand, but this was a battle waged in the moment and her granite delivered her onto a flat white surface with no texture whereupon she walked upright in the body she had called her own since she was printed out into physical space.

The sea fell away and the Face of Loss walked towards her in human shape. Tall now, armed with a sword.

Old school, she thought, and wondered where it had learned about this kind of weapon. Then she saw it wasn't a sword but an extension of its arm, fused at the wrist like a cancerous growth.

She rusted the sword and the Face of Loss stopped. It changed shape, into that of a monster, all arms and teeth, big saucer eyes and claws that could pick her brain out with the smallest effort.

Meat appeared at its feet and with salivating mouth it ate. Prab watched and as it was finishing up a net fell over it. The creature writhed and tore and growled and whined but couldn't escape.

Then it was a tiny little creature – legs and thorax and abdomen. No bigger than her eye and small enough to fly out through the holes in the net. Prab was ready, for this was what she'd anticipated.

A block of granite fell from the sky and smashed the creature into another coming up from the floor. It would be smeared into paste.

That was easier than it could have been, she thought.

The stone blocks groaned at her, old men trying to stand up too quickly. Then they cracked, and from within, ice spread across the remains towards her.

She threw fire at it and instantly knew it was a mistake. The fire turned the ice to steam which continued towards her as she rapidly retreated. It was Prab's turn to use ice and she threw it into the air, chilling the steam into snowflakes.

I'm getting nowhere, she thought.

The snowflakes clumped together and the Face of Loss stood to its feet, eyes still dead.

Casting around, Prab was reminded of the coral and thought about how to dissuade such a creature.

Taste bad.

Taste so bad it refused to eat you. How did you make information taste bad?

Prab fell back, throwing broken ideas at the Face of Loss; acid baths, poison balls, venom from snakes, cancerous growths, the castoffs from salt mining. Then she tried the more conceptual - that there were no other worlds than their origin world, that you had to die physically and end, that the universe was an empty place.

Then she was suggesting to the space around her that there was no order, just ideas that took the forms of multi-dimensional geometries, bending the world around her. The Face of Loss kept coming. It had no interest in conspiracies, in nonsense. It was indifferent to chaos and order.

It has no consciousness, her ideas tightening around her like a noose.

The Face of Loss regrew their blade and swung at her.

Prab dodged out of the way. She fashioned a sword with her own mind, two of them, then a dozen, and slung them through the air. They hit the Face of Loss, sinking in their flesh, bursting out of their back, but no blood was drawn.

The swords sank deeper still, drawn in to disappear inside its body. And still it came for her.

Please be winning, she willed at Kercher, because she wasn't going to be more than an asteroid in the wrong place to this thing.

And she hated it because she knew she was right about how to defeat it but she didn't know how to be right. How to taste bad was a question she couldn't answer.

Ducking under an attack of axes, she bent like she was a flower in the wind before evaporating into water vapour as the Face of Loss tried to boil her body with heat. From there she was a stream of boiling acid as it became a cage and burned through its container.

Outside of its trap Prab tried to return its attacks. Don't be on the defensive, she kept saying inside her head.

"We are hungry," said the Face of Loss, over and over.

She made herself a void and it became light. Each time they scuffled it drew a little closer and Prab knew she was missing something crucial.

The Operand had avoided it by hiding, by renouncing the technology that made them interesting to the Face of Loss.

She had no choice but to stay here in this place where it was emperor.

There has to be a way, she thought. She was a quark pair then, refusing to be split as the Face of Loss attempted to demonstrate she was alone and, singular, could be locked away and forgotten about.

Prab pushed back as a four-dimensional pseudo-Riemannian surface, on which an entire universe could exist, expanding away from all other points like an inflating balloon. She tried to contain the Face of Loss and for a swift moment she believed she'd managed it.

Then it was a singularity, of infinite mass contained in an infinitesimal space and the combination broke through her manifold and it was free of her. She flung matter at it, as much as possible, threw axionic bosons all around it to encase it, knew they did not care for the impact of gravity but could hold the singularity in place.

I'm trying, she thought and there was pride at how long she'd been keeping it at bay. Prab tried not to think about the inevitability of what was coming. They were alone. There was no cavalry.

We've come so far, she thought. Yet their journey had been nothing more than a long defeat.

The Face of Loss became a cloud of gravitons and reshaped the curvature of spacetime and was free.

They were both people-shaped again and this time it was close enough Prab could touch it if she wanted. She was running dry. Ideas she'd already used came into her mind, crowding out the frantic need to find something she'd not tried already.

She tried picturing the mixing of milk into water. In her idea she put all the possibility of the Face of Loss and the Arcology co-existing. Mixed together, inseparable.

Instead the Face of Loss took her image and thread through it an infection that ate at it, fed on its health until the infection had multiplied and overwhelmed her harmony.

Prab was flat on her back, the world emptied of up, down, forward and backwards. Time had gone.

All she had was this moment and over her, towering like a lightning-struck tree, was the Face of Loss, its eyes on hers, its body sharp and needle like, those spikes through her body, pinning her in place.

"We are hungry," it said one more time, and its jaw fell away to reveal pulsing red and white flesh which bulged out to envelope and consume her.

37.

The stream of quark star burned and gathered material to itself. The monofilament trailed behind Hanuman as heavy as a city, as massive as a country and it was nothing but bait.

Kercher swung right in towards the nearest ship, holding fire lest they retreat, or worse still, in case they were destroyed.

The others closed in, peeling their outsides away as they grew tendrils and fibres Kercher knew would immobilise Hanuman and slowly tear him apart in their search for the cube. All they could think about was saving Praveenthi.

This was it – they had nothing, nowhere to go.

Hanuman's strategy had been nonsense. Hundreds of days travel trying to stay one step ahead of the Face of Loss and, somehow, to elude it long enough to reach safety without being followed right in and destroyed along with everything they were supposed to find.

You lived longer than the Arcology, thought Kercher, and was inexplicably relieved and angry at the result. They're all dead now. Just like you thought should happen.

How will they be reborn?

Kercher realised they'd always assumed people would be reborn into the Arcology, but if it was all gone, then where would they return to?

It shouldn't matter but the change, the possibility of it, was so vast Kercher couldn't think straight.

The only certainty was they'd join them momentarily.

Enough, they thought, and translated three light seconds away. Close enough to watch as the filament of quark star they'd left behind whipped through the void, suddenly untethered and with enough energy to release the preons inside.

Time to go, they thought, and translated again. A light hour this time. Enough distance to watch and plan and then leave after it was all done and long before the consequences of what they'd unleashed reached their new location.

The ibits where the Face of Loss had tried to corner them changed shape, expressed themselves as a hole in spacetime and grabbed at everything within reach. No collapse, no event horizon worth mentioning, just a sudden gap in the fabric of everything and, at its heart, the Face of Loss being crushed down to nothing.

Kercher was thrilled at the destruction but knew reinforcements would be on their way.

"Praveenthi," they messaged. She was still alive, her mind still active. There were ugly spikes across her cognition but nothing a proper fight to the death wouldn't elicit.

She wasn't coming out of information space voluntarily so Kercher yanked her back. All trips down there had life belts designed to bring people home. Easier to retrieve those with consciousness because a mind wasn't a phenomenon that handled exposure to raw data well and so would always reach for a helping hand when offered – in spite of what those being dragged back might want.

A gasp. "Owww."

"Are you ok?" they asked.

"I was dead," she replied, her words slurred. "They were all over me, spikes and blades and teeth and so much flesh." She shuddered so violently Kercher could hear it.

They made calming noises, not sure what else to do.

The quark star was rippling in information space. Kercher's attempts to destabilise it working far better than expected. The impact on local spacetime was going to be catastrophic.

They'd do well to leave, but Kercher was going to keep them there until the very last possible moment. And then possibly longer. It was the only way they could think to mask their trail.

"I know how to stop them," she said.

Kercher's heart stopped.

"We have to taste bad."

"How?" they asked.

"I don't know," she replied, and the hope that had built in their skin dissipated like water in the desert.

Far quicker than they'd hoped, the ship indicated new signals in system. Five of them, one huge beast of a contact which reminded Kercher of the arms that had sliced through Akhanda.

They're really tiring of chasing you around, they thought.

"What are those?" asked Praveenthi.

"They're here for us," said Kercher.

"This is as far as we go," she said, and Kercher was grateful she understood without having to be told.

"I was going to take us away. I'd hoped to use the star to hide our departure. It's dense enough with information it might even have worked."

"They're here too soon," she said.

And again, Kercher was grateful they didn't have to explain themselves.

"I've destabilised the star," said Kercher.

"Right in their faces," said Praveenthi, her voice rasping with the effort of speaking. "It's probably a good thing Hanuman's not here."

"They won't get to eat us," said Kercher. They'd changed their navigation, targeted the heart of the quark star. Their information would be lost forever and along with them the Arcology.

Translation gates split open around them and out poured dozens of the enemy who moved through to take up position around them on all sides. Craft of all different sizes and profiles.

Like a hunt which had run its quarry to ground.

"We doing this then?" asked Praveenthi.

Kercher took a deep breath.

"Hold that thought," said a voice across the ship's system. Not Hanuman. Not anyone they knew.

IDs flooded the ship; Arcology entities.

Lights pinged on the map of the system as dozens of ships arrived. They fired immediately.

"Moving us," said Kercher and they dropped away through a hole in the enemy net where three of their craft had been vapourised in the onslaught.

Kercher received coordinates, in system. They sent them back about the destabilised star.

"You have been busy," came the response. New coordinates were provided, fifteen light years away. Inside a bespoke network with Arcology tags. The translation would be easy, stable. Safe.

"Go now," said the voice, which had identified itself as a ship without a name currently doing its best to cut one of the enemy into pieces with beams of awfully angular information.

Kercher was in no mood to retreat. Not now.

A fleet from the Arcology. Ship profiles Hanuman's systems were telling them were old enough to be archived. Cavalry arriving from the past to save them.

Would it be enough.

The battle was not one way. The surprise of their arrival had given them an initial advantage but the enemy was fighting back, more of their craft arriving every moment.

"You need to go," said the rescuer. "This isn't a battle where we wash them away. We're life boats on the open sea and you need to take hold and get on board so we can head to shore."

With a shiver of frustration Kercher relented and did as they were told.

Translation.

38.

"What in an anchorless translation are you doing down here?" said the doctor.

Hanuman was sat upright in a hospital bed having his bloods taken. The phlebotomist was a young male-presenting figure with three arms and no eyes. Hanuman could see how their skin had been altered to take in stimuli from a number of sources including light. This doctor saw with their whole body.

It explained why they were wearing a transparent gown.

"And when did you decide pretending to have a body was the easiest way to have this conversation?"

Hanuman remembered a pilot they'd known. A strange little person who flew their ship with their skin.

"Focus," said the doctor, clicking their fingers in front of Hanuman's face. "This is to be expected, unfortunately. You weren't the original target for this procedure and so no one prepared you properly. I'm only surprised your identity took this long to disintegrate."

Hanuman wondered if that was good or bad news.

"Oh, it's bad news," said the doctor. Hanuman stared at them, but they averted their gaze.

"This is a printed body?" he asked.

The doctor snorted then a serious look came over their face.

"It is not a printed body." They gestured at the room. A large pod with a bed and a screen that ran along two walls showing a view from the top of a mountain in a lush rainforest. Trees carpeted the land as far as the eye could see as huge birds wheeled slowly in the sky overhead. "This is not a hospital and I am not a doctor. None of this is real, it's what's left of your identity attempting not to be entirely overwritten."

"Oh," said Hanuman. He looked around the room and tried to work out which bits weren't real. Was there a seam somewhere, a thread he could pull to unravel it all. "Am I inside the Arcology then?"

"In many ways you could say that you have become the Arcology," said the doctor who wasn't a doctor.

"Do you have a name?"

The doctor paused for a moment. "Unlike you, Hanuman, I have not earned that honour. Perhaps this rescue will walk me further along the path to such a thing."

"What happens now?" asked Hanuman, at a loss for what else to do.

"You could surrender. Let this finish." The nameless doctor eyed him, refusing to give any sign of whether this was a good idea or not.

"What happens then?" asked Hanuman.

"Then you'll disappear, become the Arcology proper. Akhanda the second maybe. Hanuman the first. The complexities around your merging with everything we are can be difficult to model."

"And if I choose otherwise?"

Was that a small smile on their lips?

"Then I press this button here." A tube had appeared in Hanuman's arm and, at the other end was a small box with a big red button on it. "And we'll start to desegregate your identity from the Arcology. It will recover in its own time and you will remain. Perhaps like an aunt or a benevolent house deva, not entirely separate but definitely mostly yourself again."

Hanuman wasn't sure what it would mean to be himself. Would he get to leave this hospital room? Would he see that pilot for a drink?

"On balance," he said. "I think I'd like to be myself again. This room is ever so small and I'd really like to see outside." He met the doctor's gaze. "If that's okay?"

The doctor pressed the button and everything dissolved around Hanuman, including his body.

* * *

The sky was lit with fires green and blue, purple and red. Electromagnetic fields were steep like cliffs and gravity itself was rolling like a storm-driven ocean.

Then the world opened around him and he was elsewhere. Translation.

Hanuman remembered it all.

Kercher and Prab. Pilot and Interlocutor. His friends.

He remembered his name.

He remembered Akhanda.

The place where they'd emerged was silent. The stars here were distant. A spot in a volume with nothing but interstellar dust and quantum foam.

"We'll stand out here like a bonfire in a cave," he said to Kercher

"You're back," said the pilot, sounding only a little happy.

"I'm sorry," said Hanuman. It felt appropriate. He guessed their recent lives had not been ones built on the happy memories of other people.

"How are you?" asked Prab.

For the first time since taking the cube on board, Hanuman felt all right. Not great, but all right. His identity was largely crisp and explorable, his memories largely intact.

"I am on limited capacity," he said, realising it was true as the words were sent to the other two.

Then other ships arrived. Arcology ships. Three of them.

"You are old," said Hanuman. And they were, older than him by tens of thousands of rotations.

"Enough of the insults," said the lead ship. "Just because you have a name doesn't make you better than us."

Hanuman recognised them as the doctor from their dreams.

"We have somewhere to go," said Hanuman. "A destination where the Arcology can unfold itself again in safety."

"Go. Now."

No debate. No questions. These were old-school defence corps. Stories about them abounded.

Hanuman approved. Many nodes wanted to join their ranks. Most nodes didn't have the mental preparedness to do what was needed.

"And you?"

One of the six possible spots was highlighted. "This one. Well done for identifying it without us. You will be met upon arrival."

"If he identified it, so will they," said one of the others.

"It's what we have," said the former doctor. Then, to Hanuman. "Go."

Hanuman did as he was told. Inside his body, Prab and Kercher asked what was happening, but he had no answer to give them except to say they were heading for the location he'd given Kercher previously.

The system was an empty one. A single star with six planets and a minimum of detritus, most of which had been flung beyond the outermost planet to orbit in a thinly spread cloud.

Two huge gas giants. One with surface winds in excess of five thousand kilometres an hour and temperatures which meant it was currently raining glass.

Its sister was about the same size but was built of simple gases and elements. Thick storms showered electrical sprites hundreds of miles long above its surface and, somewhere deep within, Hanuman could spot a liquid helium core. It was only a whisker away from being a star.

No signs of anything alive anywhere within a light hour. The information well here was flat. Nothing of interest, nothing for the enemy to feed on.

Hanuman had the same creeping feeling of sticking out, of being exceptionally easy to find.

Then, as if unveiled from behind a screen, came an Arcology warship.

Hanuman admired the curves of its form, a teardrop shape, the fashion for which had passed into the history books probably around the same time their rescuers had been born.

This one was of the same profile. Probably the same generation. Unlike the others it had been busy remaking itself.

How did I not see it?

Hanuman's question was met with a deluge of information. The ship was one of sixty in its generation. Nearly all of them had been experimental identities grown to horizon scan for threats and crises. They had disappeared tens of thousands of rotations ago after submitting a report that predicted a poorly defined extinction-level event and declaring they were going to prepare for it. They'd not been heard from since.

None of this node's class had names – they'd not been around long enough to earn them. Although they had been cutting edge at birth, they were obsolete now. The profile matched those who'd come for them just as all hope seemed lost.

Hanuman asked himself how they'd been found.

The answer was embarrassingly simple. The cube within them was an ibit device. Integrating it into Hanuman had not changed the fact that it was wrapped up deep in information space, way down low in the raw stuff of the universe where it shone like a lighthouse on a dark night.

He'd been carrying a beacon within himself all along without realising it.

This was all new.

How do I know this? he asked.

You are the Arcology now, came the response in his voice.

He recalled the conversation with the doctor, the explanation offered to him.

It wasn't true that he was the Arcology. But he also wasn't separate from it as an identity anymore. Everything it was he had within him.

Hanuman felt like he was a river meeting the sea for the first time.

"You're who we were sent to meet," he said to it.

The ship acknowledged the assumption. "This way," it said, and turning, launched itself in towards the quieter of the two gas giants.

Hanuman followed in.

"This is a system for the Excluded," said Kercher. "I can find no signs of life."

"They are hidden," said Hanuman. He couldn't pierce whatever technology they were using to hide themselves either, but this was good news.

They sank into the clouds of the gas giant's atmosphere, electricity discharging around them and winds hundreds of kilometres an hour strong doing their best to shove them off course.

There was a lot of sulphur and iron in the atmosphere. Silicon, sodium, carbon and oxygen, but it was largely hydrogen and helium. It had eighty-four moons, a handful of which had atmospheres of their own, methane seas, ice, liquid cores and the most simple forms of life. An entire planetary system all of its own.

He saw and felt nothing until they were upon it. A huge station floating there in the darkness of the storm systems. Thin layers and platforms stretched out in one plane to give the impression of a spill of molten metal.

No tethers, no anchors, just the station hiding here minding its own business.

This wasn't technology the people here had developed themselves.

"You did this," said Hanuman. "You hid them."

"We have hidden ourselves," said the ship. "This will be the Arcology's new home."

"What about survivors?" asked Hanuman.

"You are the survivors," said the ship.

But Hanuman had the traces of trillions within him.

"Are they ready for us?" he asked.

"They have been informed of your coming," said the ship.

Hanuman realised he could give this ship a name. It had earned it and he was the Arcology now. It was within his gift to do this.

"How did you hide them?" he asked.

"They're not truly hidden," said the ship. "We have masked the information they give out. There are seams if you know what to look for. Eventually the enemy will find us here, but until then we have time to prepare and learn what we can about them."

"My crew has the best experience," said Hanuman. "They know more than anyone.

The ship didn't reply and Hanuman got the sense it wasn't interested in what his crew had to say.

A signal arrived from the station.

A video stream of a woman with long blonde hair and dark skin. Her eyes were a piercing red. Her face was built for someone who liked to box.

"You are not welcome here," she said.

"Nice," said Hanuman.

"They weren't expecting the place to be developed," said Prab. "The ships who came for us? They were expecting something uninhabited."

Which was true. At the time the cohort had disappeared, this was a backwater identified only for mineral deposits and the nascent lifeforms on the moons of the two gas giants.

The station's community was only a few thousand rotations old, established by a vote of nodes on various committees who oversaw the welfare of Excluded communities.

The station itself was a curmudgeonly node who had an ongoing interest in microbial life. It had agreed to its tenants on condition that it didn't need to provide for them.

Both sides were happy with the arrangement and the Excluded arrived to live lives they were content with.

"It's more primitive than home," said Prab as they digested the lack of reception.

The station itself had sent no messages and Hanuman couldn't raise it despite trying to get its attention. It was definitely there but was showing no interest in them or its tenants.

"Does the station know what you did?" Hanuman asked the ship. He was struggling to think of an appropriate name for it, wanted it to be right. Names meant something, had to embody a sense of who you were and the story you'd lived.

"The station agreed to host tenants. You are a tenant. It has no interest in what you do."

"We're going to unfold the Arcology here," said Hanuman. "That's not the same as a few Excluded coming here and living off the grid."

"That's certainly what the Excluded are going to think," said Prab, busting into the conversation.

"Nothing you do will disturb its experiments and observations," said the ship. "As long as that remains true it doesn't care what we do."

"The enemy will find us here," said Hanuman.

"It calls itself the Face of Loss," said Prab.

"Who cares?" asked Kercher, and Hanuman sighed with frustration.

"That is not the point," he said.

The woman on the other end of the message repeated herself.

"Hello," said Hanuman. "I am Hanuman and I am in need of refuge."

"Go away," said the woman.

"Do you have a name?" he asked.

"What I'm called isn't important, node. You and your kind aren't welcome here. We are a community of the Excluded and the Arcology agreed to let us be."

"The Arcology is gone," said Hanuman.

The woman paused. "You are the Arcology and we wish to be free of you."

"What happened to her as a child?" asked Kercher.

"Let me talk to her," said Prab.

Hanuman ceded the stream to the Interlocutor. It's her job after all, he thought.

"Hi. I'm Prab. We have a cargo of two hundred Excluded."

"One hundred and three," said Hanuman on a private channel.

Prab ignored his correction.

"They need a home. I need a home. The ship is called Hanuman and he needs a home. When he says the Arcology is gone he means it. They were invaded and exterminated. The ships here are the last of them. They are refugees. None of us are Excluded anymore because the empire which we left is gone too."

The woman listened and Hanuman could see her expression was different than when he was speaking.

"I'm sorry to hear that," said the woman eventually. "You can call me Anaisha. We'll need to vote on it. What are you asking for?"

Hanuman felt Prab's focus through the system.

"We wish to rest with you and rebuild, we wish for all the Excluded on this ship to have the choice of staying with you. I wish for Hanuman and what's left of his people to have a place of refuge here until they find a new home."

Which wasn't the plan at all. This was supposed to be their new home. A few thousand Excluded, he couldn't see how there were more, shouldn't be allowed to stop that.

The ship with Hanuman was listening in and he could feel its impatience. The Arcology itched within Hanuman, it wanted to unfurl, to be itself again.

"We will vote on these proposals," said the woman and the feed cut off. There was no invitation to dock. They were left hanging.

"How long before they tell us to go fuck ourselves?" asked Kercher.

"They won't," said Prab.

Hanuman wasn't so sure. He predicted that the Excluded here would allow those inside his body to come ashore but they would deny him, they would deny the Arcology.

He had to get the attention of the station – it did not belong to the Excluded. Hanuman also knew Prab would not approve.

There was an emergency channel upon which the station had agreed to be reached. The Excluded did not have it but Hanuman did, it was there in someone's memories floating up like a treasure from the deep.

"Station, my name is Hanuman and within me I carry the Arcology. I need to use your body as a home for the empire. The Excluded aboard your structures are denying us access. Please, we need your support and approval to come onboard."

"If we're hidden, you could build your own station," said Kercher.

If they had an infinite amount of time that statement might be true. The problem was they didn't. If they stood any chance of understanding how to defeat this enemy, they needed to unfurl the Arcology as quickly as possible and start thinking. The time to build what they needed would be an unacceptable delay.

The woman's face appeared in all their feeds, this time on the channel Hanuman had used to reach the station in private.

"Get out," she said.

"I'm sorry," said Hanuman, realising what had happened.

"You ask us to act in good faith and then you go behind our backs. Like you always do. You think we don't know what you really want? That you won't evict us as soon as you're comfortable? Leave now and the station won't make you."

"The station is Arcology," said Hanuman, feeling dumbfounded at her comments.

"You think we wouldn't have found a way to talk to it by now?" she replied, disdain written across her face in arched eyebrow and curled lip. Her eyes were wide, fixing him with her anger.

"I did not know he would do that," said Prab, cutting across Hanuman as he flailed to find the words to convince this obstacle to help them. "He has not understood that we're all actually real people. I won't apologise for him, he has to do that himself but please don't let that interfere with our plea for help."

"There are ships arriving in system," said Kercher.

"See," said the woman.

"Please," begged Prab. "Please don't abandon us. We've come so far to find someone who'll offer us refuge."

"You're here because you think this is easy, that we're a pushover."

"We came because no one realised you were here," said the ship who'd met them when they'd first arrived. "Your presence was unanticipated in our original planning."

"All of that might be true," said Prab, her words strained. "But I'm asking you to consider our request on its own, without any of the baggage the nodes we have with us are bringing. Our history isn't important, only our need."

"You have a need because of your history," said the woman. "The hubris of the Arcology brought low at last."

"You are happy trillions are dead?" asked Hanuman.

The stream went dead.

Hanuman wanted to do something, to exercise feelings of frustration and impotence.

Within him Prab wrung her hands. Her vitals showed a disproportionate response even with the stakes as they were. The woman was teetering on the brink of a collapse. Hanuman wished he could help her, could make things right.

He might be prepared to evict the Excluded from a willing station and move in anyway but if the station was unwilling then that left them with nothing if the population here said no.

"What about the other options?" he asked the rescuing ship.

"They are unprotected and we don't have the resources to build the same deception as we have done elsewhere before we are discovered. This is your only option, Hanuman Arcology."

"We wait," said Prab.

"We don't have time," said the ship.

"And what do you have?" she shot back. "We cannot rush them, not now Hanuman has amply demonstrated his bad faith."

"I didn't mean to upset them."

"No," said Prab, and her voice was calm, like an Interlocutor at work. "You didn't mean to get caught. And you were. Contrition is all well and good but better not to do the thing that requires restitution in the first place."

"I've heard it's better to apologise after than ask first," said Kercher.

Prab sighed. "Only the selfish think that's a good course to chart. If you're part of a community where you actually respect the other people in it, then you take the slower pace because you understand the strength of the bonds of which you're a part and see them as a good thing to be maintained."

"Yet you still left the Arcology," said Kercher.

Prab didn't answer the accusation.

"We should have forced our way onto the station," said the rescuing ship.

"Enough," said Hanuman. "The Interlocutor is right. We will wait for the Excluded to consider her proposal."

"And if they deny us?" asked the ship.

Hanuman had no answer.

39.

Talking to Kercher about patience and consent had reminded Prab of her mothers, of how she'd tried to persuade them about her leaving the Arcology only to then do it rather than wait for an approval she'd thought would never come.

Prab rehearsed never to be had arguments with them as she watched ships continue to arrive. No news of passengers but the numbers were heartening. There were all kinds, from small little things that would fit a dozen times into Hanuman to hulking great beasts nearly the size of the station whose silence was anxiety inducing.

They had reached thirty-three ships when the station came back online.

The woman was there, joined this time by three others. An older man, another woman and someone with smooth androgynous features like Kercher's.

They'd come with their answer.

Prab told Hanuman and Kercher to stay out of it.

"Ship?" she tagged their rescuer. "That goes for you too."

"I will speak as I believe is required. This plan was instituted long before you were coded into being and I will not see it disrupted because you think your short life experience qualifies you over me."

Prab knew that kind of attitude and it wasn't worth arguing, especially with the Excluded live and in front of her.

"Thank you for coming back to us," she began. The woman who'd first spoken to then held up a hand and Prab stopped talking.

"We have reviewed and voted on your proposals. Those proposals being firstly that we allow the Excluded onboard your ship to apply for refugee status among us. The second being that you yourselves are provided safe haven here until you're ready to move on and thirdly, that you can utilise the station's own capacity to unfold the Arcology."

Prab nodded. There was no benefit in correcting or disagreeing, that moment had passed.

"On the first," it was the older man speaking now. "We grant your request with eighty-three per cent in favour. On the second we grant the request with sixty-one per cent in favour. On the third we grant the request with fifty-one per cent in favour."

The woman who'd raged at them for trying to go over her head looked furious at the outcome, her lips pursed and her jaw clenched, but she said nothing.

With a majority in favour of just one per cent, Prab wondered at how close they'd come to being denied the chance to save the Arcology. She had no idea how many people were aboard the station, perhaps a few thousand, given its footprint, but with that kind of majority, their fate had come down to a small handful of Excluded deciding in their favour.

Trillions of lives decided on the whims of a few strangers and disaffected.

The second woman, dark skinned and with a soft patch in the middle of her forehead, which Prab knew contained a third eye capable of seeing into the ultraviolet, started talking.

"We will provide you berths for docking, but only for you. Those who have arrived after you will not be welcomed aboard. We do not see this as a problem since they are nodes and need no physical space on our station.

"Before you celebrate, there are some caveats."

Prab felt Hanuman grinding to speak but the ship kept hold of his impulses and said nothing.

"You did not mention these before," said the older ship. "This is unacceptable."

To their credit, thought Prab, the four representatives from the station continued as if no one had spoken. It would drive the old ship mad.

"Firstly. We will not accept a long-term residency here. You may stay only so long as the war does not come to us. We are not interested in your conflict and we will not become involved.

"Secondly. The station will remain a home for those who do not wish to join the Arcology. To that end no deployment of technology or decision making will be permitted that infringes upon the community here.

"Lastly, no further attempts to talk to the station will be accepted. The station has its concerns and those are not to be interrupted."

Which was a polite way of saying don't try going around us a second time.

"This is acceptable." It was Hanuman.

She knew he was right to accept, it was his gig, but still Prab felt undermined. She was reminded of why she'd left the Arcology in the first place.

"We will need to meet with you when you have docked," said the first woman.

"It would be wonderful if you could give me your names," said Prab.

The four of them exchanged off screen glances which confirmed for Prab that they were in the same room and streaming individually.

"When you dock. We will be waiting."

Then they were gone.

A docking vector was provided and Kercher took them in.

They weren't actually brought inside the station. A gangway was extended and Hanuman created an airlock to which it was attached.

When they were secure, about twenty metres out from one of the station's thin stretches of metal, Prab asked Kercher if they were coming aboard the station.

"I don't think so," they replied.

"You should come," she said. After everything, she wanted them there. It was important they hear what the Excluded on this station had to say, to learn what they thought. Perhaps even understand how they saw the Arcology.

Prab didn't think Kercher was likely to change their view of things, they were off the other side of the Arcology with their own strange take, but, she told herself, it couldn't hurt.

Besides which, the thought of being alone out there made her bones light and her stomach hurt. She needed someone by her side or she didn't know what would happen.

More ships were arriving in system as they decanted into the gangway.

"Sixty-seven and rising," said Kercher. "There's a couple from Akhanda."

Prab already worried they would be found by the enemy. "Won't more of them attract more attention?"

"The information distortion the old guard have created covers the entire gas giant, once they're inside its atmosphere, they disappear," said Hanuman into her ear.

"You can talk directly into my head if you want," she replied.

"Are you sure?" asked Hanuman.

"No," she replied. "I will probably change my mind, but it's not you I'm angry with, Hanuman. And pretending that it makes a difference how we talk to one another doesn't make things right."

"How's this?" he asked and the voice was there like he'd spoken right into her mind.

Prab winced but nodded. It was uncomfortable and she wanted to shout at him to get out of her head as she'd done every time a member of the Arcology had taken that liberty in the past.

Shivering to shake off the feeling of the uncanny, Prab sent back that it was fine and she could hear him loud and clear.

It was easy to remember why she objected though. When he was allowed to speak that way he did so by reading her magnetic field and shaping it to create the words in her mind. He didn't need to be told she could hear him because he was literally manipulating the words into her mind. That kind of transparency created a vulnerability akin to being flayed open by a surgeon, and Prab hated it.

Why talk at all if the person on the other end could look at your magnetic field and know exactly what you were thinking?

Worse still was that there was no way for Prab to do it to Hanuman. There was no central nervous system or brain to read on a ship. The transparency, the vulnerability, was all one way.

"I understand," said Hanuman.

"Then don't," said Prab.

"I won't read your thoughts, your moods," said Hanuman. "We can communicate using words."

That he'd read her thoughts to know she was uncomfortable wasn't a great start, she thought, but she'd take his promise at face value.

You can always change your mind later. Isn't that right, Hanuman?

He didn't respond.

Close enough, she thought.

"Kercher," said Prab. "You should come."

The pilot, wrapped in the covering that served as their interface with Hanuman, showed no signs of emerging.

"We can eat and drink. You need to decompress from all of this."

"I can do that virtually," said Kercher.

"I'll ask you again, have you ever had shore leave?"

"They are serving a custodial sentence," said Hanuman. "There is no shore leave."

"I'm requesting it. These are extraordinary circumstances, don't you think?"

"Fine," said Hanuman, and Kercher's interface rolled back off their body like paint peeling in the sun.

Kercher lay there a moment and she knew Hanuman had done it again; acted on someone, not with their consent. She waited, and after a while they lifted their head, looked around then moved. Stood upright they looked a little lost, a lot anxious.

"Come on," said Prab, and Kercher's vulnerable expression was packed away, replaced by the blank look of a soldier.

The end of the gangway opened to reveal a single person, thin and fragile-looking as was so often the case in low gravity environments among those who didn't really care for their physical form.

It wasn't one of the four. They were short, thin wispy hair tucked behind their ears as an afterthought, with large black circular eyes about five centimetres across.

In a high-pitched nasal voice they said, "Welcome aboard. The elected council is waiting for you."

They followed their chaperone through a long, empty passageway whose windows only showed the dark storms beyond. Across the visible spectrum there was nothing to see, but in the infrared and ultraviolet the planet was alive with activity.

After a few minutes they veered away from the outer edges of the station and the windows stopped. They emerged onto a large concourse and Prab saw people. Actual people.

They were in all shapes and sizes, except they were all, roughly, human in form. There were a few with more arms or legs than normal and the average number of eyes was above two, but compared to the Otto or the Operand, they were among their own kind.

As they progressed, people stopped to look at them. They passed cafes and people in the street, glass-fronted buildings where people were busy doing whatever it was they did here, but everything slowed and stopped as they passed by.

At her side Kercher shifted uneasily.

"It's not you," she said to them.

"It absolutely is," they replied, looking from side to side at the expressionless staring.

"I mean it's not you specifically. They must know who we are and what we've brought with us. I'd be looking too if it was me. We're going to change everything and they know it."

She knew how her family would have been regarded if they'd printed themselves out and walked the streets of Sirajah's Reach. An ache started in her hands and ended in her throat.

They weren't words designed to calm Kercher down, but she wanted them to be clear about what they were asking of these people. She thought that Kercher was one of those who would see other peoples' sacrifices as existing on paper only unless they encountered them first hand.

"What is this elected council?" Kercher asked their guide as they walked through an archway and into a huge garden. The entire place was warm and humid, moisture prickling on Prab's skin after so long on the ship.

She felt a spike of home sickness for the botanic gardens of Sirajah's Reach. She remembered picking guava and anabak fruits there during the pick-your-own windows each month. She'd take fresh crackers and would lie with her head in Mari's lap reading old histories after they'd gorged themselves on fruit and synthesised cheese all washed down with cheap sparkling wine.

The smell of petrichor in the air left her stood still, eyes wide and breathing deeply. Sirajah's Reach had none of the glory of the worlds of the Arcology, but its gardens had offered some little respite from the singular sterility of the rest of the city.

"Is everything okay?" asked their guide, looking nervous.

Prab closed her eyes and breathed in one deep, deep breath. "I'm okay," she said.

Their guide cocked their head at Prab, eyes narrowed, but after a moment they gave a tiny little shrug and turned to continue on. "They're waiting for us."

"The council?" asked Prab, forcing her feet to start walking again. It wouldn't do to arrive in tears, so it would be clenched jaw and sucking hard until the urge subsided.

"How does it work?" asked Kercher.

"Everyone here gets a vote. We decide together on matters which concern us. People vote as they see fit and anyone can bring a proposal forward for voting on."

"How many of you are there?"

"A little over a million of us."

"Wow," said Prab. She'd never heard of this kind of self-organisation. Within the Arcology the nodes let people do as they wished, but the empire was run quietly and efficiently by those nodes interested in making things work. Sirajah's Reach had been organised around interests. People who made things, bought things, imported and exported things. The Arcology had handled the infrastructure and everything else was managed with currency – those who had it getting to decide how it was spent.

Prab had never really found it effective, but because the Arcology ensured water, power and air were plentiful, she'd never really worried about the greedier citizens of the city and the selfish decisions they made.

"How does anything get done?" asked Kercher, their voice filled with disgust and disbelief.

"Local communities of a thousand or so elect representatives and those representatives decide on everything within that scope. For larger decisions those representatives come together in the council and vote."

"And whoever gets the most votes wins?" asked Kercher.

"No," said their guide. "Sometimes a simple majority is appropriate, but often there are more than two options or no right or wrong and in those cases the voting slate will reflect such nuances."

Prab thought it would take a lot of time to run a community this way.

"Not everyone is ready to decide on their lives," said the guide plainly.

"I left the Arcology too," said Prab.

"That doesn't qualify anyone for anything," came the response.

Prab shut up for a bit.

"The station delegated most of its systems to us so everything you see is created and maintained by those who live here. The botanic gardens didn't exist when we first arrived."

They arrived at a small pagoda surrounded by water. In the water were large iridescent fish, lazily holding position in the gentle flow. Large crabs picked their way through the vegetation as if they were searching for a delicate treasure. A butterfly as big as Prab's fist landed on the finial of the red wood-finish fence that ran around the edge of the waterway. A small ornate bridge painted in green and silver crossed the water into the pagoda.

Inside, on benches, were the four people from their initial interview.

Stood there with Kercher, the guide dipped their chin to the four and departed without saying goodbye. Around them in the gardens, people went about tending for the life there without any regard for what was happening so close to them.

After being watched coming into the space, Prab realised these people were only pretending at working. They were there to intervene if Prab and Kercher proved to be untrustworthy. They weren't staring with idle curiosity, they were paying careful attention while trying to look like they weren't.

It was almost comical.

"I'm no threat to anyone," she said as the older man indicated a space where she and Kercher should sit.

"You might not be," he agreed. "They, however, are absolutely a danger."

"I mean you no harm," said Kercher.

"You'll forgive us for not taking you at your word, pilot," said the woman with whom they'd first spoken.

I have to take control of this, thought Prab. "I'm Praveenthi Saal. I'm called Prab by my friends. I'm an Interlocutor, a role

I accepted after leaving the Arcology. This is Kercher. They are a pilot for our ship, Hanuman." She left out the part where Kercher was a convicted criminal serving at the Arcology's leisure for a heresy directly opposed to leaving the Arcology.

"Why are you here?" asked the one member who'd not spoken to them yet, the androgynous human. In person they were tall and thin like Kercher. Was it possible they too had once been a pilot?

Trying not to be distracted, Prab took her eyes off them and looked at each of the others in turn.

"You have granted us asylum and for that we thank you. I thank you. But if we're to become community then it would be great if we could start not with agendas but with names. You are?" She returned her gaze to her questioner.

They nodded, accepting her gentle rebuke. "I'm Relian. Head of Logistics. This is Jura, head of people." They indicated the second woman who was clearly someone used to lifting heavy objects and putting them down again. Broad shoulders strained against a wrapped shirt that folded and pulled against her body.

"I'm Anaisha," said the first woman. "We have met. I speak for the council." In person her red eyes were complimented by hands that were rust coloured, shading darker as they hit her wrists. Her sandaled feet were similar. When she smiled Prab noticed a green sheen to her teeth.

"And I'm Etheloed. I fix things." He had smaller eyes, one of which was clearly mechanical. His body was hidden beneath light pink slacks and a loose linen shirt but Prab could see from how he shifted in his chair that he was absolutely comfortable in his body.

He does not fix machines but situations, thought Prab with a chill. Those people pretending at gardening around them were waiting for his signal to intervene.

"You may or may not know what has happened and why we found ourselves asking for your help," Prab started.

"We know more than you think," said Relian.

"We know everything," said Anaisha.

Cut off, Prab let them continue. When people were exercised enough to talk over her, she always let them continue until they ran out of steam.

"You probably thought we were isolated and cut off out here," said Anaisha, and the disdain dripped from her words. "Of course you would. How could we possibly survive without the support of the great Arcology? You're probably shocked we still wear clothes and feed ourselves."

Prab could remind them she was also Excluded but it was pointless because they weren't listening. Not yet anyway. She flagged to Kercher to stay quiet and hoped they'd listen to her advice.

She did not need an argument to memorialise their first meeting with their hosts.

"We have contact with a great many other cultures and none of them try to control us or tell us their way is the right way of living."

Kercher was growing tense next to her and Prab, feeling she had no choice, reached out and tapped their leg with her fingers. It was enough to jolt Kercher out of their rising anger.

"The Operand told us you'd be coming. They warned us." The other three were also shifting and Prab could see they weren't entirely happy with what Anaisha was saying. Which was good, it gave Prab room to move when the rant finally stopped. The big red flag though was the Operand. What were they doing out here and how could they have known they'd be coming this way?

"We don't need you. We don't want you. You bring trouble to our door and ask us to handle it for you. We don't want to be drawn into your war. The Arcology can fall. The galaxy will move on and we'll be properly free."

"Are you finished?" asked Prab. Anaisha's face said she had more to say but her lips quivered with nothing more than unsaid half-formed sentences.

"The people we brought with us need your help. They are not a part of this. And please, I would remind you I'm also one of the Excluded. I am the reason those people are alive and the reason why we're asking for your help."

"Of course," said Anaisha, "because the ships with you would have evicted us and got on with their plans regardless of our fate."

Which was close enough to the truth Prab wished she'd never mentioned her role in securing their help.

"It doesn't matter," she tried. Anaisha folded her arms and the others looked on, silent now, their earlier misgivings about Anaisha's anger allayed as Prab spoke and distanced them from needing to intervene. "If there was any previous lack of clarity, we have since willingly agreed to your terms. The station has made its intentions clear. No one would be crass enough to try to evict anyone."

"We don't want you here," said Anaisha again.

"Anaisha," said Jura. "Please stick to the facts. The community has agreed to the request for asylum. We have misgivings. We are nervous, but we are agreed they are welcome."

Anaisha hissed her irritation but it was directed at the sky not her companion.

Jura continued speaking now Anaisha was silent. "We have logistics to manage. After this meeting Relian will contact your ship."

"Hanuman," corrected Prab.

Jura nodded briefly then continued. "They'll handle the capacity Hanuman needs for safe storage of its cargo. As for your people, I'm informed there are just under six dozen. Is that all you were able to save?"

Those figures couldn't be right. Hanuman told her only nine had died. They'd had more than a hundred on board. Jura kept speaking but her words were nothing more than white noise.

A hand on her arm. Kercher returning the favour. Prab looked down then up at their face, saw that they'd known in their eyes. She wanted to bite down so hard her teeth would shatter.

Noise and light came funnelling back in.

"Of course," she said. "Sirajah's Reach was caught unawares and our infrastructure relied much more on the Arcology than you do here."

She had her suspicions that the station here was disconnected from the network and this alone had saved them. They'd consider themselves better than her but if they were alive, it was as much an accident as Sirajah's demise.

"I did what I could. I am grateful you will allow them to live among you."

Prab wiped a tear from her eye.

"You did well," said Jura, and there was genuine kindness in her voice.

Prab did not agree.

"All I've done is run away. My family were still in the Arcology but they died before what was left of it could be saved. Sirajah's Reach suffocated to death while I fled, lucky enough to receive a call up from Hanuman. I watched as people scrambled to get a place on the ship only to die as we took off. Nothing I've done has worked." She'd started now and there was no going back.

"I tried to negotiate and the Otto and the Operand already knew everything. They abandoned us to our fate. I tried to understand what the enemy wanted and failed at that too. Nothing I've done has helped, Jura. I'm here, now, with only half the people who left Sirajah's Reach and I didn't even know."

"I'm sorry," said Hanuman in her mind. "They died while I was somewhere else. This is not your fault."

"The worst of it," said Prab. "The very fucking worst of it is that I know it's not my fault. How could it be? I didn't enrage an unknown hostile culture. I didn't have responsibility for Sirajah's Reach, or Hanuman, or even the people I persuaded him to bring on board. I can't pilot a ship, I am not part of the Arcology. All of that just makes it worse because I never could have done anything about this and here I am alive while all those who could have helped are dead.

"All I wanted was to be left alone to live my life, to read my books." She stopped. There was more there, but guilt and shame were driving her now and this was supposed to be a diplomatic conversation, not therapy.

No one said anything for a minute then two. Prab's body shook, her skin was pale and grey.

Eventually Jura stood up and came over to her. Kercher shuffled aside to make room.

"I'm sorry, Praveenthi. This must have been very hard."

Prab shook her head, and in that effort she tried her best to pull what remained into a functioning person. Jura sounded genuine but she didn't want to be patronised and she couldn't handle her compassion. She would get extraordinarily drunk at the earliest opportunity and find someone to fuck and then lock up her feelings deep down.

"Thank you," she managed, and wiped away the tears from her eyes. "I'm sorry. It's been hard. Look, I'm not trying to derail our conversation. I watched Sirajah's Reach die. I saw Akhanda fall."

"That's why we don't want you here," snapped Anaisha. "You bring your troubles with you."

"Anaisha," said Relian firmly, and the woman subsided.

At this point the hostility was nothing more than noise. Prab had lost her family, her friends and, now, the sense of whatever she'd managed to save in the face of that disaster.

"What you have achieved is no small thing," said Jura, and she stood, better able to address everyone in the pagoda. "You will be remembered, Praveenthi Saal, and you are welcome among us for as long as you need."

"This doesn't change our requirements," said Relian.

"I will need to properly debrief you and your pilot," said Etheloed. "But we have a luxury you have not enjoyed recently: time. Please, make yourselves comfortable, have some real food and get some proper sleep and then we can talk."

Prab could hear it was an appointment, not an invitation.

"There are medications we can issue should you need them to stymie your grief," said Jura.

Prab knew the impact drugs would have, the relief of being lifted out of an acid bath and given respite but right now she wanted nothing more than to feel that pain. You deserve this, she thought angrily.

"Before we finish, how many ships are coming here?" asked Etheloed.

"We thought we were the last," said Kercher. "Every single one of them is a surprise to us."

Etheloed nodded as if unsurprised. "Your ship may have a better idea."

Kercher shook their head. "Hanuman was damaged. He is not what he once was."

"That is true but not accurate," said Hanuman into Prab's mind, but he did not correct Kercher before the others.

"You wanted to meet us." said Prab. They'd only said things they could have said remotely. There was something they wanted to say, something they felt needed to be done in person.

"The galaxy knows the Arcology has fallen," said Etheloed. Anaisha looked like she was about to explode. "We have had people come here already seeking the station, seeking the technology here, the wealth, as they see it, ripe for plundering.

"We don't worry about them much, they have always seen us as vulnerable, but the station keeps us safe. But this enemy. It's something else, and we won't have you bring that war here. None of us will survive it. You understand that."

Prab nodded, knowing what was coming.

"Unless you have a way to defeat them, then we cannot let your ships stay. We cannot let them unfold the Arcology here. It will be struggle enough to defend against those like the Shahar without worrying when the real enemy will arrive."

"They'll come here eventually," said Kercher.

"You don't know that," said Relian.

"Even if you're right, we have time that you're shortening by your presence," said Etheloed.

"How many people have died since you arrived?" asked Prab.

"What?" asked Anaisha.

"How many people have died?"

They looked at her with blank expressions.

"None. You know how I know this? Because you're Excluded. You left the Arcology. Just like me. You took the basics, just like me. No privacy veils for us, eh?" Jura smiled at this and Prab rushed on.

"And one of those basics were technologies to extend healthy lives indefinitely."

"That technology doesn't use ibits," said Etheloed.

And you can guarantee nothing here does?" she asked.

"We are entirely physical," said Relian proudly.

"And the station?" she asked, keeping her voice gentle while grief slowly fed into purpose again.

"The station doesn't either. This is why you're so dangerous."

Hanuman was already in her ear as she thought he would be. The station was deep in information space. It's observations of the planet's moons relying on Arcology technology for their effectiveness.

"You're wrong," she said.

Anaisha was on her feet and this time no one moved to calm her down.

"What?" asked Prab, knowing she was about to poke already angry hornets. "You think the station tells you everything? It seems to me that it just wants to be left in peace. You've done that, but the problem there"–and here she looked at her fingers as if she was bored of explaining–"is that information asymmetry will get you killed. You have what you need, but the station's provided you with nothing more because it hasn't needed to and wasn't prepared to. It was unresponsive towards us, and Hanuman is an Arcology enforcer. That kind of insouciance comes from not giving a fuck, not from being a kindly old scientist."

Anaisha came right up to her, Jura moving to intercept but too slow to get between them. Prab remained sitting, her heart pounding in her chest. This was where she loved being, and despite everything going on, the thrill of having someone right where she wanted them soared in her spirit like a bright sun-bound comet.

Bending over, Anaisha poked Prab right in the chest. "You think you know what's going on. You don't even know who your enemy is."

"Our enemy," said Prab flatly. It was taking every ounce of her self-control to remain upright instead of leaning back. She wanted to get distance and then to punch Anaisha. She couldn't afford to do what she wanted.

Then a revelation.

"You know what it is."

Anaisha froze. They all did.

"You let us on here, gave us a hard time, and you knew all along."

"We don't know what you're talking about" said Etheloed.

"Don't lie to us," said Prab.

"Don't have your ship read us," snapped Anaisha.

"As if I'd need that," sneered Prab.

Anaisha stepped back, the anger transformed into something else.

Prab wasn't really paying attention. The question for her was how they could know.

In her mind Hanuman was there, asking the same thing.

"How long have you known?" asked Kercher.

"We don't know what you're talking about," said Etheloed.

"We don't know anything," reiterated Relian. Anaisha fell back further. "So there is no period of time since we've known."

"So what now?" asked Prab. "I keep asking and you keep lying?"

"You have free run of the station," said Jura, hands out in front of her, gesturing for everyone to stay calm. "We will provide your ships what they require, but our previous requirements remain in place. The Arcology to leave as soon as they are able."

Prab wasn't listening at all. It had to be the Operand. Had they colonised the Excluded here?

Kercher was on their feet.

"Don't," she said, but her heart wasn't in it because the calculus had changed.

Kercher's body hummed but they gave her one look as if to ask her to stop them.

Prab did not move and with that lack, Kercher acted.

40.

They'd counted nine people pretending to care for the garden. Plus the four of them who'd come to talk. Thirteen.

Kercher didn't care about Relian, Jura or Anaisha, despite the anger rolling off her.

Etheloed was different – a man built for conflict.

Kercher didn't head for him. The space was too close and Prab was in the way. They leapt over the rail of the pagoda, over the water and into the gardens. They could have attempted to take one of the four hostage, but it was clear these four weren't the head of the beast.

Something more severe was required to get the attention of those in charge.

Moving so fast the first gardener they reached was only just opening their eyes in surprise, Kercher tranquilised them without pausing, tagging the second and third before a half dozen seconds had passed. None of them would be up and around for about an hour, if they were in standard printed bodies.

Which left half a dozen others and Etheloed who was moving obliquely to intercept them at the fifth of the gardeners.

To their credit the fourth and fifth were a little faster, meshed muscles and implants giving them advantages that would make for great police officers among ordinary printed people.

Kercher was no ordinary person. As deadly as Hanuman and primed to go off when required.

The fourth guard was tall and thin, as if they too had been printed for piloting duties, but instead they were just fragile and lanky. They had a weapon in their hands; a modified pistol Kercher recognised as Arcology issue. Nothing lethal, before it had been tinkered with.

A palm under the jaw sent them flying and the neurotoxin they'd secreted onto their skin had them down.

Kercher met the fifth and sixth together in a whirl. They threw the sixth at Etheloed's advance and grasped hold of the fifth who managed to get a shot off. Their discharge went wide, fired almost vertically.

Kercher wondered how many of them had ever fought in earnest.

Down to three plus Etheloed.

Etheloed warned the remaining guards about coming into contact with Kercher. People were shouting at them to stop, to calm down. In their head Hanuman was demanding that they think about what they were doing.

Prab was notably silent and Kercher believed it was because she realised what Kercher was trying to do.

Besides, Kercher was not about to let these fucks lie and put the Arcology's only hope at risk.

There was someone waiting and watching this and with sufficient motivation, Kercher knew they could force them to reveal themselves.

Etheloed was the only real roadblock, and once dealt with, Kercher was confident they'd get a real conversation.

Their head of security knew what he was about. No grandstanding, no delay, just action without speaking.

Etheloed sent in the other three and as they tried to flank Kercher, the fixer ran for the pagoda.

Prab.

Kercher saw her realise moments too late. They were forced to rush the three remaining guards, who'd taken out charged batons, to get to her. Kercher could ignore them and risk being stunned to get to Prab before Etheloed or do what they had to do and leave her at risk.

The calculation was simple; Kercher was no good to anyone if they were neutralised. They could worry about Prab later.

Reaching for the wrist of the first, Kercher turned their baton against the second, spinning around an incoming body and shoving them away. The second slumped backwards and with a shift of their weight they threw the first head over heels at the third.

With a cry the first of the guards plunged into the water running around the pagoda.

Kercher left them to it, concentrating on the third who was coming back around, waving their baton carefully in a figure of eight. Kercher was simply too fast and, seeing the movement, tracked it and lunged past their guard as the baton went to their outside. A palm on the chest, a foot on top of their foot and they snapped back at the knees. Their baton stayed in their hands but Kercher touched them, almost gently, on the forehead and they were unconscious a fraction of a second later.

The tunnel through which they were seeing the world widened to show five people in the pagoda and the very last guard picking themselves up out of the water.

Kercher took a step and then saw the gun at Prab's temple.

"This is not a stun weapon," said Etheloed.

"You harm her and I will kill every one of you on this station myself and then hand it to the Arcology with my blessing," said Kercher very calmly.

They watched as those around Etheloed blanched.

Prab's eyes were wide but Kercher didn't care what she thought. This was the way it had to be.

They took a step towards the pagoda.

"Enough," said Etheloed from Prab's side.

"Release her now," said Kercher. "I won't ask again."

A big thick layer of matted paint peeled itself from the underside of the pagoda.

Etheloed dragged Prab out of the way as it fell to the floor.

"Do not interfere," said Jura, but the mat was busy changing its shape into something resembling a giant saltshaker, mottled brown and green, it was wide at the bottom, tapering slightly to a rounded top. There were no limbs, no visible organs, just a smooth surface that looked like jelly.

"Oh, yes, and let you mammals/hosts succumb to your ridiculous prey drives and shoot one another," said the saltshaker. "Honestly, I wonder why we bother with your species/type of housing. All of you are the same, big complex structures/colonies are nearly always stubborn and full of their own misplaced sense of worth/endurance."

An Operand, thought Kercher.

"That was not who I thought would be in charge," said Hanuman in their head.

"I don't think they are," said Prab.

Kercher assumed no one else was listening in to their chat but the presence of the Operand had been a surprise to all of them, so who knew what else this culture had within its colonial treasure chest.

A frond emerged from the saltshaker and snapped its fingers. "Your attention too," it said to Kercher. "You have these lovely little micro expressions/giant tells when you're talking inside your head. Micro expressions/giant tells for you are astronomical/worlds for us, makes you terribly easy to read/manipulate."

"What do you call yourselves?" asked Prab.

"Ah, a sensible question."

"You're not in charge here," said Etheloed.

"You're here by our invitation," said Jura.

"We are here/fractioned because this concerns us/you together. You might think it's smart to pretend/deceive you're neutral to all of this, to allow your childish/overgrown concerns about colonialism/symbiosis and freedom/illusion and personal/loneliness expression to justify sticking your head in the proverbial stomach of the heifer/perfect host but we aren't here because your thoughts match/converge on ours."

Kercher relaxed although only a little. They weren't sure how they'd render a colony made up of billions of lives unconscious. They weren't even sure it was a thing a colony of bacteria could be.

Etheloed did not move either.

Jura threw her hands up and sat down, she was followed by Relian, but Anaisha moved to stand on the other side of Prab.

As if she'd dare do anything, thought Kercher, who saw in the woman a tendency to let her anger carry her over others' opinions but who didn't have anything to back it up. She might break herself on someone who wouldn't be moved, but any damage she did would be a result of stubbornness, not capability.

"Kercher," said Hanuman in their mind. "De-escalate. Your strategy here was to bring this event about. You have succeeded and there is no need to continue pulling on a used lever."

It was impossible to know if the saltshaker was regarding them but Kercher sensed some change in them even as they were falling into a more relaxed stance.

"Your people are unharmed," said Kercher.

"That remains to be seen," said Anaisha but Kercher saw Etheloed nod his understanding.

The gun came away from Prab's head just after. Prab took a moment to gather her wits and then stepped away from everyone until she was out of the pagoda and on the other side of the pond.

"We should talk/share fluids," said the Operand. "It would be better if you/Praveenthi came back here so we can do that without you raising your voices."

"I'm covered in bacteria," said Kercher to Hanuman. "What's stopping them from co-opting me entirely.

"You're quite safe," said Hanuman.

"We mean/intend you no harm/colonisation," said the Operand. "We call ourselves Sea of Thought Drifting. We are but a fragment/fraction/independent state of the Sea's full host but enough of us are here that this colony represents the views/impulses of the whole."

"Where's the rest of you?" asked Prab.

"That's hardly important/classified right now."

"Call it a trust-building exercise," said Prab.

The saltshaker called Sea of Thought Drifting twirled on its base like a wobbly blancmange. "Our vessel/home/grown is docked here in the station. We came as a representative/parcel. The ocean of which we are a part resides on habitats starting eighteen light years from here and extending more than fifty in most directions.

"We have been on friendly terms with your Excluded here and on Kith's Observatory itself for nearly thirty thousand rotations."

"You see this as your territory," said Prab, with discovery in her voice.

"They know the station's name," said Hanuman, with equal wonder in his.

Prab turned to the four leaders and said, "You know the Operands are a colonising culture. The Otto and several others are integrated into their volume. They're no better than slavemasters."

"Now," said Sea of Thought Drifting. "Each to their own/ expansion impulses. We have not been waiting here for you to throw barbs about who's empire is the most oppressive/ overwhelming."

Kercher was listening with interest. They knew Prab was the lead here but they were also frantically trying to understand how they'd not spotted the bone ship within the structure of the station.

Had Kith's Observatory hidden them, did they have technology the Arcology didn't know about? What else don't we know? they thought.

Whether it was because Prab found the Arcology unpalatable or because she saw no point in enflaming things all over again, Kercher saw her body soften and change.

The Operand must have seen the same thing because it jittered about as if dancing on its base and said, "Good. Perhaps good judgement/collaboration can prevail. You are facing an existential crisis."

"And you're proposing to help fight the Face of Loss?" asked Prab.

"Goodness no," said the Sea of Thought Drifting.

"You cannot fight them here," said Relian.

"Our dear friends. If we could get a word in edgewise that would be excellent. Can you all agree to shut your individual airways for long enough for us to explain why we're here and what our interests/impulses are?"

"I'm sorry," said Prab.

"No, you're not," said Kercher in her mind, thinking it was funny to call her out.

"Shut up," she replied, without any sense she appreciated their attempt at humour.

"Are we agreed?" asked Sea of Thought Drifting.

"Please," said Prab.

"As you wish," said Jura. Slowly, Jura first, the Excluded sat down next to one another along two sides of the pagoda.

Sea of Thought Drifting shuffled to the edge of the pagoda and occupied the exit closest to Kercher with the Excluded on one side and Prab on their other.

"You can help me manufacture an antibacterial?" Kercher asked Hanuman.

"I've updated your body already," said the ship. "Just don't start making it, I cannot tell how effective they are at reading your biome."

"No need to alarm it," said Kercher.

"You have met another of our colonies/kin," said Sea of Thought Drifting. "They gave you the rudiments/uninformed of our history although your behaviour on their station left them disinclined to be transparent. They were interrupted by scavengers eager to pick over your bones/colonise you.

"So let us proceed as if they hadn't spoken.

"We are a culture/impulse that predates the Arcology by geological amounts of time. We have been spacefaring for a similar amount of time. We, like many others, understood what you call information space early. And we spread. Glorious times they were full of nourishment and expansion.

"Then our tendrils encountered the predators you are suffering under now."

Sea of Thought Drifting shivered and grew a few inches, becoming thinner in the process and for all the worlds Kercher was certain it was settling down to tell them a story.

"All of which is a long way of saying that we were travelling the stars before you were wearing clothes. We tried fighting the enemy and we pushed back and forth with it for a thousand orbits of our origin host before we understood there was no defeating it/accommodating it.

"We hid/made small ourselves and abandoned/adapted what we had become in order that what was left might continue to find/expand its way through time."

Kercher wasn't interested in hearing the tale of how they'd lost. They wanted to hear how to win. There had to be a way to win.

"When your kind appeared we approached them with a warning, Kith's Observatory heeded us and, possibly, passed that information on to the rest of your Arcology. What you did with that we do not know. We believed our duty/respect to other lives satisfied."

Kercher understood now why the station was silent – it had prepared for this disaster. The problem of allowing people in community to decide what they wanted to do was you ended up with Kith's Observatory – someone with crucial information keeping it to themselves and making sure they were okay, and no one else mattered as long as they were all right.

Kith's Observatory was the node equivalent of an Excluded. The difference being it still had all the benefits of being part of the Arcology with none of the responsibility.

"It never told us," said Hanuman.

"Perhaps we wouldn't listen," said Prab.

"There's no record of this anywhere."

"What do they want?" asked Prab, and Kercher thought she might fall apart right there. The pressure on her, the discovery that those she'd tried to save had largely been lost. All of it was taking its toll.

"It feeds on information. The denser that information the better/more nourishing. It came out of the galactic core, dark against the blaze of the stars towards the hub. We must have shone like a protein marker to a virus.

"Like you it took a long time for us to understand What we were facing/meeting/expanding into. We've met others who understood/exploited information. You are not the first."

A pause; how the Operands would meet those who came after the Arcology as well, unsaid.

"How many?" asked Kercher.

"Four others. We are the only ones who continue/remain to follow our paths," said Sea of Thought Drifting.

Kercher tried to think about this.

"Face of Loss beat everyone?" asked Prab, with slumped shoulders.

"Those others were eaten or absorbed," said the Operand. "There is no beating it, no conversation, no negotiation. It has no worlds, no places. It isn't like you and it isn't like us. It does not build, it does not think, it does not yearn and it does not plan."

Kercher knew the Operand were different to the Arcology. They were a culture of microbes whose decision making, if it could be called that, emerged out of the drives of hundreds of different types of bacteria working together in synchrony. No awareness and a consciousness of a different category than that of nervous system-based entities. A rare evolutionary outcome but no rarer than apes or spiders or cephalopods or varanusian convergence. The latter species might have individuality, but the former had community in a way the Arcology aspirationally built towards but never reached.

"It will find you/expand here," said Sea of Thought Drifting.

"You cannot stay," said Relian. "Do you see that? If you do, we are all dead."

"You would send us off to die elsewhere," said Prab dully.

None of them answered her.

"There has to be something," said Kercher. "We're hidden from them. We destroyed their ships when they came for Akhanda. We can find a way to beat them. We only need the Arcology unfolded so we can plan our counterattack."

"You're here because you planned ahead," said the Operand.

"They are right," said Hanuman. "The ships in-system planned for this."

And look where it got them, thought Kercher, seeing their defeat written large across the faces in front of them.

"We are happy to share what we know/experience with you," said Sea of Thought Drifting.

"I have heard all this before," said Anaisha with no interest in her voice.

"I would join you," said Etheloed. Relian expressed their interest as well.

Prab slumped.

"She needs time," said Hanuman.

"We don't have time," said Kercher.

"We need her. So find what time you can," said the ship, and Kercher realised it was an order.

41.

Nothing the Operand said was encouraging.

"They fought them for an age," said the old ship when Hanuman relayed the stream of what they'd witnessed. "They never prevailed. But they never found a way to hide themselves except to abandon their access to information space. There is hope yet."

"We don't know that," said Hanuman. "The facts are only that they fought them and lost badly enough they decided to abandon the very thing that made them a target. They may well have hidden themselves just as we have only for the enemy to see through it in time and continue their war."

The other ship was silent for a while.

"What do you think about how they speak of the enemy?" Hanuman asked.

Outside the ship the station was slowly rolling out connection points. Regardless of what the Excluded were demanding, Kith's Observatory was quietly providing Hanuman exactly what he needed to unfold the Arcology. By his estimates just a few more hours and they could restore as much as could be supported here.

Which wasn't much compared to that stored inside of him and buried in information space, but he expected it to transform their situation. With even a fraction of the Arcology restored they would have resources and nodes to use. They would have options.

He turned his thoughts to Prab and to her loss. There was no retrieving her parents or any part of that community. They had been excised very early in the assault, when the Arcology had understood the attack as a corruption. It had cut pieces of itself away in an attempt to keep the rest undamaged.

A foolish strategy but the best one at that point in the encounter. Sacrifice the few to save the many. The stress of that loss flared in her body like a meteor shower no matter how hard she pushed down. In time she would have to reckon properly with that loss.

"They speak of it, not they. So a culture without consciousness. Perhaps without awareness either. Yet still sentient."

"We have encountered this classification before," said Hanuman, as parts of the Arcology's history unfurled in his thinking.

"Not like this. Always a type of being contained within spacetime."

"It shouldn't be a surprise that something similar swims through information space," said Hanuman.

"And yet here we are," said the ship.

"I've been thinking," said Hanuman. "You need a name."

"I am but one of many who contributed to this strategy," said the ship, and Hanuman understood it wasn't interested in being named.

"You may not wish a name, and that is a commendable approach to honouring your kin, but I disagree and the Arcology within me demands it."

The ship was quiet – there was no arguing with Hanuman now, he was the Arcology's avatar, its one and only deva, and even when the Arcology restored itself he would sit at the front of what was to come.

If they survived, Hanuman would replace Akhanda.

"The kinds of behaviour we've witnessed with this class of intelligence in spacetime is worrying," said Hanuman, knowing the matter of names was settled but uncomfortable with forcing a name on someone who didn't want it. It could wait for another time. "It doesn't recognise sentience because it cannot. There is no reasoning with it. Our history shows we normally divert them where they will not harm citizens."

"In spacetime you can blow them up, even the big ones," said the ship.

"We did the same at Akhanda," replied Hanuman. Memories of the gargantuan curve of information space breaking across the ringworld like a claw would never leave him. For all their efforts they'd been an ant against a tree.

"What went wrong?" asked the ship.

"There was no defence readied. Even if there were I'm not sure we could have done much more than slow them down." Hanuman told the ship about the attack, about how Akhanda had been torn to pieces. He had plenty of footage.

"You're responsible for the cube," said Hanuman.

"We put the contingency in place," confirmed the ship.

"Could you not have prepared us better?"

"We could not predict the form of the disaster, only that it was possible," said the ship. "We didn't even get this world right. Kith's Observatory planting itself here like an unexpected comet has thrown our calculations out."

Hanuman thought about Sea of Thought Drifting and wondered if the colony had witnessed the Operands" war with this enemy first hand. He knew it was a mistake to think of them like that – the individual microbes wouldn't live that long, and the gestalt could not have witnessed that war to remember it. Instead, Sea of Thought Drifting was an organism that carried its memory in its physical body for all to live with. A stimulus encoded into the colony's behaviour, a kind of recall for sure but not memory by any standard the Arcology measured it.

Prab or Kercher wouldn't recognise it as being different to knowing they shouldn't bang their elbow on a sharp point.

Translating the colony's communications was handled by autonomous systems deep within Hanuman's insides but they worked hard to turn the idioms and concepts used by other cultures into those used by the Arcology. It meant that for cultures where intelligence wasn't built around individual consciousness, the gap between what that culture was saying and what Hanuman saw could be substantial.

That the Operand knew more than the Arcology about this enemy was obvious, but what they knew felt beyond understanding.

"Could you communicate more directly with the Operands?" he asked the rescuer ship.

"Any of us can," said the ship. "The question is whether we have the time to make the changes necessary to our sentience and then do the work of translating our own experience back into something we can use."

"What would be your advice then?"

"We should be preparing for war." The rescuer ship was without hesitation.

"You heard Sea of Thought Drifting," said Hanuman. "They could not beat it across eons of conflict."

"The Arcology is not the Operands."

Which as a statement was both entirely true and entirely unhelpful.

Hanuman could see nearly twelve hundred Arcology ships in system. The initial flood of arrivals had slowed to a trickle, down to ten or so arriving an hour. They were being neatly folded into the veil the ships had created to hide them. An armada of sorts as each of them were refitting for conflict.

Most of the arrivals were those who'd been outside the Arcology when it was attacked. Twelve were from the rescuer ship's generation. It reported high losses but that this was to be expected.

Hanuman guessed they had as many ships now as they'd had at the defence of Akhanda. Enough to defeat any culture they'd ever encountered except the one they'd not known of until the fight was brought to them.

With this combined might present in one place, the rescuer ship's advice made sense. Yet Hanuman didn't think it was the right course of action.

"There is no gain in fighting an enemy whose agenda and strategy we do not understand," said Hanuman. "We would throw ourselves against the ocean and hope for the sea to roll back as a result."

"I'm sure they'll care when they find us."

Not preparing was stupid, Hanuman knew that.

"Then lead the preparation," he instructed the ship. It wanted to do this and he didn't want to get involved with something when he could feel the nub of insecurity rubbing at his thoughts.

The rescuer ship took the job willingly and faded from Hanuman's identity.

Hanuman's contemplation was interrupted by a communication from the station telling him the connections were in place and they could start the process of rolling out the Arcology.

Which sounded simple, but first they'd need to build the computational capacity for the Arcology to exist here in the physical world which would then allow it to properly exist within information space.

Hanuman expected them to have a fraction of a fraction of a percentage of the Arcology supported here. Nevertheless it would allow them to progress, to build back over time.

Many nodes had speculated about the possibility of transcending into information space entirely but no one had proceeded to make that possible. The Arcology remained anchored in physical space as much as its citizens existed almost exclusively within information space.

It's an arrangement with significant weaknesses, thought Hanuman.

Thanking the station's pixies for the update, Hanuman started the processes for building what he needed to restore the Arcology. Hours to go, but what was hours spent preparing compared with being alive again.

He had high hopes that given time and space, the Arcology could rapidly come to some decisions about what to do next.

"You're the Arcology" was a refrain he wasn't happy with despite it being more or less true. Hanuman was only just at the beginning of understanding what it meant to be so tied into the fundamental being of the empire. Once, he would have observed nodes such as Akhanda and recognised how much deeper and broader they were than him.

Oceans to his pond. And he had been fine with that difference.

Now he was a pond discovering it was actually an ocean and, to his own confusion and puzzlement, he knew the task ahead of him was to plumb his own depths, his own reaches, and see of what he was now capable.

Around him more than a thousand nodes waited for his instruction and he wasn't ready to give it, to accept the role. He could feel it growing within him, the sense of responsibility, of inevitability.

Hanuman did not want to lead anyone to their death, certainly not as both his first and last act as leader. It was not the plan had had laid out for himself.

Being a warship had been hugely satisfying. Becoming something more, something he didn't understand and, given the current situation, might never get the chance to, did not make for contentment.

Other nodes would have been happy to be in his hull, but he regarded these changes, that he wouldn't have opted for if they'd been offered, as having been forced upon him.

His name felt apt in so many ways. In the stories the monkey king always discovered a new power, which was really an old power he had forgotten he was capable of, just at the right moment. Life is no story, he thought. Best to know your limits early so you can prepare.

The hope to be someone so self-aware was laughable.

"Send me the raw data of Sea of Thought Drifting's communications," he instructed his little sprites, and they delivered reams of material to sift through. Maybe there was something in what the colony was saying that would give them a clue.

Hanuman left it alone, splitting his focus across that, the building of the substrate needed to unfold the Arcology and, finally, they thought about Prab and Kercher.

Instead of being with Prab, the pilot was working with the locals to decant the survivors of the trip from Sirajah's Reach onto the station.

Hanuman closed off the sections of himself with dead bodies inside and prepared them for rendering down to ash and ejection into the planet's atmosphere where they'd circulate for millions of years as echoes of what was lost.

There was no record in his systems of when so many had died. His sprites shrugged and explained they'd been busy trying to stop him dying – everything else had been an afterthought. All he could find was a window of time between the attack which had killed the first few and then Hanuman's realisation that so many more had perished too.

A hole in his identity that no prodding or poking would restore. Worse still, apart from fleeting hard to grasp images, he could not remember what had happened to him in between those two moments. The stories the sprites relayed were almost unbelievable but here they were, and here he was, part Arcology, part himself, part Hanuman. Two new identities from the ashes of his old self.

His deaths had been multiple and had come in many forms, he realised.

Hanuman wanted to talk to someone about death because no one died in the Arcology. Like him, nodes embodied as warships acknowledged they were the ones most at risk, but they proceeded as if it could never happen to them.

The rescue ships who'd turned themselves off until the Face of Loss invaded had trusted to fate that they'd ever wake up. He found it easy to dismiss their choice as one none of them associated with dying but it was there nonetheless.

Even elected deaths among the Arcology's citizens resulted in those so doing being stored somewhere in perpetuity, their consciousness spooled down, inactive, but maintained.

Kercher's archaic belief in needing to die notwithstanding, Hanuman could see how the edges of the Arcology would fray from this experience. Once restored, vast swathes of its citizens would never even know their lives had been interrupted, the timelines they lived on would exhibit no disruption. The millions of missing would be missed only by those who'd known them and in a population of trillions it wouldn't move the needle. Statistically speaking. The truth of it was the gaps would be noticed by families and friends, lovers and enemies alike. The questions would come, the investigations, the committees.

Knowledge of this catastrophe would spread gradually, but spread it would.

The first to understand would be those who ventured near the "Surface" of the Arcology, where it met the physical world. They would see information suggesting something had gone awry. Those few would see something no one had contemplated – that the Arcology could end, and end in the blink of an eye.

If they survived this, then Hanuman could foresee entire social trends around death, around preparing for uncertainty taking root as those nodes who cared for the empire's future tried to digest what had happened to them in this first contact.

What direction those reflections would take them in were largely forecastable, but Hanuman had no interest in knowing where the Arcology was headed. He only really wanted to be a warship on the borders, the Arcology's voice and hand among its neighbours.

Undertaking decades of social engineering, healing and societal-level manipulation in the name of cultural stability was of no interest to him at all.

Right now Prab was alone somewhere in the station. The location irrelevant compared to the fact of her isolation. He'd asked Kercher to attend to her and the pilot was, instead, doing a job any dock engineer could have managed.

And what about you? he asked himself.

He had died. And been reborn.

Don't start down Kercher's line of thinking, thought Hanuman. Best to think of it as having engaged properly in samsara.

But Hanuman didn't feel reborn, just overwhelmed. Algorithms on the edge of a divide by zero overwhelmed.

"Kercher," he said.

"Kind of busy here," said the pilot.

"We are all busy, pilot," said Hanuman, and Kercher stopped what they were doing to pay attention.

As they should have done the first time, thought Hanuman.

"I'm looking for her friend," said Kercher. "Mari."

Hanuman scanned the manifest and saw Mari was still alive. She'd yet to be decanted, was in the last dozen people to be brought off.

"Fine," said the ship, reluctantly. It was a good idea. Prab had shown a close attachment to this woman on Sirajah's Reach. "Make sure you're there when she's woken up and doubly so for when she meets Prab."

42.

Prab let the others fuck off. She refused to go with them at the edge of the botanical gardens, choosing instead to remain there for a while and think.

It turned out that reflection was a very bad idea. Unwanted memories, of parents, friends, books she'd left behind. None of it was welcome, but there it was anyway.

She could imagine Hanuman relieved and happy at the news the Arcology would be restored. She could imagine all those within what the cube had saved as eager to carry on with their lives.

Except for her parents. Except for those who'd died outside the Arcology's close embrace. Except for the dead aboard Hanuman.

Prab found herself on the main concourse leading towards the gardens. She turned down a corridor and emerged on another long street and guessed the station was built around a hub and spoke design with the gardens at the heart of the inhabited sections.

The station's sprites readily provided a map which laid out the three-dimensional space intuitively. They were unusually helpful and while she was pondering this one of them shyly informed her that Hanuman's sprites liked her and so they were keen to help her in any way they could.

The station was big. Much bigger than it had appeared when they'd ridden in on Hanuman.

A million people took up a lot of room and she reckoned she'd seen no more than a few hundred of them. The idea of so many living in this station, itself floating in perpetual darkness amid the storms of the gas giant within which they were hidden, wasn't something she could process.

Every face in the garden and on the street reminded her of her parents, of her brothers and sisters.

If she slowed to take in features and force the recognition that these people were nothing more than strangers, then Mari's face would come to mind and she'd be staggered all over again.

She needed a drink.

The station's guide pixie appeared in the air before her and, at her request, led her to a bar that served, in her words, dirty drinks and didn't care who drank them.

It was a low-slung but brightly lit den of people with visible augments and bodywear. They didn't look up as she entered.

Prab clocked replacement arms, legs, eyes. A couple of flattened noses, tagged and sculpted ears and a lot of shaved bodies as if hair itself brought uncomfortable associations. Her augmented system tagged them as engineers and system workers who did the filthy jobs like mending broken pipes, replacing valves and scrubbers. The kind of work the Arcology would have autonomous machines perform but which, here, the Excluded undertook.

Conversations were loud, determined, passionate. There was anger here and after standing at the bar for a minute listening, she realised they were discussing her and the rest of the crew she'd arrived with.

"What do you want?" asked the bartender, a person with heavy muscles, a few scattered tattoos that slithered over their skin proprietorially and a single eye that was the starkest lilac.

"To forget everything," she replied, and they laughed.

"I won't bother introducing myself then."

A bottle was handed to her along with a single shot glass and as she looked around, a hand came over her shoulder to point at an empty booth along the back wall.

Thanking the bartender who she decided was probably a man, Prab slouched into the booth and drank one, then two, then three shots without tasting the liquor she'd been handed.

There'd been no charge. She was sober enough to ask the station about currency.

They didn't use it here. Kith's Observatory provided them enough energy to manipulate basic elements into whatever they needed and so the idea of scarcity and, hence, needing to own things, was redundant.

On a whim, as her scalp prickled with the first flush of alcohol, Prab checked and found that less than thirty per cent of the population had registered occupations and those that did were engineers, scientists and gardeners.

She saw a few scattered artists among the wider population but nearly everyone else passed their time without logging it as labour.

This, then, was a worker's bar.

As far as the Excluded communities she knew went, Kith's Observatory was close to utopian. By which she meant it was close to the model of the Arcology.

The station registered no cultures present outside of the Arcology. Which, given the patronising lecture she'd received from an Operand, wasn't true.

She wondered what else was happening here under the surface.

"Not your problem," she said out loud, and took another shot.

The bottle was half empty when Hanuman appeared in her feed.

He'd chosen an avatar, brown hairy skin, black hair, deep black irises and a monkeyish face with bulging cheeks and thin lips. His arms were thick like tree trunks. His nose just a little too flat to be standard issue. A golden glow limned his projection as he sat opposite her.

"I asked Kercher come to find you," he said as an apology.

"I'm fine," she said, and twisted the bottle in her hands.

Hanuman's avatar was appearing only in her vision, projected there by Hanuman himself. She could ask for him to go away, or at the very least to stop co-opting her audio-visual processes, but there seemed little point.

There seemed little point to anything.

"I'm not okay," said Hanuman.

She raised her glass to toast him. "There's a queue."

A glass appeared in Hanuman's hand and he saluted her.

"You can't get drunk," she said.

"I can't get drunk," he said, but the glass didn't disappear.

"So, you want to talk then."

"I think I want to be quiet," said Hanuman.

"You're busy doing other things," she said.

"Parts of me are. The part that is here with you wants to be quiet."

"I'm here to destroy my mind," she said. She'd rather destroy herself but she was certain the station would intervene if she attempted anything so definitive.

They sat quietly for a while. Prab listened to the bar, listened to the life and it dragged at her heart like a rake, left her bleeding and drowning without dying. After a while she didn't hear their words, only the cadence and the sentiment.

These people don't understand, she realised. Or they didn't care. Perhaps one was because of the other.

She hated herself for thinking they'd understand soon enough. All this happiness would burn and these people would stop their noise and celebrations, their casual, unthinking joy.

"What did you want?" asked Hanuman

"We've been over this," said Prab.

"I mean, why did you leave the Arcology, Prab?"

"Can we please not?" she said.

"I don't care about your history," he said. "I'm trying to understand what you wanted."

"What's the point of me?" she asked angrily. "How about I don't care?"

"I'm sorry," he said.

"Don't be fucking sorry," she said, and there were tears that wouldn't be denied even as she reached the bottom of the bottle. Her mind was full of cotton and her mouth was sharp and dry.

A plate was thunked onto the table. It was the barman. His eye was a fiery violet.

"You look like you need to eat," he said, and was gone before she could tell him to take the dish away.

"He's right," said Hanuman.

"Oh. Good."

"You have family beyond those you lost."

Prab fixed him with a baleful glare.

"No one dies in the Arcology, Prab. You have generations of people stretching back."

"How many of them did the Arcology excise?" she asked bitterly. It wasn't even the point. Her mothers were estranged from their nearest family members because they refused to live in techno-utopian cities, preferring to live their lives in fantastical worlds where dragons and sea serpents roamed freely. Places where rivers and mountains, forests and oceans were alive, had their own spirits. Even if they were alive they had nothing in common. It was doubtful her more distant family even knew she existed. She'd certainly never spoken to any of them.

"You're not alone, if that is what worries you."

"I didn't leave the Arcology because I was lonely," she said.

"Then why? What did you think you'd get from it?"

Focussing was difficult but she could still talk just fine.

"I didn't want anything from it. The first time I left? I wanted to go places the translation network wouldn't take me. I wanted to visit worlds in the physical whose cultures were real, not simulated.

"There's something plastic about everything the Arcology builds even when it's real, even when it's accurate or genuinely emergent. The physical has other cultures, Hanuman. People who've never been worried about the things we worry about, who've tackled their problems without our ideas. I wanted to see all that and come back. There was no plan to stay away for good."

"What changed?"

Prab stared at her glass, at the empty bottle.

"My family never approved of me going sightseeing as they called it. Why not explore the Arcology, they'd ask. They kept on talking about its reach, how it had an infinite number of expressions, that I could never get bored."

"Lots of citizens spend their time exploring. Many of them make their own worlds," said Hanuman.

"Yes, they do," said Prab.

"You disapprove?" he asked.

"I don't care," said Prab. "I wanted something other people had made, and not other people who were just like me."

The ship didn't prod her.

Prab waved at the barman but he was busy serving other people. She wanted more to drink because she was not drunk enough, not by a long shot.

At a loss she tried the food. It was colourful and pretty, flowers daintily set upon small dark brown cubes that oozed a smell that made her mouth water. Around them a lively transparent green oil dripped into small pools. Picking one of the cubes up with her fingers, she popped it in her mouth and was instantly transported by the savoury, gummy taste on her tongue. The punch of salt and umami was enough to leave her sitting there, mind blank for a moment.

The rest of the dish was gone a short while later, leaving nothing but her lips covered in a thin film of salty grease she didn't want to remove.

"That looked good," said Hanuman.

"I made the mistake of calling the Arcology a simulation to their faces," she said.

"It is not a simulation," said Hanuman, and she felt the defensiveness in his tone.

"Yes, that's what they said."

"I'm sorry," said Hanuman after a moment.

"Other cultures think we uploaded our minds to a computer," said Prab. "They look at people like me and assume I've grown tired of living in a virtual world, that this body I'm wearing matches some authentic version of myself. It's impossible for them to conceive that I was born in the Arcology and this body is one I chose and refined to suit my taste, that it's the most artificial thing about me."

"That you're an intelligence created by other intelligences doesn't seem too difficult for them to understand," said Hanuman.

"Oh, they know you and the nodes are just that, but seeing a biological body, they short circuit. They are unable to hold it in their thinking that I'm wearing this body like a glove, rather than integrated into and defined by it."

"How does this relate to your story?" he asked.

She sniffed. "Boring you, am I?"

"No," he said hastily. Then stopped. "Funny."

The bar tender finally saw her waving and brought a second bottle to the table along with a bowl of seeds and nuts. He nodded approvingly at her plate and cleared away the empties.

"I thought it was my family. You know, pushing me to stay within the Arcology. But it wasn't. I realised pretty quickly that the Arcology didn't want me outside. I wanted to know why."

"And what did you find?" asked Hanuman.

"Chaos, uncertainty. Death." There it was again.

"That's all outside you though," said Hanuman.

Prab looked around. "Really?"

"This is now." The ship stopped short of telling her it didn't count, but she heard it anyway and, fuck him, he was right.

She tried again. "I found the Arcology gently and quietly overturning cultures it didn't approve of. Correcting those who it believed thought wrongly about things. Hollowing out those who acted in ways it thought weren't progressive."

"And you object to us stopping slavery where we find it?" asked Hanuman.

"Of course not," she said. "The Operands can call their client relationship with the Otto whatever they want, but we were asked if we were selling slaves. There's no avoiding that and there's no accepting it."

Hanuman waited.

"It was the subtle stuff, the cultural pressure to conform, the use of our languages to trade with." She shut up, feeling small minded for being angry about a culture that had just been through the worst kind of trauma.

"It doesn't explain what you were doing as an Interlocutor on a world at the edge of the Arcology."

The accusation was she could have been doing more. Should have been significant in the way the small niche she'd carved for herself wasn't.

"I was fine, you know? Living a life where I helped ordinary people survive when pressed by some culture on one side and the demands of the Arcology on the other. I did good work for them."

"And now? Will you do that here?"

"There won't be a here," she replied. "If you leave then the people here won't need someone like me, and if you stay we're all dead."

Hanuman huffed a chuckle that was half snort, half despair.

Prab shrugged, not feeling sorry for calling it how it was.

"When we lose things, Prab. It makes us wonder what we were doing ignoring such apparently obvious risks. It's normal. The question for you is, what will you do with that realisation?"

"What realisation?" she asked, waiting for the answer like someone watching a dead body in case it moved again.

"That there's no going back. What are you going to do next?"

Rather than answer the therapy-textbook-snorting ship and tell him where to go, Prab grabbed at the bowl of nuts and put a large handful into her mouth.

Unlike the meal these exploded in her mouth with the dry manky taste of rotting fish and putrid guts. The alcohol in her gut decided it had had quite enough of her bullshit and came right up her throat and spewed forth and through the space where Hanuman's image was overlaid on her vision.

The bar fell quiet.

Then erupted in cheers and robust applause.

Moments later the barman was at the table with a mop and bucket together with a roll of damp cloth.

"Here," he said. "Free to you in exchange for you cleaning up your shit." Then he was gone.

Prab wasn't listening. Her mouth was on fire, her throat inflamed and her eyes watering. It was all she could do to stare at the ground at her feet.

"Tasted good then?" asked Hanuman.

"It tasted like Kercher's underpants," she said.

"I didn't think you'd know."

"Hanuman. I had it before."

"What?"

"How to beat them. How to send that smug shit, the Face of Loss, scurrying for the empty space between the stars. It's the taste." She shook her head, which was a bad idea because she was rewarded with a throbbing headache that shouldn't have arrived for several hours.

"And how do we do that oh drunken princess?" asked Hanuman, but she forgave him because inside the words there was a seriousness she could respect.

"We make ourselves taste so bad they never want us near them again."

43.

It took hours for the people on board Hanuman to be decanted properly. Kercher was done with it long before the task was complete.

Those being woken fell into a pattern they were unprepared for and rapidly grew to hate even while there was no escape.

The first of them set the pattern for what came next.

A man called Sarun, Excluded, an engineer specialising in self-repairing systems. He'd worked on the substrate at Sirajah's Reach, specifically on the intersection between the world's non-Arcology systems and the Arcology itself.

I'm a pilot, Kercher told themselves as Sarun fell out of the pod.

"Where am I?" asked Sarun.

"Sarun?" asked Kercher. There was a script for waking people from stasis. Disorientation and lethargy leaving them requiring a few minutes to find themselves again.

Sarun nodded.

"Brilliant. Take a seat over here." They were in a section of the ship where Hanuman had printed out a wide, deep sofa and low table. The seat took up one complete wall – the room wasn't very large. The pale blue and cream colour scheme gave the sense of bright futures. Luminous red poppies and vibrant orchids were splashed across the wall and over the furniture. Not quite enough to leave wall and sofa merged but enough to give a sense of the wild rather than the inside of a ship hunkered down in a millennia-long storm.

There was no sound apart from Kercher shuffling and Sarun scratching at his chin.

"Where is everyone?" asked Sarun.

"You are the first to be woken," said Kercher. "We're on a small station whose node had agreed to give you residency."

Sarun accepted this in silence.

"There are about a million people here, all physical. Upon leaving here, you'll be met by a guide who'll take you to your new home."

"When do we go home?" asked Sarun, cutting across Kercher's words.

Kercher swallowed. The script suggested answering all questions without committing to details. How were they supposed to talk about Sirajah's Reach without that world's end coming into focus?

"We can talk about that later," said Kercher, and winced at the sound they made.

Sarun nodded. "Can we speak to them?"

Kercher knew Sarun had been one of those arriving late, that he knew what was happening, had experienced the panic. Had he forgotten, was it just the disorientation playing its part?

"Fuck," said Sarun, and Kercher heard the mental barriers crack and collapse from across the room. "They're all dead."

"We don't know that," said Kercher, following the script which suggested responses in their mind. Then, because Kercher wasn't built this way, they veered right off. "Actually, we do. You're right. They're journeying along samsara."

Acknowledging what Kercher knew to be true felt good. Being factual felt right. The little prompts flowing across their vision were screaming for a return to the script.

Sarun started weeping.

"What am I supposed to do?" he asked Kercher, and in his eyes there was more than just a request for a task to keep him busy.

Kercher checked on the guide, an average-sized woman in khaki with a large over-the-shoulder bag she clutched like it was a sickly child, and saw they were outside. With a sigh of undisguised relief, they brought the guide in and handed the weeping Sarun over.

Sarun did not look at them as he left.

This process was repeated with only small variations several dozen times.

Some of them wanted to know why Kercher hadn't done more, why they, personally, hadn't saved the whole of Sirajah's Reach.

Others couldn't process the news and would ask after individuals who weren't on the manifest one by one as if perhaps, if they kept checking the world might change and grant them the smallest bit of mercy.

What surprised Kercher was the anger so many of them felt. It was undirected, unfocused, but very definitely there. Kercher could imagine the sense of loss, the sense of despair, but the idea that they'd be angry literally wasn't on the script.

Mari was the sixty-first person to be decanted.

By then Hanuman had dealt with the dead and reshaped himself so the compartments in which they'd transported the rescued were folded back into his preferred shape.

Mari was no different to the others except she quickly remembered Praveenthi.

"She's on the station waiting for you," said Kercher.

"And you?" asked Mari.

"Me?" they asked.

"How are you? Sirajah's Reach wasn't your world. It wasn't mine either." She stopped there and Kercher imagined the truth of that statement turning on her tongue. "What's happened? How did we end up here?"

She wasn't the first to ask this, but she was the first to direct the question at Kercher rather than asking the universe at large with a glazed expression slapped across her features.

"I'm fine," said Kercher.

She tutted. "Neither of us are fine. I am going to find Prab and expect to be inconsolable very quickly. But who do you have?"

"That doesn't matter," said Kercher. They thought of Prab and the idea was surprising and tenderly welcoming at the same time.

"Pilot, can I use your name?" she asked, and Kercher felt like a child under the tone of her voice. They nodded.

"Kercher. You're a pilot. You're serving sentence for a crime the Arcology deemed worthy of physical existence rather than rehabilitation within its walls. You're alone and limited and have been through an experience I am sure I can't imagine. If you're here with me rather than talking about all this to Prab, then I'm not leaving until you've told me something."

Kercher didn't reply. How could she know they were thinking of Prab?

"Anything," she said kindly, and then, with a smile. "I don't need your life story. I just need to know you're alive in there."

"We lost," said Kercher. It was the plug in the dam.

As if following her own script, Mari didn't ask for more, but Kercher spoke anyway.

"I thought we could win but we can't. I thought we were indomitable. They came from nowhere and dismantled everything and they don't care what happens. I've seen hostile cultures and they're different." They shook their head. None of that was relevant. "I'm here because Prab needs someone to give her what I can't."

"And what's that?" asked Mari.

"Hope," said Kercher.

After that Mari tried to have Kercher talk further. She seemed more interested in how they felt than what the future held, but Kercher was done with it and with her.

When she was gone, led away by her guide with a lingering look over her shoulder, Kercher stopped decanting the remaining survivors and sat alone in the reception room with the lights off.

"What's going on?" Hanuman asked later, as if his attention had been elsewhere.

Perhaps it has, thought Kercher.

Hanuman asked them to finish decanting those few still on board.

"I can't," said Kercher.

"Yes, you can," said Hanuman.

"What happens next?" asked Kercher.

"When they're awake and off me we need to reconfigure my body for combat. After that I'll need you to liaise with the people on the station and then the ships of the fleet. There's a lot to do, Kercher, and you can't be hiding from it."

"And then?"

"What's going on?" asked Hanuman.

"We can't win," said Kercher.

"Is that what bothers you?" asked Hanuman.

"What bothers me is that even if we do win, I will remain your pilot. After all this I remain a criminal, an outsider."

"We can effect some kind of commutation of your sentence," said Hanuman smoothly.

"And then what?"

"Kercher. We don't have time for your sudden introspection."

Kercher banged their hands on their thighs.

"What do you need?" asked Hanuman.

"I wanted to talk about my faith without persecution. I want to be free to die."

"You talk of defeat, which would certainly mean death, and yet if we survive you want to die?"

"Enough," said Kercher. If Hanuman was going to be like that there was no point continuing the conversation. "I've got work to do."

"I'm sorry," said Hanuman. "I'm trying to understand what's happening for you."

"I'm working out my sentence," said Kercher coldly.

"I've told you we can fix that."

Kercher stood up. At the door to the room they stopped, hand resting on the wall, the sensation of it grounding them heavily so their chest felt leaden and their legs tired.

"Fixing it. Is this what it takes to be able to get what I want?"

"Is this what you want?" asked Hanuman, and the words, simple and plain, were the hardest they'd ever heard.

Did it matter if they died now? Was such a principle any kind of guiding force with what lay ahead?

Kercher could see how their beliefs had been vital and inflexible benchmarks to them when it didn't matter, when the idea of dying was a distant peak to be climbed someday. Now, with everything at risk, they struggled to find solace in the idea.

Yet they couldn't abandon it. It's not enough, Kercher thought, and realised there was more to what they believed, that there had to be more to it.

They wished the people who they'd been in community with before their detention were here. They needed to talk to someone who understood.

"I don't know what I believe," they said to Hanuman.

"You're changing your mind?" asked the ship.

"No. Never." They opened the door and the corridor beyond was already different. Hanuman was capable of operating in multiple shards and clearly other parts of him were busy with other tasks.

Kercher wanted to be angry at not having Hanuman's complete attention but knew it was a meaningless concept. They had everything of Hanuman that mattered. That Hanuman's identity allowed them to be in many places at once didn't diminish what was happening here and now.

"I mean I believe, and that won't change, but I can't explain to you or to myself why it's important. It feels so one note and that's not how it is. My people could have explained, could have told you the stories in which what I believe make sense."

Hanuman appeared in the corridor. A human-shaped avatar with hairy brown skin and shining black hair, luscious lips and bright open eyes the colour of bottomless glacial pools but with bristly, pudgy cheeks.

"It's easier to talk to you like this," he said. "And I know the stories. I have them on record. I can share them if you want them."

"Isn't that forbidden?" asked Kercher. "Encouraging the prisoner in their recidivism?"

Hanuman clapped his hands together. "Haven't you heard? I'm the Arcology now."

Kercher was at a loss. Where to go now they were out of the reception room?

"There are still a dozen people waiting," they said.

"They never needed you," said Hanuman. "You told me you were here to find Mari for Prab."

Kercher had lost themselves in the process and when Mari had been escorted away, they'd turned to decant the next person without pausing. It was easy to repeat themselves, harder to think of being with someone who needed care.

"I want to be for more than this," they said. "I'm printed into a body which curtails my creativity, narrows my focus, my freedom in ways no prison cell could. I want to fight, Hanuman, and in losing I'm left bereft. I want to win, I will sacrifice my life without thinking to beat my enemies. To beat your enemies. This isn't enough. You talk about me coming back inside the Arcology but what does that mean?

"I can't accept what the Arcology represents. I'm not sure I've been able to for a long time. As far as rehabilitation goes, this sentence has failed."

"It was never meant to rehabilitate you," said Hanuman. They approached Kercher, coming alongside them. "We should get out of here and talk properly, but we don't have time for that. I'll make you a deal. I'll explain the nature of your punishment and give you a choice, if you'll help me beat this enemy."

"And what if we can't beat them?"

"Then you won't have to worry either way."

Kercher laughed and its raw wildness caught in their throat. "Fine."

"You weren't printed into this shape to help you realise you were wrong. The Arcology never worries about that. What's the worst you could do? Actually end yourself? So what?

"You were printed into the shape you have now because we needed someone like you on our borders. You're okay with dying. That's a rare trait among our people. The weird cohort of nodes who prepared for this disaster aside, the Arcology had no idea this was coming, but it's always needed people like you on its edges. It always will. So here's the choice. I can print you a new body, one with more capacity for being alive, for having agency beyond how to strategise for combat. In return I want you to stay with me when this is all over."

"To remain in your body, outside the Arcology?"

"The Arcology is many things, Kercher. We are it, here, right now. As much and as authentically as Kith's Observatory in its silence, as much as Prab who thinks she's left us behind. The Arcology is legion and in its diversity we are strong."

"You could have asked me," said Kercher. "Why didn't you ask me?"

"Your fascination with actual death isn't healthy. No one believed rewarding the idea was a message we wanted to send to ourselves. But a choice can serve many ends."

Kercher was speechless. They didn't know where to start with what Hanuman had revealed. Their punishment a utilitarian process by which they were used according to the very end for which they were being penalised.

"You probably think I should thank you."

"I think you're furious and I think that's a natural response to what I've just told you. Yes, we treated you as a resource, but we also gave you what you wanted, a chance at a proper death. All these things can be true, Kercher. Life isn't full of binaries, it's full of entropy and uncertainty and ensemble acts of randomness that give the impression of order. Should we have found a different punishment for you and left ourselves poorer as a result?

"Who benefits from that?"

"Why would you stay in this ship?" asked Kercher, deciding they'd think about all this when Hanuman wasn't there cheerleading their imprisonment as a moral good. Because fuck him.

Hanuman smiled and Kercher felt queasy. "Most nodes are embodied, Kercher. It's the citizens of the Arcology who choose to live inside its walls."

"Akhanda," said Kercher.

"Had a ringworld as a body. There's something about being truly embodied that's different to living inside our systems like ghosts, building illusions to keep ourselves entertained."

"You can't mean that," said Kercher.

"Perhaps now," said Hanuman, and the smile faded. "The truth of the matter is the nodes who run the Arcology? All of us have physical bodies of some kind, be they stations, ships, entire worlds. Or they did have."

"And now?"

Hanuman frowned. "So many of them are gone."

"They have what you denied the rest of us."

"And you wish you'd died with them?" snapped the ship.

"No," said Kercher, and it was the truth.

"Prab has just said something interesting," said Hanuman, looking off to the side.

Kercher waited.

"How would you like to taste so bad the Face of Loss pukes out their dinner?" asked Hanuman after a moment.

44.

The old cohort rejoiced at Prab's insight. The few ships remaining scattered among the fleet assembling in the gas giant's atmosphere. Hanuman could feel their sense of purpose and, underneath it, the possibility of hope driving them onwards.

The big question to answer was simple – how to taste bad to an enemy that wanted to consume information, and by all accounts, the denser the better.

Prab had said coral. A sedentary colony species that consistently battled for space just by existing. The biology of physical examples involved numerous tactics for defence and expansion. The one that fit with what they'd experienced at Akhanda and with the Face of Loss' own expression of hunger was the deployment of their digestive systems alongside nematocysts to stun and harm their neighbours.

It was complex behaviour with no sentience, no identity, no mind involved but which resulted in a living creature actively engaging in competition and, for lack of a better term, warfare.

Hanuman could see all kinds of flaws in the analogy, not least that this was a galaxy-spanning enemy with ships and translation technology that had built itself a person-shaped avatar to try to communicate with them.

He didn't understand why it had tried to communicate. It seemed to him this was the biggest hole in their understanding. Hostility was pretty simple in the end, and even the why didn't really change the outcome if you succumbed.

However, communication was something else. It cost time and energy and information to build a body and put it somewhere.

Hanuman was getting lost in the weeds when something changed.

It was the station, Kith's Observatory.

"Hanuman," it said, its voice a dry drawl. "We should talk."

"I thought we might go the whole time without you raising your head."

"I would have preferred that, but your substrate is ready and that means life for all of us is about to change."

The Arcology could be unfolded. The empire restored, kind of.

The Arcology would exist again within information space. A glorious save of trillions of lives. Yet all those who had existed in the physical were gone, their worlds, their stations, their ships consumed by the Face of Loss. An enemy who had made no demands except to inform them that it was growing and it was hungry.

"When you do this, that neat little veil your cohort has constructed around us is going to tear like a hydrogen gas cloud in a super nova. I'd tell you to not do it, but you're the empire's poster child, aren't you?"

Which meant they'd have an unknown amount of time to prepare their defences.

"It's coming for us one way or another," said Hanuman.

"And your plans?"

"Taste bad," said Hanuman.

The station laughed, a sound like boulders being ground to dust.

"You think the Operand didn't try that?"

"They hid," said Hanuman.

"You're going to fight them then, in information space and in the physical?"

"The fleet is preparing. If we lose the physical, we lose our expression, but what point saving that if they conquer us within the substrate?"

"And your little ones?" By which the station meant people like Kercher and Prab.

Hanuman didn't see what they'd do. When the entire Arcology was at stake, what could two people printed into bodies two metres long do to affect the outcome?

"It was her idea, to taste bad," said the station, as if following the same channels of thought Hanuman was sailing along. "Yes, I've been paying attention."

"What would you do?" asked Hanuman.

"You might persuade the Operand to stand with you. They are a surprising culture, full of little secrets the Arcology never guessed at."

Hanuman considered Sea of Thought Drifting. "They're done with this," he said.

"Then give them a reason to take it back up."

"They're slavers, Kith."

"Then find an accommodation. Their slaves aren't members of the Arcology."

Despite Kith's advice and aside from the absolute red line on enslavement, Hanuman didn't think they were relevant to what was about to happen. The station took his silence as encouragement and the channel closed off. Kith was gone back to their own solitude.

Hanuman didn't expect them to help when the Face of Loss finally showed up.

Instead of spooling up the Arcology, a small word for the unfolding of an entire empire, Hanuman warned the fleet their time was nearly done.

Some of those who heard asked him to delay, but most responded with a fatalism that did not bode well.

"They will find us eventually," said the cohort ship. "A month will not save us if a day does not."

Hanuman wasn't sure he agreed but if they were to prepare, they needed the vast knowledge of the Arcology unfiltered by his own limitations.

Having provided a dose of perspective to the bubbling hope among the fleet, Hanuman started to think about the battle that would unfold within information space. The physical would be a repeat of Akhanda. They could expect all those ship profiles plus the light-second-long arms of informational chaos that had cut chunks out of Akhanda.

Yet the enemy's approach in information space remained unknown. The Face of Loss was physical and although Prab had related her fight with it within information space on their flight from Akhanda, that provided no real insight into the struggle to come.

So Hanuman shifted ten per cent of the nodes in the fleet to prepare for information warfare. They would need to fortify themselves then the rest of the fleet from being overtaken and either destroyed or turned. After that they were to think about how they could take the fight to the enemy.

Hanuman had no idea what tasting bad would look like but he made that their problem too. The sense of purpose worked to undo the sombre assessment he'd provided about their time being up and the fleet broke into little pieces as they started strategising across their various tasks.

Satisfied he'd done what he could for now, Hanuman turned his thinking back to restoring what he could of the Arcology now Kith had confirmed the station was ready to support him. In bringing some small part of the Arcology back to life, he was prepared to run the risk that the benefits they'd gain from the millennia of knowledge and the wisdom of billions outweighed the risk of the Face of Loss arriving and destroying them immediately.

When he was sure the fleet, currently fourteen hundred ships, was aware he was about to begin, Hanuman initiated the process of unfolding the Arcology.

The cube, whose remnants he'd sealed off as a memento mori within his systems, had accessed seventeen dimensions, squashing the Arcology down, freezing it in place so none of those within understood their lives had been put on hold.

Undertaking the reverse of that wasn't as simple as undoing a knot by pulling on a thread.

"You have a local rotation," he announced to the fleet. "Then what we can support of the Arcology will be restored. After that the enemy will know we are here and will come for us. We must be ready."

A dozen members of the fleet, mainly those whose hulls were ill designed for configuring as warships, stopped their other tasks and set themselves to understanding what tasting bad would look like. Given their exclusive focus, those other nodes who'd been playing around with it stopped to concentrate on the battle to come.

"What do I do?" asked Prab.

"The fleet will handle this," said Hanuman.

"I fought them in information space," she replied. "I can be useful."

Hanuman understood her motivation but he saw nothing she could bring.

"It was my idea," she said. "You'd have nothing without me."

"I don't know what to do with you," he said. "You should spend time with your friends. Try to find some space to sleep."

"Just like that," she said bitterly.

"What do you propose?" he asked. "In information space there are a thousand ships here with depth of experience you cannot match. An ability to work with raw information in ways your identity can't begin to grasp. In the physical you're in a printed body that needs oxygen to survive. You are no ship."

"I just." She stopped and looked away from him, her eyes wide and her focus in the distance. "You're going to drop me. Now I've served the purpose you wanted for me." The grey despair in her voice sank through Hanuman's systems and he wished it was otherwise, but she had nothing to give them. At least Kercher would be piloting him when the time came.

He had no choice but to leave her behind.

"I'm an Interlocutor," she said.

"We do not need an Interlocutor. I'm sorry Prab but you should know none of this would have been possible without you. For that I will be grateful for as long as we have left."

"I should find my friends and toast the end of all things, that's your advice," she said.

Hanuman didn't care. He couldn't care because it would make no difference. He had an empire to restore and a war to lose.

45.

The air felt different.

Prab groaned and rolled over. The flat she'd been delivered to, she didn't remember who by, was small. A single room with a bathroom off to one side, a single window looking out onto an actual street and a tiny space for sitting when she wasn't asleep.

Whoever put her here hadn't attempted to get her into bed and for that she was glad. The sofa was smooth and a little too slippery to be comfortable but the only thing which mattered to Prab was the state of her head.

Her head didn't hurt but painkillers wouldn't sort dehydration and that sticky taste in the mouth from having drunk too much unidentified booze.

It was someone arriving at the door which had woken her. Their electronic handshake pinging into her mind like a hand reaching through a letterbox.

Not having a change of clothes, Prab answered the door worrying she smelled of her own vomit. It wasn't her finest hour.

It was Mari.

Her friend looked haggard. The only real upside was Mari also was very much alive.

They embraced and Prab realised Mari was the first person she'd touched with genuine affection since leaving Sirajah's Reach.

"You're alive," said her friend. "Are you okay?"

"Nothing some drugs, water and fatty foods won't fix."

They left the flat and bulged out onto the street. It wasn't really a street, just a large corridor decked out with windows like the one in her flat running up and down both sides.

It was wide enough that there were people stood talking to one another and they didn't need to move for Prab and Mari to pass them. She was conscious of eyes on them as they walked. At her side Mari talked about nothing and didn't need any answers, for which she as grateful.

Her nose led them towards the smell of sizzling fat and her stomach grumbled its utter commitment to this decision.

Coming upon a canteen full of people eating, a short man with six fingers on each hand and no discernible neck squeezed them in between two other parties who moved up without acknowledging their arrival.

There was no menu, and the food, which smelled divine, was delivered a few minutes later while Prab was still trying to figure out how the canteen worked and how to talk to Mari.

Mari was patient, her small talk having run dry and venturing nothing more substantial in its wake. They knew one another too well to talk without purpose when it mattered.

The food was delicious, a meaty flavour with something starchy on the side in a thick white sauce that was sweet, salty and a little acidic. It looked like something she'd thrown up the night before but as it filled her belly and revived her head it was just what she needed.

Around them people chattered. The only subject was the arrival of the Arcology.

No one mentioned the Face of Loss, no one talked about the Arcology's fall, just what it would mean for them, here and now that the Arcology was moving in.

It was hard to listen to because with each expression of fear for their own lives Prab wanted to stand on the table and tell them to get some fucking perspective.

That none of them would be here in a few rotations' time was the only thing keeping her in her seat.

"I've heard some of what happened," said Mari when the platter they'd been given was mostly empty. She looked right at Prab, who found she couldn't return her gaze. The dull shine of the cutlery was much less demanding. "It must have been awful."

"I remember the crowd pressing against the ship as we took off," she said, the images of blood and gravity and so many ends right there at the front of her mind. "It didn't get any better after that."

She could hear their screams in her head.

Mari reached a hand across the table but Prab didn't take it.

"I've watched everything fall away," she said. "I've done nothing to help and now they don't even want me in the room." She didn't mention her family, the electricity of their loss scorching her if she gave it even a moment. Did Mari feel the same?

"I don't believe that," said Mari. She reached under the table and brought up her backpack. "I brought you something." From inside she brought out a small book with hard covers and gold lettering embossed on the front and spine.

Prab thought about her own backpack full of books on the ship. She'd not given it a second thought since stepping aboard on Sirajah's Reach.

Prab took Mari's gift with both hands and absently opened the front cover. "Timaeus' *History of the Retorick Archipelago*. I love this book." She finally met Mari's gaze. "Thank you."

"It was the only thing I could grab before you yanked me off the street. I knew something was wrong and I guessed you'd be involved. You saved my life, Prab."

And missed millions of others, thought Prab.

"You did what you could. There's no shame in not being able to do more. It's more than I can claim. I'm alive because you chose me. Don't take this the wrong way but I'm going to live with the guilt of surviving for the rest of this life."

"To survivor's guilt," said Prab with a grimace.

The table next to them emptied and was immediately taken by someone on their own. A big, long body that folded uncomfortably into the space.

With a sigh Prab looked over before realising it was Kercher. It was good to see them and a smile crept unbidden to her lips. Kercher tipped a greeting.

She introduced them.

"You're the pilot?" asked Mari.

Kercher nodded uncertainly. Mari reached out and clapped them on the shoulder. "Well, thank you too."

"Hanuman told me you don't want to stay on the station," they said to Prab.

"What?" said Mari. "Where are you going to go?"

"I want to fight," said Prab.

"You hate the Arcology," said her friend. "I'm the one who's supposed to love it. It's our thing."

Prab looked at Kercher and saw understanding in their eyes.

"What exists between the Arcology and myself doesn't matter, Mari. I want to make a difference."

"And what about you, pilot?" Mari asked Kercher. "You still loyal as a prisoner?"

"He's offered me a new body," said Kercher.

Prab nodded. "You should accept his offer."

"He said some strange things to me, Praveenthi."

Mari was watching their conversation and looking uncomfortable.

"What is it?" asked Prab.

"They're a criminal, Prab." The implications were clear and Prab was both disappointed and not surprised because she'd once felt all too close to Mari's attitude.

"I'd be dead without them. We all would," said Prab. "Kercher's my friend." The statement felt the least of what she could say but the words dragged at her heart as she said them and tears welled in her eyes. "I think you'd like them. They're a prickly arsehole, to be honest."

Mari gave Kercher an appraising glance. "One of us then."

"I don't want to leave the Arcology," blurted Kercher.

Mari smiled but it was thin. "My dear, you never will."

"What happened?" asked Prab.

Mari put the palms of her hands on the table as if to push to standing. "All of this? How can I continue, Prab? Everything I thought was wrong."

"He said you haven't left either," said Kercher to Prab.

"Who?" asked Mari.

Prab knew who'd said those words and Hanuman wasn't really wrong. It was a hell of a realisation to make given where they were headed.

"The thing you learn when the world ends is that the ways you defined yourself are so much bullshit. All of it relies on everything around you being the same tomorrow as it was today because without it the shape you squeeze yourself into makes no sense."

Mari pursed her lips and sat up straight.

"Don't be like that," said Prab. "You know I'm right. All those delineations you and I would spend time drinking and ranting about? They're wrinkles, nothing more. We just don't like to think about it." She took a deep breath because all of this pressed in on her and talking about it was hard. "I've had no choice, Mari. I've seen it all fail, have literally fought the enemy face to face. I was proud of being Excluded." She waved at the people in the canteen, her hands open and inclusive.

"Was?" asked Mari, her voice sharp edged.

"I thought I was outside the Arcology. I'd given up my conveniences, lived my own life. All I was really doing was using it to tell a story that made me feel good. Fuck, I sound like such a child."

"So what? You're going back to them?" asked Mari, and she looked ready to break something.

"We never left, Mari. Look around you. You're alive because of them."

"I'm alive because of you," said Mari.

"And them," said Prab and pointed at Kercher, who shrank back from her outstretched finger. "And Hanuman. And the lost Akhanda. And everyone else who died so we might live. They were all Arcology. Even these people here are Arcology, they're just getting off on calling themselves something different."

"I don't understand. Leave it to them. It's their war. Stay here, Prab. Stay with me," said Mari crisply.

"It's not about what I want," said Prab, then stopped. "Don't you see? I'm nowhere, Mari. I'm not outside because life without them is unthinkable. But I'm not inside their tent either. I thought about it. I want the Arcology to exist because the alternatives seem fatal for us, but where does that leave me? Most of all I want to be out there because my family deserve someone to remember them. They all deserve better than this."

"Hanuman says the Arcology knows all this, made space for you because of it," said Kercher quietly.

"That hardly helps," said Prab.

"I know it's been difficult, Prab," Mari started.

"You know?" asked Prab, cutting across her oldest and dearest friend. "You know? What do you know? While you were asleep my parents were killed. Gone forever. While you were asleep the rest of Sirajah's Reach died. Suffocated to death. While you were asleep Akhanda, the great ring world and hub of the Arcology, died. I watched it all. I had no choice. Yes, I saved you, Mari.

"What's burning away my insides is that I saved anyone. That I left more to die, that the choice was mine. Did I save you because it was right, because you're my friend or because I didn't know what else to do? What about those who I might have chosen if I'd had more time to think and those I sent messages to but who didn't make it to the bay in time? Don't sit there and tell me you know what I think when what you really mean is you want me to start thinking like I used to, like you still do.

"There isn't any going back."

"That's not fair, Prab. You really think I can't feel shitty about this? Look at me. I'm the one who liked the Arcology, who remained a part of it when you rode around on the back of how Excluded you were without your privacy veil and with your parents who wanted you back. My word you dined out on it. We are both hurting."

"We're not the same," said Prab and felt her words cut sharp as knives. She wanted Mari by her side more than anything but her mind, her heart, would not allow her to remain near. The idea of being close to Mari filled her with hatred so intense she wanted to scream.

"I can't stay here," said Prab. "I can't do nothing."

"If you stay, you'll be with me," said Mari.

"I don't want that," said Prab, eyes firmly fixed on the table.

Mari stood up, staring down her nose at Prab. "I'm sorry, Prab. I can't sit here. Not right now. You think you have the monopoly on misery, but you don't. You're floundering, grasping for something to make surviving feel okay. It won't be okay, but pushing me away isn't fair. Is this really how you want to remember our relationship?"

She waited a moment then and Prab could see her expression, the open eyes, the trembling mouth, and knew her friend wanted to be stopped, but Prab could not move.

Mari turned slowly, hesitantly, and left, Timaeus' history sitting on the table the only sign she'd been there.

Kercher didn't move.

Prab played with her hands, pulling at her fingers while the world swirled all out of focus in her head, a noise and flash of events and people and thoughts she couldn't slow down.

"Why won't Hanuman let me help?" she asked Kercher eventually.

"What would you do?" asked Kercher, but it wasn't dismissal, they were ready to argue for her, to help.

The question had no answer and her shoulders slumped.

"We aren't going to win," said Kercher. "He knows that."

"So I should just wait for it?" she said angrily.

"I understand the need to fight even when there's no chance of winning," said Kercher.

"Loss is not inevitable," said a voice.

Prab looked up and saw how the canteen had emptied as they'd been talking. A few people were still there but they were subdued and at the edges. A substantial ring of emptiness surrounded them on all sides.

The voice belonged to the saltshaker-shaped Operand, Sea of Thought Drifting, who glided in through the open door behind Kercher.

"Do you mind?" they asked, before deforming themselves to take up residence as a bland human-sized blancmange on top of the table.

"You lost against them," said Kercher.

"Ah, straight to the point in the way only a single mind/ loneliness can manage," said Sea of Thought Drifting. "We did/have. You are right/perceptive. It doesn't mean we didn't try/fight/resist a lot of things before we surrendered/adapted. Willingly by the way. It doesn't know we surrendered/adapted only that we stopped competing with it for ibits within information space/the ground of being.

"You single minded organisms/hosts are always built around wiping out competitors. Others don't have that luxury; coexistence/co-option is the perpetual state of things and we learn to abide by our own rules/impulses."

"How does that help us now?" asked Kercher.

"Praveenthi/this host had a very communal thought. How to taste bad/set boundaries. Your nodes are running about all over the place trying things, simulating outcomes, speculating but they can't get their identities to behave as it will because they keep insisting on thinking/rationalising. It doesn't think/plan. It spreads/grows and consumes. You've come into its feeding ground, so what does your planning brain/loneliness predict?"

Prab shook her head. "I'm only hearing what I already knew," she replied.

"But they're not listening to you," said Sea of Thought Drifting.

"And you can make them?" asked Kercher.

"Don't be silly, your culture is arrogant/short sighted, it cannot conceive of others having wisdom it does not already possess. Easier to add new energy to the universe than to penetrate your assumptions about how things work."

"And?" asked Prab slowly.

"You're useful/good seedbeds," they said.

"Will you get to the point?" said Kercher.

"We know how to make you taste bad."

"And you didn't think to tell us earlier?"

"We were deciding whether you were worth it," said Sea of Thought Drifting.

"Nice," said Kercher.

"What made the difference?" asked Prab.

"Nothing you'd understand," said the Operand, and she had the distinct impression it wasn't entirely happy with its choices.

"You know what? I don't care," she said. "How do we do it?"

"Sting them back," said Sea of Thought Drifting.

"That's what we're planning on doing," said Kercher.

The Operand shivered and it was like watching a huge jelly wobble. Prab realised they were laughing.

"No. You're attacking a fruiting body and expecting the creator/roots to notice and understand. It is incapable of either of those responses."

"Then what?" asked Prab, holding a hand up to stop Kercher who was ready to spit unwise words.

"In simple terms you can do to them what it's doing to you."

"Consume the consumer," said Prab. "I understand the concept."

"We don't expect you to understand the details."

"And you do?"

"We do not speak of how things are in the same way you do but we can provide information in a way that your nodes can translate, understand and build."

"But it didn't work," said Kercher.

"It did/does," said Sea of Thought Drifting.

Prab didn't believe them.

"How long will it take us to do this?" she asked.

"We can't tell, it will be completed when it is completed."

"Yet here you are betting on the future," said Kercher.

"We are drawn to the possibility that we might once again explore/expand into that from which we've withdrawn/adapted. Our agenda here is purely one of growth and you giving us the chance to pursue it."

Prab thought she understood. Aiding the Arcology might afford them the chance to return to information space as they were before. She wanted to worry about what that might mean, about what secrets the Operands were holding onto about this enemy and why they'd retreated from a war they claimed they'd been happy fighting.

Yet to be useful, to force her way back into Hanuman's presence and have him acknowledge her. Prab's heart sped at the thought and her worries could find no purchase.

"What do you think?" asked Kercher.

"Give us what you have," said Prab. She opened a location for them to deliver the information and sent it to the Operand's systems, assuming they were the same as those they'd used when they'd first met them on their bone ship.

Sea of Thought Drifting sloughed off the table, rebuilding themselves on the floor so they had a tripod of legs.

"A forest of competing interests," it said. "How interesting our growth shall be." With that they swung their new legs into motion and were gone from the canteen.

Kercher stood and followed them out of the door.

Prab guessed the Operand have given her enough data to occupy the nodes for weeks. Yet the most important piece was contained in a small folder at the surface of the deep well of calculations and it was a message for her explaining what was needed.

Kercher reappeared a few moments later. "They've shuffled off."

Prab was already on her feet. "We need to go because this is going to take time. We have to stop Hanuman from unfolding the Arcology until we're ready."

"It's too late for that," said Kercher. "Can't you feel it in the air?"

And suddenly the change she'd felt made sense.

"Fuck," she said, and without waiting for Kercher, sent to Hanuman on every channel at her disposal that he needed to meet with her.

46.

Details of the Operands' stingers quickly spread across the fleet. Swiftly followed by uproar.

Some wanted to know why the Operands had withheld this information.

Others wanted to punish them while still more didn't believe it despite the fact Hanuman and others had verified the calculations.

And so Kercher found themselves back out in space, their body wrapped in Hanuman's hull, drifting him from one spot to another as he sought to meet in person with the nodes who dissented.

While they were busy negotiating the cooperation of large parts of the fleet who still felt a grand gesture of going down guns blazing was the optimal strategy, the Arcology that could, continued to unfold.

The process was like a flower budding and it wasn't until everything was over that the Arcology would be itself once more. Still, thought Kercher, it's on its way.

With Hanuman as the newly appointed avatar of the Arcology the rest of the fleet looked to, Kercher was inclined to believe him when he said the pilot could have a new body and choose the future they wanted.

Shuffling Hanuman from one spot to another left Kercher with a lot of time to think, and all of it was spent reflecting on this opportunity – to stay outside or return to the Arcology.

Hanuman's point about what the Arcology really was set to one side, Kercher found the choice harder than they'd anticipated. Being outside the Arcology, even if it was piloting one of their warships, had changed them.

At the beginning of their sentence they'd resented the Arcology and the processes that had led to them becoming embodied and exiled, as they saw it, in the physical.

Much of that feeling had drained away and Kercher couldn't pinpoint when it had started because when Hanuman made his offer, Kercher realised they'd been drifting along to an unspecified sense of listlessness for a long time.

Going home wasn't the foregone conclusion it should have been.

Without doubt there were people waiting for them to come back – those who'd escaped the prosecutions entirely or those whose sentences hadn't been as severe as Kercher's.

To see them again and pick up where they'd left off brought waves of comfort and good feeling to Kercher's heart.

And emptiness. How could they go back after what Hanuman had said? Was the ship manipulating them into staying longer, was any of it even true? All this was before they thought about what kind of body they might choose. Kercher thought about it the only way they knew how – as a soldier.

Hanuman had no need for Kercher. Delegating ship systems to a biological interface was inefficient. Suboptimal, the nodes would call it. Hanuman was arguably better off without a physical pilot no matter what benefits Kercher might bring.

And, by his own words, Hanuman was in a position to rewrite Kercher's sentence or commute it entirely. No one was going to argue with the node who saved the Arcology, who became its avatar.

It wasn't altruism behind Hanuman's suggesting Kercher remained in a printed body. Hanuman said he needed Kercher.

Kercher couldn't figure out why. Which left them thinking about their own future.

Strategically then, Hanuman was being honest for reasons which Kercher recognised they didn't completely understand, but whose benefits the ship would accrue only if Kercher remained in the physical. Fine.

The trap being that to be the kind of body that was useful, they had to stay as they'd been made and not reclaim those parts of themselves stymied and erased in being printed out as a pilot.

If they returned to the Arcology they'd frustrate Hanuman, but what did they think of as their own win condition? It was here Kercher realised they didn't want to return home. The belief they'd considered their life's journey was too small for them now. It felt like a failure of imagination.

I still believe, they told themselves, but the idea of death being necessary wasn't enough. It had to sit in some larger idea or it was meaningless. It just had to.

Kercher had seen enough death to know that without ideas within which it could be understood, samsara was just an excuse.

And samsara wasn't an excuse.

Kercher knew they wouldn't find their answers inside the Arcology and so here, at its edges, was their opportunity to figure out why the founders had believed in the cycle of life and its importance in the journey of a person's atman towards its highest self.

They felt bad for Praveenthi. After her bombshell had been digested, Hanuman had once again thanked her only to set her to the side all over again.

She had been distraught and then very, very angry.

Kercher understood her feelings entirely but they were powerless to persuade Hanuman because, when they thought about what she brought to the situation, her strongest contribution had already been made.

There was no role for an Interlocutor when talking was done with and only violence remained.

The information bulwark, as many of the nodes in the fleet were calling the defensive technology given to Praveenthi by Sea of Thought Drifting, would be built by nodes and then activated by nodes. Praveenthi, in her little printed body, had nothing to offer them.

She would be celebrated if they survived but until that moment she was done.

Kercher was glad they'd not been part of the conversation where Hanuman shoved her aside for a second time.

All the while the Arcology continued to unfold.

Estimates were that the portion of the Arcology that could be restored would come alive properly a few hours before the Bulwark was ready.

If the Face of Loss was searching for them it would be then the battle for their future would be fought. It would be then they were most vulnerable.

Empty now of refugees, Hanuman had retrofitted himself purely for information warfare. His weapons fell into two categories; those for delivering the Arcology's most advanced physical destruction and those which would allow confrontation directly within information space.

There was a faction already advocating for moving the arcology truly into information space if they survived this encounter. The calamity could have been avoided, they argued, if the Arcology had been entirely outside of the physical, after all, it was the destruction of so many worlds and their information-processing capabilities which had been so disastrous.

Such ideas were fine, thought Kercher, but they were distractions from what needed to be done now. They suspected many of the nodes feared what was coming to Kith's Observatory and rather than prepare for their own deaths they were prevaricating about issues which could only have meaning if they survived.

Which, if they didn't get their shit together, they wouldn't.

They weren't interested in the discussion between Hanuman and factions like these. Much of their dialogue occurred on channels and in mediums too esoteric for Kercher's limited body to even access let alone understand. What they could access was as tedious as large numbers of people with different agendas trying to cooperate sounded like.

How they built anything remained a mystery, thought Kercher, in one of the more depressing moments where delegates were arguing about how to argue.

Hanuman let a lot of these conversations progress without directly intervening and this too Kercher thought was a waste of time. Why not just smooth things along and get to the meat of the matter.

"How to talk to one another is the meat of the matter," said Hanuman.

"How to fight this war is the meat of the matter," said Kercher.

"Both these things are true," replied the ship, and at that point Kercher bailed, dragging themselves happily back to the physical and their endless simulations about how this fight could go.

One thing Hanuman had mentioned repeatedly, although never more than as a single thought at a time, was how the Face of Loss had tried to communicate with them. The ship seemed puzzled by this fact pattern.

Why would a non-sentient non-conscious entity try to adopt the manners and form of someone like Praveenthi or Kercher. First of all, why not mimic a node? The conditions for the spontaneous emergence of inorganic sentience were easier to construct than for organic life. The latter needed evolution to arrive at sentience. Inorganic life was almost entirely an epiphenomenon of organic life. At least as far as the cultures the Arcology had encountered through its existence. Not a single inorganic culture had arisen spontaneously. The prerequisites were some basic manufacturing and fabbing technologies which didn't arise naturally through evolution.

Which was a distraction, Kercher realised. The matter at hand was not why the Face of Loss had mimicked organic intelligence but why it had mimicked intelligence of any kind at all.

They had no data from which to draw conclusions and Kercher wondered if setting aside Praveenthi was a mistake, because she could be tasked with understanding what the Operands were getting out of helping the Arcology.

Kercher was certain they were hiding something and had been convinced since their first encounter on the Otto station.

You can't be sentimental, they told themselves. They could feel the desire they had to be near Praveenthi, to help her and find a chance to talk to her again. Such thoughts weren't helpful when trying to plan a battle.

Kercher had devised two schemes of engagement. The first, and least likely to be enacted, was that they were able to establish the Bulwark but the enemy assaulted it anyway. If the strategy worked and the Bulwark was damaging to them in a way physical combat wasn't, then they'd only have to protect it. The Bulwark had dozens of weak points – where nodes would be required to bring it into existence and then sustain it. If those nodes were killed, then the spots where they had been would become gaps in the Bulwark's coverage. If enough of them fell then the Bulwark itself would collapse entirely.

They'd need defending.

The nodes working on this insisted the enemy was not the kind to understand about weak points and so defences could be targeted rather than overwhelming.

Kercher wasn't so sure and was running alternatives where the enemy clustered around the nodes that needed defending. None of the outcomes were good. Perhaps this is why the Operand abandoned this strategy despite its superficial benefits.

The second set of simulations were what happened if the Arcology came online but the enemy arrived before the Bulwark was established around the planet.

Precious few of the fleet had been at the fall of Akhanda even if they came with their own survival horror stories. The sprites in the fleet had formed their own communities already, they always did, trading themselves among their nodes as if they were nothing more than club houses. Those sprites who'd been on Hanuman kept sending unsolicited reports to Kercher; on what other nodes had done, where they'd been, on the cultures they'd negotiated with to survive and a dozen other subjects. They'd arrive with no fanfare, no commentary and no sense that Kercher was a prisoner the sprites should keep at arm's length.

They didn't question this largesse – it seemed pointless to ask why they were being treated like one of the family.

Which left Kercher working with a smaller subset of those who understood what they were facing properly. Among them were a few dozen pilots, and Kercher happily created a subnetwork for them to talk directly.

They quickly divided themselves into cells of six, except for Kercher who, being on board Hanuman, was given a guard of two complete cells but kept out of their direct communications. Their two guard units were appointed a pilot named Waveby and another called Sharma to speak on their behalf.

The basic message being, "Tell us what you want us to do."

The blank-faced commitment to Kercher and their cause felt unearned and almost ridiculously satisfying. And Kercher's brain hated it even as their body hummed along with pleasure. Understanding why they were treated different didn't translate into liking it. Kercher would rather have been a member of a cell with the chance to get to know their fellow pilots as comrades.

The most they got were formal reports and requests for tasks and goals and strategies.

There was no small talk, no banter.

"Officers don't banter with those under their command," said Hanuman when Kercher complained.

They physically returned to Kith's Observatory in time for the Arcology to finish its restoration. The atmosphere in the moments before was one of quiet held breath and contemplation, shrouded in the planet's black helium storms.

Then everything opened like a bright day as the Arcology spread its wings through information space, flooding their comms and their systems with its presence.

Like a receding wave, the portion of restored Arcology was back within itself immediately after, leaving a thousand stunned ships swirling drunkenly in its wake.

Kercher, who'd snapped out of the network the moment they'd been dazzled, tentatively rejoined to find hundreds of nodes joyously celebrating the return of their home.

No one mentioned that they'd managed to bring back a tiny portion only. That any restoration had occurred at all seemed to be triumph worthy of abandon.

"Now we wait," said Hanuman to Kercher. "Are you ready?"

"As much as possible," said Kercher, scanning across everything available for signs the Face of Loss had arrived.

For a while nothing happened.

Kercher's system dialled back the adrenaline and cortisol but the pilot felt wired and exhausted all at once. They refused to relax, believing that the moment they did the enemy would be upon them.

"There's something happening on the station," said Hanuman.

Kercher tried to see what the ship was highlighting, but communication with Kith's Observatory went dark the moment they tried.

47.

Hanuman inserted himself into Prab's optics.

There, in front of her right in the middle of the street, was the Face of Loss. The figure was the same as before.

No. That wasn't true. The body had more definition, the face was less plastic, more fleshy than before. The eyes were the biggest difference. The last time they'd seen it floating in space a few metres away from Kercher's position in the cockpit, the eyes had been lifeless.

Now they had everything to them the living held themselves. Darting, small movement, irises and cornea that adjusted to the smallest changes of light.

Hanuman immediately let the rest of the fleet know their time was up. Huge numbers of ships moved across the plane to agreed staging posts. They were going to fight the enemy across the system and not within the atmosphere of the gas giant – it was too small a theatre and Hanuman worried they'd be cornered and wiped out if they hunkered down defensively.

"What are you doing?" asked Prab, sensing him in her feeds.

"I have to see this," he replied.

"I did not give you permission," she said.

"Not this again," said Hanuman, remembering how she'd insisted on his speaking to her without using magnetic field manipulation.

"Out," said Prab.

"Please can I stay?" Better to ask permission than leave, he thought. She'd soften and allow him to remain.

The Face of Loss waited calmly as if listening in to their disagreement and Hanuman was again concerned they'd missed something in their analysis of what this enemy wanted.

"You don't get to choose when I'm useful," she said.

And then he was out, Prab completely dropping out of the network.

Hanuman scrabbled for the station's feeds but found Kith's Observatory was hiding itself as well.

Groaning with frustration, he called on Kercher.

"I need you in the station. Now."

The pilot acknowledged the request. "I can't get there in time," they said.

Hanuman rolled their anxiety back and tried to listen to what Kercher had said. They were currently inside Hanuman who was adjacent but not connected to the station.

By the time Kercher could get to Prab's location, whatever was happening there would be done.

All he could do was start the machine running.

Docking with the station, Kercher disembarked anyway and Hanuman set to waiting.

48.

Prab had been walking when everything changed.

She'd been out for an hour or so, had messaged Mari to ask to meet, been ignored and was skirting the edge of the botanic gardens when the lights in the street went out.

When they returned the Face of Loss was standing there, head angled weirdly to one side like a puppet with slack strings and hands on hips.

She froze. The air was chill on her eyes and all through her insides a demand that she fled, that she do something, anything at all, cried out loud and shrill.

"We came to talk," said the marionette. Its words were slow, methodical and spoken with a voice that was rough, as if the speaker didn't quite know how to work their mouth.

None of this made sense to Prab. If there was anyone else in the street they were keeping out of this conversation. Prab wished they'd join her, wished she wasn't alone.

Then Hanuman had been there and she'd discovered that, actually, there were people she didn't want with her right then. Talking to the Face of Loss wasn't the logical thing to do and she didn't care. Fuck the Arcology and its casual exploitation of those it needed.

She wouldn't let it happen again. She'd left her family for exactly this, she thought, knowing it wasn't really true but feeling its new truth in her gut. Rejecting Hanuman was easy in comparison.

Better to be alone. Better to face a monster than trust those who didn't trust her.

"Talk," she said.

The head snapped to the other side, too fast for it to be without pain.

Hands fell to its sides and the Face of Loss took a step forward.

Prab took a step backwards and then following half a dozen steps in which one came forward and then the other, she found she'd retreated.

Then the Face of Loss retreated a step. Prab did not close the gap.

"You speak here, like this?"

"You speak," she replied, unwilling to give it anything more. For all she knew the battle had begun outside and here she was trading single syllables with a poorly constructed flesh puppet.

"Listen to us," it said, taking a step forward.

Prab retreated again, aware this street only ran a few dozen metres before it hit junctions into other corridors designed for normal station use rather than repurposed into common areas. They were narrow spaces and she did not want to get trapped in one of them with this thing on her heels.

Which meant she had to stand here and face it.

"I'm listening, but you stay there," she said.

Another step forward, another step back.

"You shouldn't have died," it said.

"You shouldn't have attacked us," she replied.

The Face of Loss' body stuttered, its shape blipping into something inhuman, bulging with flesh in the wrong places, its clothes moving as if they were part of its body not something worn over it.

Shocked, Prab stumbled back and found her back against a wall. Cold steel under her fingers as she reached, hoping for a door, without taking her eyes off the approaching monstrosity.

Then it was in a person shape again, its edges solid, the blurring and movement absent.

She realised the door was a couple of metres to her right. She could dive for it, hoping it opened as it should and run for it. Sometimes a plan that made no sense became the only one available and despite knowing it ended badly, she couldn't see any other option.

"We need you," said the body.

Prab dived right and found the door, which opened as she got close. She was through.

She ran. The door closed behind her then slipped open again and the Face of Loss was chasing her. It kept pace but didn't close in.

Bringing up a map of the station she plotted a course for the spot where she knew Hanuman would be berthed when he returned. Perhaps he was there already.

Her breath was quickly gone from her lungs and Prab heaved her way through passage after passage with burning chest and thighs that wanted to stick nails into her brain. She passed people, pushing, calling for them to get away. Whatever she needed for a clear run.

Then the doors she needed to get through wouldn't open.

The station's systems told her the door didn't exist. She checked twice then three times, stood there looking at a sealed bulkhead as the system said it was a clear passageway.

Screaming with frustration she turned to see the Face of Loss was there watching her, five paces away but not making any attempt to get hold of her.

"We need you," it said a second time and, unlike before, it held up its hands, palms outwards, to suggest it meant her no harm.

Prab felt like a frightened dog being soothed and refused to be manipulated so easily.

"Stay the fuck back," she said. If the enemy wasn't about to murder her in cold blood, she'd treat it like it had something to say.

To her surprise the Face of Loss stopped moving.

Kercher was on her channel. "Where are you?" they asked.

Prab brought up the map of the station only to discover she wasn't on it anymore.

Panicking she told the pilot where she had been heading.

"I've passed there," came Kercher's response. "No sign of you and no locked doors either."

Prab turned around, staring at the walls, and realised something was wrong.

Placing a hand on one surface she thought hard about it being soft like marshmallow and, with a little sigh of terror she watched as her fingers sank into the wall.

"I'm in information space," she said.

Kercher didn't reply.

The Face of Loss coughed and she turned to find it a pace closer. With a lunge it would reach her.

"I will fight to my last breath," she hissed at it.

"No fighting," it said. "You shouldn't have died. It was not understood."

Prab thought about how to fight, about what weapons she had at her disposal.

"That's quite enough," said the drawling tone of Sea of Thought Drifting, and there, in information space, was the salt-shaking microbial colony. As in physical space, the colony appeared bland and smooth skinned, but it moved so quickly Prab had trouble following it.

Before she truly understood what was happening, the Operand was on Face of Loss, covering it like a giant wad of phlegm. Wherever they touched the Face of Loss' skin burned and turned red.

The enemy showed no pain but it stumbled and fell back. The fight between them created no sound, and in that eerie quiet the Sea of Thought Drifting slowly digested the enemy until there was nothing left but the Operand's transparent body.

When they were done, the Operand twirled back towards Prab.

"We are here to help," they declared proudly. "But we can only do it with your collaboration/vulnerability."

"What do you need?" asked Prab.

"Give us space inside your physical body. With access to the Arcology we can unite/synthesise and defeat/reprimand the enemy, give you time to establish your Bulwark, also our technology, and then, from here, we can strike back at the enemy/reprimand decisively/overdue.

They were asking to inhabit her, to turn her into one of their client cultures. If she gave them this then they'd have an entrance into the Arcology itself.

Unless you remain Excluded, she reminded herself. It was risky but seeing what they'd done to the Face of Loss here in information space she was certain that with their aid the Arcology could defeat their enemy and survive.

"Hanuman," she called, opening her channels.

"No," said Sea of Thought Drifting. "You must decide this/ here, not your inorganic overlords/patrons."

"He is no one's overlord," she replied. Did the Operands understand the difference? Did it even matter?

"You're still alive. What do you need, Prab?" asked Hanuman, the relief in their tone palpable.

"The Operands are here in information space. I am too. They want to help us."

"No," said Hanuman.

Prab felt like she'd been punched. "What?"

"They are not to be trusted," he replied. "They gave up their technology, they were defeated and now run their sphere of influence built on the backs of slaves who likely don't even realise they've been made into slaves."

Hearing the words brought the world back into focus for Prab and she felt her surroundings turn hard and real in her mind.

"We will be fine," she said to the Operand.

"You will all die/cease your paths," they said, their tone cheerful. "It would be a waste of your entire existence to be consumed now."

"Set your slaves free," she said.

"This is not a negotiation," they replied. "Accept our offer/ strategy here/now or accept it when many more of your nodes have died in a fruitless/immature defence of your last outpost. We will have what opportunity provides."

"I think you want this, and I think you will negotiate," said Prab. "We will take our chances." She hoped she was right.

Sea of Thought Drifting wobbled once then vanished, leaving Prab all alone.

"Hanuman," she said. "I'm here in information space. The enemy brought me here. I'd like to come back out."

She felt Hanuman's presence envelope her and then, in the moment between closing and opening her eyes, Prab was back in her physical body, stomach heaving and legs working out if they'd allow her to stand.

49.

Returning to the ship without Prab, Kercher learned all that had happened to Prab. That she was still alive lifted them, but why Hanuman hadn't brought her to the ship was beyond explanation. Could the ship really believe their situation hadn't changed?

Whatever his thinking, Hanuman was disturbed, and that uncertainty flowed through his communications with the fleet.

What were the Operand doing?

Had they really appeared in information space alongside Prab and the enemy with no ceremony at all?

Hanuman instructed the station's council to keep Praveenthi under supervision until such time as he said otherwise. The ship was clearly concerned something was happening with her that needed caution.

"Why not bring her onto the ship?" Kercher asked, but Hanuman only tutted at the suggestion as if Kercher was missing the entire point.

Hanuman had Kercher take them out of the planet's atmosphere and plant them quietly in one of the gas giant's icy rings which were hundreds of kilometres wide but only a few tens of meters thick.

Kercher assumed it was a whim because their profile stuck out like a sore thumb and within information space the rings, the planet and most everything within three light minutes were effectively invisible. The star and the Arcology's ships stood out like green shoots against the informational desert of open spacetime.

Three hundred nodes were busy building the Bulwark they'd adapted from the information provided by the Operand.

"Why do you trust that and not this?" asked Kercher.

"Because we can do the maths on the Bulwark," said Hanuman. "It is the thing itself and it's partly our design, not theirs. An idea we've taken and made into something else."

Of the remaining ships, many of them were veiled in small pockets waiting for trouble with a few dozen dotted around the local volume up to a light hour away waiting on the Face of Loss to appear in system with their ships.

Within information space many of the nodes had generated small defences to protect themselves from infiltration. Otherwise, they'd thrown calculations at the ibits across the system to keep them busy by forcing them to prove the multi-dimensional version of Tarski's undefinability theorem that arithmetic can't define itself by arithmetic by crunching the raw numbers. The task would occupy the ibits until the end of the universe without resolving and, effectively, locked them out from being used by the enemy when they arrived to launch attacks through information space.

Kercher worried the enemy would appear on top of Kith's Observatory, ready to repeat their destruction a second time. The preparations around them suggested Hanuman and the other nodes expected something different to happen when the enemy finally arrived.

"This is no conventional engagement," said Kercher.

"We haven't ever been at war," said Hanuman. "Not properly. I've been sailing what archives are now available. We haven't fought in earnest since we discovered translation, the ibit and how to live inside information space."

This is the first time? thought Kercher.

"We've simulated countless wars," said Hanuman, as if that explained things and made them better in the saying. Which it didn't – there was no substitute to almost dying to sear lessons into one's identity.

When Sea of Thought Drifting treated them like they were insufferably arrogant it had a point.

A loud scream through the comms channels. "Contact."

The Face of Loss had translated in on the far side of the star to the gas giant – the wrong place if they were hoping to catch the strategic advantage. A large volume of ships and attendant vessels. Images showed several large craft, as massive as Kith's Observatory and accompanied by hundreds of smaller ships.

"Kercher?" It was Praveenthi on a secure channel. "Are you there?"

Kercher let her know they were listening.

"They don't want to fight. I think they did all this by accident."

"Some fucking accident," they replied.

"Listen to me. I don't think they understand what they're doing to us. I don't think they understand us at all. They have no concept of mind, no theory of consciousness. I think they're super close to the Operand. They may even share a common ancestor."

"The Operand have no problem talking to us," said Kercher.

"No, we've developed a way of understanding the intent of what they're communicating, besides the Operand live in the physical and that gives both sides some common ground. They're like the Face of Loss; they have no theory of mind, no consciousness, no intentionality. When I was in information space Sea of Thought Drifting deliberately stopped the Face of Loss before it could tell me what they wanted. They were going to tell me what they wanted, Kercher. Don't you get it? We can't get into it now but look for the right moment."

"The right moment for what?" asked Kercher.

"Are you all right?" It was Hanuman.

Praveenthi was gone, the connection cut on her side.

"I'm fine," said the pilot.

"Then pay attention. We're taking a large part of the fleet to engage them on that side of the star. Make the physical battle there rather than here. Are you ready to go?"

The battle in information space was already underway. Readouts suggested the Face of Loss had moved to reshape the system only for their grasp at ibits to fail against the Tarski gambit. Their immediate response was to pummel the Arcology's firewalls in the hope of finding a way into their worlds.

He didn't think it would take long and then the battle would be twofold, within the Arcology itself and here, in the physical.

Kercher didn't hesitate. "Ready."

They translated.

Into chaos.

The sky was lit with fire, projectiles and explosions.

Kercher arrived, moved towards a fifth the speed of light and then immediately swerved to avoid being turned into granite by a stray beam from a nearby node.

The Arcology had wasted no time in laying waste the moment the enemy arrived in system.

Whatever Praveenthi had wanted them to do had no chance now.

A chance for peace missed.

Of the three huge craft the Face of Loss had brought, the first was being carved into pieces by the concentrated firepower of more than a hundred nodes. Around them a similar number were protecting their flanks from counter attacks.

The foe had clearly not expected such a response as their craft were, unexpectedly, out of position for a firefight and were only now responding to the onslaught by repositioning their flights to engage.

Kercher was delighted. Their heart pumped hard to see the Arcology finally have the upper hand. This same vibe of triumph was filtering through the fleet, most of whom had not yet encountered the enemy directly until now.

Hanuman took them in with a group of a dozen other nodes all of whose bodies were of similar size and configuration. Kercher had never seen a dozen Arcology warships working in concert – there had not been a culture known to them that demanded such a show of force.

These dozen targeted the second of the great vessels, their approach covered by dozens of others laying down suppressive fire all around them. Wherever their weapons struck the enemy splatters of their vessel's surfaces turned grey before splintering away.

It took moments for the strike force to puncture the enemy vessel, high energy beams blasting into its insides now the information barrage had peeled its defences apart like skin from an orange.

Coming up and around the shattering vessel, Kercher felt good to have the cockpit shaped for them alone once more. They felt balanced, in the moment and ready for anything.

A fleet of the walnut-shaped ships emerged from translation gates and opened fire. Their concentrated assault tore apart dozens of nodes and ripped a hole in their assault. Three of

Kercher's companion warships were carbonised, the nodes within collapsing as their bodies turned from complex adaptive matter into the stuff of trees and diamonds.

The Arcology's fleet pivoted, closing the hole with dozens of small translations. They'd planned for this across a thousand simulations.

Within information space, Kercher saw the enemy crashing against ibits busy calculating Tarski's unsolvable problem. It was gratifying to see the enemy stumble.

Kercher tracked the ships engaging and hoped those whose job it was to stay hidden until needed heeded their orders.

The third of the great vessels, shaped like an hourglass with one bulb larger than the other translated away.

The fleet did not cheer; it was too soon, and the battle was only just begun but there was no doubting the sensation of hope and pleasure that rippled across the comms channels.

Kercher was one among hundreds scanning for where the enemy hourglass would appear next.

The pilot's guess was inside the gas giant on Kith's Observatory's doorstep. They had no idea how the station would respond but it didn't matter. Three dozen ships fit for short range carnage were ready and waiting.

In the meantime, they had the remains of the enemy fleet to mop up.

The large hourglass vessels had deployed wide-ranging counter measures that had blunted the greatest excesses of the Arcology's weaponry, their own version of denying them access to information space and its ibits. However, with two of those vessels dead in the sky and the third seemingly fled, those remaining buds and walnuts were wiped out within minutes.

The largest ship did not reappear.

Combat ceased and Kercher heard nothing but nodes taking stock, counts of the lost, memorials being readied as seconds ticked by and nothing appeared in system. Requests came flooding in asking if that was it, if there was more to come. Some expressed shock this enemy had overwhelmed Akhanda. Still others warned that their simulations showed more to come.

Hanuman demanded the comms show discipline but the disbelief and easy win remained like a shadow across their display.

The Arcology had gathered the largest fleet it had ever fielded and even so, this felt like they'd missed something, were blind to the real weight of the threat.

The fleet idled and it was then Kercher realised where they were making a mistake.

Others came to the realisation at the same time because before the pilot could warn them off their complacency, comms were arriving from across the system.

As a hundred channels opened asking what was happening and how did they prepare for the next wave, those floating through the debris of their first encounter scattered.

It was not quick enough. The ink of empty spacetime tore open, a hole that looked like a planet, spherical and utterly dark. From it came a long thick arm the same as the one that had torn Akhanda asunder. Thick as a moon, flowing through the system faster at superluminal speed, an arm emerging directly from information space to wreak havoc on the fleet.

The arm was an impossibility; information existing unexpressed in the physical and each time they told a part of it to express as carbon or chalk or sunlight, the raw information of the universe itself was being funnelled in to replace it.

It lashed through the remains of the two great vessels and as it did so it caught dozens of nodes in its reach, smashing them to pieces. This thing had broken the great ring world to pieces, it would smash Kith's Observatory to shreds without the least effort.

The fleet sparked with panic, ships taking evasive manoeuvres to return fire, calling for help, crying with dismay. Others translated away and then translation stopped working as an interdiction field rolled out from the great arm. Unlucky or just too slow, more ships were smashed aside before they could tack out of the way.

"They're interdicting us," said Hanuman and there was fear in his voice.

The comms chatter screamed across the spectrum. Kercher filtered all of it except their pilot channel. What nodes were doing was incomprehensible to them and where it wasn't they didn't need overwhelming with the fear of civilian ships pressed into combat discovering the enemy had come for them personally.

"The big bastard's appeared between the fifth and sixth planet," said a pilot only five hundred rotations into their sentence called Nimue.

The gas giant was the sixth planet.

"It's heading towards Kith's Observatory."

"We're minutes away," said Hanuman into Kercher's mind.

"Do what you can," said Kercher to the other pilots. A chorus of acknowledgement, grim and resigned but no less committed for the lack of hope. Kercher was suddenly, unexpectedly, inordinately proud of their pilots.

By their calculation there were two hundred ships within range of the giant vessel before it reached the atmosphere of the gas giant. They would deal with it. They had to deal with it.

"All those who can hear me, target the arm," ordered Kercher, and their pilots swept out of the groups they were in and converged on the great arm.

Nodes complained directly to their channel, demanding the pilots fall back into the abandoned groups but Kercher ignored them. This was no debate.

"Its surface is covered in raw ibits," said Hanuman. "It's why those nodes who touched it were killed."

A contact poison, thought Kercher.

"Do not touch the enemy," said Kercher to anyone who was listening. Of the rules of space combat, not touching your enemy shouldn't need to be articulated but there they were.

Their weapons made no impact, splashing information across the arm and turning it to carbon or iron or silicon. Those injuries were shrugged off, replaced with new materials dragged out of information space by whatever was driving the enemy's forces. The arm hadn't translated into the physical. Kercher could see how it was still half within information space.

Who knew where the Face of Loss was channelling this monster from but it could feasibly have an infinite amount of information at its disposal. Kercher was sceptical they could do enough damage in one go to overwhelm the arm's ability to reconstitute itself. They didn't blame those who'd fled at the sight of this unbreachable monster.

"I have an idea," said Hanuman, and sent Kercher a schema for what they needed to try to do.

The enemy had its own agenda though and the arm, initially thrashing through the wreckage of its own people, tore the gash in spacetime wider still and aimed right for the system's star.

Kercher coordinated the pilots nearby and had them intercept.

Reports were coming in from the volume around the gas giant. Hundreds of enemy ships were translating into the space around their remaining large vessel, sacrificing themselves to keep it intact. The Arcology's forces were struggling to get through without shredding themselves in the process. "What does the Arcology reckon?" they asked Hanuman.

"We're giving it everything we've got Kercher, but there's the second front in information space that's equally demanding. If we lose here, we lose our expression but if we lose there, we lose ourselves."

Ships around them started falling silent.

Within information space the Face of Loss had breached the Arcology's defences and those inside were fighting a grinding battle of oceans against mountains, sunshine against ice and satisfaction against hunger on the scale of an entire civilisation.

The defenders were building entire worlds in which to fight conceptually, rule sets, ideas, philosophies grubbed up from history, from imagination, from out of nothing in the hope it would give them an edge, would slow the enemy down.

Was the Face of Loss fighting in the physical a feint? Destroying the system's star would certainly do the trick. Yet was consuming the Arcology within information space if they failed in the physical the real aim?

Kercher thought of Praveenthi, of how she'd figured something out and how she'd ended up overtaken by a world beyond her control. Was she watching this in despair?

Hanuman directed Kercher to lead the fleet towards the gash in spacetime.

Kercher informed the fleet of the formation they needed and the weapons they'd be using.

The Arcology could destroy stars if they needed. Right now they needed to stop the enemy from doing it first.

The arm was snaking its way through the system and bringing the rip in spacetime with it as it translated a few light seconds at a time. It was the first limitation Kercher noted to their ability to manipulate information space.

From their hiding places, half the remaining Arcology nodes sank into information space and to support the war there.

"We can't win this," was a repeated message. Useless except as a cry for unsupplied help, for absent hope. Those tasked with protecting the construction of the Bulwark were pulled away to engage in both the physical and in information space.

"Make them pay dearly," said Hanuman. "We need time. Get us time."

But with so many assigned to the latter they were now hours from the Bulwark being completed and this would be over long before then.

"Kercher," said Hanuman. "You need to take down the arm. I have to support our people in information space."

"You're taking the entire Arcology to war," said Kercher, realising what Hanuman was proposing.

"Do this for me," said the ship.

"My pleasure," said Kercher and, gathering the remaining pilots across their channels, told them how they were going to tackle the great arm of the enemy.

They took the fleet that was within range and, each time the enemy translated, used that window when their interdiction was down, to move themselves. They translated ahead of the arm so they were orbiting the star.

Drawing energy from the star and the information well within which it existed, they built a web of chaotic information, ibits in tension with pieces of mutually exclusive information. Drawing those conflicts together was the informational equivalent of putting the north pole of a magnet against another north pole.

The potential disruption grew and grew but they contained it inside the star's own information, the distortion causing the star to bulge like a stressed balloon in the physical.

The arm ignored their activity, sliding its way in towards the star like a snake through water.

Kercher knew it had only one goal; to destroy the star and in so doing the gas giant that orbited it. If the gas giant was obliterated then what was left of the newly reborn Arcology would be shredded in the destruction.

One by one their pilots indicated they were ready, excitement flashed across the channel at Kercher's tactics.

"On my mark," said Kercher and, allowing their body to be one with the ship, took them in towards the arm with fifty ships in their wake, a flock of birds diving towards the ocean.

They sprayed around the arm, spreading out like seedlings blown by the wind and as they did so each ship opened unanchored translation gates against the surface of the arm as it moved again.

Then they were out and trying to get away.

Kercher took Hanuman's body up and across the arm. They folded space and darted away, out from the star towards the gas giant. Behind them the arm of the enemy convulsed as along its length dozens of locations tried and failed to translate.

Then, like a bone under too much pressure, the arm snapped, breaking across its width like dead wood. Instead of reaching the star the arm floundered then jittered then disintegrated as all that raw information dissipated away.

Cheers erupted across Kercher's channels. Hanuman sent congratulations from within information space where the arm's destruction arrived like a shockwave across the enemy's forces.

Maybe we can win this, thought Kercher, allowing themselves a moment of hope.

Behind them the star flickered then broke into two as space was sheered apart by a second arm. The plasma of the star, disrupted and broken by something beyond gravity and matter, blasted its insides out in a silent gush of light and fire. The new arm coiled around the burning remains of the star as if it might pull it back together, but it was too late for that.

Kercher could only watch, silenced by the destruction, by the snatching away of their victory.

The light of this event wouldn't reach Kercher for three minutes but their displays were showing the informational changes wrought by the arrival of the enemy's new arm.

Dismay and despair ruptured the fleet's sudden hope as minds turned to escaping. Was it even possible, could the Bulwark, or what had been constructed, leave before the gas giant was destroyed by its star's disintegration? A walnut appeared alongside Hanuman then a second and a third. The sky opened in a blaze of white and a fourth gigantic hourglass vessel shifted into sight.

Kercher counted seven hundred nodes left. Fully half their number were already gone. They took their ship out of the plane in which the enemy was arriving, called on those ships who'd moments before had been celebrating to follow them. They swung like an arrowhead away from the arriving fleet.

It didn't matter that the gas giant wouldn't survive this, it didn't because matter the Arcology was done. Around them the fleet was being taken apart. Throughout the system those who'd been hiding emerged to fight, to protect those who remained.

The last of their reserves, and it wouldn't be enough.

We're watching the end of all things, thought Kercher, and for the first time the idea they would vanish struck at them hard.

"We're losing here," they said to Hanuman.

"We're losing everywhere," said the ship, and showed statistics of the battle in information space. The enemy had devoted untold resources to information space and was dismantling worlds faster than the Arcology could create them, overwhelming their defences not with concepts but with static, with thunderous light that quenched the very possibility of coherence and resistance.

They were forty per cent done on the Bulwark but all construction had stopped.

A scream of rage crossed the channels and from the station, Kith's Observatory announced his anger at the system being destroyed.

"Tens of thousands of rotations of research for nothing," he yelled at everyone who would listen. Then the station was moving, firing, attacking the enemy who'd made it into orbit around the gas giant.

Kercher reckoned it was nothing more than a momentary stalling of the enemy, Welcome but irrelevant.

"I'm proud of you all," they told the other pilots. "Give a good account of yourself before the end."

Their pilots acknowledged the message, sending back their own admiration, their honour at having fought together to the end.

While they watched lights spluttering out as nodes and ships and lives were extinguished by the enemy force. One by one their pilots fell silent as they died.

Behind them, at the centre of the system, the star began the process of breaking apart. Gravity was trying its best to draw the star back together but that arm remained ensconced there as if ignorant of the damage it had done

"Praveenthi," called Kercher.

"I'm here," she said.

"We're finished," they said.

"It was good to not dislike you anymore," she replied, and Kercher laughed.

"Same," they said.

Around them the system was growing quiet, the information landscape sparse. The survivors had broken off into two groups, one inside the atmosphere of the gas giant along with Kith's Observatory who'd been damaged such that he couldn't do much more than maintain a steady position just inside the clouds.

The second group was with Kercher.

They weren't firing and, to Kercher's surprise, the enemy had stopped engaging them too.

The arm through the star rolled itself up and vanished back into information space.

The two parts of the star reached for one another, flames of plasma arcing through the void, but it wasn't enough and, slowly, they fell away. The end of this star would play out over the next few days and weeks but like any physical body, such decay occurred only when it was already dead.

"I'm sorry, Praveenthi," said Kercher.

"You could call me Prab," she said.

"Okay," they said.

"The Face of Loss is by the station," said Hanuman. "They're inside information space. Inside the Arcology. They're coming for me." He sounded terrified, lost.

Kercher closed their eyes and prepared for the end.

50.

Prab sat in the room they'd put her in. The council had been apologetic, resigned, angry and almost none of that was directed at her.

The woman who'd been so hostile upon their arrival, Anaisha, had been transformed by the inevitable into someone with compassion and empathy. She'd remained after the others had left, holding Prab's hand and wishing the world could be different.

Prab watched her as the door closed, finally sealing her inside her apartment.

The battle was happening without her and her punishment for defying Hanuman was to die alone and without warning.

Then Kercher was in her mind telling her how bad it was, how obvious their deaths were.

"Well, isn't this all too predictable/obvious," said a now familiar voice.

A translation gate opened, the size a mouse might need, and through it came Sea of Thought Drifting in the shape of a sausage squirming across the floor like a landed trout.

When it was there, restored to its preferred saltshaker shape, it quivered for a while before speaking again.

"We had hoped/expected your people would get the Bulwark established. We had hoped/suspected you would cooperate. Our hopes were too wide. Not that we hope/yearn, we are a people of opportunity/impulse, always ready to move, to adapt when the circumstances are right. Not for us your tedious blindness/inattention that drives your looking to the future and planning for it. What stupidity/seed's vision is sung of your kind and their notions of blindness/knowing what's to come."

Prab knew why they were there.

And she was prepared.

"Yes," she said.

"Yes, is it?" said Sea of Thought Drifting. "You too can be a creature of opportunity/now it seems. Are you not worried about the future/blindness?"

"It is because I am worried," she said, forcing herself to step towards the Operand. "Because I want them to live."

"We are all food for others. In the end."

"It does not have to be the end today," said Prab, hoping it was true.

"We cannot build the Bulwark," said Sea of Thought Drifting. "We can create enough time for the rest of you to complete their task."

"What is the price?" asked Prab.

The saltshaker shifted colours from pale cream to bright pink. Prab's translation software suggested this was a sign of both pleasure and surprise.

"Oh, oh, oh. Thinking ahead has its merits/funny. The price, the agreement, the opportunity is for us as it is for you. We will find space/existence inside your Bulwark."

Prab expected more, expected demands listed in alphabetical order. Instead, co-existence, nothing more.

Nothing less, she thought. They would be inside the Arcology, inside its defences, given space to re-establish their own use of translation technology. It suddenly seemed an idea with many downsides.

"Tick tock, macro-organism," said Sea of Thought Drifting. "Your time to prepare is running out, your friends are ending. What will be your answer? Will it matter what you say, or will you be so long in deciding the opportunity is gone?"

Prab thought about Kercher and Mari. She wanted them to live. They were all she had left.

"I can't offer you the Arcology," she said.

The saltshaker melted like ice cream in an oven.

"Oh, ho, ho, ho. This is between us giant one. No inorganics here, just you with your pretend body and us with whatever shape we want. Your biome is lacking something Operand flavoured and we would bless you with our presence, to make your life complete, to bring you into the wisdom of our kind. What say you?"

"How do we do this?" asked Prab.

"That's the spirit," said the Operand, and a small tendril built itself out from the saltshaker, no wider than a straw, bright green and rippling it extended until it was at Prab's mouth.

She stood still, holding her muscles tense, her breath steady. Her eyes watered from all the things she could imagine. Being their slave, under their control, lost to herself.

But the others will live, she thought, and parted her lips.

"Good host," said Sea of Thought Drifting, and the tendril slipped between her teeth and a drop of something touched her tongue. "All you need to do is swallow us down/in, down/become, down/us."

It sounded manic to her, gleeful.

Regretting her choice was too late to change it, Prab swallowed.

Nothing happened.

"You expected to disappear? You expected to become a puppet with our will driving you? Is that how your existing biome operates?" The next words didn't translate but the software suggesting it was calling her a stupid ruminant.

A second translation gate, this time just about large enough for her if she stooped.

"Come," it said.

And Prab followed.

51.

Hanuman was fighting his last fight inside information space. In the physical the battle was over. The Arcology was defeated, its nodes unwilling to throw themselves away for the sake of glory and waiting instead to be consumed as their home, their heart, was devoured.

The enemy had stilled, its vessels floating in silence, their weapons cold.

Yet inside information space he put to work every citizen unfolded in their restoration of the Arcology. If they were to die then it would be fighting for their lives. The nodes alongside him stopped fighting, instead lending their processing power to support him as he drew on the Arcology itself in one last desperate stand.

Billions fought with weapons beyond anything conceived as possible in the physical. Pushing back against the noise of the enemy, forcing it into coherence and into defending itself in turn.

Dragons and demons, knights and rockets battled alongside love and hate, quadratic equations and triple points. Ripples of appreciation defeated closed gates and the intentions of works of art were deployed against walls without seams.

This subset of the restored Arcology, largely without even knowing, were transformed into a network so vast the galaxy itself wouldn't have held them had they been unrolled into the physical world.

Billions and billions of ideas were being turned against the simple thought of hunger.

Because the Face of Loss was there, a body with long black hair and an awkwardly bent neck appearing in world after world, in simulation after simulation to consume them.

Hanuman was at the centre of this network, vast and without equal, coordinating ten million conflicts, losing here to lure the enemy in, counter attacking there to ensure they could close the gap.

Yet whatever he tried, the enemy's hunger was insatiable.

Hanuman looked at the Bulwark and how it would operate and took its tricks into information space. He tried to make them taste bad and, to an extent, it worked, because the enemy slowed, turned away and rolled back as much as it kept on fighting.

Where Hanuman was successful it wasn't clear to him why. Sometimes trying the same thing twice yielded different results and no battle was repeated successfully. The Face of Loss didn't seem to learn from pain or defeat but that was because it had no strategy Hanuman could discern.

He'd reviewed the events at Akhanda, at all of their worlds, all their stations, from all their nodes and saw the same thing over and over again – the enemy ate everything they put against it, as if the very existence of the Arcology could sustain it.

Shards of himself were fighting hand to hand with armies composed of endless versions of the Face of Loss who'd trapped Prab in information space. Other parts of the Arcology were dressed as photons melting the ice of the enemy, or as grass breaking up its earth with roots and vigour.

Bit by bit the enemy was finding its way towards the heart of the Arcology, to the place where all nodes came from time to time to bathe themselves in the unified thought of the entire empire.

Hanuman dwelled here now, for better or for worse, and with each defeat a part of him felt them crawling towards him and what he had become.

More translation gates opened and Hanuman prepared for another wave of the enemy. Yet in the physical, combat had all but ceased, the enemy floating inert as the star collapsed.

Instead, through came dozens of the bone ships they'd encountered in Otto space. Some were curving ribs, others stout knuckles but most were the long, tapered femurs they had met that first time.

The Operand were here and they were using translation technology.

It wasn't shock he felt at their arrival, at this use of a technology they'd claimed abandoned, but anger.

Here to pick over our remains, he thought, but frowned as they aimed for the enemy fleet instead. He saw then something fundamentally shared between the Face of Loss and the Operand. As if they were two sides of the same coin.

Was this what Prab had discovered?

The Face of Loss drained away from the Arcology, their ships translating across the system to engage with the Operand even at the cost of being smashed from behind by the Arcology.

Seeing the change, Hanuman called every remaining Arcology vessel to the gas giant. This was their chance. Had the Operand done this to save them? Was the distraction provided deliberate or were they operating to a different agenda?

It hardly mattered.

Within information space the same was happening. On the verge of washing over Hanuman and the remaining defenders, the Face of Loss had simply vanished from its vantage within the Arcology, the only sign they'd been there degraded worlds, dismantled systems and ruined lives.

"We are leaving," he told them, almost unable to say the words for fear the next moment might prove him wrong.

"We can finish the Bulwark," others replied.

"We should join the fight," came still more.

"We can finish the Bulwark anywhere," he said, and the implications of what he was saying spread like lightning across the network.

And so, in the space provided by the Operands' arrival, the Arcology took what it had built and, identifying a system half way up the galactic arm it had once called home, they left. First the scouts then the rest of the fleet until, at last, Hanuman was left alone in the system with Kith's Observatory.

"Are you coming?" he sent, but the old station had fallen silent once again.

"We need you," he tried again, although they'd already distributed the Arcology's substrate across a hundred and three ships to ensure nothing like what happened to Akhanda could happen a second time.

"I will die here with my experiments. If you don't leave now, you'll join me," said Kith's Observatory, their voice filled with bitterness.

"Come with us you old fool, start again."

Kith didn't answer him, and Hanuman knew the node would die here when the star failed.

Instead of leaving, Hanuman stayed to watch. The battle between the Operand and the Face of Loss raged across the volume, spreading beyond this system and its dying star, light days beyond the outer debris cloud captured by the star and deep into information space.

Hanuman recorded how they fought, tagged techniques and manipulations the Arcology hadn't dreamed of and sent them home. From this we will rise, he thought.

If only to be able to defend themselves against the winners of the war playing out in front of them.

For the first time Hanuman had a sense of the scale these foes were capable of. If the Operand had been hiding their star in a cloud all this time they'd done so with aplomb. He could see ideas the Arcology had only just begun to sense the shape of developed as if they were as obvious as aleph numbers. Just how long had these two civilisations been traversing the cosmos?

The Face of Loss brought two of its light-minute-long arms to bear but the bone ships were a match for the enemy and in the darkness their conflict glittered like diamonds cast across cloth.

Hanuman had trained against other Arcology warships in countless simulations but, eventually, nodes stopped playing these games because they became not about the game, the discovery, the adaptation, but in how to play against someone who knew you as well as you knew them. It was a different kind of warfare, based on intimacy rather than materiel, and Hanuman recognised its marks among the Operand and Face of Loss everywhere he looked.

That the Face of Loss and the Operand had tested one another before this battle was obvious in how every move seemed to be known, how every tic and preference, every habit and lazy choice was expected. Dropping into information space Hanuman found two forces desperately busy trying to consume one another. The Operands attacked exactly as the

Face of Loss, huge expressions of gnawing emptiness that could only move forward by eating everything they came into touch with. Hanuman realised they weren't simply two cultures who'd clashed and then stayed away from one another, they were a family in conflict with themselves. Two lovers fighting over the shape of the universe.

At some point these two were one, he realised. If the Operand were different now it wasn't choice, or contemplation, that had changed them but necessity.

If so, he wondered what had brought them out now to save the Arcology, for why else would they have come?

"Hanuman?"

It was Kercher.

"Where is Prab?"

Hanuman didn't understand the question. She would have been evacuated along with everyone willing to leave Kith's Observatory.

"I've checked the manifests," said Kercher, and Hanuman knew what hadn't been said.

He opened a channel.

"Prab? Can you hear me?"

"Why are you still here?" came the reply. Voice only, no visuals.

"What did you do?" he asked, his systems flinching with the thought of what she had allowed to happen. He knew he was responsible for leaving her vulnerable.

You had no choice.

"Finish the Bulwark and then we can talk."

"I will not permit slavers and ravenous monsters inside the Arcology," he said flatly.

"Finish. The. Bulwark," said Prab, and their communication was cut off.

52.

The system was a binary, early in its life, low informational content. Both stars were bright yellow with strong green emissions, but as with all stars, there was no hint of the green to the visible eye.

Thirty-seven planetary bodies of which eight were gas giants and the rest icy rock pebbles. This wasn't counting the hundreds of moons.

None of them were conventionally inhabitable but then, as it stood, the Arcology had precisely no citizens requiring physical space at this point in time. Those Excluded who'd been evacuated were currently sleeping and would remain so until a solution could be found.

They were far from the top of the list of tasks to be completed. Realistically it would be thousands of rotations before they were woken for their next morning.

Assuming the Bulwark held.

The scouts had found nothing of interest and by the time Kercher brought Hanuman in, they were gone, away to the wreckage of what had come before to salvage what could be salvaged.

They would build the new upon the old.

The Arcology's distributed substrate built by the fleet to replace the hardware provided by Kith's Observatory was holding up fine.

In total five hundred and fifty-four nodes had left Kith's Observatory. Of their pilots, Kercher had counted in just twenty-eight and not one of those whose names they'd learned had made it. It wasn't anywhere near enough, but it would have to suffice because they were all they had.

Kercher wondered how many more stragglers were still out there waiting for a call home.

The Arcology itself remained intact if battered.

For the first time those of the general population who'd been unfolded had been informed of an assault and perhaps thirty per cent had been conscripted to fight the battle against the Face of Loss inside information space.

All of that was fine but Kercher could only think about one thing, about one person. Prab.

Sacrificing herself so they could live.

Useful in ways Kercher couldn't have imagined. Yet fundamentally they missed her. She'd been cutting, short tempered and self-absorbed, riddled with guilt no right-minded soldier should feel and desperate to prove herself in a way Kercher knew would never be satisfied. All of it had combined into a package they'd enjoyed knowing.

Hanuman was idling in a complicated looping orbit close to the system's two stars. Drenched in all kinds of radiation, Hanuman had been silent for hours while the fleet worked on completing the Bulwark.

Without any ceremony the Bulwark was activated. Each and every node in its network coming together in a complicated dance both inside information space but also in the physical. Kercher had watched them weave and lace through one another's spaces like a hundred mating birds dancing for the future of their species.

Hanuman showed them what it was, a kind of digestive tract turned inside out and covering the idea of the Arcology. It would dissolve the very nature of anything approaching the Arcology in information space.

No one was quite sure how elastic it was, whether the Arcology could expand properly or whether they were better remaining crunched up, limited for now.

Millions of citizens instead of trillions.

It had taken the informational potential of millions of stars and tens of thousands of light years of space time to express the Arcology at its height. Right now they were unfolded in the tiniest fraction of that.

The outcome of the battle between the Operand and the Face of Loss remained unknown. No amount of looking in the direction of that lost system revealed anything except the dead star. The conflict had ended and the two sides were gone from any place the Arcology could observe.

The Face of Loss had not come after them. The Bulwark, humming through information space with its promise to digest any who came near its undulating contours, found no sustenance.

And then a bone ship was in system. Translating in smoothly as if it was arriving into part of a well-anchored network.

It swung around the system until it matched Hanuman's orbit, followed by dozens of nodes who'd observed its arrival and decided they would see what there was to see.

Kercher knew what was coming and ensured they were inside information space when Prab showed up, an avatar appearing across a dozen or so public comms channels.

"We did it," she said by way of greeting. Her shape remained human but her skin was laced through with green and navy-blue veins, her eyes had lost their sclera. Regardless, Prab it was, her expression that strange, confused, anxious confidence Kercher remembered hating on first sight.

"What are you doing here, Prab?" asked Hanuman.

"The Operand have a request," she said.

Kercher could see something different about her, in the way she held herself. Taller maybe? Settled perhaps.

She has a purpose now, they thought.

They tried to send something private, a request to meet and talk.

"When we're done here, we'll have all the time," said Prab immediately into their channel.

"I cannot grant it," said Hanuman.

"Why don't you shut the fuck up and let me ask," said Prab.

Hanuman's body bristled and Kercher bit back a laugh. It wasn't their place to suggest Hanuman was getting exactly what his behaviour deserved.

"Ask your question," the ship said.

Kercher noted just how many of the nodes shadowing the bone ship were ready to open fire.

"The Operand formally request to join the Arcology as a peer to its existing citizens and nodes."

"And their slaves?" asked Hanuman.

"Their client cultures will be given a free choice to come along or choose their own path."

"I don't believe them," said Hanuman.

"This is the offer, Arcology. We have moved substantially in your direction since we last spoke."

"Praveenthi Saal," said Hanuman. "She is an Excluded, a member of the Arcology. I demand you release her and leave."

Prab snorted with derision. "Hanuman, it's me. The woman you locked in a room rather than listen to. The Operand and I have come to an arrangement. As part of that they've agreed to amend their presence in their existing biomes."

"Why?" asked Hanuman.

"You offer them a better opportunity."

The world exploded in chatter, a thousand conversations across twice as many channels except for Hanuman who remained closeted within his own thoughts.

Until recently Kercher would have been able to comfortably predict what the ship would choose. Except it had failed to defend its home, been swallowed by the Arcology, lost its identity and lately been brought back to life. Now everyone around them treated Hanuman as if he was the arbiter of their destiny.

Hanuman was going through some changes of his own.

"How would you integrate?" asked Hanuman emotionlessly.

The ship might be unsettled and volatile but he remained himself and Kercher knew this kind of busywork question meant he already knew the answer he would give.

"We will share our informational biome with you. We have no identities as you think of them but we are unified and our way of engaging with existence will benefit you as yours will benefit us.

"It is only together we can defeat the enemy," answered Sea of Thought Drifting's melodious voice.

Kercher thought Hanuman might refuse to make the decision, that he'd force a vote across all the active citizens of the Arcology.

Instead, cutting through the cacophony of voices talking over one another, each with an opinion on what should be done, Hanuman answered with one simple word.

"Yes."

The ships around them dropped away, most of them returning to their recently abandoned tasks. Others opened translation gates and left the system without announcing where they were going.

Losing them was painful. Kercher hoped they'd be back. However, with the Operand inside the tent, the first outside culture to join the Arcology, they reckoned they'd be all right for now.

When they were done and Prab had sent a time and location for catching up – that awful bar on the Otto planet made of gold, Kercher checked the translations of their conversations twice because the system struggled at several key points when Prab was communicating.

The spot he found most interesting was in the Operand's naming of the Face of Loss, suggesting something along the lines of wayward children who tried to take too much from a good opportunity.

The Face of Loss was gone for now, but it would be back and the Arcology had agreed to intervene in a fight between a collection of parents and their children.

Flexing their skin inside their mesh as they thought about it, Kercher hoped they lived long enough to see the day.

53.

The Otto station was as Kercher remembered it. Kercher was waiting in the bar where Prab had gotten them drunk for the first time since the start of their sentence.

"New body I see," said Prab, arriving with a couple of Otto in tow. They hung around until she sat alongside Kercher and then ambled off.

Kercher watched them go and wondered whether they'd been escorting her, protecting her or serving her.

Prab behaved as if she'd not seen them at all, giving Kercher an appraising look as drinks were put on the table between them by an Otto holding a couple of trays.

Kercher looked down at themselves. Still long and thin, no kind of pilot would choose otherwise. The changes were inside. A new endocrine system, different brain chemistry and rejigged apportion across the various sections.

"I had an anxiety dream," they said.

Prab smiled. "I didn't realise you could be nervous."

"Nor did I," they replied. "New body, new problems."

"But you prefer it," she said.

"I do."

"I'm the same. It's strange not needing to eat. I feel like I'm back inside the Arcology some days. I'd love to eat but it's only really for pleasure now and they don't have chefs so this is about the best I can get." She took a long swig of her drink.

"They're family," said Kercher.

She nodded.

"Did we choose the right side?"

"I don't think so," she said.

Kercher looked at the drink in their hands. They weren't getting drunk today.

"What do we do about it?"

"Nothing. For now. The Face of Loss choose to exist inside information space. The Operand wanted to live in the physical. Like the Arcology. They fell out over it, couldn't agree on which road to follow."

"They lied to all of us," said Kercher.

She shrugged. "The Face of Loss realised it had hurt you only when it was too late. It was trying to meet you but destroyed you instead. For their part, the Operand realised the Arcology could provide a way for them to tip the scales against their children."

Kercher didn't like what she was saying.

"We can't worry about it now," said Prab.

"Then what?"

"We worry about today."

Kercher was silent.

"I mean we drink and eat and you tell me what it's like to work for the leader of the Arcology and I'll tell you what it's like to have become"–she gestured at herself–"this."

Kercher put their hand on top of Prab's. "It's good to see you," they said.

Prab smiled and nodded.

54.

Hanuman was slowly expanding the Arcology. In the weeks since the Bulwark was established, they had found and been found by hundreds of nodes. He could almost believe they would find themselves again and things would go back to the way they had been before the Face of Loss. Before Sirajah's Reach.

Those few surviving nodes who'd woken from hibernation to meet the threat had been among those to leave when he'd welcomed in the Operand.

They had not come back.

Hanuman did not think about them. He was too busy managing a growing Arcology and trying to understand what it meant to lead the Arcology.

He wanted to be a warship.

Although meeting other nodes, building the Arcology's substrate, managing its citizens' rampant anxiety about the Operand and the process of integrating the Operand themselves, Hanuman split off a small shard of himself.

This small shard set itself a task of working on the Arcology's future. It worried about many things but it had one goal – understand the Operand and the Face of Loss and extricate themselves from their conflict.

Current projections were suggesting it might take them a couple of hundred thousand rotations to do this.

Others suggested it was too late, that the ingredients had been mixed and it was now the best he could hope to influence the taste of the cake when it finally came out of the oven.

There were few people Hanuman felt comfortable talking to about himself. Too many nodes either regarded him as an avatar, to be venerated and obeyed while others regarded him as the kind of authority they did not want to work with.

He wondered how Akhanda had done it without wanting to throttle both sets.

Of those few it was Kercher who kept Hanuman feeling like himself.

"Leadership comes with no thank yous," said the pilot. "Just expectations, confusion and disagreement.

"You can meet expectations, dispel confusion or resolve disagreement. Any two of those three, but not all of them."

Hanuman wasn't sure Kercher was right but then the pilot saw just about everything he did, so perhaps their perspective was no less informed no matter how depressing the outlook.

Prab lurked in his systems, but Hanuman had found ways to avoid meeting her without a formal body of work to keep them occupied.

However, Kercher insisted he meet his Interlocutor and apologise if nothing else.

Three rotations ago they'd expanded the Bulwark to encompass a third star system. Hanuman was there now, wallowing in its radiation and feeling the patter of the solar wind on his shell.

Hanuman invited her to meet. No agenda, just to talk. He was more nervous than he'd anticipated.

Prab arrived on a bone ship whose profile matched that of Sea of Thought Drifting. Translating into the system with a few planets between them in a way which felt respectful.

"I'm here," she sent.

"Will you come aboard?" asked Hanuman.

"I will," she said.

He irritated Kercher by reshaping the cockpit to recreate her old seat. The pilot grumbled but their body was clearly ready to spend time with her again.

"Come along then," said Kercher. "I've everything ready for you."

ACKNOWLEDGEMENTS

Ah, acknowledgments should likely be as long as the books themselves. In an effort to make sure that isn't the case, I'll try and keep this short but add the caveat that many people were essential to the birth of Hanuman and the long winding journey that brought this one to life - I know who you are and thank you. More specifically, John, without your precision hustle I feel like I'd still be on endless sub eating myself alive. To Eleanor who pointed at a pitch doc and said 'I love that one.' To Simon and the rest of the team at Angry Robot, who just got it.

This story doesn't exist without Iain M Banks whose stories transformed my world as a teenager. Your passionate commitment to punching up remains an inspiration.

Lastly, but far from least, to Rachel, if I can get you reading past bedtime, then I know I've got something good. Without your encouragement none of this would be possible.